ACCLAIM FOR ANNIE SOLOMON'S PREVIOUS NOVELS

M

DEAD SHOT

"Solomon's psychologically rich romantic thriller balances grisly imagery with tender moments and is entertaining, through and through."
—***Booklist***

"Gripping . . . Solomon's characters are convincing and compelling . . . good suspenseful fun."
—***Publishers Weekly***

"A riveting and edgy romantic suspense that you'll want to read in a single sitting."
—BookLoons.com

"4 Stars! A creepy edge of danger threads through the story . . . fascinating. Solomon and suspense are a perfect match!"
—***Romantic Times BOOKreviews Magazine***

"Compelling . . . The plot is well-written, the action fast-moving, keeping the reader in suspense to the last page."
—**MyShelf.com**

more . . .

"Talk about edge-of-the-seat! I have never read a book with such relentless suspense . . . A superb example of showing over mere telling of a story. I highly recommend *Blackout*."

—Romantic Reviews Today

BLIND CURVE

"4 Stars! Riveting and emotionally intense."
—Romantic Times BOOKreviews Magazine

"A perfect ten . . . nail-biting, intense drama that will leave you breathless with anticipation."
—MyShelf.com

"Annie Solomon does such an outstanding job creating taut suspense. From the very first page . . . to the riveting climax, you can't help but be glued to the story."
—RoundTableReviews.com

"An action-packed novel . . . a feast for suspense fans, and the added mixture of romance . . . another winner for an author who clearly has a gift and is on the rise."
—TheRomanceReadersConnection.com

TELL ME NO LIES

"Infused with raw emotion and a thirst for vengeance. Excitement and tension galore!"
—Romantic Times BOOKreviews Magazine

"Full of simmering emotions that lovers of romantic suspense will devour."
—Rendezvous

more . . .

"Another success! Miss Solomon's latest novel is a testament to her gift for crafting intelligent, sexy novels."
—RomanceReadersConnection.com

DEAD RINGER

"Just the ticket for those looking for excitement and romance."
—*Romantic Times BOOKreviews Magazine*

"An entertaining . . . exceptional . . . emotionally taut tale . . . offers twists and turns that kept me enthralled to the last page."
—*Old Book Barn Gazette*

"Thrilling and edgy . . . *Dead Ringer* delivers excitement, suspense, and sexual tension . . . Highly recommended."
—RomRevToday.com

LIKE A KNIFE

"A nail-biter through and through. Absolutely riveting."
—Iris Johansen

"Fast-paced . . . exciting romantic suspense that . . . the audience will relish."
—*Midwest Book Review*

ONE
DEADLY SIN

ANNIE SOLOMON

ONE DEADLY SIN

FOREVER

NEW YORK   BOSTON

Cover design by Diane Luger
Book design by Giorgetta Bell McRee

Forever
Hachette Book Group
237 Park Avenue
New York, NY 10017
Visit our Web site at www.HachetteBookGroup.com

Forever is an imprint of Grand Central Publishing.
The Forever name and logo is a trademark of Hachette Book Group, Inc.

Printed in the United States of America

First Printing: May 2009

10 9 8 7 6 5 4 3 2 1

To Mimi, Sundra, Lindsey, and all the rest
at Panera's West End. Thanks for the coffee and
the warm welcome every morning.

ACKNOWLEDGMENTS

I'd like to thank all who helped get this book into proper shape, particularly my agents, Kelly Harms and Christina Hogrebe, and my editor Michele Bidelspach.

As always, my appreciation goes to Agent Pat Hamblin of the Tennessee Bureau of Investigation for all her help with the criminal justice system. Also to Lieutenant Doug Whitefield of the Wilson County Sherriff's Office for his tour of the Wilson County Criminal Justice Center's jail, including a trip in the "pickle suit." Thanks for all you two do to keep us safe.

To Stephanie Floyd for introducing me to wildman "Panhead" Phil Hipshire, whose help with the world of motorbikes was invaluable.

To my writing pals, Trish Milburn and Beth Pattillo, who read some of the early drafts, and picked me up when I was down, thanks for being there.

Finally, to Larry and Becca, who are always along for the ride, whether it's bumpy or smooth, I couldn't do it without you.

~1~

She came at night, creeping into town like a shade. Darkness suited her. It evoked the past, that black hole of fury and mystery. Recapturing it required dark arts.

There was irony, arriving at midnight. Pulling into the cemetery at the traditional witching hour, leaving the street lights behind. She inched forward, navigating through stars, those pinpricks of light. And memory.

The stars were out that night, too, long ago when the doorbell clanged and shattered the silence into before and after. She'd heard it through her bedroom door when she should have been asleep. But who could sleep with her father accused and missing, her mother an inconsolable machine of tears?

She remembered the darkness through her window, the moon a sly smile in the sky, the black a background against which the grown-up voices rumbled below.

And then her mother's scream.

Unhuman, animal, a throat ripped out, a universe hacked and splattered into pieces. A sound so feral the memory of it still gave her shivers.

No one screamed now. Nothing broke the silence but the hum of her wheels rolling down the winding cemetery road, a path between graves.

At last she slowed. Stopped. Turned off the engine.

And picked her way over the dead to her destination. The last thing she'd seen in this town. The last image of home. Now, it was the first thing she'd see on her return.

The black angel.

She swept a penlight over the sculpture. Remembered the gargoyle face seen with ten-year-old eyes. Twenty years later she saw the face was meant to be kind. But it was overshadowed by massive wings that spanned up and out, looming over the headstone like a vampire bat.

There had been hot arguments over that angel. Even banished to her room, she could hear her mother and her aunt fighting.

"It's frightening. Unholy," her aunt had said. "A mark against his name."

"They put the mark there, not me."

"They who?"

"I don't know!"

"You can't do this, Evelyn."

"It's done." Her mother's voice was harsh and strained. "It stays until the stain is gone. Until I can prove it."

Until I can prove it.

Poor Mother.

There had been no proving. It was all too hard, too heavy. Like life itself.

She bent down, ran her fingers over the headstone. Mud had dried and caked over the words cut into the marble. She found her penknife and scraped it away, blowing to clear the residue.

Charles Swanford.

Hello, Daddy.

She traced the rest of the inscription, not needing to see it because it was incised in her memory. *Beloved husband and father.* And the quotation: *They make haste to shed innocent blood.*

Innocent blood. She rose to face the angel. They needed a black angel, her father and mother. They were weak. Unprepared for the pressure life steamrolled over them. People who retreated and hid. Ran away. Died.

But they had her now. She snapped off the light, leaving the darkness to coil around her like a shroud. Edie was back. And she'd make everything right.

2

"Edie Swann." Red McClure looked from the job application to Edie, who stood on the other side of the bar.

She held her breath, waiting to see if the name struck a chord with him. Did he recognize it? She'd debated using her real name. It wasn't that dissimilar from the one she'd left Redbud with, so a false identity might have served her well. But using an alias picked at her. She wanted to come back as herself, right under the nose of the whole damn town, betting that the twenty years between then and now would have blurred memories. So far, she'd been right.

The look Red gave her was open, friendly. Free of shadows. It was a good round face, a plus for a bartender. One that invited small confidences.

Not that he was going to get any from her. "That's right."

She'd seen the help-wanted notice for Red's in the *Red-bud Gazette*. Wondered if the bar was named after the town or after the owner. When she got there, the thinning red thatch atop his freckled face was her answer.

He perused the application again, maybe for the third time. Edie tamped down her impatience.

"You've been around," he said. "New York, Boston, Chicago, St. Louis, Nashville."

She shrugged. "Still trying to find my Eden." She put that out there, waited for some hint of recognition, and got none. A shiver of satisfaction ran through her. It was hot outside, deep and thick with summer humidity, and the bar was air-conditioned to the hilt. It would be great once she started working, but right now her bare shoulders in the tight leather vest were freezing.

"And you think you've found it in Redbud?" Doubt trickled into his voice.

"You never know." She smiled, giving him the blazing one she showered on customers. It worked like it always did. Well, that and a few other tricks of the trade. Like putting her elbows on the bar and leaning forward so her cleavage was even more visible.

"These are good places." He tapped the paper, referring to the list of priors that was her bar girl résumé. "I know some. Well, by reputation, of course. Though I've been to the Sassafrass in Nashville. Quite a scene. You won't get that here. This is a neighborhood place, just folks relaxing."

Neighborhood was an exaggeration, seeing as it was on the edge of town, a bare half-mile from the Hammerbilt HVAC plant. The only neighbors were the truckers offloading steel sheeting and the steady stream of shift workers without whom Red's would be dead.

"What I'm looking for." And to underscore her assurance, she looked around the place. A clutter of small tables, high on the outside, low in the middle, stools at the bar. All squeezed into a cave of a room, dark and cool enough for hibernating. "Someplace comfortable. I'm tired of wandering. Be thirty in a few months. Time I put down some roots."

"And you picked Redbud?" As if no one in his right mind would choose this tiny spot on the highway to settle down. Not if he had the options she'd obviously had.

She laughed, her story already worked out in her head. "Actually, Redbud picked me. Ran into some trouble with my bike and had to shell out a handful to get it fixed. Redbud was as far as the rest of my cash could take me."

"Well as far as bartenders go, you've got the pedigree."

"What about the job?"

He pursed his lips. "Can you make, ah . . . one of those apple martinis?"

She paused. Didn't think there'd be much call for mixed drinks here. "I do a killer appletini." She vaulted over the bar. Looked for the vodka and the apple schnapps. Found the former, not the latter. She asked for it.

Red-faced, the bar owner said, "Don't have it. Don't get much call for it here. Just—"

"—Wanted to see if I knew what I was doing?"

He nodded.

"Okay. Give me a second." She took the time to peruse the shelves, found some brandy, a kid's carton of apple juice in the bar fridge, and a lemon. She mixed the drink over ice, added a dash of vodka, and poured it into an old-fashioned glass garnished with a lemon twist. Made a second drink adding ginger ale and poured it into a highball glass. "Apple blossom. Apple blossom fizz." She pushed the drinks toward him. While he sampled, she found a bottle of crème do cacao, blew off the dust, mixed it with vodka in an ice-filled shaker and poured the drink into a martini glass. "Chocolate martini. What do you think?"

He grinned. "Yeah, but can you draw a beer?"

She gave him that smile, leaned against the bar again. "Like nobody's business."

They shook on it, and agreed she'd start later that night. "Got a big to-do in town," Red said. "The guy that heads the plant is leaving to run with the big dogs at IAT—International Ambient Technologies. They own Hammerbilt."

"Oh, yeah?" Edie faked mild interest. But anything about Hammerbilt got her attention.

"Won't be much alcohol at the picnic, so figure there'll be a lot of spillover here. You should stop by the park. It'll be a big send-off. I'll introduce you around." He handed her a flyer with all the particulars. She saw the honoree's name and her heart started to thud. Sometimes the gods were smiling.

"Thanks." She pocketed the flyer. "Maybe I will."

She needed a place to flop, and Red showed her a room above the bar. He apologized for the dust, but they worked out a deal, and once the place was cleaned up it had everything she needed. Bed, hotplate, a table that could serve as living and dining room. Not what she'd call homey, but then again, she hadn't really known homey since she left Redbud behind.

Oh, there'd been home—Aunt Penny's apartment with its mess of three rooms, Edie's the one with the pullout bed. Then again it had been a long time since she'd had a yard and a tree to swing on. It wasn't as if she'd miss it.

Not like she had at first.

But that was years ago, and this was today. And she had things to do.

She hauled her bags up the iron stairs that overlooked the back alley. No one would bother her here. Perfect site to start things swirling.

She stuffed the few hanging things she'd brought with her—a couple of dresses in case she needed them—into the tiny closet. Cleaned up some abandoned crates lying in the alley and lugged them to the room to serve as a dresser.

By noon there was only one last thing to put away. Reaching deep inside an inner pocket of her duffel, she pulled out a plastic bag. Hefted its light weight in her hand, jiggling the forms inside. The corners of her mouth twisted into a small dark smile, and she upended the bag onto the bare mattress.

A dozen tiny black angels spilled out.

~3~

Redbud was built by immigrants and easterners coming west to Tennessee for adventure and prosperity. They brought with them the square plan and built the town around it. As it grew, newcomers desperate for space stretched the boundaries, not always sticking to the order. Behind the original town with its neat map of squared-off avenues around a central quad, the streets were akimbo, alleys snaking off into meandering roads like a maze hiding secrets.

The signature redbuds, which once grew wild on the outskirts, had gradually given way to homes and progress. Town fathers had added them later, planting the trees in orderly rows to line the central square and its expansion—Redbud Park. Spring had long gone, though, and with it, the beautiful pink buds that had given the town its name. Now the trees bloomed green, and if you didn't know what they were they could have been mistaken for anything. But Edie remembered what they were, and as she walked among them to get to the park, she pictured them fuzzed with pink.

Looked like the whole town had turned out to celebrate Fred Lyle's departure from the Hammerbilt plant. Redbud Park was festooned with balloons and banners that read "Thank you, Mr. Fred!" in bright blue letters. Four grills on one side of the park kept up a steady stream of hot dogs and hamburgers. A small bandstand stood across the way, but it was empty now. According to the notice she'd read in the window at Red's, the music wasn't supposed to start until later that evening.

She plunged into the crowd. Various sponsor signs greeted her. The Redbud Community Church manned a dessert table. A teenager was handing out old-fashioned cardboard fans with Runkle's Real Estate printed on one side. Red had his own corner—lemonade, water, and iced tea by the looks of it. No alcohol for Mr. Fred.

People weaved around her as she stood still, pivoting to embrace the feel of the place. She was sure she remembered the swings in the corner—*higher, Mommie, higher!*—and the water fountain and monkey bars. Or did she? Memories were tricky. Sneaky. She'd grab for one, and it dissipated like a handful of smoke.

New children clamored over the playground now, also screaming at their parents to be pushed higher. She found herself riveted by their innocence. It seemed foolish to be so guileless. As if the universe spared the young any more than it did their elders.

A microphone shriek drew her attention toward the bandstand. A kindly-looking white-haired man was tapping the microphone.

"Citizens of Redbud," he began. "We are here to celebrate a lifetime of service to this town. For twenty years he's been plant manager at Hammerbilt and an asset to this community, holding our future in his hands with expertise and commitment. It's been an honor to work with him and with Hammerbilt's corporate parent, International Ambient Technologies, and now, on the eve of his well-earned promotion to CEO over all of IAT's North American holdings, I can only say, thank you, Mr. Fred."

Applause and whistles broke out as Fred Lyle ambled to the microphone. But not everyone approved. Behind her she heard a few snorts and at least one muttered, "Bullshit."

She turned, searching the crowd for the nay-sayer, but couldn't find him. Meanwhile, Fred Lyle had started speaking. She let his self-congratulatory words drift over her as she conjured an image of him from years ago. But only the name and the hush it brought to her memory lingered. The living room in the old house. An impression of drapes hanging closed. Lamplight and shadows. The couch where she'd squeezed herself into the crook of her mother's listless arm. And Aunt Penny creeping in.

"Evelyn, Mr. Lyle is here." Her voice was low and gentle, as it had been for days. Like they were all at a school play and the lights had just gone down. Then, with a firmer tone. "Go to your room, Edie."

She must have refused. Maybe she snuggled deeper against her mother's body, hoping the physical touch would keep her mother from drifting away. Whatever Edie did, she didn't go to her room. Not until Mr. Lyle appeared. At the sight of him, her mother's body had stiffened. Become present and focused. And suddenly there was anger in the room. Huge, massive currents of rage. Afraid she might hear that scream again, Edie had scurried away.

Now, she gazed at the man in front of her. An ordinary

man. Thinning hair, glasses. A good man. A good citizen. Harmless.

But Edie Swann knew better.

"Bullshit!" This time, the voice was louder. Edie turned to see a tall, thin man with a greasy ponytail shake a fisted arm in the air. "That's a lie!"

People around the man frowned. "Shut up, Terry," one of them said.

"I fucking won't shut up," he growled, and stalked toward the other man, who backed up quickly. "That's what they want," Terry barked. "To shut me up. But I know stuff. I know what goes on in that place, and it ain't all caring and concern."

More of the crowd eased away.

"At Hammerbilt we're proud of the work we do," Fred Lyle was saying. "Proud of our commitment to our town and the people in it."

"Bullshit!" Terry yelled, this time loud enough for everyone to hear.

Lyle stumbled, adjusted his glasses, and continued.

"You're drunk," a man in the crowd said to Terry. "Go home." He put a hand on Terry's shoulder, and Terry whipped around. "Don't you touch me."

"I just think you should—"

Terry swung, someone swung back, and before Edie could blink, the circle of people around her had collapsed into a free-for-all. Someone cuffed her chin and she stumbled back, nearly lost her footing. A woman screamed. People were shoving and Edie struck out, trying to keep a perimeter of safety around her. Her fist connected with something, sending a shock wave up her arm.

"Jesus." A large, sandy-haired man scowled at her,

rubbing his jaw. In the seconds it took to realize what had happened, she realized something else. The man wasn't just big. He was beautiful. Tight-jawed and wide-mouthed. Muscled shoulders and lean, powerful legs. And just now all that hard masculine energy was scowling. At her.

He grabbed her arm in a merciless grip and pushed forward into the crowd, taking Edie with him.

"Hey—let me go!"

He ignored her, shouting into the crowd. "All right, stop it. All of you!" His voice was loud and authoritative as he waded into the shoving throng.

"Let—me—go!"

Instead, he jerked her closer to him. She stumbled against his rock-hard ribs, and her teeth cracked together. Meanwhile he addressed the huddle of men still struggling with Terry. "I said cut it out!" He kicked one man away and with his free hand, pulled a second man back. "I'm counting to three . . ." The rest saw, heard, sheepishly slowed, then stopped. Only Terry still fought, even if it was just air.

One of the fighters glared at Terry, then said contritely, "Sorry, Chief. But this asshole—"

Chief? Edie stared. Not likely Native American with all those Nordic bones. What other kind of—

She groaned silently and looked him over. No uniform, no badge. Just a pair of well-worn jeans and a T-shirt molded over a broad, enticing chest. Then again, did the chief of police in a small town wear a uniform?

"Don't think you can shut me up, Holt," Terry said to the bigger man. "Ain't no one can shut me up."

"And we all know it, too," the man named Holt said. "Come on, you can tell me your troubles on the way." He put a friendly arm around Terry, who tried, unsuccess-fully, to shrug it off. Edie noted Holt's arm had slipped up to Terry's neck, more of a hold, like his grip on her—tough and unbreakable. With both of them prisoners, the chief walked off.

"Hey!" Edie stumbled along. "Where are you—"

"You can continue, Mr. Fred!" Holt shouted.

"Thank you, Chief," came Mr. Fred over the micro-phone, and began droning on again.

Edie tried twisting out of his grip. "You gonna let me go?"

He looked down at her. "You assaulted a police officer."

"I did not!" She heard the screech in her voice and forcefully calmed down. "I was defending myself. Not my fault you stepped into my fist."

He grinned. "That what happened?" He turned Terry's head toward him. "That what happened, Terry?"

"I don't know," Terry grumbled.

They'd reached the edge of the crowd and the curb where a black SUV was parked. Edie found herself shoved into the front, while the lawman dealt with Terry in the back. As soon as Holt's back was turned, Edie got out of the car.

"Don't make me chase you." Holt didn't even bother turning around. "It's my day off and I already did my run for the day. Twice in one day makes me grumpy. And you don't want to see me grumpy."

She was debating this when he slammed the back door on Terry, and Red ran up.

"You okay, Edie? Holt, what the hell you doing with my new bartender?"

"Ah, so that's who she is. Well, why didn't you say so?"

He grinned at her again, and she was flummoxed by the twinkle in his eyes. Were they green? She looked closer, caught herself. Scowled.

"You didn't exactly give me a chance," she said.

"True. My bad. It's just not good for my reputation to be hit in the face by a girl."

"I need her tonight, Holt."

"Expecting a crowd?"

"You bet I am."

Holt rubbed his jaw again.

"You're not seriously going to arrest me for injuring your pride?" Edie said.

"You do have a pretty mean left hook."

"The better to pull two beers at once."

"Yeah?"

"Holt—" Red was sputtering.

"Okay, okay." Holt laughed. "Just wanted to find out who the little spitfire fighting the whole town was." He leaned against the car door. Inside, Terry began banging against the window.

"You could've asked," Edie said.

He acknowledged as much with a shrug. "Now where's the fun in that?"

Asshole. The word was halfway out her mouth when Red took her arm and pulled her away.

"Edie," Holt called out behind her back as she walked off with Red. "Nice to meet you."

She turned to face him, walking backward. "Can't say the same."

Holt watched her stomp off, a tough, dark-haired woman in a town of soft blondes. Not that he minded blondes. He'd married one. But Cindy had always been modest, her butt carefully disguised in soft skirts and loose trousers. The one walking away from him swayed proudly in tight jeans. Round, juicy, touchable. He had to tear his gaze away before someone accused him of gawking. Hell of it was, he was gawking.

In a rush to stop, he whirled around, called his deputy to come get Terry Bishop, then looked out over the park, the clumps of colored balloons, the clusters of townspeople. But all he could see were Edie's firm breasts encased in her leather vest, the tattoo peeking out of the shoulder. And that mass of dark hair piled loosely on top of her head—like one of the Ronettes from his dad's record collection.

Not exactly what he should be bringing home to Mom. Or a five-year-old.

His pulse picked up again. Edie whoever she was spelled trouble. Big-city trouble. He'd been away from Memphis for five years now, and though loath to say so out loud, he missed it. The speed, the lights, the strange characters. Not to mention that adrenaline rush of danger. His body hummed the way a missing limb itched.

He forced himself to recall the rest. The junkies, the dealers, the pimps and gangs. And the dead. Always the dead. Strung out in alleys, outside clubs, on the street in midday, in hospital beds. Especially in hospital beds.

The dead had chased him back to Redbud.

Deputy Samantha Fish showed up in a squeal of brakes, siren and lights flashing. She jumped out of the car spic and span, her uniform pressed, her hair slicked back in an efficient bun.

"Yes, sir." She practically saluted him.

"At ease, Deputy," Holt said dryly. But getting ex-army Sergeant Fish to ease up was no easy task.

"Yessir." She still stood ramrod straight, even while looking past him at the back of his SUV. Terry continued making a racket. "That the miscreant?"

"That's him." Gingerly, he opened the door, surprising Terry, who was in the middle of banging on it. The drunk fell out and landed on his face, making it easier for Sam to cuff him.

"Stow it, Bishop." She hauled him upright with a powerful arm that could more than handle Terry's inebriated state. In fact, it could more than handle most men. Holt suspected if he ever got down on the mat with her, he'd come up second, even with the thirty-odd pounds and five inches he had on her.

Terry stumbled to his feet, grinned at her.

"Hey, Sam."

"That's Deputy Fish to you," she said with a stern frown.

"Aw, c'mon, Sam. Let's have a beer."

She lugged him toward her car. "Beer's what's got you into trouble in the first place."

"Yeah, but it's hot, and I'm thirsty."

That was the last whine Holt heard because Sam shoved Terry inside her car and drove off with him. A night in the new town jail would keep him off the streets and out of Red's.

"Daddy!" Miranda ran up and hugged him around the knee. His mother, Mimsy, was right behind her. The sight of his women sent a warm ripple through him. What was he doing hankering after a dark mistress when he had his own blonde tribe to surround him?

"You said ice cream," Miranda scolded in a clear tone that brooked no arguments. She'd inherited her mother's fine translucent skin, the kind that had fascinated him about his wife. He used to trace the blue veins beneath the tender skin, marveling at how fragile she appeared. But Miranda was not her mother. Even at five she was demanding where Cindy had been persuasive.

He swung his daughter up to his shoulders. "And I meant it, too."

Her small fingers grabbed the top of his head. "I want chocolate."

"I like a woman who knows what she wants." He kissed her knee, and winked at his mother. "Where's Dad?"

Mimsy rolled her eyes. "I don't know why that man calls it a game when it's clearly life and death to him."

"That bad, huh?"

"The last I saw, he was arguing over whether Babe Ruth or Joe DiMaggio was the greatest hitter ever."

Holt smiled. Some things never changed. Not in Redbud at least. There was comfort in that, even if it was a little predictable. He looked around. The picnic was still going strong. Laughing faces, kids screaming, the smell of hot dogs and popcorn. His town. Where he was born and raised. His place in the world. And now it was Miranda's place.

Uneasiness tried to wriggle its way up his chest, an asp searching for his heart. But nothing could go wrong in a place like Redbud.

He hugged Miranda's knees closer to him. Maybe that was the problem.

4

By ten, Red's bar was one note short of rowdy. Which suited Edie just fine. She didn't have to scrounge for the information she wanted; the place was buzzing with the fight and Terry Bishop, as she learned his last name was. Not to mention her own part.

"Hey—you're the girl the chief dragged away."

"That's me. Barely got to town and already notorious." She swiped the bar clean in front of the three newcomers and gave them that welcome smile. "Edie."

"Give us a couple, Edie."

She poured the beers and set them in front of the group.

"Andy Burkett," said the one in the middle, a small wiry man with a shock of thick, unruly hair that continually fell over his forehead. "Run Myer's garage."

"Yeah? So what happened to Myer?"

As one, the group pointed to the floor. "Six, seven years ago," said Burkett. "Bought it from the widow. Thought, hell, whole county used to calling it Myer's, why change?"

Now that was a hell of a thing, Edie thought, recalling her own decision. "What's in a name anyway, right?" Only everything.

Burkett shrugged and introduced the other two men with him. He nodded to the stodgy one next to him. "That good-for-nothing's Howard Wayne and the other one"—he thumbed to the scarecrow on the far side—"that's Russ Elam. They work over at the plant."

"Celebrating Mr. Fred's good fortune?" Edie asked them. Russ and Howard were both wearing greasy Hammerbilt ball caps. Was the factory truly the darling of the town?

Howard readjusted his hat and snorted. "Long's they don't close the plant, that's all I care 'bout."

Edie tried not to look too interested. "Oh? That in the wind?"

Andy shoved Howard. "Nah. Old Howard's just a scared old fart." The *scared* sounded like "scairt," and the *fart* disappeared in a joint guffaw that Howard took good-naturedly.

"You work on Harleys?" Edie asked the mechanic.

"Shoot, yeah. When I get the chance," Andy said. "Why? You got one?"

"A 1200, raked two over, lowered in the rear with a chopped fender and a beauty of a chrome package." She couldn't help the pride creeping into her voice.

The three men raised impressed eyebrows.

"Wouldn't mind taking a look-see," Andy said.

"I'll stop by one of these days," said Edie. They beamed at each other.

"So . . . hear you got into it with Terry Bishop," the

skinny one—Russ—said. "That why Chief Drennen hauled you away?"

For a minute, the world stopped.

"Did you say Drennen?"

"Yeah. Holt Drennen. The police chief. Why?"

She shrugged, coming up with a story fast. "Used to know a Drennen in St. Louis. Any relation?"

Howard, the squat one, answered. "Nah. All the Drennens from around here are still here." He leaned forward. "So give it up. How come Holt hauled you away?"

She leaned forward, too, taking the nearby customers with her. "I was protecting myself, and he walked into my fist." She straightened and said with mock somberness, "Don't like anyone getting in the way of my fist."

The three men laughed, and she winked. Left to fill more empty glasses. Think about that name. Drennen. But Holt was too young to be . . .

"I need three Buds, one light, and an RC and rum." Red's other employee leaned over the bar with her tray. Lucy Keel was tall and straight-boned with a smoker's tang to her voice and a head of red hair that swirled around her long skinny neck. She was sixty if she was a day, hard and tough-skinned and, when Red introduced them, said she'd been working the bar for the last thirty years. "Through two owners and three husbands, a bout with breast cancer, and a car wreck. So I don't take no bullshit and I ain't looking for friends. Get me my drinks fast and we'll get along fine."

Edie'd been jumping all night to get Lucy her drinks. She didn't want to piss the waitress off. She didn't want to piss anyone off. Just do her job and blend in. Nice and slow. Easy. One of the gang.

"Well, lookie here." Lucy elbowed Edie as she popped the tops on the bottles of beer. The older woman nodded in the direction of the door. "Law's after you again," she smirked.

"Well hey there again, Edie." Holt Drennen sidled up the bar with an older version of himself.

Her heart jolted, but she quickly recovered and scowled at Holt.

"You here to get in her way again, Chief?" Lucy called over her shoulder as she whirled away with the drinks.

Holt grinned. "Maybe."

"We hear she packs a wallop!" someone down the way yelled out.

Holt rubbed his jaw. "Want to see my bruises?"

The room laughed.

Someone came up to the pair and slapped the older man on the back. "Nice to see you, Chief."

"You, too, Henry," the other man said.

"So what can I get for you?" Edie interrupted the love fest. Holt was still in his jeans, the sleeves of that T-shirt stretched tight over hard shoulders and muscled biceps. She recalled the feel of him, big and powerful. Found herself staring at those arms, the big hands tapering down to long, slim fingers.

"You want a beer, Dad?" Holt asked.

Dad. The word snapped her back. Everything fell into place.

"That's what I'm here for."

"Draft or bottle?"

"Pull 'em, girl," the older man said with a grin. "We want to see you work."

She grabbed a couple of mugs and filled them. Set them down in front of the two men. Holt introduced his father.

"James Drennen, Edie . . ."

"Swann," she provided, along with a quick handshake.

"Swann," Holt said. "Don't think I know that name. Dad?"

James gulped his beer. Eyed her over the rim of the glass. "Nope. Can't say I do."

Edie changed the subject. It was their name she wanted to talk about. "Two lawmen in one family. Impressive."

"Only one." James pointed to his son. "I'm retired."

"Oh, so you 'inherited' the job." She emphasized the word and gave Holt a pointed look.

"I campaigned like everyone else," Holt said mildly, clearly not bothered by the implication of nepotism. Then he grinned, and there was a devilish gleam to it. "But it doesn't hurt to have connections around here."

"Not to mention ten years with the Memphis PD," James pointed out.

"Oh, yeah. That, too."

Which told her exactly what she didn't want to hear. Not some yahoo with a badge, but a cop who might actually know what he was doing. And who looked too damn good doing it.

"You got Terry Bishop in lockup?" she asked.

"He'd only hurt himself if I let him wander around," Holt said mildly.

She took a breath. Nothing ventured and all that. "What was he so worked up about? Something about the plant? Said he knew things. Any idea what?"

The older Drennen snorted. "I wouldn't trust a thing Terry Bishop says."

"Especially when he's got a six-pack in him," Holt added. "Got fired from Hammerbilt. Been shouting about it ever since. Not much to do around here if you don't work at the plant."

"Quit monopolizing her, Chief," someone called out, and Edie left to fill more orders. Just as well. Couldn't pump the local law for information without it seeming strange. Especially coming from someone who'd just arrived in town.

5

Red closed the place down at two. A couple of hours less than Edie was used to, but that was okay. She had things to do.

Edie, Lucy, and Red worked quickly to tidy up. When Lucy was done, she plopped in a chair, took off her nurse's shoes, and rubbed her feet. "My second husband used to massage my feet," she said absently.

"Yeah?" Edie popped an orange slice in her mouth. Not much call for condiments but she liked to keep them stocked and fresh.

"You ever been married?"

Edie shook her head. "Got too much to do."

Lucy nodded sagely. "A man'll slow you down, that's for sure."

"Hey," Red said. "Watch what you say. The enemy is listening."

"Now, Red, you ain't the enemy," Lucy said. "Just an ole annoyance." She cackled at her own joke. Slid her shoes back on and lifted her chair onto the table. "Well, you're a good sport, Edie. And you work fast. Keep it up." She headed for the door. "See you tomorrow night, Red."

Edie shook hands with her boss. "Thanks for the job."

"You earned it tonight." He clapped her on the back and left.

Edie turned off the lights, locked up, and slipped out back for a breath of air. There were things to do before she closed her eyes in Redbud that night, but first there was darkness to soak up. She leaned against the back of the building, breathed in the night. The sound of Red's car heading away drifted past. And then nothing. Not even the sound of traffic buzzing. Too far off the highway for that. Just the whisper of her own ghosts to keep her company.

"So I hear you got car trouble, Edie Swann."

The voice came out of the cavernous black, ghostly and disembodied. She jumped.

"Whoa there, woman. It's only me." Holt Drennen stepped closer.

"Jesus." For a minute she'd thought she was being haunted. Given who she was she had every right to be. But it was only a living soul. She smacked Holt in the middle of his wide, hard chest. "Don't sneak up on me like that."

"Man, didn't anyone teach you to use words instead of your fists?"

She eased back against the wall, her breathing back to normal. "Didn't anyone teach you when to go home?"

"A police chief's work is never done."

She said nothing, knowing the truth of that all too well. And what would he say if he could look into her heart? His work with her was only beginning?

She should keep her distance. Cool as an arctic dawn. Yet she wasn't cool. Her heart thrummed a hot, steady beat. Her finger drummed against her thigh keeping time. And her head whispered a single word. *Danger. Danger.*

The recklessness her aunt always criticized stirred, molten and thick. She was intimately aware of his big body next to hers. She imagined them together, the song of it, low and sultry. It was crazy, this instant attraction. She didn't even know the man. She should send him away. It was late. She was tired.

She was tempted.

"Thought this was your day off," she said.

"Technically that was yesterday."

"So you're back on duty." She peered closer and made out some kind of emblem on his shirt. A star? A uniform jacket? Thank you for small miracles. She didn't like the idea of him skulking around in jeans and a T-shirt. He looked too delicious in them. And if he kept it up, he might discover more than she wanted him to. "And I'm your early morning task?"

"Gotta check out all the newcomers."

She paused, careful now. Was he serious, or just bantering? "Want my social security number?"

"Nah. Red's got it if I do."

Her shoulders stiffened. Had he already scoped her out? If he'd discovered who she really was, why not say so? No, he knew nothing. Had discovered nothing. She was just . . . a newcomer, as he said. And she could almost smell his attraction. That was something she could manipulate, couldn't she? Draw him in. Pillow talk could be useful.

And he was considerably gorgeous.

"So what *do* you want?"

He peered down at her, and though she couldn't see

well enough to know the expression in his eyes, she felt them piercing and hungry. She shivered.

"Truth?" he asked.

"Night's the perfect time for confession."

"Can't sleep. Been here five years and the quiet still gets to me."

"City boy?"

"Nope. Redbud born and raised. But city spoiled. Can't get the hum out of my head. Thought I'd see if Red was still open."

"Drinking on the job, Chief?"

"Coffee, Edie Swann. Just a lowly cup of coffee."

Her pulse picked up but she didn't show it. Coffee alone with Holt Drennen was more than a temptation. It was a dare. And she was too damn weak-kneed when it came to daring herself over men. "Well, Red's closed up, but I'll reopen if you want." She yawned, hoping he would take the hint.

He did. "Thanks, but it's late. Don't want to keep you from your beauty sleep."

She put a foot on the bottom iron stair. "I'll owe you one."

He nodded. "I'll collect."

She felt his eyes on her back as she climbed up, the clang of her feet on the metal echoing between them.

She got to the landing at the top, inserted the key, and opened the door. Turned to say good night, but the dark had swallowed him up.

Safe, she let herself lament that she hadn't given him that cup of coffee. Or invited him to follow her up. But the regret lasted only a moment. Long enough to ensure he'd cleared out. Time enough for her to complete her task.

She did it with shaky hands. Not from fear, because she believed in the righteousness of her mission. But because something about Holt Drennen, chief of police of Redbud, lingered in the air. Like a tantalizing smell to wind that drew her off course.

She'd always liked big men. The way they could crush you and didn't. The heft of them. As if no storm could blow them down. Holt was a big man. Hard-handed when he needed to be. But good-humored, too. It was the gleam in his eyes that made her look twice. The twinkle that said the world might be a serious place, but we don't have to give in to it.

Then again, he hadn't lived her life. Hadn't heard his mother scream out her soul and her mind. Hadn't watched strangers bury his father.

She ripped off the protective strip from the envelope seal. Pressed it tightly. Crept down the iron stairs to the alley where her bike was parked. She kicked the starter and the engine snarled awake. The abrasive howl bolstered her, reminded her of the strength she owned, bone, sinew, and brain.

She leaned to the left, kicked the bike off the stand, and roared off.

6

The morning after the town picnic, James Drennen pulled into the abandoned rock quarry on the east side of town. His hands were sweating and his mouth was dry, and he ignored both. He saw immediately he wasn't the first to arrive. Everyone knew Fred Lyle's Town Car. He recognized Kenneth Parsley's car by the fish on the bumper, and Dennis Runkle's Corvette stood out even without the Runkle Real Estate sign on the back window. But he would have known who gathered there regardless of those familiar indicators. Their little group had been forged in deception and blood, and it wasn't likely he'd forget any member. Several of their group were missing, of course. But you can't call the dead back to life. Or so he'd have thought.

He parked his truck and walked to the flat rocks overlooking the pit. Fred Lyle was already pacing, his skin bloodless and strained.

Reverend Parsley perched on an outcropping, calmly staring into the abyss. He'd put on the pounds in the last twenty years and his chin had disappeared into his neck.

But he still had that air of rectitude that never seemed quite on the level to James. But Parsley's self-assured piety had vaulted him to the head of the community. No one was closer to God than Ken Parsley, Mimsy liked to say, and he'd tell you so himself.

As usual, Dennis Runkle was on the phone, mouth going fast, hands gesturing emphatically. On his wrist, a thick gold Rolex winked in the hot sunlight. James couldn't remember ever seeing him stand still. But even nearing seventy he still seemed the little weasel he'd been in high school, though he'd had the last laugh on all of them. Biggest house in town, fastest car, sexiest ex-wives.

Runkle, Parsley, Lyle, and him. James stopped a moment to watch the motley group. All of them kept well away from the edge. He understood. He didn't want to go anywhere near the pit himself.

"Jimmy!" Fred spotted him and stopped pacing long enough to close the gap between them. "What are we going to do?"

"First, we're going to calm down."

"Calm down? Are you crazy?"

"James is right." Ken Parsley ambled toward them. In deference to the heat, he'd removed his suit coat, but his sleeves were still buttoned at the wrist. Without the coat you could see his rotundity more clearly. His slacks were hiked over his round belly, like Humpty Dumpty's, but his height and huge broad shoulders somehow carried it. "We have to remain calm. Think this through."

Fred threw up his hands, retrieved a handkerchief from his pocket, and mopped his face. "Runkle!" He threw the real estate agent an angry glance.

Runkle held up a hand, and Fred uttered an annoyed

growl. But ten seconds later, Dennis Runkle strode over. More like raced. But then, that was the man's natural gait. Why walk when you could run?

"That Jansen property is going to kill me," he frowned. Redbud's self-styled Donald Trump, he'd bet on Hammerbilt's growth, buying out the Jansen farm for a new subdivision. But with the audit market tight, development money was scarce. He'd already been the key investor in the new condos on Redbud's west side—an eyesore to some with its repetitive concrete and fake wood façade, a symbol of progress to others. Dennis Runkle was firmly with the latter, reputedly moving his town square office to the west side, though some would say unit sales were languishing.

"Okay." The little man rubbed his hands together. "What's so all-fired important? I got a business to move, things to do."

They formed a misshapen circle, Parsley towering over Runkle, and James looming over Lyle. James could feel the impatience and edginess of the group. Or maybe it was just his own anxiety poking through.

Fred reached into his pocket and pulled something out. He opened his fist. In the center sat a tiny black angel.

The atmosphere stilled, then tensed. Everyone stared. No one reached out to take the thing.

"How did you get that?" the reverend asked.

"Came in the mail," Fred said.

"Did you bring the envelope like I asked?" James asked.

Fred took a rumpled envelope out of his pocket. Turned it over for everyone to see.

"Well, hell, Fred," Dennis Runkle said, "Isn't even stamped. Someone stuck it in your mailbox. A prank."

"What kind of prankster would know?" Fred insisted. "You're the only people who do. Did one of you send this?"

They avoided each other's gaze. It had been years since they'd spoken about any of this and the habit of silence was hard to break.

"Of course not," Ken Parsley said at last.

James looked down at the little toy in Fred's hand. He, too, avoided touching it. "What is it? Some kind of plastic?"

"Probably," Fred said.

Runkle scratched his neck uneasily, an allergic habit he'd had since first grade. "It's a prank, I tell you. Some kid. You're getting all worked up over nothing." Who was he trying to convince—Lyle or himself?

"A week from now I'm due in Chicago," Fred Lyle said. "I'm taking over IAT's entire North American operation. Do you know what would happen if this gets out?"

Thick silence rocked the quarry. Only the sound of the hot breeze whistling between the stones could be heard.

"Maybe it's time we told," Kenneth Parsley said at last.

"And then what?" Fred said. "Aside from what it would do to me personally, there are implications for the plant. IAT is looking for sites to close. That threat is still as potent now as it was twenty years ago."

"That's what we told ourselves then," Parsley said. "We can't keep using the same excuse. One day the truth will come out. Better to hear it from us."

"No. Absolutely not," Runkle said. "Do you know how much money I have riding on this Jansen thing? I need that plant to stay open. The past is over and done. I say we leave it buried."

"James?" Fred Lyle turned to him. "You're the lawman here. What do you think we should do?"

"First off, I'm only an ex-lawman."

"I don't suppose you'd relish being arrested by your son," Runkle said with pinpoint accuracy.

James's lips tightened. The thought sent an ice pick of dread through him. "You leave Holt out of this."

"I'm just saying—"

"Don't," he snapped. "My son has nothing to do with any of this. And he never will. Never." He forced the angry fear out of his voice. "I'm sorry, Reverend, but I'm with Dennis on this. Digging up the past won't help anyone and it will hurt us and the town. Then everything we did will be for nothing."

"Besides," Runkle said. "We took an oath, remember? Never to tell. Never to betray any one of us."

Parsley sighed, but nodded.

"So, we're all agreed?" James looked at each of the group in turn.

"Silence is golden," Runkle said.

"That still leaves us with who sent this and why," Fred said.

James nodded. "Let me look into it. Shouldn't be too hard to find a source. Find the seller, you're one step closer to finding the buyer." James gave them a taut smile. "Now, go home. All of you. I'll let you know when I find out anything."

He walked them to their cars. Organized their departure, making sure a good ten minutes passed between vehicles. Runkle was the first one gone. Hurrying back to close more deals, James guessed. Fred left next, and finally Ken Parsley. Then there was only James's dusty pickup left. He checked his watch. A few more minutes and he could leave like the rest. Put this behind him. But he walked to the edge of the old quarry instead and faced what he wanted to avoid.

He hadn't been here in a long, long time. Not since . . . well, he didn't want to think about that day. Finding the body at the bottom, broken and bloody. It had been a scorching summer, triple-digit temperatures, and there'd been no water in the basin to break his fall. The whole ordeal of climbing down, rigging the body to lift it out. The terrible scream of that poor young widow.

He shivered in the heat.

He still remembered when the quarry shut down. How old had he been? Ten? Eleven? Seemed like the whole town had closed up and vanished. His wasn't the only father who missed every Little League game the summer of 1954. All the adults talking in hushed tones, as if someone had died. The moving van that took his best friend to Chicago where his father had found work. There were lots of empty desks when fifth grade started.

And then Hammerbilt announced it would build a new plant in Redbud. It was like Christmas twice in one year. The worry lines in his mother's face turned to smiles. He had a ham sandwich in his school lunch instead of the usual bologna.

But the fear lingered, even if only way down deep in the back of everyone's mind. They were as close to the edge as he was right now. If Hammerbilt went the way of the quarry . . .

He looked away from the dried-out pit. The sun had

baked the surrounding stone white hot. It hurt his eyes. No, he didn't want to think about the bad times. He'd done what he had to do. What was best for the town and everyone in it.

He conjured up the little black angel that had stared at him from Fred Lyle's fist. Well, stare away, sweetheart. Redbud was doing just fine now. And so were the Drennens. He had his son's love and respect and damn anyone who tried to take it away.

~7~

Except for Holt's early morning ramble to Red's, the day after the picnic was like any other in Redbud. He performed street patrol then went to his office.

But that exception was a big one. Much as he'd like to, he couldn't get Edie Swann's small tight body out of his head. Standing there in the dark with her, his pulse had buzzed. It had been a while, but he remembered that buzz. Waiting on a street corner doing a drug buyback. Walking into a strip joint with his fancy pants on, knowing he was lying to everyone in sight, and knowing, too, if they found him out, he'd be one more body dredged from the Mississippi.

He hadn't felt that hum in years. Not since he turned in his shield and came home. Became "chief" to no one but himself.

Well, that wasn't entirely true. His dad had a couple of part-time deputies, and when necessary, the Volunteer Police Auxiliary. But the deputies retired when his dad did, and the VPA consisted mostly of men in their eighties.

Of course when he needed serious assistance there was

always the county sheriff or the State Bureau of Investigation. They had helped last year when a group of druggies thought Redbud would be the perfect nowhere place to set up headquarters.

But mostly Holt was on his own. At first, that had unsettled him, but he'd grown used to it. He'd grown used to a lot of things. And Edie Swann was starting to unravel that cozy blanket he'd wrapped around himself after Cindy's death.

At least he wasn't a one-man force anymore. Before the bottom dropped out of the market, rumors that the plant was in line for expansion had fueled development, which would have generated more people and more traffic. Holt had used that to talk the council into funding a full-time deputy's salary.

"Show the governor we're not only committed to growth, we're committed to planning for it," Holt had said in his presentation eighteen months ago.

Six months later he'd hired Sam. Newly separated from the army after two tours in Iraq, she had the seriousness and stability the job required. Sometimes a little too serious, maybe—going by the book was a religion with her. But she grew up in Corley County, so small towns were familiar territory. If he ever moved on, she'd make a good replacement. And for now, she provided backup. They switched off weekends, working every other Saturday. Which was why he had been in the alley behind Red's a few hours ago, his uniform on, sniffing at Edie Swann's door.

At least a fling with Edie would break the routine.

And when was the last time he had sex with anyone but himself?

His phone rang, the sound piercing the early morning quiet. He checked the time. Six. Like every other work morning since Miranda had learned to dial.

"Hey, pumpkin. Sleep well?"

"Yup."

"What are you doing?"

"Eating Froot Loops."

"With milk?"

Silence.

"You have to have milk, baby doll."

"I can't lift it."

"There's a glass in the fridge. I poured it before I left."

More silence. "Okay." He heard the pout in her voice.

"Good girl."

"I love you, Daddy."

"Me, too. Don't wake Nannie."

"I won't." At least, not on purpose.

He hung up with the sweetness of her voice in his ear and the rightness of his life back on track.

He pushed off his chair and headed for the back room. For years Redbud had gone without a jail. If Holt's dad needed to arrest someone, he called the state police or the county sheriff. A workable solution, given the crime rate, but an inconvenient one. Part of Holt's expansion of the police department included a new jail cell in what used to be a storage room off the one-room police department. The single office was right on the square in the Redbud Municipal Building along with the mayor's office, the Chamber of Commerce, the city clerk, and anything else of an official nature.

Currently, Terry Bishop was the jail's only occupant. He sat on the edge of the cot inside the cell, head hanging low over his knees. His ponytail had come undone and hair stuck out all over his head. He looked as bad as he probably felt.

"Morning," Holt said.

Terry jumped. Groaned. "Jesus, Chief, you don't have to shout."

"Think you can behave yourself?"

"I could use a cup of coffee."

Holt unlocked the cell. "Claire's is open," he said, referring to the coffee shop on the square. No way he was letting Terry have so much as a glass of water on the city's dime.

Terry grumbled, but managed to shuffle his way out of the cell.

"I were you, though, I'd skip the café and head straight home. In fact, if I were you I'd stay there the rest of the weekend. Think about the right way to conduct yourself in public."

Terry took the hint and headed for the door.

Holt grabbed his uniform jacket. Time to take a ride and check the traffic into and out of town. Saturdays weren't as busy as the weekdays, but it never hurt to make sure folks going somewhere knew to keep to the speed limit.

Edie didn't sleep much. A couple of hours and she was awake again. By six she was dressed and out. Ten minutes later she parked the bike off the central square where she could see the front of the municipal building, but where anyone coming out might not see her. She leaned against a tree and yawned. Like anyone, she liked her sleep. But she figured she could rest later. When everything was over and done.

Half an hour later Terry Bishop stumbled down the steps of the building. When he reached the sidewalk he stopped to stretch and rub the back of his neck. He looked grubby and tired. With all that beer and a night in jail he probably smelled bad, too.

What the hell. It wasn't as if she hadn't smelled worse. She started the bike. Caught up with Terry on a side street a block away.

He slowed when he saw her coming. Put a hand to his forehead to shield the morning sun.

"Need a lift?" she asked him. He stared at her. "You don't remember me."

"Should I?"

"Yesterday. At the picnic. You, me, and the chief . . ."

"I was wasted."

"I know. I was there." She stuck out her hand. "Edie Swann."

His handshake was flabby. "Terry Bishop."

"I know who you are."

"Yeah? So why do you want to give me a lift?"

"I thought you had some interesting things to say yesterday."

"About—"

"Fred Lyle. Hammerbilt."

He scowled and started walking.

Quickly, Edie parked the bike and ran after him. "Wait a sec! Hold up!"

He continued walking and she kept time with him. He shot her a suspicious look. "You trying to set me up?"

"Why would I do that?" Edie said. "I'm interested. Really."

"You a reporter or something?"

"No. Like I said. Just an interested citizen."

"No one's interested in me."

"Look, let me give you a ride home. We can talk better there."

That seemed to alarm him even more. "I don't think so." He picked up his pace, and with her shorter legs, she could barely keep up.

She stopped trying. "You change your mind," she called, "I'm over at Red's. Stop by. I'll buy you a beer."

He neither accepted nor rejected the invitation. Didn't even acknowledge it. Just kept walking.

Edie watched him go, back hunched, hands stuffed in pockets. For all she'd gotten out of him she could've stayed in bed. She headed back to her bike. He was mouthy enough the day before with a few beers in him. If nothing else, there was always Red's.

On his way out of town Holt spotted Terry racing away from someone. Holt slowed. Recognized Terry's companion. Now what did Edie Swann and Terry Bishop have to say to each other?

Maybe she was apologizing for getting involved in Terry's business yesterday. Holt smiled. From the little he knew about her, Edie wasn't the apologizing type. He stowed the question in the back of his mind. One of these days he'd ask her about it.

Which meant, he realized, that he was going to see her once more.

Sure he would. Next time he went to Red's . . .

He grinned again, mostly at his own self-delusion, then continued out of town. Traffic was slow for the first half-hour, but picked up. Wal-Mart was an hour west, and people were getting a jump on their Saturday errands. He watched them slow down when they saw him, and after a half-hour or so, he headed back to the east side where he got his second surprise of the morning. His dad coming back into town.

Holt waved him down.

"What are doing over here, Dad?" If Redbud had a wrong side of the tracks, this was it. All the development had taken place on the west side, leaving this older section to crumble. Not much out here but the old quarry.

James got out of his truck, stuck his hands in his pocket. "Nothing. Driving."

"Something worrying you?"

"Just restless."

"Want your old job back? I can deputize you any time. Just say the word."

James smiled. "I'm fine, son. The sun's up. Gonna be a beautiful day. Just wanted to see it start."

"Miranda okay?"

"Pretending to drink that milk you left her."

They exchanged smiles, both acknowledging and accepting the way the little girl manipulated her men.

"Well, don't let me keep you." James clapped Holt on the back. "See you later?"

"You bet."

James gave a thumbs up as he got back in the truck. If the man had been upset about something he sure looked fine now. He was right. It was a fine morning. Gonna be a fine day.

8

Amy Lyle never could be sure what woke her that Sunday morning. She was usually a heavy sleeper, but then so was Fred. Thirty-five years sleeping next to the man, and he was rarely restless. So maybe it was some kind of wifely sixth sense that had her eyes wide open at two in the morning, made her hurry out of the room without her robe when she saw his side of the bed empty. Or maybe it was the worry she couldn't seem to shake. Fred had not been himself these last few days. Something was bothering him. She hoped to God it wasn't his heart again. The doctor had been clear about the toll stress could take on him, but whenever she asked, Fred always told her he was fine. *Fine.* Was there ever a more feeble word?

Maybe there had been a noise, some kind of sound that had penetrated the walls of their home. The place where they'd celebrated anniversaries and birthdays. Raised their children. The place she'd been racing to leave. So busy looking ahead she'd never stopped to see where she was.

And now she was here, in the kitchen with the police

chief, while Fred lay still and silent in the den. Both waiting for the ambulance to arrive. Not that Fred would need an ambulance. Not anymore.

"And you didn't hear him leave the bedroom?"

Amy looked blankly at the man in front of her. Chief Drennen. There'd always been a Chief Drennen in Redbud.

"Mrs. Lyle?"

"Yes?"

"Did you hear your husband leave the bedroom?"

"No."

"But something woke you."

"Yes."

"And you don't remember what it was?"

"No."

He seemed to want something more from her, but she had nothing more to give.

"Do you recognize this?" He held up some kind of plastic bag with a tiny angel inside. All black with spread wings. Amy's eyes welled up again. Fred could have used an angel tonight. "I found it in your husband's hand, Mrs. Lyle. Have you seen it before?"

She shook her head, bewildered. "It was in Fred's hand? But . . . why would Fred be holding an angel? Especially if it didn't"—she stopped to gather her control—"didn't help him. Look out for him." Her voice broke.

"I don't know." The sheriff's voice was gentle and sympathetic. He handed her a tissue. "I'm . . . I'm very sorry for your loss."

She dabbed at her eyes. "Thank you."

"Just a few more questions. Are you sure you've never seen this angel before? In your husband's desk or study? On his dresser?"

She shook her head.

"Does it mean anything to you?"

She shook her head again.

"Some religious significance, perhaps?"

"Fred wasn't a very religious man."

A woman ambled into the room, and Holt stepped back to let her grasp Amy's hand. He was relieved she'd come. Hally Butene had lost her own husband a year or so ago, and the Lyles had rushed to be there with her those first wrenching hours. Now it was Hally's turn.

"I am so, so sorry, dear," Hally said in her trademark gravel of a voice. A tall, slim woman, she wore classic clothes that hung well on her slender frame. Her white hair was cut short and chic and her large horn-rimmed glasses looked fashionable as well as functional. Her husband had been the plant comptroller until he died, and even in the throes of grief Holt had never seen her look disheveled or dowdy. Even now, in the middle of the night, her slacks and shirt were well pressed and she carried herself with quiet dignity.

She wrapped Amy in a tight embrace that hid the constant trembling in her hands and the slight quiver of her head.

"Can I take her upstairs?" Hally asked Holt. She spoke the words with raspy precision, as though she fought to pronounce each one. The Parkinson's might have taken a toll on her body, but sharp intelligence still glittered in her eyes.

"Yes, we're done for now."

Hally nodded, wrapped an arm around Amy, and led her away.

Holt walked to the den where Sam was finishing her

pictures. A couple of EMTs from the county hospital and Doc Ferguson, the county coroner, stood on the sidelines waiting. Doc had already given an opinion as to time and cause of death—heart attack most likely; it was Lyle's second—and there wasn't much else to do. Except for that strange little angel.

Holt held the evidence baggie up to the light, stared at the thing inside. What did it have to do with Fred Lyle? Why was he clutching it in his hand? A kid's toy, it looked like. Something out of a Cracker Jack box. But more sinister. The black angel. The devil's angel.

He shook off an ominous feeling. Nodded to Sam. "Okay. Let's get Mr. Lyle out of here."

News of Fred Lyle's death rocketed through Redbud and obliterated the party mood of a few days before. Edie felt the pall settle over Red's. Heads were lower, voices more thoughtful. Business was sluggish. Even Lucy's sharp tongue was curbed. She leaned against the end of the bar chewing ice from her empty glass.

Edie refilled it with Coke. "So . . . think it's true about the black angel?" Lucy had been around a long time, and if Fred Lyle's death was going to loosen tongues, might as well start with hers.

"That they found a black angel on Fred Lyle's body?" Lucy snorted.

"About what it means."

"It's just nonsense. Men being gossipy fishwives."

"I heard it had something to do with trouble at the plant."

"Look, are you going to believe the bunch of old ladies here?"

"C'mon, Lucy, give."

The older woman sighed. "Oh, all right. But don't say I didn't warn you." She settled herself against the bar, sipping her drink. "Years and years ago, they say someone got in trouble over at Hammerbilt. Money trouble. Embezzling. Cooking the books. Something like that. Some said he was innocent, but most were sure he wasn't. Then he proves them right by killing himself."

No fun to hear her own history played back as if it belonged to a stranger. But she urged Lucy on. "And that ties in to the black angel—how?"

"The family—his wife, mother, who knows, they buy this angel for the grave. And overnight the thing turns black."

Edie laughed. "Get out of here."

"I told you it was nonsense."

Red leaned in. "You can go out to the cemetery and see for yourself. Big old black angel, like a devil's messenger standing over the grave." He gestured her in closer. "They say it'll turn white again when he's proven innocent."

Lucy rolled her eyes. "They also say only a virgin can survive its touch."

"Guess that leaves you out," Red said, and Lucy whacked him.

"Hey—Edie!" To her left, someone signaled an order. She hustled over to the other side of the bar and served a couple of beers to her regulars—Russ Elam and Howard Wayne.

"You heard about the black angel they found with Fred Lyle's body?" Howard asked.

"Nothing but," Edie said. "Not to mention a lot of stuff about a dead man's grave."

"Gives me the creeps," Howard said. "Could be some kind of devil worship that backfired."

"Shut up, Howie," Russ said. "It's too early for Halloween."

"Yeah, but I've seen that grave," Howard said. "And the black angel standing over it."

"Well, keep swilling that beer, you'll see a whole bunch of black angels," Russ said, and everyone nearby laughed.

Edie twisted her mouth into a smile, but she wasn't laughing. Fred Lyle got what he deserved, didn't he? The ruckus his death provoked was only justice doing its work.

She scanned the bar, seeing who else she could pump for reaction. Someone new had arrived.

Holt Drennen. He wore his uniform, or what consisted of his uniform. Those sexy jeans and the black T-shirt with the chief's star over his breast. About the closest thing to a uniform was the hip-length black jacket with the star on the sleeve and his name on the front. And if she was in doubt about who he was, there was always the handcuff case attached to his waist at the back. And the utility belt with whatever else a cop carried these days. Asp. Mace. Ammo. Holster.

"I'm here to collect that coffee you owe me," he said to her when she sidled up to him at the bar.

She put a cup in front of him and poured it from the carafe Red kept hot. She put sugar and milk in front of him, but he sipped it black and eyed her over the rim of the cup.

Holt could see she was in her element—wiseass smile at the corners of her mouth and a wink for everyone. He'd seen her laughing with the guys from the plant. He liked the look of that grin on her face. Black hair falling into her eyes and over her shoulder. Half of it up, the other half wild and sleep-tossed.

But he hadn't come for the look of her. Okay, not just for the look of her. He'd come to see what the town telegraph was saying about Fred Lyle's death. He'd had hints of it all day. The dismissive look in Sam's face when she came back from lunch. Scoffing at rumors but buying them, too. Hedging her bets on the afterlife and messages from beyond the grave. If feet-on-the-ground Sam was shaken he could only imagine what the rest of the town was saying. Red's was the perfect place to find out.

"So what's the big talk tonight?"

She washed a couple of glasses. "Fred Lyle. Black angels. Did you know there's a angel over a grave somewhere, turned black overnight?"

"Yeah, I heard that."

"Is it true?"

"Well there's a black angel in the cemetery. But I have a feeling there's a logical explanation." He paused dramatically. "Oxidation. I hear it happens. Naturally."

"You don't believe in magic?"

"Not so much." But he remembered finding the black angel in Fred Lyle's hand. An uneasy shimmer ran through Holt.

"They're talking devil worship, too."

Holt frowned. That's the kind of talk he was hoping to avoid. "Seriously?"

Eddie shrugged. "Just passing it on." She grabbed a bar towel and began to dry the glasses she'd washed. "So what's Lyle's death going to do to the town?"

"Besides give everyone something to talk about for a while?"

"Lyle was heading up the ladder. Didn't that put the plant on the map? What will happen to Hammerbilt without Fred Lyle to lobby for it?"

Holt ran a finger around the rim of his coffee cup. Her question implied a deeper interest in the town than he thought she had. And a deeper understanding of the connections between Redbud's various economic sectors. So maybe she was serious about putting down roots. Oddly, the thought depressed him. Like caging a wild bird. "There'd been talk of expansion and Redbud was ready for it. Lyle's promotion might have put the town at the top of the list. Now, with the economy in the ditch, it's anyone's guess."

"Seems like the town's betting on it. I saw someone's building a country club on the north side."

"Why not? Golf course, pool. Even us hicks need our relaxation."

She gave him an ironic smile. "You play golf?"

"I like a game with a bigger defense."

"So what's your poison? Football? Basketball?"

"Why—you going to challenge me?"

"Maybe."

He laughed. Downed his cup and rose from the bar stool. "Thanks for the java."

"Any time, Chief. Want to keep the law happy."

"I'll remember that." He gave her a mock salute and sauntered out.

And Edie watched him go. All the way to the door and out into the night. Didn't his back view look just fine.

~9~

Two days later, the town buried Fred Lyle, and in honor of the funeral, Red closed the bar. Edie used the day off to visit the Redbud Public Library.

All copies of the *Gazette* had been stored, but issues before the turn of the new century were still on microfiche. The librarian led Edie to a back room, showed her how to search the shelves for the dates she wanted and how to use the microfiche machine. Edie thanked her, waited for her to go, then pulled out the box dated July 5, 1989.

She didn't have to do much searching. The article was right there on the front page. Familiar words burst out at her. Charles Swansford, Accounting Manager, Hammerbilt. She skimmed them, searching for the unfamiliar. But it wasn't until July 8 that she found it.

Arlen Mayborne, accounting assistant, was quoted as saying, "He was a nice man. Easygoing. I never would have suspected a thing." And the comptroller, Alan Butene: "This is a tragedy on many levels. For me personally, I've lost a friend and a colleague."

What did it all add up to? She could never get her mother to talk about the day her father died. Where had he gone? Who had he seen? And had any of it forced him to the edge of despair? What had happened between leaving the house that morning and throwing himself over the edge of the old quarry that afternoon?

If she could only figure that out, she would have the answer to the biggest question of her life: why? Why did he step off that ledge? Was he guilty of mismanaging plant funds, as everyone said? A coward? She didn't want to believe that. Her mother never did. But what else could she conclude?

She was staring at the microfiche machine when she felt a presence in the room. A child stood in the doorway gazing at her. One of those beautiful kids, with perfect features and silky blonde hair cut bluntly at her chin.

"What's that?" She pointed to Edie's shoulder, and Edie looked down at the tattoo emblazoned there.

"A swan."

"Why do you have a swan there?"

"It's my name. Edie Swann."

The kid took that in, continued staring at her intently.

Edie never saw herself as the family type. Kids made her nervous with their innocence and trust. This one looked really young. Five? Six? Edie swallowed, not knowing what to say, and wished the kid would go away.

Instead, she walked in, right up to Edie's chair. "Can I touch it?"

Geez. "Uh . . ."

The little girl took that grunt for permission, and before Edie could stop her she'd climbed up on her lap. Tiny fingers traced the outline of the blue and gold wings. "How did you do that?"

At least this was easy. Informational. "It's called a tattoo. You go to a special store and they use needles and ink."

"Does it hurt?"

Truth or lie? Experience had taught Edie that kids were too sheltered by half. "Yeah," she said. "It does."

"So why'd you do it?" Her wide green eyes seemed to peer right into Edie demanding an answer.

"You ever do something you know might hurt but you do it anyway because it's fun or because you want to see if you can take it?"

"I jumped off the swings in the park once."

"You hurt yourself?"

She nodded solemnly, and Edie shrugged as if to say, "See what I mean?"

"What's that?" The girl pointed to the pinup below the swan.

"Betty Boop."

The kid giggled. "Betty Poop."

"Very funny," Edie said dryly. But couldn't resist a smile.

"Miranda!" A small, compact woman with a head of short blonde curls, messy yet attractive, stood in the doorway where the kid had first stood. The mother? Edie took a closer look. Youthful, but not young.

"Good Lord, Miranda, what on earth are you doing? You know you're not supposed to wander off." The scolding seemed to roll right off the little girl. She didn't budge. The woman turned to Edie. "I am so sorry she bothered you."

"I didn't, did I?" Miranda asked Edie.

"Uh . . . no." What else was she going to say? And besides, Edie realized, it was true.

"Come on, now, get down."

Miranda hopped down from Edie's lap. "Can I have a swan on my shoulder, too?" Miranda asked the older woman.

"What?" The woman looked confused.

Edie pointed to her shoulder. "I think she means this."

"A tattoo?" The woman laughed. "Miranda Drennen, you never cease to amaze me."

The name caught Edie off guard. "Drennen?"

"Oh, yes, bless your heart. I'm sorry. I'm Mimsy Drennen. Miranda's my granddaughter." She extended a hand.

"Edie Swann." Mimsy's grip was firm and brief but not unfriendly. "Any relation to the chief?"

"That's my daddy," Miranda said.

"Your . . . daddy?" It never occurred to her that Holt might have a child. She gave the kid another look, trying not to stare. Holt's green eyes looked back at her.

"Do you know my son?" Mimsy asked.

"He's the chief of police, isn't he? I'd guess most people know who he is." Edie said it lightly and hoped Mimsy wouldn't see the answer for the dodge it was. Interest in Holt was bad enough, but his mother and his kid? That had to be a full-fledged disaster. But before she could figure out a way of avoiding it, Miranda intervened.

"I want a swan on my shoulder," she demanded.

"Absolutely not," Mimsy said.

"Why?"

"Tattoos are for grown-ups, that's why."

"I want to be grown up," Miranda said.

"Don't I know it. And much too fast if you have anything to say about it." Mimsy lifted the girl up. "Come on, child, we've got to get home."

Miranda waved over her grandmother's shoulder, and against her better judgment, Edie found herself waving back.

She returned to the microfiche thinking of Holt. Lately she'd been doing a lot against her better judgment, hadn't she?

~10~

Fred Lyle's funeral left Redbud quiet all over town. Holt sent Sam to direct traffic into and out of the small town cemetery, which would overflow with family, friends, and plant workers. While the rest of the town was burying one of its own, Holt ran a street patrol. No better time for a robbery than when half the town was away.

But Redbud was silent and calm, its houses small and tidy. And on the east side they were shabbier, strewn with automobile parts and kids' toys. But he saw no broken windows or signs of vandalism that hadn't been there before. Nothing out of the ordinary until he got to one weedy yard. Leaning against a detached outbuilding that was once a garage stood a motorcycle.

Holt knew the house well, had cleaned up several drug operations there. He'd have to talk to Runkle again. The grass needed mowing, the house needed painting. It looked forlorn and abandoned. No wonder one scumbag after another thought it the perfect place to set up shop.

He parked. Got out of the car and crept up the front

steps. The door was locked, the curtains drawn. Slowly, he eased his way around back.

Someone was sitting on the back stoop, turned away from him. But he'd recognize that head of hair anywhere.

"Edie?"

The surprise on her face mirrored his own. "What are you doing out here?" she asked.

"Just what I was going to ask you." He crossed to the stoop, stood with a foot on one step.

"Meeting a real estate agent. Dennis Runkle."

Holt's eyebrows rose. "Real estate? This place?"

She shrugged. "It's affordable."

"Not when you look at the repair bills."

"It's criminal the way this place has been neglected. You definitely should be arresting someone."

"I did. Cleaned up a drug gang here. Saw the bike out front. Thought someone was starting it up again."

She raised her hands. "Not me. Just looking for a place to live besides Red's."

"So the bike's yours?" He glanced at her curiously. Jealously even. "Nice ride you got there." He let that float away. Gestured to the run-down house. "So . . . planning on staying a while?"

Edie scanned the yard. She'd come straight from the library, not knowing what she'd find, but not expecting this. The grass had given up fighting with the weeds, which were knee high in some places. Her grandmother's house was riddled with neglect and abandonment.

"I don't know." She rose, pushed through the weedy thicket to the elm tree in the south corner. "Maybe." A souvenir of better times, remnants of a tire swing hung from a branch. The thick rope her father had used to fasten it had been replaced by blue nylon. While most of the tire was gone, that indestructible nylon noose hung on. She pushed the piece of black rubber still attached to it. Squeals of laughter echoed in her memory.

Holt joined her. "Wouldn't be hard to fix. New tire, new rope. Back in business."

If only fixing the rest was as easy. A wave of sadness rolled over her and she turned back to the house. White paint peeled off the back wall and rust spotted the metal edges of the screen door.

"Don't think I'll be needing it," she said. Maybe this was a bad idea. Too much memory could drown her.

Well, drowning was always a risk. Wasn't that why Aunt Penny never brought her back here?

"Why can't you leave the past where it belongs?" she always complained, even in those last days.

"Because it's with me. Always," Edie had replied, handing her a glass of water with a straw. Her aunt had shriveled to almost nothing, stopped eating, barely drank anything. She wanted to die, and it made Edie furious. As if egging on the anger, Penny waved the glass away, shifted in the hospice bed, and turned her face to the wall.

Edie gritted her teeth. "Please," she begged. "You're the only person who can tell me now, the only one left." Her voice cracked. Tears of anger and frustration began to sting, and Edie swiped at her eyes.

With a grunt of pain, Aunt Penny turned to face her niece. "You'll be all right, cookie," she whispered. "You're strong. You'll be fine."

"Easy for you to say," Edie said. "You're not the one who'll be alone."

Her aunt managed a choked cackle. "I'll be the one dead."

"You and everyone else."

Her aunt patted the bed weakly. Edie sat, and her aunt took her hand. "Why do you tramp through the world with your fists up? Don't you know there are some things can't be changed? No matter how hard we wish for them."

"I just want to know what happened. Please."

"All right. Don't have the strength to battle with you anymore. Though I don't think it'll bring you much peace."

And after all the times she'd asked, Penny had finally given her what she wanted. A week later she was dead. Edie stayed to see her buried, packed up the apartment, gave away her clothes. A month after the funeral she pulled into Redbud. Alone, adrift, and ready for payback.

"If you're serious about buying, I'm sure you could do better than this." Holt pushed the tire remnant, and they watched it swing.

"If I had the cash, you mean."

"If you had the brains," Holt corrected.

Just then the voice called out, thick with false cheer. "Halloo?"

"Back here," Edie shouted.

A small, energetic man with a golf course tan emerged around the corner. He wasn't young, but he was well-preserved. Expensively dressed. And the hand he extended to shake had a thick gold bracelet on it.

"Miss Swann? Dennis Runkle." A wide smile accompanied Runkle's outstretched hand. He looked from her to Holt. "Nice to see you, too, Chief. Problem?"

Holt shook his head. "Just making sure you don't sell Miss Swann a bill of goods."

Runkle chuckled. "Oh, I warned Miss Swann about the condition of this property. And she said she was looking for something out of the way."

"I like to work on my bike," Edie said to Holt, using the explanation she'd given Runkle. "Too many neighbors complain about the noise."

Holt seemed satisfied with that, but he cautioned Runkle on keeping the house maintained and Edie on purchasing it. "Buyer beware," he told her.

When he was gone, Runkle turned to Edie. "Front or back?"

She chose the front and he guided her to the door. "Watch your step, here, young lady." Runkle inserted the key, had a little trouble with it sticking, but eventually got the door open.

Suddenly she was surrounded by the familiar and unfamiliar. Roses still clung to the walls, but the wallpaper was dirty and faded. Nothing like the bright, airy foyer she remembered. Instead of the homey smell of Sunday dinner, the air was stuffy and reeked of mold. And the house was much smaller. As a child it had seemed gigantic to her. Now it was stunted and dwarfed by time.

She followed the real estate agent to the kitchen. A rust stain marred Grandma's sparkly-white porcelain sink.

"Not much to look at," Runkle said.

She pulled at the oven door, and it opened with a squeak. "Well, I don't cook much." She remembered chicken swimming in a sea of gravy. Mashed potatoes.

Her mother smiling as they sat down. Her father holding the chair for Aunt Penny.

"Want to see the rest?"

He led her up the stairs to the bedrooms, and she ventured her first real question.

"So who owns this place now? Why'd they let it get so dilapidated?"

"Not much going on this side of town. House hasn't been lived in for a long time. Twenty, thirty years ago used to be the Bellinghams lived here. Old Mrs. Bellingham died and the property was sold to settle the estate. I bought it five or six years ago, kind of a speculation. Development's going to come to this area one of these days. Been renting it on and off, though the last lot was a horror, as the chief said. One of these days I'll just tear the thing down and put it out of its misery."

Bellingham. Her mother's maiden name. The answer to every security question she'd ever been asked.

She floated to the room she'd stayed in when she slept over. Her mother's room. Not that she would have recognized it. There was no trace of the white dresser or the pink chenille bedspread. An iron bedstead and a bare mattress occupied the space now. Looked like prison gear.

"Seen enough, young lady?"

She nodded and they trooped down the stairs. "I'll think about it."

"You do that," Runkle said with a wink. "Wouldn't blame you a bit not wanting to live out here. Still got that condo in town, if you change your mind. Nice hardwood floors. New appliances."

They left the house and walked to the curb where

Runkle's car—a neon-blue Corvette—sat. "You just let Dennis Runkle know how he can be of help."

And now the real reason Edie had set up this appointment. She fingered the tiny treasure inside her pocket and leaned against the passenger side door. Examined the car with bright eyes. Guy who owns a car like that had to be a little machine proud. "Nice wheels."

Sure enough, he brightened. "You like cars?"

"Who doesn't?" To distract him, she pointed to some gizmo on the dash. "What's this?"

Runkle went off on a lengthy explanation of torque and rpms, explaining it as if she'd never heard the terms before.

Okay by her. While he was busy with show and tell, she slipped her little gift under the briefcase he'd laid on the front seat.

"Impressive," she said when he paused for breath.

"Best money can buy." He smiled proudly and reached for the briefcase.

Edie froze. Waited breathless to see what would happen. How he would react. A small thrill of anticipation ran through her.

But he only snapped the case open and brought out one of the Runkle Real Estate fans she'd seen at the picnic. He handed it to her, pointing at the logo. "Got my phone and email there. Keep in touch, young lady. I'm sure we can find something for you."

"Thanks." She gave him the smile she usually saved for customers and watched him go. He waved as he drove away.

When he was gone, she pulled out the crumpled list she'd carried everywhere for the last few weeks. Aunt

Penny's list. She stared at the five names like they were the magic keys to unlock the kingdom of revenge.

She'd seen Lyle at the picnic. Now Runkle. Three more to go.

The fun was only beginning.

～11～

Dennis Runkle was a satisfied man. Despite what Edie Swann had said, he had a feeling that black-haired mess of a circus act would end up taking the Bellingham house.

He paused leaving his latest appointment—another old relic on the east side. Time wasn't right for east side development. But it would be. Yes, indeedy. Long as Hammerbilt stayed open. And if he could get this monstrosity at a good price, he'd own two nice properties on the east side of town, this and the Bellingham house.

He trotted down the sloping steps to the curb. Why did he keep referring to it as the Bellingham house? As he'd told the Swann woman, the Bellinghams hadn't owned it in years. Not since . . . well he'd had enough of the past in the last few weeks to last him another twenty years.

Black angels, indeed.

Well, now that they'd buried poor Fred Lyle, talk should die down.

At the bottom of the steps, he took a moment to admire the convertible's blue shine. He inhaled good fortune. Thought about the woman he'd just left inside the house.

Poor thing. Now that her mother was dead she was free. Better late than never.

He remembered her when she was in school. Never pretty but always kind. What they used to call a good girl. And now. White-haired, dried up. Life had passed her by.

He had an odd impulse to go back and ask her to dinner. Or lunch, maybe. Yes, lunch would be more appropriate. He might even enjoy talking with a woman closer to his own age. He'd enjoyed talking with her just now.

But he couldn't imagine her sitting next to him in his gleaming Corvette. He'd look ridiculous. He needed someone pretty and young sitting there.

So he suppressed that fleeting impulse and opened the car door. Was about to toss his briefcase inside, when his smile chilled. Something on the passenger seat. Something small and black.

Tentatively, he leaned over the driver's side and poked at it. The thing rolled on its back, and sent a ripple of apprehension down Dennis Runkle's spine.

A tiny black angel. Just like the one Fred Lyle had received right before his death.

What the—

He slid behind the wheel. Stared at it. How long had it been there? Up until the afternoon he'd had folders and papers piled up on that seat, ready to move them to the new office. Had someone tossed it in days ago and he hadn't seen it? Or had someone placed it there today? A few minutes ago.

He looked around. No one on the street. He started the engine and slowly rolled down the road. No one hiding behind trees or shrubs.

He started to sweat.

Anyone could have done this. In good weather, he always kept the top down. He liked to show off.

But now . . . He'd been foolish to expose himself all this time.

He sped away and as soon as he saw a public lot—Myer's Gas Station—he pulled in, quickly raised the car top, locked it in place, and rolled up the windows. Feeling safer, he sped off again, blasting the air-conditioning. He was absurdly hot.

He glanced at the dark little creature, so like a devil's messenger. Another shiver ran through him.

What did it mean? Some kind of voodoo?

Suddenly, he grabbed the figure, yanked open the glove compartment, and threw it inside.

But still, he couldn't breathe easier. He couldn't breathe at all.

He gripped the wheel. His throat was closing up. He gasped, desperate for air, and clutched his neck. The car swerved violently. Panic overwhelmed him, and in a violent jolt, he understood what was happening. But the knowledge came too late.

Holt got the call over the radio while he was doing his afternoon patrol. By the time he got to the accident site there was a small crowd. The town fire truck was there, along with their volunteer crew. A county ambulance stood by. Sam had already set up a perimeter and was holding the curious back.

He drew her away from prying ears. "Status?"

"Dead," she said.

"I can see that." He glanced over her shoulder to the

wreck. The showy blue convertible was crunched like a tin can against a telephone pole. Dennis Runkle's body was crushed against the steering wheel.

"Pretty straightforward. Plenty of eyewitnesses," Sam said, gesturing with her head toward a group separated from the rest. Holt recognized Andy Burkett, who ran Myer's garage, but he didn't know the others. "Same story all around," she said. "He was going fast, lost control, and wham." She whistled like a mortar traveling overhead and exploding. "I tracked the skids. They jibe with what the witnesses say."

"Any indication of why he was speeding?"

"Idiocy? I mean, the man was seventy if he was a day. Had no business driving a powerhouse like that to begin with."

"Ageism, Deputy Fish? Not much of a theory."

"Okay, so maybe the brakes failed."

"Wouldn't be skidmarks if they had." Holt signaled to Andy Burkett, who ambled over. "You said he was driving fast. Anyone following him?"

The mechanic shook his head. "Just raced down that hill toward the square like a demon was after him."

"You see one?"

"No, sir."

"Sam, check with the others." She went off, and Holt turned back to Burkett. "Can you stand by? We'll get the body out and you can tow the car."

"Sure thing, Chief."

Between Holt, the EMTs, and the volunteer fire department, they got the driver's door open and Runkle's body off to the county morgue.

The rest of the witnesses confirmed Burkett's story,

which left Holt mentally finishing his accident report, case closed. He gave Burkett the okay, and the mechanic called the garage and had someone bring the tow truck to the wreck.

The crowd of onlookers had thinned, but there were still a dozen hardy souls who would stay until the bitter end. They watched silently as Burkett hooked up the wreck and stood by while the driver started the winch. The crushed metal clanked as it was hauled upward, and the briefcase on the seat fell onto the car floor.

"Slow it down!" Burkett yelled to the driver.

The winch jerked to a stop, and the glove compartment popped open. The owner's manual, papers, and other odds and ends fell out, then shifted from side to side as the pulley started again, slower this time.

"Hold it. Hold it!" Holt held up a hand, and Burkett shouted to the driver to stop.

"Something the matter, Chief?" Burkett asked.

Holt barely heard him. "Sam," he said softly. "Get me an evidence bag from the trunk of my car. And some latex."

She was back seconds later with the bag and the gloves. "What is it?"

Instead of answering, Holt put on the gloves, leaned in through the now-open driver's side, and picked something off the floor of the car.

"Lord God a mercy," Burkett said with solemn awe.

Sensing something momentous, the crowd edged closer, and Burkett blurted, "It's one of them black angels."

People started murmuring, and Holt snapped his head up. "Get those yahoos away from the car," he said to Sam. But it was too late. She ushered them back, but they'd all heard. He gave the crowd his sternest, coldest look. "Go home. All of you."

Folks grumbled and shuffled, but neither he nor Sam gave ground, and one by one they pulled each other away. Finally only the tow truck was left. Holt sent Sam back to the office to write up her report while Burkett finished hoisting the convertible and had it towed to the garage.

"What do you want me to do with it?" Burkett asked Holt. "Someone going to claim it?"

"Not yet. Listen, I want a full workup. Brakes, fuel line, transmission, you check everything. And I mean everything. If that car's been tampered with I want to know. I want you to do it personally, okay? No one else."

The intensity in Holt's voice communicated itself to Burkett. He nodded gravely. "Yes, sir."

"And Andy—you keep it to yourself. You have notes or paperwork, keep them locked up. I hear any of this talked around, I'll know where it came from."

"Won't be from me."

"Good. When you're done, you call me. No one else. Got it?"

Burkett nodded, and Holt handed him a card with his contact information on it. Though he tried not to show it, he felt tired and dispirited. The death of two city leaders so close together was daunting. And the black angel lingered like doom over both.

~12~

As always, Sam Fish did as she was ordered: went to the office to write out a report. She didn't particularly like writing reports, but following orders was a way of life. Otherwise things got all screwed to hell. Not that they couldn't get all screwed to hell on their own. She'd seen that for herself in alibabaland. Her mind automatically scolded her. Iraq. She meant Iraq. Of course. No disrespect intended. Sir.

She sighed. Couldn't seem to shake the army. Maybe she should have stayed in. If her mama hadn't gotten sick she probably would have. A lifer. Well, things don't always work out the way you planned. And law enforcement was a good job. Holt a good boss. Not bad to look at, either.

Her face heated, and she immediately dismissed that thought. It was her mother's fault, always telling her to loosen up. "How you going to get that handsome man to notice you?"

Well, what was wrong with a starched uniform? Sam never did understand that whole wrinkled look. If you couldn't make yourself neat and presentable, how were you going to make the world around you that way?

She let herself into the office. Frowned at the clutter on Holt's desk. He might be movie-star cute, but they'd never suit. She'd always be running behind him, straightening up the mess he left. Just looking at his desk, she was tempted. But she resisted. He left her alone, only right she do the same.

She got out the report forms and started filling them out. She'd seen her share of bodies, but thought she was all through with that when she came home. She'd imagined a life of corralling Terry Bishops—drunks and drifters mostly. But here she was, two dead men in less than two weeks. And both with black angels.

She looked up from the form, stared into space. A coincidence or a connection? She wondered what Holt thought. In all the time she'd been his deputy, they'd never had a real case. Was this the first? Goose bumps ran up her arms. A real investigation. Wouldn't it be sweet to go after the bad guys again?

When Holt finally made it home, Mimsy had dinner waiting. She sat him down at the kitchen table, the same table he'd eaten at his whole life, and put a cold beer and bowl of chili in front of him. How many meals had she made for him? He looked around at the kitchen. Saw the nick in the counter where an illegally thrown football had knocked over a glass bowl. The corner by the phone where messages, store circulars, and coupons had mounded into a junk pile. Home. Family. The natural order of things.

Dennis Runkle's smashed-up body invaded the scene

in his head. Stroke? Another Redbud VIP felled by a heart attack?

It could be the car. Something mechanical, either accidental or . . .

Or what? Murder didn't happen in Redbud.

And yet . . .

Two deaths. Two black angels.

Unnatural. Supernatural?

He pushed the bowl of chili away. Man, oh man, now they had him thinking crazy.

Miranda rushed in, dressed for bed in her favorite nightgown with the lace ruffle around the edge. No one could accuse his child of not being a girl. "Daddy!" She hopped on his lap, and his gloom vanished. Hard to be gloomy when Miranda was around.

She put her arms against his neck and squeezed. "You're late."

"Sorry, darlin'. I was working."

"I got a fattoo."

"A what?"

"A fattoo. Look." She pulled the neck of her nightgown down to bare her shoulder. Showed him some kind of picture she'd drawn there. "It's a swan."

He laughed. "Why in the world—"

"Don't worry, it's just marker." His mother bustled into the kitchen. "It'll wash right off." She shot Miranda a long-suffering look.

"I don't want to wash it. Do I have to, Daddy?"

"That's what life's all about, baby girl. Doing stuff you don't want to do." He nicked the tip of her nose. "So why a tattoo?"

"Miranda made a new friend today," Mimsy said.

"Really." Holt could only think of one person with tattoos. But where on this planet Earth could Miranda have met Edie? "A new kid?"

"Oh, it wasn't a child," Mimsy said. "It was . . . well honestly, I don't know what she was. A phantom from past. *My* past. Black hair all teased up and going every which way. Thick black eye makeup. I used to know a dozen girls like that."

He looked down at Miranda. "So you met my friend, Edie."

"Friend?" Mimsy said. Her eyes bored right into him. Matchmaking was one of her favorite hobbies.

To put any ideas to rest, he explained, "She's Red's new bartender. Where did you meet her?"

"In the library," Miranda said, oblivious of the undercurrents running between her grandmother and her dad. "Playing with the big machines." She drew the size in the air with two hands.

Holt looked up to his mother.

"Microfilm," she explained.

What was Edie doing digging in the library's microfilm room? She didn't look like the studious type. In fact, he had trouble imagining her sitting still long enough to get any use out of a library.

Miranda tugged at his shirt. "Can I get a real one?"

"A real one what?"

"A fattoo!" The tone implying her father was not all there.

"Oh, sure."

Her face lit up, and he hated to spoil that excitement, but hey, he was the dad. It was his job. "Some day," he added.

She pouted. "When?"

"When you're older."

"How old?"

"Thank God you came home," Mimsy said. "I've been running around those questions all day."

"How old?" Miranda repeated.

"When you're old enough, I'll let you know." Holt swept her up. "Come on, you." He took her upstairs and put her to bed.

Covered in a comforter with pink doodads over it, she looked up at him with wide, innocent eyes. "Maybe I can get a flower," she said.

He grinned. She was nothing if not persistent. "We'll see."

He closed her door and went across the hall. When he moved back to Redbud, he'd been a mess. No job, no desire to get one. His parents had taken him in and he was too tired to protest or do anything else. In fact, their kindness had been a welcome relief.

But he couldn't bear going back to his old room, so he gave that to Miranda, and Mimsy had transformed it, burying his boyhood under a weight of pink ruffles and lace. Now, he bunked in what used to be the spare room, a narrow compartment that Great-aunt Ida used to sleep in when she came to visit. Far from lavish, it was clean and utilitarian, and suited him fine. He hadn't added much to it in the five years since he'd been back. In the beginning that had been a hedge against making the room and the move permanent. But it had become permanent. He'd planted his feet and they'd stuck.

He opened his laptop. Spent a couple of hours searching for places to purchase black angels. Found a gothic clothing store, a 1946 movie, a rock group, but no retailers. Which meant he wouldn't be able to trace the things through the net. That only left the rest of the wide-open universe.

At a momentary dead end, he tramped downstairs to the den, where his father was ensconced on the couch across from the TV. Holt paused in the doorway, taking in the room.

Like the kitchen, the den was worn and lived in. Old basketball trophies and plaques still decorated the bookshelves along with pictures that swept the realm of his life. His own high school yearbook picture where he looked impossibly young and goofy. Prom night with Cindy. Their wedding, her smile sweet and gentle and happy. And Miranda. A red-faced infant. A toddler with him and Cindy. And then . . . with just him. There were pictures of his parents' life, too. James and Mimsy on a cruise. At the foot of the Eiffel Tower. In front of a tent in the Smokies. It was all a jumble, one on top of the other. But the pictures never changed. Just like home was always home.

It was precious. Even more so after today. Holt had seen his share of violent death, but it never went down easy. The images of the day circulated inside his head— the blue sheen of Dennis Runkle's vanity car crunched and scraped raw. His body, crushed and bloody. In case Holt ever forgot how fragile we all were. How fast everything could be taken away. How vital it was to hold on to what was important.

He wondered what his dad would have done if Mimsy had died before she turned thirty, leaving him with a year-old baby. Would he have slunk back to his parents' home?

Wouldn't have been an option. His father's parents were long gone by the time James Drennen had married and fathered a son. He'd started with nothing and made a good life for his family. Holt was proud of that.

Now James sat on the sofa staring at what should have been the Braves game. Instead, a diamond ring circled in close-up on the muted screen.

"Thinking of adding to your jewelry collection?" Holt strolled in and sat beside his father. "Dad?"

"Oh, hey, Holt," James said.

"Hey yourself. What're you watching?"

"Hmm?"

"The TV. What are you watching?"

James looked at the screen. He didn't even remember turning it on. "Damned if I know."

They sat in silence for a while, watching the ring sparkle and circulate. James tried to pull himself together, but his heart had been pumping like a gusher ever since he'd heard from Mimsy, who heard it from Patsy Clark, who was at Claire's when Runkle plowed into that tree.

What did Holt know? That was the thing that kept James's mouth dry and his palms clammy.

James clutched his hands together and leaned over his knees. He didn't want to look at Holt while he fished for information. "Heard you had a rough day."

"Not the best, no." There was weariness in Holt's voice, and James felt sorry for it. But not sorry enough to change the subject.

"Get everything cleaned up?"

Holt didn't even ask how his dad knew what happened. He just nodded, accepting the fact that the town's informal telegraph system was swift and efficient. "Car's at Myer's. Body's at Ferguson's."

Myer's meant a search for mechanical problems. Doc Ferguson was the county coroner. So that meant an autopsy. "How fast until you hear the results?"

"I told both to put a rush on, but you know how things get done around here. When they get done."

That meant—what? Days until James could relax. He nodded, stared out at the room again. Didn't see anything.

"You okay?" Holt asked. "First I find you at the crack of dawn wandering on other side of town, now you're watching QVC."

Christ, he had to do better than this. He sighed. "Guess it's unsettling, all this bad news coming one on the heels of the other."

"Tell me about it," Holt murmured. "Look, Dad, how well did you know Dennis Runkle?"

James froze. "Me?"

"Whoa, slow down," his son laughed. "This isn't an interrogation. Just thought you could, you know, throw some insight my way."

James tried to loosen up. "I didn't know him much at all. Just to say hello to. Or, you know, city business."

"Much of a drinker?"

He told the truth. "Never got a call on him. Never heard he had a problem. Why? Think he was drunk?" Wouldn't that be helpful.

"Don't know. Maybe he was just driving too fast. Man that age should know better."

"Hey"—James tried a chuckle, and it came out choked—"one day you'll be a man that age."

"Well, I hope I'll know better by then," Holt said dryly.

James paused. How to bring things around to the next concern? Couldn't think of any way other than outright asking. He took a breath. "You find anything on that black angel?"

Holt groaned. "Aw, geez, Dad, you're not going voodoo on me, too?"

Voodoo? Was that what the town was saying? "Just asking. Not saying there's anything to it. But there's going to be talk until you can come up with an explanation."

"Talk I can handle. And I'll find an explanation. One that doesn't involve black magic or the devil. You can count on that."

James nodded. As long as it didn't involve him either.

~13~

Arlen Mayborne still worked at Hammerbilt, although no longer as an accounting assistant. He was head of the department now and Edie had little trouble getting in touch with him.

She told him she was a business writer doing a story on the economics of small-town America, and arranged an appointment with him on her first day off. A shift must have ended because cars streamed out of the gates as Edie pulled in.

The plant itself was a sprawling complex that seemed to stretch for miles on the north side of town. Edie stopped to give her name at the guardhouse and to get directions to the office area. Once there, she asked for Mayborne at the reception desk.

She sat in a vinyl-covered chair to wait. Copies of *HVAC Today* were scattered over a nearby coffee table. The hard clink of metal on metal drifted in from a distance along with the industrial odor of steel, grease, and sweat.

Edie had eschewed makeup, leaving her face pale and

unremarkable. Her hair was up, but she'd taken care to keep it neat and presentable. Black slacks and a blazer completed the discreet costume. Her arms were covered; she didn't want her body art to distract.

And it didn't. Mayborne gave her a perfunctory smile when he came to get her, but there was nothing in it that said, who is this freak? A look she often got in her usual getup. Not that she cared. She was a freak. Had been all her life. And it all started here, somewhere in Hammerbilt.

She followed him down a corridor, past the mailroom, and around a corner, rigid with anticipation. Would she run into anyone she knew from the bar? Mayborne had never turned up at Red's, and she could only hope he never would. But Howard worked here. So did his friend, Russ. Would they recognize her in her nunlike costume? She gripped her hands waiting for someone to shout, "Hey, Edie!"

But no one did, and by the time they reached the accounting department, she had loosened up enough to feel the tension in her neck and shoulders.

The accounting department was a wide room with four desks and a private office to one side. Gray metal file cabinets lined the walls, a copy machine and a paper shredder stood in one corner. Cold and impersonal, the place smelled of paper and copier ink.

Two men in dull white shirts and Wal-Mart ties, neither particularly crisp, occupied two of the desks. A woman in a lumpy stretch top sat outside the private office. Department secretary? The other woman was young—younger than Edie. Wearing a suit that hung on her bony frame, she looked barely out of high school. Of the four, she stared frankly as Edie came in with Mayborne.

Was this where her father sat? A place like this could drive anyone to despair.

Mayborne led her into the little office, offered her a chair, and sat behind the desk. He was a thin man, tall, with a concave chest that hung inside a too-large shirt. A pair of gold-rimmed glasses perched on his nose. The lenses were dirty and spotted but he didn't seem to notice. Edie tried not to.

"So what would you like to know, Miss Swann?" He gave her a polite smile that stretched his pale skin. Atop his head thinning red hair looped in lean curls.

On the drive over, she'd plotted the route of the interview, starting with the innocuous. She took out a notebook and pen, held the pen poised over the paper. "Tell me about coming to work for Hammerbilt."

"Well now, I came right out of high school in the spring of '86," he said. "Completed my accounting degree at night. Hammerbilt had just started a program to help employees who wanted higher education. Still running, too, I'm proud to say."

She pretended to take notes. "When was that?"

"A year or two after I came. One of the previous department heads, Swanford, he started it."

Her pen skidded to a such a hard stop it poked a hole through the paper. She hadn't expected her father's name to come up so easily. She forced herself to breathe normally.

"Swanford? Can you spell that for me? I'd like to get in touch with him."

A tiny pause. "Well, sorry to say, he passed. Years ago. Very tragic. Took his own life."

As it always did, her stomach clenched at the phrasing. "How awful. Why?"

He leaned over the desk, lowered his voice. "Rumor had it he was caught with his hand in the cookie jar, so to speak."

"Embezzlement?"

"Never proved, mind you. He died before it could come to trial. And frankly, I had trouble believing it at first. But you never know, do you? Innocent men don't do themselves in." He sat back abruptly. "You're not going to write about this, are you? It happened so long ago. Don't want to dredge it all up again. Terrible time. Terrible."

She flashed him a sympathetic smile. "I can only imagine. Must have been pure chaos here. Schedules just go out the window when something like that happens, don't they?"

He nodded. "Mrs. Garvey was in a complete frenzy, if I remember correctly."

Her attention focused. An unfamiliar name. A new lead? "Mrs. Garvey?"

"Hannah Garvey. The department secretary."

"How can I get in touch with her?"

"Oh, she passed, too. They're all going, the old ones."

She tried not to show her disappointment. The one lead he'd given her, and it was a dead end. Literally.

"Even Mr. Butene, the plant comptroller," Mayborne mused.

Her heart squeezed. That was a name she recognized. "Oh?"

"Died a few months after poor Hannah. Fell off a ladder. Did you know how high a percentage of fatal accidents take place in the home?" He shook his head. Sighed. But Edie only hugged her pen tighter.

Another name crossed off, but this one for good. Three names gone and she was no closer to uncovering the truth. When would she catch a break? Disappointment turned into annoyance. Waste of time. Total waste of time.

Then again, maybe not. She'd passed a mailroom on her way to the accounting department, hadn't she? An idea began to form.

"You must have seen a lot of changes in the plant and the town," she prompted, and while Mayborne talked about his years at the plant she had time to firm up her idea.

When Mayborne wound down, she said, "You must like it at Hammerbilt to have been here so long."

"Plant's been good to me. And, well, to be honest, not much else to do in Redbud."

She rose to go, extended a hand. "Thank you for your time."

"Happy to do it. You send me a copy of that article, now." He gave her a card with his name and address on it. She pocketed it, and he came around the desk.

"No need to see me out. I know the way."

He waved her off, and she put her plan into action, heading back to reception with a bit of a detour. She'd been going to do this on her way back from the plant, maybe take a ride over to the next town. But how could she resist using Hammerbilt to send her next little package?

She slipped into the mailroom. A woman was sorting mail, but she didn't look away from the wall of cubby-holes she was filling. Edie spotted the container marked "outgoing," and dropped the small padded envelope from her purse into the basket.

Just in case, she kept her head down and gazed at the floor as she swept out of the mailroom. Gazed down and smiled.

Then she raced back to Red's and arrived in a party mood, humming as she ran up the iron steps to her room. She knew exactly what she would do to finish off this glorious afternoon.

She flung open the door, stripped off the confining clothes she'd worn to see Arlen Mayborne, and shoved on a pair of cutoffs and a tank. Got her headphones and flipped through her CDs for the one she wanted to listen to. With a pail of water borrowed from Red, a sponge and her bike cleaner, chrome polish and wax, her terry-cloth towels and chamois, she was all set.

Back in the alley, she smiled silently to the bike. Hello, Beauty.

The water was cold but that was fine in the warm summer air. She sponged down the bike, then sprayed it with Showbike and cleaned out the grunge. After the dirt was gone, she started on the chrome, buffing and polishing the handlebars and down those gorgeous legs. They were going on a little trip tonight, and she wanted the bike to look its best, all shiny and new like the metal had captured the sun and couldn't help but glow.

God, she felt free. She'd been inside the monster, right there in the heart of Hammerbilt. Even used the plant to send her latest little bomb. And it felt good. So good.

She pictured the recipient. Would he quake and stagger when he opened the package? Would his heart go off on him, like Lyle's did? And Runkle? What had he done?

She hoped he'd trembled with fear, desperate to know who planted his little missive. She wanted to shake them all up, the guilty and the innocent—the whole town if need be. Then maybe the truth would stumble, tattered and worn, maybe, pale but alive, into the light.

For the past twenty-five years Runkle Real Estate had worked out of a small storefront two blocks off the town square. Over the years the business had expanded and outgrown its original space, but it wasn't until a prime location near the new west side condos opened up that Runkle thought seriously about moving.

When Holt arrived at the old storefront off Main he found it a mess of boxes and files, stacks of books and papers, phones and computer wires that created a minefield of junk to negotiate.

Marydell Figgis, one of Runkle's agents, greeted Holt with swollen red eyes. "I just can't believe it." A large, middle-aged woman, Marydell came with a full bust, plump cheeks, and short blond hair inexpertly fixed. A hundred years ago she would have looked at home in a farmyard, a wide apron over her ample chest holding grain for a flock of chickens. Now she squeezed into a pantsuit and sold the land her ancestors once farmed.

She blew her nose loudly. "Another week and we'd be moved." She shook her head. "I just can't believe he's . . . he's gone." Her voice cracked and Holt shifted uncomfortably under the emotion.

He cleared his throat. "I'd like to ask you a few questions."

She inhaled a shaky breath. "Of course." Glanced around for a place they could sit. Couldn't find one. "All the chairs are already gone," she said lamely and looked as if she was going to burst into tears again.

"That's okay," Holt said quickly. "This won't take long." He plunged right in. "Do you know what Mr. Runkle did yesterday? Did he have any appointments?"

"Oh, I'm sure he did." She scanned the room again. "He keeps his own schedule. We all do." She fished through some boxes. Came up empty-handed. Crossed to the other side of the room and dug around some more. "I'm sorry. I can't seem to find . . ." She straightened. "We have a sign-out board and the schedule is usually posted. But with the move and everything . . ."

Holt spied a couple of PCs on the floor. "What about a computer? He keep his schedule there?"

"Oh, no. He was very old-fashioned. Wrote everything down in a book."

"And the book is . . . ?"

"Should be here." She gave him an apologetic looked. Dabbed at her nose again. "Somewhere. I do know he was going to show the old Bellingham house on Dogwood."

Where Holt met Edie yesterday. "I'm interested in what he did after that." Holt took out a card, handed it to Marydell. "I'd appreciate you making a special effort to find that appointment book. My number's on the card. Let me know when you do."

Marydell held a hand to her heart. "I'll do whatever I can." She sniffed. "I just can't believe . . ." He left her shaking her head, a round apple of a woman in the core of the mess.

Back in the car, he drove around to Red's. The bar was closed, but he wasn't interested in the bar, only the bartender. He made his way around the back to the alley and stopped dead.

Edie was wearing a skimpy pair of overalls cut way above midthigh. Some kind of stretchy sleeveless thing covered the exposed areas below the bib but the rest was as God had made her—golden skin covering her arms and legs and shoulders and neck. It was a sight to take a man's breath away.

She was busy when he got there, her back turned so she didn't notice him. Her bike was out, a pail of water, a couple of chamois strewn around. Her hair was piled on her head but as always some of it had floated down her neck giving her that sexy bed head look.

She was working like a demon, scrubbing the body of the Harley with a sponge the size of her, headphones square on her head. They were large, not those little iPod doohickeys. Hers looked like the noise-canceling kind, which meant he could probably shoot off his weapon and she wouldn't hear him.

So he stood there, enjoying the view. She leaned over the bike to get every inch and her ass, as sweet and ripe as any he'd ever seen, stuck out and pulled in, out and in.

He swallowed. Or tried to.

She turned to squeeze out the sponge over the pail and saw him. Jumped ten feet. Flipped the 'phones off her head. Glared at him.

"How long have you been here?"

He grinned. "Long enough."

She frowned, hands on curved hips. "See your fill?"

"Not by a long shot."

She tossed the sponge into the pail. Came toward him. "What can I do for you, Chief?"

If she only knew. "Heard you were at the library the other day."

"So?"

"So you don't seem like the bookish type."

"You shouldn't go by what people look like. That's stereotyping. Not what we want from local law enforcement."

"Uh huh. What were you doing there?"

She eyed him. "I like history," she said finally. "Just wanted to know a little more about the town. Didn't know it was illegal."

He smiled. "Not illegal. Just not efficient. I've lived here all my life. You got questions, I probably know the answers."

She gave him an arch look. "That some kind of invitation?"

Holt blinked. Realized it was. "Yeah," he said, warming up to the idea. "I can show you around."

She thought it over. Returned to the pail and the bike without answering. He followed. Nodded toward the headphones.

"What are you listening to?"

Another playful look. "What do you think?"

He shrugged. "Metallica? Nine Inch Nails?"

She laughed. "Now what is it about me that makes you think all I listen to is heavy metal?"

"I have no idea."

A mischievous expression crossed her face. "Want to find out what I'm really like?"

He should have resisted the opening, but didn't. Slowly, he ran his gaze down her body and all the way up. "You mean beneath the tattoos and what little else you—"

"Yeah, Chief," she said dryly. "Beneath everything."

He leaned against Red's back wall, crossed his arms, and cocked his head.

"I'm going to a concert tonight," she said. "Come with me."

He straightened, not sure he'd heard right. "You asking me on a date?"

"A date?" She picked up the chamois and returned to polishing the bike. "Just a return of favors. I take you to a concert, you fill me in on the ins and outs of Redbud."

Briefly, Holt watched the swan on her shoulder jiggle as her arm moved up and down. "You got a deal," he said. "Meet you outside the office."

She stopped and shot him a wide-mouthed smile. "Pick you up at seven," she said, and went back to work.

Holt was almost at the car before he realized he hadn't asked her what he'd come to ask in the first place. He jogged back. Her headphones were back on, but he managed to position himself so she saw him before he scared her again.

She thumbed the 'phones off her head and they curled around her neck. "You're making a pest of yourself."

"About the other day. At the house with Runkle. He say where he was going after he left you?"

"No. Why?"

"I'm trying to trace his steps those last few hours."

"Last few hours?"

"You haven't heard? He ran his car smack into a pole."

She inhaled a sharp breath. "Is he all right?"

"Only if you call dead as winter all right. Found another black angel, too."

She paled. Stumbled a little and grabbed the handle-bars to steady herself.

"You okay?"

She nodded. "I just . . . just saw him. How could . . . I mean . . ." Her voice trailed off in a tone of disbelief.

"Yeah, I know. It's been a shock all around. Sure he didn't say anything?"

She shook her head.

"All right then. See you tonight."

Edie watched Holt leave through a fog. Quickly, she finished the bike, doing a half-assed job of it, but no longer caring. She gathered her things, ran up the stairs, shut the door, and leaned against it.

Water splashed on her leg. She looked down. Her hands were shaking.

She set the pail on the floor. Thought of Runkle's sharp, tanned face and practiced smile. A little while ago, she'd been gloating. Hoping the guy was shaken up. Now . . .

Dread circled around her. Was some unseen hand weighing in on her search for justice? Who knew what she knew? What secrets she kept? Her heart was beating hard enough to rip through her chest.

It had to be a coincidence. Two elderly men—the chance they'd kick it one right after the other had to be high. Right?

And anyone could crash into a tree. It had nothing to do with her. Nothing.

She crawled onto her bed, wanting to crawl under the covers and hide. Let the world go on without her.

Then she remembered. Holt. The concert. Her big plan to pump him for information. She groaned. The last thing she needed was a night of fencing and flirting with the town police chief.

She should call him. Cancel.

But how to explain? I can't come because the two men I sent those black angels to—ha ha—turned up dead?

Her stomach swirled. She rolled over on her side. Drew her knees up to her chest.

Two men. Two black angels.

And the third one. Already on its way. Too late to take it back. Too late. Too late.

~14~

Edie picked Holt up in front of the municipal building. For the ride to Nashville, she'd worn a pair of jeans but her concert clothes were packed in her saddlebags. When Holt had told her to pick him up downtown she had a quick thought that he'd show up in his uniform, but he wore a pair of khakis and a white shirt open at his throat. Not exactly Metallica costume, but then they weren't going to hear Metallica. Of course he didn't know that.

"Ready?" she asked when she pulled up to the building. He was waiting for her at the curb.

"For what?"

"For whatever."

"I didn't bring my asp with me. Or a can of mace."

Her mouth twisted. "I think we'll be safe."

He eyed the portable seat behind her. "Where'd that come from?"

"Lick 'em and stick 'ems. Suction cups. Come on, get on, they'll hold you."

He looked like he didn't believe her, but he swung a leg over. "Okay. I'm trusting you, now."

Well bravo for him. She zoomed away, glad the noise made conversation impossible. She'd tried to work herself up for this, but couldn't quite make it. They jogged along, bouncing with the ride, and her insides shook and pounded, which only fit her mood. As if she'd been poured into an industrial mixer and the motor set to an endless "on."

She still hadn't absorbed the shock of Dennis Runkle's death. Surely it had nothing to do with her. It had to be exactly as it seemed—a terrible, awful accident.

And if it wasn't?

What if she'd set something in motion? Or rather, someone? And how did she tell them this wasn't what she intended? Her head hurt thinking about that. Because if Runkle's death wasn't a giant coincidence that meant there was one more body out there. Two if you counted all the names on her list. And who knew if her list was the master? Maybe whoever was out there had a bigger list. With more names on it. Maybe even . . . she shuddered. Hers.

Because if her angels were connected with the deaths she'd be implicated, wouldn't she?

She set her face into the wind. What the holy fuck had she started?

The ride to Nashville was about an hour. Normally, she would have taken the back roads and given Holt a real spin, but now she just wanted to get there and get the whole night over with.

But she could never resist the magic of the road for long. Fifteen minutes into the freeway, the rhythm of the engine took over like it always did. The standing world sped by and blurred into nonexistence. Angels and death faded away. Wheels and speed were the only things left. As she breathed in the warm summer evening, she relaxed against the body behind her. Holt's chest walled her in, his strong arms wrapped around her waist, long fingers pressed into her belly. How could she feel nothing?

She couldn't. Not with his mouth at her neck, his heart at her shoulder.

She found herself breathing hard, and not only from the thrill of the ride. And once she pulled off into the downtown exit and parked, she saw he was affected the same way. His eyes shone under the city street lights, and she sensed he was in the same jacked-up mood that hit her every time she got on the bike.

She grabbed one of her saddlebags, slung it over her shoulder. "Enjoy the ride?"

He laughed. Full-throated and excited. "Are you kidding? God, I forgot what that felt like." He shook his head, marveling. "That was fantastic. You've got to let me take her home."

She eyed him, curious. "You don't strike me as much of an adrenaline junkie."

Something crossed his face. A kind of melancholy look, briefly there and gone. "Used to be. I had a bike. Not a Harley, but it was a pretty decent Yamaha."

"Yeah? What happened?"

"Drove Cindy nuts. I finally got rid of it."

"Cindy?"

"My wife."

She'd wondered when he'd tell her about Miranda's mother. "Divorced?"

"Dead."

She almost tripped, that was so unexpected. Ten thousand questions flooded her head, but Holt tensed. Looked as if he'd rather choke than talk about his wife. So she continued walking up Broadway, past the honkytonks and then south down Fourth Street. How had she ever thought he didn't know what loss was? That the teasing gleam she liked so much was all there was to him? She felt a rush of shame for misjudging him. Still, the questions, silent and unasked, continued to linger between them.

"Look, we all have our sob stories," Holt said at last. "Just to get mine over with, leukemia, five years ago, Memphis. Moved back here because I needed help with Miranda. You?"

She paused, debating what to say, how to say it, whether to say anything at all. "Can't compete with that," she said at last.

His mouth curved into an ironic smile. "Yeah. I usually win the prize." He gazed down at her. Exhaled. "So . . . now we've got that over with, when are you going to tell me where we're going?"

She turned the corner and led him toward the huge neoclassical style building. Nodded toward it.

"I thought you said we were going to a concert."

"We are."

"At the courthouse? Or is it a very, very, very big bank?"

She laughed. Flourished an arm in the direction of the building. "May I introduce you to the new Schermerhorn Center."

He looked at the massive building dubiously. "And they do rock concerts there?"

"I didn't say that."

He paused when they got closer. Hard not to. The

Apollo fountain fired the plaza, its beautiful spray gleaming. Lights around the imposing entrance with its impressive set of steps made the limestone glow. He stared at the pediment over the building.

"Hades dragging Eurydice out of Orpheus's arms and back to the underworld," she told him.

"Who's the other woman?"

At Orpheus's back a woman sat on her knees, crumpled, devastated, reaching out in anguish. "Grief," she said.

They climbed the steps, joining other concertgoers. Once inside, he turned around, taking in the Spanish marble, the mammoth columns, the chandeliers with their round, fat bulbs. Edie smiled to herself, happy that Holt was as affected as she was the first time she'd been here.

"And the acoustics ain't bad, either." She winked and left him to gawk. Disappearing into the ladies room, she changed into the clothes in the saddlebag, packed her jeans and bike boots inside. Then she checked the bag and rejoined Holt in the lobby.

His eyes widened when he saw her. The black dress was made of a silky material that never wrinkled. It had a knife-pleated skirt that swayed against her hips and legs as she walked, a smoothly tight bodice that showed off her breasts, and a narrow belt that shone at her waist. The sleeveless shoulders were cut so deep they revealed her collarbone on each side. It was her favorite dress. Elegant but sexy. Not to mention the spikes she had on her feet. A far cry from the jeans and leather he'd mostly seen her in.

She burst out laughing at the look on his face. He tucked her hand firmly on his arm. "We're not going to a rock concert, are we?"

"Ever hear of Brahms?"

He gave her a sardonic look. "Once or twice. I think."

She took out their tickets, handed them to an usher, who led them to their seats. "His Fourth Symphony is one of my favorites."

He gawped at her. "You weren't listening to Metallica, were you?"

"Beethoven. 1812 Overture."

His eyes narrowed. "You're enjoying this, aren't you?"

"What?" she said in mock innocence. "Overturning your assumptions?"

"Surprising people."

She put a hand over her heart. "I confess."

"So . . . this Brahms guy." He returned her mock innocence with false ignorance. "What's so great about him?"

The lights dimmed. She nodded toward the raised stage in front of them where the musicians were taking their places. "You tell me."

Edie had heard Brahms's Fourth many times, but she always forgot the way it struck until the lush, passionate waves of the first movement swelled up and over, drowning her in a sensation that was as physical as it was emotional. Enveloped in sound, she forgot about Holt, forgot everything, the same way she forgot on the Harley, immersed, wet, flooded with something unearthly, something she could only grasp when she was deep inside the music or flying down the road.

And in the midst of this otherworldly haze, as the thick notes seized her chest and belly and made her body shimmer, she felt someone grab her hand. Hold on as if clinging to life.

Holt.

And if she didn't know instantly that he understood, it was there in his glittering eyes, the breathless rise and fall of his chest, the crazed fervor with which he squeezed her fingers.

And later, much later, after the music had ended and she had her breath back in her lungs and her jeans on, and they were walking back to the bike, she knew he'd been moved beyond speech. From the minute the last note sounded he hadn't said a word. Didn't seem capable of speaking.

But just outside the parking garage, he stopped, turned to her, and with a slow, deliberate pull, drew her close. And closer still. He searched her face, a look deep and profound. And slowly, oh so slowly, he kissed her.

It was like no kiss she'd ever had. Quiet and raging. Hungry and yet, oddly, humble. He took her mouth as if he was taking her soul. Tenderly. Knowing how precious it was. She was.

Like the music, it made her want to cry. Or to roar with joy. Or both or neither. Only let it never end.

And when it did and he pulled away, unhurried, lingering, he cupped her face with his slim fingers and strong hands. "Thank you," he said simply. "Thank you."

~ 15 ~

It wasn't natural to have a piece of music change one's life, but Holt woke the day after the concert as if something overpowering and important had happened. The universe had shifted on its axis. The moon had switched places with the sun. Things were no longer as they were, and it was jolting to discover that despite these strange and monumental alterations the world went plodding on. And Sam, straight, by-the-book Sam, was as unaware of it as everyone else, calling him on his day off as if everything was the same.

"About those black angels," she said.

Holt needed a minute to come down out of the stratosphere and tune in to Sam's channel. Oh, yeah. Black angels. Right. She was supposed to be researching possible retailers. "What've you got?"

"Nothing. Not in Corley County at least."

"Okay." He ran a hand over the back of his neck. Could still feel prickles there. "Spread a wider net. Forget the county, go for the bigger markets. Nashville, Knoxville,

Chattanooga, Memphis. Hell, try Jackson even. Murfrees-
boro. Johnson City."

"I'll be dead before I finish all that."

"Keep notes and I'll pick up where you leave off."

"Then we'll both be dead."

Sam told him she'd leave her progress on his desk and
signed off. Stared at the computer screen but made no
move to keep searching. Something in Holt's voice made
her uneasy. She had seen him leaving on that bartender's
bike the night before. Didn't like the idea of him hanging
around her. Talk about messy. That woman always looked
like she didn't own a comb *or* a brush. Holt deserved better. Not to mention poor motherless Miranda. Sam didn't
like to think of herself as a snob, but that child deserved
more than a bartender for a momma.

She sighed. Well, hell. None of her beeswax. Won't last
anyway. Holt's got a head on his shoulders. That romance
was bound to go sour. Just don't ask her to clean up when
it did.

Soon as he was done talking with Sam, Holt heard
from Andy Burkett down at Myer's. Nothing wrong with
the brakes on Runkle's car. No one had tampered with
the transmission, the fuel line, or the steering mechanism.
Mechanically, the car was in great shape.

Unfortunately.

Holt had been hoping for an easy explanation, and now
he was left to fall back on natural causes—a heart attack
or a stroke. But Doc Ferguson was taking his time.

A shower, clothes, breakfast. Miranda was glued to the
TV, but she made sure he remembered his promise to take
her to the park. By that time the old rhythms had reestab-

lished themselves, and he was no longer sure he'd gone to a concert last night let alone been enchanted by the music and the woman who'd conjured the spell. But the morning was bright and if the sky seemed bluer or the babies in the park more endearing it was only the final trick left over from the night before.

When he and Miranda arrived, a girls' soccer game was in full swing in one corner of the park. Holt followed Miranda to the sidelines, where she watched intently. Next year, she'd be old enough to join the league. He tried to imagine his blond baby out there kicking the ball.

"Hey, Holt." Bunny Carter smiled at him. A divorcée, she had pride of place on his mother's list of suitables. Bunny dressed well, kept in shape, worked at the plant, and had the requisite fluff of light hair. Plus she had two kids, a girl and a boy. The girl was a couple of years older than Miranda, and was out there on the field, legs pumping. "Getting Miranda ready for next year?"

He returned her smile. Despite what he knew about the town's machinations regarding his marital status, and the fact that a smile would be telegraphed and interpreted and discussed over tea and whatever Redbud's constantly dieting female population ate with it, he couldn't help himself. In fact, he seemed to be smiling an awful lot this morning. "I don't know. She seems interested. We'll see."

Bunny eased closer, lowered her voice. "Terrible about Mr. Runkle. Figured out what happened?"

"Not yet."

"Is it true you found another black angel?"

He suppressed an impulse to glare. She was ruining his buzz. "It's true."

Either he didn't do a good job of keeping his feelings

off his face or she was unusually intuitive. She stepped back. Smiled. "You should bring Miranda over. Brittney would love to give her a few pointers."

Uh huh. Not to mention Brittney's mom.

"Thanks," he said, friendly enough. "Maybe we will."

"How about this afternoon?" Man, she went for the kill.

"I'll see how the day goes." He tugged Miranda away, and Bunny waved.

He bolted to the swings.

"Too fast!" Miranda said.

Instead of slowing down, he hoisted her to his shoulders. "There's a swing opening up. Better grab it before someone else does."

He helped her climb on, then pushed. As always, he began slow, and as always, she urged him to go faster and higher. He complied to the point of safety, but not with his full attention.

What was Edie doing right now? He pictured her tousled black hair, that wicked smile, the dare-you look in her eyes. Now there was a black angel.

Instantly, his thoughts leaped and soured. Two dead men. Two black angels. Where the hell did those things come from? And who was sending them?

The obvious explanation jumped to the top of the list. But a serial killer? In Redbud?

The idea seemed preposterous. Ridiculous. And yet . . . A feeling of foreboding ran through him.

But . . . both deaths were easily explainable. A heart attack and a car wreck. Not exactly the usual script for a serial killer. First off, the two men died in very different ways. A serial killer doesn't change the way he takes out his victims.

Unless . . . maybe Runkle lost control of the car because he had a heart attack, too. That at least would connect the deaths.

And why these two men? What did Fred Lyle and Dennis Runkle have in common? Runkle was a native, but Lyle had come to Tennessee as an adult, to run Hammerbilt. They were both wealthy by Redbud standards, but they weren't exactly friends. Lyle had been married to the same woman for decades. Runkle had run through three wives that Holt knew of. All much younger than Amy Lyle and none too interested in the community work Mrs. Lyle did.

Only one thing linked them. The black angel.

Holt knew about the local legend. The black angel that would turn white when a guilty man was proven innocent. But what did it have to do with Runkle and Lyle? The details were fuzzy, but wasn't the guilty party connected to Hammerbilt? If so, that could involve Lyle, but not Runkle.

Or maybe it had nothing to do with either of them. Maybe someone was using that ghost story to throw him off. Those thugs running the drug ring he'd cleaned out had spread a story that the house they'd set up their operation in was haunted. Kept people away for months. Was someone doing the same now?

Miranda was at the height of her swing, and getting a little too wild. He opened his mouth to tell her to slow down, when all of a sudden she did the craziest thing.

She jumped off.

"Miranda!" He ran to where she'd landed in a heap.

His heart was racing and the taste of fear curdled in his mouth. "Are you all right?" He ran his hands up and down her arms and legs. One knee was scraped, and she seemed dazed, but unbroken. Relieved, he hugged her swiftly to him, then anger overtook the relief and he pushed her back. "Are you nuts? What is wrong with you? You could have broken your neck." He grabbed her shoulders and steadied her. Her eyes were wide and solemn, and she looked right into his. "Why did you do that?"

"I wanted to see if I could."

He gaped at her, speechless. Then, "Well don't. You do that again, we won't come back here for a month. Understand?"

"Okay, Daddy."

"Enough swinging," he grumbled. "Come on." He held out his arms. "Let's get us some ice cream."

Scolding forgotten, she leaped into his open embrace, and he swung her around while she squealed. The possibility of a maniac loose in Redbud suddenly seemed both foolish and remote.

Claire's closed early on Saturday, so there was always a rush at lunch. A favorite place for the postsoccer set, the small space was crowded.

"You'll have to wait," Darcy, the owner, called over to Holt as he stood by the door. She hurried past, menus tucked under her arm. A wide-mouthed blonde with a low-cut blouse that showed off an impressive chest, she wore earrings the size of Texas that swung above her shoulders as she galloped by. Someone named Claire must have owned the place once, but who or when was lost in the fog of time. As long as he could remember, the place had been called Claire's, and no matter whose name was on the deed, he guessed it always would be.

Holt stooped to scoop up Miranda. "Hey, darlin'. Come on up here so we won't be in the way."

She didn't protest, sitting high in his arms to look around. Her gaze caught on something.

"What?" he said.

She pointed.

An old-fashioned soda counter ran down one side of the rectangular space. Opposite it was a string of ancient booths. Seated in one was Edie. She was eating a hamburger, a perfectly normal event. Yet he was struck dumb by the sight of her. In the middle of Claire's the memory of their moonlit kiss rose high and fast with a rush of unexpected heat. Standing like a statue, he couldn't keep Miranda under wraps. She scrambled out of his arms and hurtled to the booth.

He got there in time to hear Edie say. "It's a honey."

"What's a honey?" Holt tried not looking at Edie, fearing he wouldn't be able to stop, but it was impossible.

"My fattoo," Miranda said proudly. "I did it myself."

"I can tell." Edie shot Holt an amused look. "Great job."

Miranda slid into the booth next to Edie.

"Whoa there, Miranda," Holt said, wishing he'd thought of that. "Anyone ask you in?"

"It's fine," Edie said.

"We don't want to ruin your lunch."

"She's finished," Miranda turned to Edie. "Aren't you?"

"When you're right you're right," Edie said. "Sit down, Holt."

He didn't need a second invitation.

"This is my daddy," Miranda announced.

"I know," Edie said.

Darcy strode up to the table. "See you found a seat," she said to Holt.

"I have a fattoo," Miranda said. "Wanna see it?"

"Never mind the fattoo," Holt told his daughter. "What kind of ice cream do you want?"

They got the orders placed, and Miranda settled down to do exactly what Holt was doing: stare at Edie. Edie caught Holt at it, but appeared not to notice the heat flooding his face. Which was good because he was beginning to embarrass himself.

"I had a great time last night," he said.

"Me, too," Edie said.

"Do it again?"

"What's that?" Miranda pointed to Edie's head.

"What's what?" Edie felt around her head for what Miranda could be interested in.

"That." Miranda touched a hair pin.

Edie slid it out. "A bobby pin." She tugged a few strands of Miranda's hair back and pinned it back.

"I wanna see," Miranda said, and Edie fished in a purse—more like a leather backpack—for a mirror.

Miranda admired herself, looking pleased. "Take a picture, Daddy."

Edie raised a brow at him, but he dug out his phone and snapped a photo, handing the phone to Miranda to see. She giggled, then held up the phone and took one of Edie.

Holt watched her endure Miranda's chatter. She was a good sport to put up with all the manhandling. He'd never seen his daughter so taken with anyone. Would she have been this way with her mother? Interested in all the girly things she did, like bobby pins and fattoos?

Not that Cindy would ever in a million years have had a tattoo.

But still she would have had a lot of girly things to pass on. For a minute a clutch of sadness hit him that Cindy would miss out on all that. Bobby pins, lipstick, bras . . . Panic overrode the sadness. How the hell was he going to handle that when the time came?

Darcy appeared with Miranda's ice cream, a huge hot fudge sundae she always ordered and never finished, and put his coffee in front of him. The caffeine had a calming effect.

"Eat slowly," he said as his child dove into the confection.

In two seconds her mouth was full, her face dotted with whipped cream.

He took advantage of the silence to repeat his question to Edie. "So . . . how about it? My turn to show you all of Redbud's secrets."

She shot him a wry look. "Didn't know the town had any."

He waggled his brows. "You know what they say about small towns, don't you? Smaller the town, bigger the secrets."

"My daddy found a baby angel," Miranda said, wielding the long sundae spoon with ungainly enthusiasm.

Alarm fled across Edie's face. "Another one?"

He shook his head, and suddenly the mood seemed to solidify. Darken. And though he loved his child beyond life, he wished she could have kept that little bombshell for another time. "She must have overheard me talking."

"It was black," Miranda said. "Teeny tiny. It's evidence." Except she pronounced it "ebidence."

"That's enough, Miranda," Holt said. "Eat your ice cream." Miranda was trying to pick up a dollop of ice cream that had plopped onto the table. "With your spoon."

Edie touched his hand across the table. The contact sent a sizzle through him. "What's it mean?" Worry lines scored her forehead. He wanted to reach out and smooth them away.

"I don't know. Nothing, I hope. A prank."

"Any idea why both men were found with . . ." She shifted her gaze to Miranda and back to him. ". . . with one?"

"I'm working on it."

"Uh oh," Miranda giggled as she dropped ice cream again, this time on her shirt. Half her face was streaked with chocolate but Holt knew it would get worse before it got better, so he refrained from reaching over with a wet napkin to clean her off too soon.

"I have to shove off," Edie said abruptly, and made a move to go.

Miranda's face fell. "You can have my ice cream." She offered the sundae, a sticky, messy bribe to make her stay.

"Thanks, but I've got stuff to do. You enjoy it. Give your dad some." She leaned in and said in a low voice loud enough for Holt to hear. "He's been eyeing it."

Miranda looked at Holt dubiously.

"Come sit next to me." Holt slid the sundae to his side of the booth and Miranda followed it.

Edie got out, started to head in the direction of the door, but Holt wasn't going to let her run away. He reached behind Miranda to grab Edie's wrist as she passed. "When's your day off?"

"Wednesday, but—"

"Pick you up at eight."

He saw rejection plain in her face, and the words getting ready to spill out her mouth.

"Eight." He squeezed her hand. "No arguments. We had a deal, remember? I owe you one."

She acquiesced, gracefully if reluctantly. "But nothing fancy."

"Hey—it's not every day a guy has to compete with Brahms." He let her go.

"Can I get some bonny pins?" Miranda said when they were alone again.

"Sure, darlin'. Finish your ice cream first."

But she pushed it away. "I'm full."

Same old, same old. He cleaned her up, not really paying attention. His mind was too full of other things. Black angels of all kinds.

Edie sped straight to her room over Red's. She yanked down her duffel and jerked out the package of angels hidden there. She'd begun the day in a swirl of elation, hung over from the night before. That glorious, unhinged night of music and man. She'd even walked all the way to Claire's, reveling in the sun and the sight of the town enjoying a day off. She'd thought of Holt and that amazing kiss, wondered when she'd kiss him again, and whether it would be as improbable, incredible, and extraordinary. And never once did she think about death or black angels.

And now, God, now.

She didn't want to think about kissing Holt. She didn't want to think about the panic that threatened to erupt out of her throat. Did she truly have an avenging angel on her side? And if she did, when would Holt find out?

She stared at the tiny black figures. She'd wanted to stir people up. Catch everyone off guard so they'd be distracted enough to tell her what she wanted to know.

But she'd never know now.

She realized this just as starkly as she realized something else. Something more sinister and frightening than anything she could have thought up herself.

She was marking people for death.

It was crazy. Insane. No, that was her mother. Not her. Not Edie Swann. She was strong. Her own woman. Making her own destiny.

But still, gazing at the black angels, she couldn't help feeling a ripple of horror. Something was happening in Redbud. She didn't know what. She didn't know why. And she didn't know who.

But one thing she did know. She wasn't in control anymore.

~16~

From the cab of his pickup James Drennen watched the front of the parsonage. Nothing had moved in the quarter-hour James had sat there. The door was closed and the drapes over the windows pulled tight.

But that's the way the right Reverend Kenneth Parsley liked it. Dark. As dark as his soul.

In all his years as police chief, James had never actually been inside the parsonage. He'd driven by often enough on patrol, and every time the house was the same. He often wondered what the electric bills were like, given that Parsley seemed so averse to natural light. Or maybe it was just light itself and the house was as dark and gloomy inside as it appeared from the street.

Then again, secrets didn't do well in the light, and the reverend had a few whoppers to keep.

James brooded over that hard truth, remembering Parsley's desire to confess. There were only two of them now. Two who knew what had happened. Two who could tell the truth. But that truth would destroy James. It would rob him of his son's respect and the town's esteem. It would make everything he'd ever stood for a joke. It would make the town ashamed of itself.

His clammy palms slid over the plastic of the steering wheel. He couldn't let that happen. Nothing was more important than keeping that from happening. Nothing and no one.

Not even a man of God.

When Wednesday night rolled around, Edie wished more than anything that she hadn't agreed to the date with Holt. She stared at the rack of clothes that constituted her wardrobe. Couldn't think. Didn't want to. Because all that circled her head was that single harsh word. Dead.

Would Holt know? Would he smell it on her like some lethal perfume? She'd drenched herself in deodorant but still she wasn't sure she'd obliterated the stench.

That was crazy talk, though, wasn't it? The smell of death wasn't on her. She wasn't seeing things, people, ghosts. Communing with the spirits. Yet she felt haunted. Pursued. By whom? What?

She punched the wall with a fist, ignoring the pain. Who was out there?

She looked around wildly, sucking at her knuckles. Heart racing. Sweat on her upper lip. No one. Nothing. She was alone. Utterly alone. She swiped at her face. Had to get ready. Wear . . . something. Holt would be there soon.

What did he know? What should she tell him?

Nothing. Nothing! She would not make a big deal out of this date. She would not shave her legs, smooth lotion over her arms and knees so she'd smell enticing. She would not primp or spend time on her hair for once.

She would resist. She'd been stupid to take him to that concert. She had to resist all the temptation Holt Drennen symbolized. The cute kid, the real family, true love and all that crap.

And if she was stupid enough to give in, the least she could do was use the occasion to extract a little 411 out of him.

But that's what she'd said last time. And the minute she'd felt those arms wrap around her waist, she'd forgotten every bit of sense she had.

Not tonight. Tonight she'd keep her distance. Aware of the danger, she'd stay in control. The thought sent a blast of icy calm through her. Control. That's what she needed. The upper hand. Steer the conversation her way. He'd promised to tell her the town's secrets. What did he know about what had happened twenty years ago? About the black angels? About her? Most important, could he lead her to whoever was out there watching her every move?

It was weird the way Holt's chest hummed thinking about his date with Edie. He hadn't felt so wrought up since high school. Even his mother noticed, and finally said something that afternoon.

"You've been jumpy all day. Whatever is going on with you?" She was standing at the open door of his room. How long he didn't know because he'd been too absorbed to notice.

He laughed, shrugging it off, but silently cursing his nervousness. "Nothing's going on." His love life was none of her business, much as she tried to make it so.

"Nothing my eye. You've been standing in front of that open closet for days."

In truth it had only been a couple of minutes, but even that was unusual for him. He sighed. She knew he was going out tonight. Had to make sure someone would be home for Miranda or he'd get a sitter. But he hadn't told her or James where he was going or with whom. The concert was still his little secret. He'd told them he was going to a movie, alone, a thing he'd done before.

Now, he looked at his mother and thought, better get it over with. She'd only hound him the rest of the day if he didn't.

"Got a date," he said.

For a moment, his mother was dumbstruck. She stared at him open-mouthed.

"Ma, you okay?"

Suddenly a bright smile broke out over her face. "A date? Really?"

He rolled his eyes. "Yes, really."

She bolted into his room, squeezed his arm. "Christy Hale said she saw you talking to Bunny Carter on Saturday, but I had no idea." She clasped her hand to her chest. "Oh, Holt, this is wonderful. Bunny is such a—"

"It's not Bunny, Mother."

"—nice— What?"

"It's not Bunny. I'm not going out with Bunny."

The expression on Mimsy's face cooled. "Oh?" But only for a minute. Eagerly, she warmed up again. "Who is it, then? Patty Jane? I didn't think you liked her that much, and she does go on and on, but still she makes the most glorious peach cobbler and if she's the—"

"It's not Patty Jane."

His mother faltered to a stop. She crossed her arms and drilled him with a look. He knew that look.

"You sure you want to know?"

"And why wouldn't I?"

He smiled. Kissed her forehead and escorted her gently to the door. "Because she hasn't been vetted yet. And I don't think she likes peach cobbler, let alone knows how to make one."

"But—"

"It's Edie."

"Edie?"

"Edie Swann." And at her astonished expression, he added, "And I promise the world will keep spinning. That is if I can get back to getting ready." Quietly, he closed the door and went back to thinking about where in the world to take Edie Swann tonight.

There wasn't a decent restaurant in Redbud. If you wanted heavy silver, a white tablecloth, and good wine you had to go into Nashville. Which wouldn't be so bad except he wasn't sure Edie Swann was ready for a romantic dinner with him. And he didn't want to scare her off when he'd barely started. He could go to Ashland City. Take her for catfish and fries. Or the roadhouse out on Highway 20. But the chances of running into someone from Redbud in either of those places was high, and he didn't want their date to be the latest topic of conversation at Claire's.

Once again, a ripple of nerves ran through him, and he laughed at himself. Could he get more adolescent? Was he this nervous when he took Cindy out for the first time? But then, he'd known Cindy all his life. And it was during school and Friday night was basketball. Easy decision. Basketball, Dairy Queen. A Redbud tradition. But it was summer now, and school was out. No basketball. And the Dairy Queen was way too public.

But the memories of high school rolled over him and suddenly he knew exactly where he'd take Edie Swann. He'd promised her secrets. Tonight, he'd deliver.

James ambled into the kitchen from the garage. Kissed Mimsy on the cheek. She was setting the table for supper.

"Where've you been, Jamie?"

He waved a hand vaguely. "Oh, here and there. Stopped in at Claire's for coffee."

"And what's the hot topic today?"

"Black angels. Dennis Runkle. What's going to happen at the plant now that Fred's gone."

"I don't know why you bother. You're retired. You don't have to keep your ear to the ground anymore. Just more worries than you need."

"Still my town, Mimsy girl."

She paused in setting out the silverware. Shot him a fond smile at the long-standing term of endearment. "Always will be, I guess."

Her face softened, and the moment lengthened. James thought of all the years he'd given to his town. The things he'd done, and would do again. They all came down to this moment, this woman. His family.

Mimsy seemed to understand. Then again, she always did. She crossed over from the table, put her arms around his neck, and looked up at him with the green eyes that had hooked him from the moment he'd seen them.

"I love you, James Drennen."

He bent to kiss her, and her sweet, familiar lips softened under his.

"Yuk."

"Hey—no lovin' in the kitchen, you two."

James smiled as he and his wife broke off their embrace. His son and granddaughter stood in the doorway, the little girl high in her father's arms. Lord, she favored Mimsy. Everyone said she took after Cindy, but James knew better. Miranda had Mimsy's beautiful green eyes, her golden hair, and that stubborn chin. He could almost see God's hand working the gene pool and extending the strength of the generations down one more link in the chain.

"No place better," Mimsy said, and kissed him on the cheek again. "As for you," she laughed at Miranda, "come over here, you scamp. Help your old grandma get supper ready."

"You're not old," Miranda said, jumping down from Holt's arms and skipping over to Mimsy.

"Well I'm glad you think so. Here." She handed Miranda the napkins. "One at each place."

"Who's not eating tonight?" James asked, looking at the three plates.

"Holt has a date," Mimsy emphasized the word "date."

James raised his brows at his son, but Miranda answered before Holt could.

"He's going on a play date with the swan lady."

"The swan—?"

"Mama knows all about it," Holt said with what James sensed was a certain forbearance. "You can talk it over all during dinner. And after dinner. And in bed tonight.

I got a feeling it's going to be a big topic of conversation. But I've got a few more things to do before I pick her up. So—" He swooped down to pick up Miranda. "You be good to Nannie and Pawpaw, okay?"

"I'm always good," she said, and everyone laughed at that whale of a tale.

Holt winked at the group and fled out the back door. It was good to see him that happy, even if it was with the mysterious "swan lady."

"Okay, you two. Wash hands, and we'll eat."

James ushered Miranda into the bathroom, and while they were drying their hands Mimsy popped her head in.

"Almost forgot," she said. "You got a call while you were gone. Amy Lyle."

The name set off a thundercloud inside him. But he met his wife's eyes in the mirror with as much calm as he could muster. "Problem?"

"She wouldn't say. Just asked you to call her back at your convenience."

They walked back to the kitchen together. "Sure hope it's nothing." Mimsy helped Miranda to her place at the table. "That woman's been through enough just now."

James's thoughts roiled. They'd all sworn never to tell anyone. Had Fred Lyle broken his word? An odd aching cramp rumbled in his stomach. What else could Amy want? And why now?

Dinner was nearly unbearable. He managed to get enough food down to keep Mimsy from asking questions. He helped clear the table as he always did, and loaded the dishwasher while Mimsy put away the leftovers. They left the pots soaking and Mimsy took Miranda upstairs. And finally, he was able to make that phone call. Shoulders tense and neck tight, he punched in the number Mimsy had scrawled on a piece of scrap paper.

Amy Lyle's voice was low and soft. "Oh, Chief, thank you for getting back to me."

James had long ago stopped correcting people who still called him Chief, and he didn't do so now. Besides, if Amy Lyle proved troublesome, he could use whatever power the title conferred on him.

And yet there'd been neither anger nor accusation in her voice.

"What can I do for you, Mrs. Lyle?"

"Oh, please, call me Amy."

"All right, Amy. How can I help you."

"It's about Fred."

James tensed up again. "What about him?"

"Chief, can I speak in complete confidentiality?"

"Of course."

"I'd like to hire you. To investigate something for me."

"I'm not licensed for investigation, Amy. I'm retired."

"I know that. But you must have lots of contacts. And this is a family matter. I want someone I can trust. Someone that knew Fred, and—"

"Why don't you tell me what it is you're trying to find out."

Her voice lowered. "Its . . . it's his will. He left a . . . a bequest to someone. I'd like to find this someone and see why Fred did such a strange thing."

"Can you tell me who it is?"

"Do you agree to help?"

James hesitated. It was likely this had nothing to do with the secret he'd shared with Fred. Then again . . . whatever stones needed unturning, better he did it than anyone without a vested interest. "All right, Amy. I'll see what I can do. So who is this person?"

"Her name is . . . Eden. What kind of name is that? It sounds like a . . . like a stripper's name." Amy Lyle's voice cracked. "And Fred left her . . . he left her a lot of money."

James sucked in a breath, rocked once again by a past that wouldn't let go.

"I'm afraid, Chief. I'm afraid my husband may have had a . . ." She swallowed. He heard tears in her voice. "A secret life. I need to know. I need to know if my whole married life has been a lie."

He could have reassured her. In fact, he was surprised she hadn't recognized the name herself, given the publicity that had surrounded that name twenty years ago. Then again, most people had long forgotten the details. They hadn't happened to them, after all. And he didn't want to remind anyone either. So he didn't say those reassuring words to Amy Lyle.

"Okay. Give me a few days," he said instead. "Let me see what I can find out."

"Thank you." She took a long shuddering breath. "I won't have any peace until I know the truth."

He set a date for a second meeting, hung up, and sat back in the old desk chair.

Damn Fred Lyle. What the hell had he been thinking?

~17~

Holt had to drive halfway to Nashville to buy the wine he wanted for the evening. Redbud had plenty of beer for the asking but a good French red was hard to find. The drive gave him something to concentrate on besides Edie, and by the time he arrived at Red's, parked the car, and walked around back to the alley stairs he'd reached a modicum of calm.

Which lasted until she opened the door.

The smile died on his face, the greeting expired on his tongue. After that dress at the concert, he should have been prepared. But he wasn't.

Every man's fantasy stood in the doorway. Scarlet draped her white shoulders, dipped low to reveal a tantalizing hint of soft breasts. Legs that went on forever were encased in tight black jeans that ended in heels like knife blades. He should tell her to change her shoes or bring along another pair, but he couldn't. Didn't want to. He wanted her just like she was. Hair tumbled and sexy, the swan sailing on her shoulder, the pinup girl dancing on her arm.

While he stood there speechless, a slow, wicked smile stretched across her face. "Well, hi there, lawman."

He managed to find his voice, but it came out hoarse and he had to clear it before he could return her greeting. "Hi there yourself."

"We gonna stand here all night?"

His face heated and he hoped to heaven it was dark enough to hide the stain. "Uh . . . you ready?"

"As I'll ever be."

He let her lead, enjoying the back view as much as he'd enjoyed the front.

She paused at the car door, and he closed in, his hands on either side of her shoulders trapping her. He nuzzled an ear, inhaled her scent. Spicy. Enticing.

"God, you smell great."

Again, that sly smile. "Glad you approve."

Oh, he approved all right.

"How about we unlock the door?" she said.

"Mmm, I don't know. I'm having fun right here."

"Not too public for you, Chief?" She emphasized the last word, an ironic reminder of his position in the town.

He smiled. Right now he didn't care who he was. President, emperor, God himself. As long as he had Edie Swann to himself all night. But he stepped back, used the remote on his keys, and the doors clicked open.

Edie slid inside the car. So far, so good. Exactly why she'd done what she swore she wouldn't—dress for success. Or, in this case, stupefaction. If she could keep it up for the rest of the night she might actually find out what he knew.

But when he slid behind the wheel and was sitting beside her and they were alone in the small space, it was her own stupefaction she had to worry about. His muscular legs stretched out to work the pedals and she found herself riveted. The shirt he wore—dazzling white against the tan of his skin—was rolled back at the wrist revealing the strength of his forearms. That hint of skin left her imagining what the rest of him looked like. Huge, brawny, powerful. The thought of those arms holding him up above her took her breath away.

Mentally, she shook herself. Get with the program, girl. She'd worked hard to make herself irresistible, better not let her own hormones blow it.

To distract herself, she asked, "Where are we going?"

He shot her a glance filled with amusement and heat. "You said you wanted secrets."

A pulse leaped inside her. Could it be that easy? Quickly, she looked away, unable to concentrate under those penetrating green eyes. "About those black angels?"

He frowned. "No. Why?"

She backpedaled fast. "No reason. It's just . . . well, that's the secret everyone's talking about. And going out with the police chief has to have some perks. No theories yet?"

"None I want to speculate on."

"Come on, I have to give the boys down at Red's something. Foul play?"

"I'll tell you one thing, it's not black magic."

"But you must have some—"

"Look, Edie, it's my day off. And I'm here with this gorgeous woman—"

That stopped her. "You think I'm gorgeous?"

"Yeah, big surprise, I do."

Her heart beat a little faster, poor foolish thing.

"And you don't want to talk about black magic or black angels."

He sent her a hot glance so full of possibilities she shivered with anticipation. "Maybe I don't want to talk at all."

A few minutes later he turned off the highway. Wherever she imagined they'd go it had always involved lights and people, waiters, a building at least. But she saw none of that here.

They passed a sign that said "road closed" but Holt kept going.

"Uh . . . the sign . . ."

"Been up for years. No one pays attention to it."

"Not even the police chief?"

"Especially the police chief. He might have to investigate."

"That what we're doing?"

"No, darlin', not tonight."

He parked the car, got out, and opened the trunk. She joined him and he handed her a folded blanket, then slung a canvas tote over his shoulder, grabbed a small cooler and a flashlight, which he turned on. "Come on." He grinned at her.

He lit the way, and she followed him down a sloped gravel path. Her sharp heels sank into the pebbles, but she managed to stay upright until they got to a series of wide flat stones at the end. Holt set down the cooler, but when she began to spread out the blanket the uneven surface tripped her up, and she would have sprawled face-first if Holt hadn't caught her.

"Hang in there, sweetheart." His arms went around

her, buttressing her body and sending a lightning bolt through her.

"I should take off my shoes," she said hoarsely, not moving.

"Aw. They look so good, though." He didn't move either. Just looked down at her as if he was hungry and she was dinner.

Gazing up at him, she was happy to be gobbled up. "You don't want me to break my neck, do you?"

His hand stroked her throat. "I can think of a lot better things to do with your neck." His thumbs worked up her chin to the edges of her mouth.

An owl hooted in the thick dark, breaking the spell. She remembered who was supposed to be the hunter and who the pursued.

She stepped away, and his hands left her. Immediately, she wanted them back. But she felt around for the blanket, which she'd dropped, and Holt shone the flashlight on the ground until she found it.

He helped her spread out the cover, then took out a lantern from the canvas tote and turned it on. They sat, and the light made ghosts of their bodies against the rocks and cliffs surrounding them. Ahead lay a dark, black abyss.

She pulled her knees into her chest; something inside her chilled. "What is this place?"

"Redbud Quarry," Holt said.

The chill congealed into horror, but Holt went on.

"Been abandoned for years. But it's a favorite Redbud secret. Our own lovers lane. In good summers the rain fills the pit and the kids swim here. It's been too dry the last few years for that, but it's quiet, and I figured there wouldn't be much action in the middle of the week." He reached into the tote. "I've got wine, cheese, fruit. Chocolate. Everything a girl could ask—"

She jerked to her feet. Tottered forward.

"Edie?" She heard him scrambling behind her but she kept moving.

"Hey, wait a sec. Hold on." He grabbed her arm, jolting her to a stop. "The pit's only a few feet away. You want to fall over the edge? Here"—he shoved the flashlight at her—"take this."

Her hand closed around the light's metal barrel and it lit the air in front of her. She gaped into the darkness. Inched to the edge. Looked over. Even with the light she couldn't see the bottom.

Is this what her father had seen? Had he jumped into the black, not knowing where his journey would end?

But no, he'd done it in the middle of the day. He knew exactly where he was going and how fast he'd get there.

"Edie?" Holt stood next to her. "What's going on? You all right?"

No, not really. She hadn't been all right in a long, long time. "Fine. I'm fine."

"What the—" He turned her away from the edge to face him. His fingers traced her cheek. "You're crying."

"I am?"

"Yeah, Edie, you are."

She swiped at her face. Found it was true. Muttered a swift curse.

"And shivering," he said.

"It's cold." Another lie, but he didn't correct her. "And I don't like heights."

He stared at her. Deep enough to scar her soul. "Okay,"

he said at last. "Bad idea. We'll go." He turned to leave, and quick as a whip, she clutched his hand.

"Wait." She took a breath. Running was what her parents did. She was stronger than that. "No. It's . . . okay. I'm fine." Face your fear and it can't control you. Run, and it chases you the rest of your life. "Let's stay."

He hesitated, and she pulled him beside her again. Raised her chin. Faced the abyss. "Wonder what it's like down there."

"Hard. Rocky. No fun."

She pictured it. The white-hot sun searing the cliffs. The leap into space, a liberation. The blistering blue of the sky disappearing into the jagged edges of the pit walls. The end that loomed closer and closer. The welcome relief of the rock, the moment of pain, then . . . nothing left. Nothing.

Nothing but a fragile wife and a young daughter.

Something touched her, and she jumped.

"Whoa there," Holt said. He'd put his arm around her again, pulled her close. "Sure you want to stay?"

She turned in the circle of his embrace. Gazed up at him. Stars framed the blackness around his face, and this time she let herself sink into the heat of his gaze. Remembered the music and what it had led to. And, above all, why she was there. "Absolutely sure."

And to erase all thought and all doubt, she pulled his head down. Merged into the velvet of his mouth. Pain faded against a flush of pleasure. He tightened his hold, deepened the kiss, his tongue caressing hers. And like before, everything disappeared but him. The image of the pit, the broken body, her own broken life, receded. And in its place was Holt, alive and strong, those powerful arms caging her, keeping the past at bay.

"So," he said softly, his big hands cupping her face, "you going to tell me what's wrong?"

"How much time we got?"

"Long as you want, Edie." He stroked her lips, and she shuddered. Tried to focus on him, on her mission, but it was all blurry and her heart was pounding and the core of her was needy and wanting.

She ran her hands along the magnificent plane of his chest. Up to his shoulders, wide enough to block out the night. To block out anything. She ground her hips against his, felt the hard length of him through the jeans, and . . .

She pulled away, breathing as if she'd finished a marathon. "I think . . . I think we should catch our breath." She needed to keep her head, and when he was around her head kept exploding.

She led him back to the blanket, and he poured her a glass of wine in a paper cup. She sipped the wine, nibbled cheese, ate a strawberry. And before he could start on her again, she started on him.

"What's Memphis like?"

"Big. Dark. Exciting."

"No black angels there, I bet."

"Plenty of dead, though."

She thought of his wife, and pushed past his grief. She wasn't here for comfort. "I think there's a connection between the deaths and the angels?"

He reached over to cup the back of her head. Stroked the hair away from her face and shoulders. "Both men were over sixty. It could all be a coincidence. Maybe someone was giving black angels away as a promotion."

She absorbed the jolt of his touch. Craned her neck back to press against his hand. "You really don't know, do you?"

He ran a finger down her cheek and over her lips. "Know what?"

"Anything. About the black angels."

"Maybe there's nothing to know."

"Maybe." She took his finger in her mouth. Sucked it in then out. Then in again, her tongue and lips capturing him in a tight, wet embrace. She watched his breathing increase, the desire fill his face. Slowly she let his finger go, and he leaned over to kiss her.

"And like I said," he whispered, "I don't want to talk about it tonight."

She accepted that as easily as she accepted his mouth. It was sweet and tasted like wine. Relief spread, melted into reprieve. *He doesn't know.* The thought sang in her head, freed her from all obligation to her mission. She slid into his lap, letting the heat of him fill her. His tongue was thick and lush against her lips, and once again her body swelled with a rush of pleasure so intense it was a new feeling. Every inch of her crackled and spat, pulsed and beat in a hard rhythm. Her breasts tightened against his hard chest, and her hands fisted against his back.

Then, in a swift, heart-jolting movement that pulled her off the ground, he swooped, lifted her, and pressed her against the cliff wall. The pain on her spine felt good. Strong and hard. Like he was. A flip of his thumb, and her jeans were unsnapped, gone, panties, too. He put a hand between her legs, groaned when he felt her creamy and wet. He unzipped his jeans, freed himself, and she saw the thick, proud span of him jutting out from his body. He raised her up so she could wrap her legs around his waist, and with a cry, embedded himself in her.

She shuddered, gripped his neck and shoulders, his length deep inside. Retracting, advancing. The heat and sweat like a blanket of ecstasy that nothing could penetrate. He reached the core of her, the sting of pleasure raw, ragged, a rocket trip to some other plane, some other universe. A galaxy where there was nothing but the thrust of his body against hers, the undulation of desire, the sweet, sweet kick of the coming explosion.

And when she did come, it was like that fall down the pit. A smashing of everything she'd ever felt or needed or wanted. He stopped moving, letting her feel the waves of pleasure pumping against him. His body quivered with tension, holding himself back until he couldn't stand it, and with a single thrust, he came, too, joining her, bucking and groaning, and holding on to her body as if he'd break every bone if only she had any left.

And then, silence. Quiet. Return to earth.

"Jesus," he breathed.

"Ditto here, lawman."

He slid down the cliff wall—somehow or other their positions had changed—and held her in his lap. Eyes closed, she drifted away, snuggling against the big shoulders and chest.

And realized, suddenly, and with a huge burst of panic, what she'd done. Lost control. Lost herself. Lost her purpose. And as suddenly, she remembered.

He doesn't know. Not about her. Not about anything.

And God, he'd felt so good.

His touch sent a shiver through her. "What's this?" He caressed the spot just over her right breast.

"Ink," she said without looking. She knew what he was circling. The tiny perfect apple, scarlet and bright, a dark serpent coiled around its heart. "Temptation."

"Temptation, huh?" He moved from the tattoo to her nipple, softly massaging the tip. A breeze she hadn't noticed before wafted across her bare legs. She closed her eyes, drifted into the night, the bud between her legs still buzzing with the bloom of him inside her.

They dozed and woke, drank more wine, and by the end of the second bottle, the past had happened to another person, a sad little girl who bore no resemblance to the woozy, loose-limbed woman who lay on a blanket staring up at the endless stars.

She leaned against him, caressing his shoulder with the back of her head. "You know, when I imagined this, I—"

"You imagined this?"

She smiled into the night. "Oh, yeah. But I figured on a bed."

"A bed, huh?"

"I know where we can get one."

In half a second they were packed and heading to the car. Minutes later, he was pulling into the alley behind Red's. They ran up the metal stairs, breathless and laughing. He kissed her at the door, making it impossible to find her key and insert it in the lock. When she finally did, they tumbled into her room, lips locked. He kicked the door closed and they fell into the bed.

He stayed until just before dawn, when he kissed her breasts, then her mouth, and her chin. And her mouth again. "Gotta go," he whispered. "Want to be home when Miranda wakes up."

She stretched, then propped her head on one arm to watch the muscles shift in his thighs and ass and ripple across his back as he picked up his clothes and got dressed. It was sad to see him cover up all that splendor.

But she was a big girl. "No problem."

"When will I see you again?"

"When do you want to see me again?"

"In an hour?"

"Can you make that twenty minutes?"

He sat at the side of the bed, and she slid over so her head was in his lap. He stroked the hair back from her forehead. "My folks always have a party for the All-Star game. It's Tuesday. Can you get the night off?"

"National League or American?"

"Are you kidding? There is only one league. National."

"Ah, the loser."

"The underdog. And be careful with that word around the Drennen house. We've been known to arrest people for disparaging our boys."

"I'll risk it."

"So you'll come?"

"Will you drive me home afterward?"

"Only if you let me stay a while." He bent down and kissed her. Sighed. Stood. Let himself out.

The clang of his feet on the stairs faded into silence. She plopped back down, closed her eyes, ran a hand down her naked body. Feeling full and replete, she caressed her mound, swollen with the remnants of sex and desire. She smiled to herself, remembering Holt's big hands there.

She was in trouble. Real trouble.

And what was worse, she didn't care.

∽18∽

The next few days floated by. Edie tried to put weight on her feet, but nothing seemed to keep her on the ground. No one died, no one blamed her for those who had. And when she saw Holt—mostly at Red's, and in the alley behind Red's and the room above Red's—she couldn't stop the sunspot that exploded inside her.

Lucy noticed it and didn't even try to leave it alone. "What's with you and the chief?"

"Nothing."

"Yeah, I can see that nothing all over your face."

Edie just laughed.

And in the downtime, when she should have been investigating, she put it off. No more deliveries. No more questions. The past was over, wasn't it? As dead and buried as those final names: the one from her list—plant comptroller Alan Butene—and the one she'd heard from Arlen Mayborne, department secretary Hannah Garvey. It seemed a sign. A note from the universe telling her it was time to take Aunt Penny's advice and move on.

Then she got a phone call. Seems Hannah Garvey had

a daughter, Ellen, and Arlen Mayborne had been talking Edie up to her at church.

"To tell the truth, no one's expressed interest in Mother since she died." Ellen Garvey's voice was elderly but clear. "Of course, she'd been sick for so long, and people do forget an old woman . . ." She drifted into a sigh. "I haven't had the chance to entertain often, but I'd be happy to tell you whatever I can. And I make a wonderful chicken salad."

She seemed so wistful, Edie didn't have the heart to refuse. They agreed on a time, and for the next few days a distant alarm rang in her head. She got her orders mixed up, and bit Lucy's head off when she complained. Edie was so restless that Holt wanted to know what was bothering her. What could she tell him? That she had a feeling something awful was about to happen? That their time together was just the lull before the hurricane hit? That some old woman Edie had never met could change everything?

Not likely. So she just shrugged and denied. And stalled.

And at the appointed time, found herself back on the side of town near her grandmother's, staring up a small hill at the wide, rambling structure that dominated it. On the east and west sides a sharp set of wings jutted out. In one corner, a round turret gave it a fairy tale touch. Edie tried to imagine a fantasy childhood there, with lost princes in the tower and herself to the rescue, cardboard sword in hand. But whimsy was never her thing. Besides, did anyone have that kind of childhood anymore? Maybe it was as much a fantasy as the fantasy of having one.

A long series of steps led up from the street, and a pulse

thrummed insistently in Edie's throat as she climbed up. Did Ellen know anything? Did her mother leave notes behind? A secret diary, a scheduling book, something that would point a finger at someone or something? Edie cursed, not sure she wanted to know.

A bramble of shrubbery formed a wild, improvised arch that created a dark tunnel and obscured the front door. Edie paused. It seemed like the passageway between now and then. Between happy and unhappy. She'd made peace with the past, hadn't she? What good was the truth now?

She turned around. She'd call Ellen Garvey. Say she was sick or something.

She stopped. Turned back again.

Hell.

She gritted her teeth. Plunged into the cool dimness, then out the other side into sunlight again. Face to face with the house front, she saw sadly that the shutters were falling off, the porch was rotting, and ivy had climbed the walls and cracked the stone in places.

Another old house in need of a loving hand.

Ellen Garvey answered the door so quickly Edie wondered if the other woman had been standing behind it waiting. She looked . . . old. Could she be seventy? Older? The skin on her elbows and upper arms sagged in the short sleeves of a dark blue dress with a wide sailor's collar trimmed in white. A lunch at the country club type thing. And so girlish, it looked out of place on Ellen's shrunken frame. But she'd clearly made an effort to look nice—there was even a small bow in her gray hair.

Despite herself, Edie was glad she hadn't disappointed the older woman.

"Come in, come in." Ellen swept aside to let Edie pass. "Everything is just ready," she said brightly. "I hope you like tea punch?"

The enthusiasm took Edie aback, more comfortable with an ironic air that allowed everyone to keep their distance. Dutifully, she followed the older woman into a formal room with a long, dark table and large, heavy chairs. Two plates were already set on one end. White china trimmed in gold, linen napkins, and heavy silver utensils. Ellen had gone to a lot of trouble. Did that mean she had something important to reveal? Edie clutched her hand into a tight fist, squeezing out uneasiness.

Ellen, too, seemed unsettled. She flicked a nervous glance at Edie. "I set us up in here. The kitchen is cozier, but I haven't had much occasion to use the dining room. You don't mind?"

Although the two of them jammed into one end of the massive table was a little bizarre, Edie found herself wanting to be kind. "Of course not."

Reassured, Ellen beamed. "I'll just get the salad."

While she was gone, Edie noticed a cracked arm on one chair. A chandelier hung over the table, but had neither candles nor bulbs in it. Paint was chipping off the walls.

But Ellen apologized for none of this. She came back with a platter of chicken salad and deviled eggs. A pitcher of tea punch and a plate of tiny, ladylike biscuits that were still warm and so tasty they broke through the sawdust in Edie's mouth.

Her hostess glowed when Edie complimented her. "Did you enjoy them? I'm so glad." She sighed happily.

"I haven't entertained in a long, long time. Mother was too ill, you see."

The first mention of Hannah Garvey sent a buzz through Edie's chest. "Yes, you mentioned taking care of your mother."

Ellen sighed wistfully. "She depended on me. She raised me and sister on her own after my father died when I was a baby. Sister left to marry, so all we had was each other."

No wonder Ellen seemed starved for company. "And your mother worked at Hammerbilt?"

"For forty years. She was dedicated. Gave her life to that plant."

"So you've lived in Redbud all your life."

"Right here in this house." She leaned closer, dropped her voice. "Oh, I had a beau. Don't let folks tell you I didn't. I wasn't a wallflower." She fiddled with her hair, patting it with shaky fingers and a sigh. "But things didn't work out. Alvin got transferred, and . . . well, Mother needed me, you see." She gazed around—almost obsessively, Edie thought. "So, here I am, in the house I grew up in. Not very fashionable these days, I suppose. But it's home."

What was that like? To live in the same house, the same town all your life. How differently would Edie have turned out had disaster not struck and her father not died, her mother not gone mad? Would they all have lived happily ever after in Redbud? She'd avoided checking out the old homestead. Avoided the sight of it altogether. Her grandmother's house was close enough. But here was a woman who knew about roots. Knew what it was like to be planted, to grow and thrive in the same soil year after year. A wave of envy ripped through Edie, and she found herself finally asking the question she'd managed to avoid,

"Do you remember anything about the Swanford family?"

Edie held her breath, but Ellen frowned. "Swanford?"

"Charles Swanford. He died tragically years ago. Took his own life."

Ellen gasped. "The man who threw himself into the old quarry? My goodness, yes, I remember. What an awful time that was. Mother was so upset."

"Did she—" Edie took a breath. "Did she ever say anything about why he did it or give any indication that she knew anything about it?"

As hard as it was for Edie to ask, the answer came easily enough for Ellen. "Not that I recall, but it was so long ago. And if I remember correctly"—she paused to think—"I believe she retired shortly thereafter. And then, she got sick . . ."

Edie licked her lips. "Did she . . . have any papers from Hammerbilt?"

"Papers?"

"Maybe . . . a scheduling or appointment book. A steno pad?"

"No." Ellen shook her head. "I'm afraid not."

"Could I . . . would you mind if I looked at her things?"

An unusual request, no doubt, but Ellen only looked sorry she couldn't grant it. "We sent everything off to the Goodwill. There was a box of Hammerbilt things, but I threw it away. It was mostly good luck cards and little mementos she'd been given when she retired. Nothing important to anyone but Mother. Certainly no appointment book."

"Are you sure?"

She gave Edie a kind smile. "You're welcome to look in her room. Of course, she was down here for the last ten years. Couldn't climb the stairs, you see."

Ellen showed her to a large room at the end of the upstairs hallway. It was clean and neat with empty drawers and a closet full of old shoes and winter clothes.

"I keep my off-season things here," Ellen explained.

Edie closed the closet door, closing it, too, on her quest. Hannah was gone, and whatever she knew was gone, too. Nothing left but the stale air inside a room she hadn't occupied in a decade.

The weight of the last few days lifted, and Edie felt suddenly giddy and untethered. She thanked Hannah's daughter, and made to go, but Ellen wouldn't hear of it until she'd had tea and a lemon square. "I made them myself," she said with pride.

With more enthusiasm than she'd given the rest of the meal, Edie ate the cake, admired its tart sweetness, and sipped a cup of tea, before finally escaping outside. She was free. Free! She almost twirled with relief. Nothing left to discover, no one left to ask.

Except, of course, that one, final name on her list. The one name she couldn't bring herself to think about, let alone approach. And now she didn't have to.

She could leave James Drennen alone, put his connection to the past back there where it belonged, and concentrate on his wonderful, gorgeous, sexy son.

* * *

Edie's smile was back in place that night. Every song on the jukebox was platinum, every customer her best friend.

"Well, look at you," Lucy said. "Someone got some, I think." Her brows waggled.

"I were you," Edie said, plopping a pitcher of beer on a tray with an arch grin, "I'd watch that thinking stuff. Burn right through that brain of yours."

Lucy hooted and went to deliver her beer. And in the midst of all the good feeling, James Drennen walked into Red's.

Holt had never told Edie outright to keep their relationship on the down low, but she sensed that the pairing of Redbud's most eligible bachelor with the town's tattooed lady might not go over well. Which was why she didn't talk about him, no matter how hard Lucy pried.

So when Holt's father slid onto a bar stool, Edie couldn't help a bump of anxiety. He wasn't a regular. In fact, he hadn't been back since that time weeks ago when he came with Holt. She would have slipped him an angel then if she'd had them with her. Now, she was glad she hadn't. But that didn't mean she wasn't a little nervous around Holt's father. Especially when he showed up out of the blue. Alone.

"Hello, Edie," he said pleasantly, and ordered a beer.

She pulled it for him, hoping he wasn't there for "the talk." How she wasn't the settling-down type, and Holt needed a mama for his baby girl, and not a hoochie mama either.

"You doing okay?" he asked when she set the beer in front of him.

"Couldn't be better."

"Good. Good. That must mean you're taken with our little town."

Uh oh. He sipped the beer, and she braced herself. "I like it fine. Just fine."

"You a small-town girl?"

"Some. Part city girl, too." She wasn't going to lie to him.

"Which is the bigger part?"

She'd spent ten years in Redbud, the rest everywhere else. "City, I guess."

"Oh, yeah? Where?"

"Chicago. St. Louis. Worked a bar in Nashville, too."

"Looking for Eden?"

The name alone was enough to send an ice shard through her chest. But it was accompanied by a cold, piercing look that froze whatever blood she had left. And suddenly "the talk" she'd expected turned into something very different. And very deadly.

She wanted to avoid those eyes but didn't. She shrugged. Forced a smile on her face. "Who knows? Maybe."

James Drennen, ex-sheriff, father of her lover, last name on her list, gave her another pleasant smile, then drank his beer.

"Hey, Edie!" A customer waved her down to the other end of the bar, and when she returned, the only thing left at James Drennen's place was a five-dollar bill.

And along with it lay every last slick of dread she thought she'd eradicated.

Holt's father knew who she was.

~19~

The rest of Edie's night passed in a horrified blur. Had she heard James correctly? Had he told Holt yet? Twice she spilled a drink, which made Lucy and Red both stare at her.

"What's wrong with you tonight?" Red threw her an extra towel for the cleanup on the second one.

"She's got a bug up her ass named Drennen," Lucy grinned.

Edie didn't bother telling her she was right . . . and wrong. It was a Drennen, but not the one she had in mind.

The minute last call was over, she hightailed it to her bike and set off out of town, not bothering with a helmet. Speed grabbed her by the throat, blasted her cheeks, shot through her hair.

Would anything in Redbud ever go her way? Something here, some sick streak of karma, was working against her just as it had her parents. She should have stayed away. Should never have come. Aunt Penny was right.

She passed the edge of town, inhaled the hot night air,

and forced herself to calm down. Look at her, full of regret, and her not the regretting kind.

At least, she didn't use to be.

She tried to look at the up side. Wasn't there always an up side? If she hadn't come to Redbud, she wouldn't have met Holt.

Some up side. More like a sucker's play. Because if James Drennen knew who she was, he'd say so. Eventually. And then Holt would know she had lied both about who she was and about her connection with those black angels. Would he understand? Forgive even? Or would everything explode around her and he'd walk away?

Or worse, lock her up.

Her stomach churned. To outrace the gloom, she turned off the highway onto a country road and accelerated into blackness. The moon made shadows of the landscape slipping past her. A dark void of fenced-in fields. Humps of trees. She wanted to charge forward. Surround herself with the thick, inky air and get away as fast as possible. Now, before it all ended the way it inevitably would. Badly.

She poured on the speed, needing to devour the miles. But unexpectedly, the road curved, forcing her to turn wildly. She pumped the brakes to slow down and heard a dull pop. In the same instant, the hand brake went spongy, and her heart thrashed. She'd lost control of the front tire.

She thrust down hard on the foot brake. Her rear tire skidded out from under her. Oh, God. Something slick was all over the road.

Beneath her, the bike careened, spinning out of control. The bike went one way and she went another. The scream of metal over pavement screeched in her brain. Panic overwhelmed her, and her last fleeting thought as she flew through the air was she wouldn't have to worry about Redbud or Holt anymore. Not if she was dead.

~20~

Edie groaned. Moved her neck. Something scratched, itched. Grass. She was lying on grass. She inhaled the smell of fields and manure. Remembered in an instant what had happened and where she was.

Her bike.

She tried moving arms and legs. Her right elbow ached but everything worked. She rolled over slowly. Sat up. Bones creaked. Her head swam. But somehow, she wasn't dead.

She stood, wavered, leaned against the fence at her back. After a moment she tried a step. Hallelujah, her feet worked. She limped over to where her bike had landed against the fence on the opposite side of the road. Hauled it upright.

And realized her hands were shaking. Her whole body was trembling. She made herself breathe through the rush of feeling. Happy to be alive? Scared spitless to be almost dead? She grasped the handlebars, steadied herself against the solid metal. Eventually, the emotion faded enough to let her think again.

She found the flashlight she kept just for these emergencies and scanned the brake lines with it. Put a finger through a jagged slit in the front line. That explained why she'd lost control of the hand brake. Also what she'd skidded on—leaking brake fluid.

She ran the light over the rest of the bike. The rear fender was dented but otherwise in decent enough shape, considering. She wiped the rear tire clean with a rag. Tested the foot brake. It was fine. If she was careful, she could make it back to town using the rear brake alone. Get Andy Burkett to fix the front brake line. He'd been wanting to get his hands on her bike anyway.

She let out a long, slow breath. Too much drama for one night. Holt's father nearly exposing her. Nearly dying. After tonight she needed a week or two of nothing going on.

But she wasn't going to get it. Not, it seemed, in Redbud.

All the way back she thought of that jagged cut. She could have sliced open the brake line on the road. A rock, a nail. A stray piece of glass from a broken beer bottle. There were plenty of them around Red's.

Then a new thought occurred, and every drop of saliva in her mouth turned to sand. She always parked her bike in the alley. Anyone could have gotten to it. Even— she gasped as the picture of him rose in her mind, sitting on the bar stool, all pleasant smiles and knife-blade words—James.

The shakes began again, and she had to stop to calm down.

People were dying all around her. Was she next?

21

In the days that followed, Edie couldn't shake the jumpiness. She took the bike to Myer's, but Andy couldn't tell whether that cut had been intentional.

"Could be," he said with a shake of his head. "Could as easily been something you picked up on the road."

Accident, her brain screamed. Yeah, right. Just like all the rest.

"Lucky you didn't break your neck," Andy added.

True, that. But was her luck someone else's disappointment? Was someone stalking her? Looking for a way to get to her the way they got to Fred Lyle and Dennis Runkle?

Was that someone Holt's father?

Since that night at the bar, he'd made himself scarce. But he hadn't spilled his secret either. If he had a secret to spill, and hadn't just been making idle conversation.

God. Could anyone blame her for being jittery?

Holt noticed it, too. Blamed the accident—which he'd learned about by way of the bruises on her right side and Andy's big mouth—and lectured her about the dangers of speed. To get him off her back, she asked if he was going to send her to traffic school, and he grinned in that sexy, evil way of his.

"You hurt yourself again, I just might do that."

The day of the Drennen All-Star party started bright and sunny. A far cry from the way Edie felt when she woke. She'd tried to come up with a reason not to go, but every time she started making noises about not showing up, Holt threatened to drag her there in handcuffs. She always backed off, knowing persistence would only lead to questions she wasn't prepared to answer.

But the thought of facing James rattled her. Who knew what he had planned for her? Maybe he was waiting for a public venue for his tell-all. Or maybe he had something even worse up his sleeve. Just to be sure, she'd take a cab. Pick up a can of mace. Something . . .

She shuddered.

Holt said there'd be a crowd. What if James hadn't tampered with her bike and it was someone else? The thought that she might be shaking hands with whoever had almost killed her sent her into a tailspin. Especially since she didn't even know if someone *had* tried to kill her.

She grabbed her hair, shook her head. Growled into the empty room as if that could shake things loose.

Nothing doing.

She kicked off the covers and slid out of bed. Look at her—the whole thing was driving her nuts. She longed to be free of the weird, scary, sticky web. If only she hadn't come to Redbud. Hadn't delivered her little goodies. Would those two men be alive? Would she be safe?

She paused on her way to the bathroom, an idea blooming hot in her head. She'd started things, hadn't she? So wasn't it up to her to end them? She could throw herself on Holt's mercy and decency, and tell him herself who she was and what she'd done. Tell him her suspicions about the bike accident. If she took him into her confidence she'd take the stinger right out of his father's behind.

She chilled. It was a risk. But not telling was equally risky. Either way she was heading down the trail to losing Holt. Not to mention her life.

A wail crawled up her throat. She wasn't ready to let go of either, and that was frightening in its own right. So much easier to drift without attachments.

Too late now.

God, she'd made a lovely mess of things.

But hell, if she had to be cut loose better she did the hacking than someone else.

She showered quickly, threw on some clothes, and let herself out of the apartment. If she was going to end things she had to end them. Cut the last link to the mission she'd come to town with and now wanted only to abandon.

She straddled her bike and took off, heading for the neighborhoods just off the square.

The Redbud Community Church occupied the corner of East and Courthouse, so wasn't hard to find. She pulled into the drive and parked in the lot behind the church. It was empty except for a ten-year-old Saturn. The preacher's? For a moment, she hesitated. What would she do if he was there? Pretend she'd come to pray? Confess? If she asked for her angel back, she'd reveal herself. Then she remembered. Clergy were like lawyers, right? Anything she said would be confidential. But still . . .

She swallowed. Better get it over with.

She tried the back door; it was open. Inside, the sound

of a vacuum cleaner told her that whoever owned the car was probably behind the noise. Relieved, she crept away from the sound, exploring hallways until she found the offices. A discreet gold plate on one door labeled one the Reverend Kenneth Parsley's.

Edie paused to listen for the vacuum. It was still a ways off, but she hesitated. What if Parsley had walked to church and was behind the door? Did she really want to do this?

The answer was a definite no, but she torqued her courage and knocked lightly anyway. No answer.

Slowly she opened the door. Peeked in. Empty. Quickly, she plunged inside, closed the door behind her. Books and papers littered the desk. Shelves of books lined the walls. A credenza in the corner held stacks of magazines. It would take hours to search everything.

What the hell had she been thinking? That he would have kept the black angel in his office in a place where anyone could find it? Yeah, right. She'd mailed it from Hammerbilt weeks ago. He'd probably thrown it away by now.

But some stubborn do-the-right-thing impulse made her continue just in case. First, she listened at the door. Was the vacuum cleaner closer? She looked back at the office, cursed her idiocy, and bolted to the desk.

She yanked open the middle drawer. Pens slid to the front and rolled back. Pink phone slips, a pamphlet on spiritual healing, and several pads of sticky notes. Three side drawers yielded Bibles, a hymnal, a thesaurus, and a folder of old sermons. Ditto the top of the desk. A closet held a raincoat, a nylon jacket with the church's name embroidered over the left breast, and a pair of ratty running shoes. She checked all pockets, turned the shoes upside down. All she found was a peppermint and a scrap of a flyer announcing a Run for Jesus.

Okay. She'd had enough. Her better self was appeased. Time to rock and r—

"Hey, what are you doing?"

She froze. Caught her breath. Her mind raced for a reasonable excuse for being there. She pasted a smile on her face, whirled to confront whoever was there, and found Terry Bishop standing in the doorway with the vacuum cleaner.

A pretext popped into her head the minute she saw him. "Looking for you."

"In the preacher's office?"

She glanced around. "Is that where I am? I was just trying to figure out what you'd cleaned and what you hadn't."

He gave her a narrow-eyed look. "What do you want?"

"To talk to you."

"About what?"

"You know something, don't you? Something about Fred Lyle and the Hammerbilt plant."

"What if I do?"

"Information can be dangerous, Terry. But if you share it, you share the danger."

"What's in it for you?"

"Satisfy my curiosity."

He twisted the vacuum's power cord between his hands, stared at her with sullen menace. "Curiosity can get you killed."

The bald threat set her pulse racing. Was he behind the

attempt on her life? He always seemed to have a grudge against her, though she didn't know why. Then again, there must be a lot she didn't know. She forced herself to smile again. "I do something to piss you off?"

He didn't answer. But something in his face softened, and she took advantage of it. Advanced on him. "You do know something, don't you? You should tell. You'll feel better if you do."

But instead of pushing him to reveal what he knew, she'd pushed him in the opposite direction. His eyes hardened. He dragged the vacuum cleaner into the office and plugged in the cord.

"Leave me alone," he said and turned his back on her.

She repressed her instinct to scream, keeping her voice calm and cool. "Fine. But do me a favor, okay?" She paused to see if that elicited a response. It didn't. She continued, "Keep an eye out for the preacher."

He wrapped a hand around the handle of the machine, flicked a suspicious look her way. "What's that supposed to mean?"

"Nothing. Just . . . make sure he's okay."

"Why wouldn't he be?"

"I don't know."

"You think I'd do something to him?"

"No, that's not what mean. It's just . . . a lot of people have died recently."

He thrust out his chin belligerently. "I didn't have anything to do with that."

"I didn't say you did."

He took a threatening step toward her. "Get out of here."

"Okay. Okay." She held up placating hands. "I'm going. But if you ever want to talk, I'm—"

He switched on the machine and the rest of her sentence was lost in the noise. Okaaaay.

She left the office and, just to make sure, vowed to check her bike before mounting. Overly cautious? Whatever. She wasn't going to let carelessness cost her everything. Catastrophe might be on the horizon, but she wasn't going down without a fight. And you could bet it was going to be a damn good down-and-dirty brawl.

~22~

The Reverend Kenneth Parsley was having a rough day. His Sunday sermon—which he wrote in longhand and usually had in draft form by Tuesday so his secretary could type it—was still only a blank page, though he'd dutifully sat at his desk in his church office all afternoon.

Using a handkerchief, he dabbed at the sweat on his forehead and behind his wide neck. Lately, he was always sweating. Maybe it was the heat, or he had some kind of flu bug. Or, as his doctor said, he needed to lose a few pounds. Either way, he couldn't concentrate. Tired of looking at the empty yellow pad, he shoved it in a desk drawer, and stood. The air inside his office was stuffy. Or maybe it was his head that was stuffy. Or his immortal soul.

Deep inside him, his belly twisted at the thought, and Reverend Parsley told himself it was a hunger pang. He thought about a snack, but no matter how much he ate, he was always hungry. Ever since that meeting at the quarry, nothing satisfied. And then with Fred Lyle keeling over and the terrible accident that took Dennis Runkle, it seemed as if the world around him was toppling. As if the Lord himself was finally passing judgment.

Then why hadn't he passed judgment on him? Wasn't the hypocrite the worst offender? He rubbed his face, tired, too, of the endless recriminations. God forgive him for a coward. Forgive him and show him the way to redemption.

Without, of course, exposing him.

He shuddered to think of the public humiliation, and concentrated instead on the good he'd done and could still do. Hadn't he fought the Lord's battles here on earth, bringing umpteen people to the Savior? Only last week, he'd ushered the Tewksbury boy into God's grace. Wasn't that worth something on the balance sheets?

Maybe that's what he should talk about this Sunday. Life as a balance sheet, with hope that the good outweighed the evil we do. Relief washed over him. Yes, that's what he'd do. Eagerly, he plopped back down and reached for the yellow pad. The minute he picked up his pen, though, words deserted him and he couldn't think how to begin.

He jerked to his feet again. He needed something to munch on. An energy boost. There'd be cookies in the church kitchen. And he could use the walk. The exercise would clear his head. Help him pray.

He took the long way around, giving himself ample time. And if he was avoiding the sanctuary he didn't admit it. It was only that everything was so tight. His shirt collar pinched his neck, the sleeves imprisoned his shoulders. Even his skin pressed tight against his skull. He needed to loosen up. That's why the words wouldn't come. He ducked into the men's changing room behind the baptismal pool. Unbuttoned his shirt and wet a paper towel, which he dragged across his face and neck. He thought about last Sunday's baptism. Tried to recapture the joy, but it was out of reach.

He left through the baptistery door, down the ramp that led to the pool. He'd always liked the way the light from the stained glass at the front of the church gave the water a godly glow. Usually, it was serene and calming. Today, it just looked green.

He blinked. Of course it looked strange. There shouldn't be any water. The thing should have been drained days ago. They'd had trouble with the pool before. He thought Terry Bishop had fixed it.

He frowned. He should have his head examined for giving that good-for-nothing a job. And now he'd have to track him down. Terry was not the easiest person to corral.

And then the idea struck him. That this was not an ordinary chore. Perhaps it was no coincidence that the pool remained undrained and ready for use. He needed a cleansing, didn't he? Maybe this was the sign he needed to get back on track. The message that God had indeed forgiven him.

A pulse began to batter at his throat. Was he crazy? Or was he the sanest man on earth?

Carefully, he removed his shoes. Didn't bother going for the waders, which were just inside the changing room. Just took off his socks, laid them neatly inside his shoes, and slid his ponderous bulk into the pool. The water should have been heated but it was cold and shocking. Another sign. He needed a shock, didn't he?

He dipped under, saying the familiar words silently. *I*

baptize you in the name of the Father, the Son, and the Holy Spirit. He bobbed up, sputtering, then went under again. *Lord, cleanse my soul and make me worthy again.* He stayed under a little longer the second time, putting his life in God's hands. When he came up again, he was gasping for breath. Chugging down air, he wiped the water off his face. Was about to go under a third time, when he noticed someone watching.

A flush went through him at the picture he made. Fully clothed, soaking wet, dignity spoiled. All of a sudden, he remembered the prayer meeting. He'd have to race home to change. "I was just—" he cleared his throat. "We're having a problem with the drain."

The smile that greeted this explanation was indulgent, then grew until it morphed into . . . a sneer? A devil's head? Kenneth Parsley stared, his mouth suddenly dry.

"What are you—"

But the next words were lost in a sizzle of pain that continued for an eternity and ended in everlasting darkness.

～23～

Holt escaped the swarm filling the Drennen backyard, and leaned against the side wall of his childhood home. It was a perfect evening. Warm, but for once, not blazing, and the crowds had turned out. The men were mostly inside watching the pregame show and arguing with each other about players and stats. But there were plenty who preferred it outside where the smell of chicken on the grill filled the air.

Not him. At least, not right now. He gazed up the driveway into the hodgepodge of cars and trucks up and down the street, troubled by what Doc Ferguson had just told him.

He noticed his dad's big, black pickup cruising the street, and wondered where his father had disappeared to. He pulled into the drive, and James leaned out the driver's window. "Too crowded back there?"

"I don't see you sticking around."

"Had to go into town for more ice." He jumped out of the cab and came toward Holt. "So?" He nudged Holt with an elbow and grinned. "What's bothering you?"

Holt smiled back. "You a mind reader now?"

"Could always tell when you had something on your mind." He went around to the truck bed and opened the tailgate. A stack of bagged ice lay heaped against a side wall. "Give me a hand?"

"Sure. But how about we wait a minute. I just got the autopsy report on Dennis Runkle."

That caught his dad's interest. He braced an arm against the truck, baseball cap pulled low over his forehead. "What was it—heart attack or stroke?"

"Anaphylactic shock."

James's thick, unruly brows rose.

"Did you know he was allergic to peanuts?" Holt asked.

"Peanuts? Hard to believe that could kill a man."

"Doc says otherwise." Holt swooped a rock up from the ground and tossed it in his hand. "Thing is, Dad, people with these kind of allergies can survive an attack. If the allergy is severe enough they usually travel with a self-injectable dose of epinephrine. Doc said Runkle did."

"So how come he didn't use it?"

"That's what I'd like to know. There were no traces of it in his blood."

"Find the needle?"

Holt shook his head. "Sam's out at the accident site now, checking. Damage was pretty severe though. It could've been destroyed in the crash. Maybe he reached for the thing in a panic, which led to him losing control of the car and then the needle flew out of his hand on impact and was crushed beneath the wheels."

"Or maybe someone took the dose in anticipation of the shock."

Holt looked at his dad. The thought had occurred to him, too, and it didn't sit easy.

"You found a black angel on him, didn't you?" James asked.

"Yeah, but . . ." Holt shifted. The facts still didn't seem to add up. "Pretty wild way to kill someone. Not exactly foolproof. Even if we could find someone with an ax to grind and we could prove he used it, what does it have to do with Fred Lyle? He had a heart attack."

They stared at each other in the bright light. James's eyes were hooded under his cap. "You got a tough one there."

Holt tossed the rock away. "Yeah. Then again, maybe it's just what it seems—a terrible tragedy that's no one's fault."

James clapped Holt on the back. "That's it, son. Keep it simple. At least till you find out otherwise."

Holt nodded and grabbed a couple of bags of ice. James did the same. They tramped off to the backyard together, but Holt felt unsatisfied and at loose ends. Trouble was, he wanted Runkle's death to be an accident. He wanted to close the book on the enigmatic black angels and concentrate on the live one coming soon. He made a mental note to ask around about Runkle. Did his employees know about his allergies? Did his ex-wives? He totted up a list of people who might have known more than they should.

"That girl of yours show up yet?" James asked.

"She'll be here," Holt said with more certainty than he felt. Edie had tried to slither out of coming, but he'd stood firm. By now she was officially late, and if that meant she was on the road to standing him up there'd be hell to pay.

They dumped the ice in the coolers by the picnic tables, and his dad disappeared into the house to check on the beer status. His mother was holding court in a corner of the yard with a group of women. Her book group or knitting club or her poker night girls, as she called them. She was talking a mile a minute. Not unusual for Miss Mimsy, he thought fondly, though he should be annoyed with her. She'd taken it upon herself to invite all of Edie's so-called rivals. Bunny Carter, Patty Jane Ellis. A few others dotted around the yard. Oh, she'd given him the excuse that Miranda would need kids to play with and the women had children more or less his daughter's age. But he understood her machinations.

Out of the corner of his eye, he saw movement. A new arrival. He turned, settled down when he saw it wasn't Edie, then went over to greet the newcomer.

"Mrs. Lyle, so glad you could come." Inviting Amy Lyle had been his father's idea. His parents hadn't social- ized with the Lyles before Fred's death, but now that Amy was alone, he suggested it would be neighborly to invite her.

"Please call me Amy."

"Okay, Amy. Let me take you over to my mother. She'll introduce you around."

"Thank you." She followed him toward the circle of women with Mimsy at the center. On the way, he noticed Amy scanning the crowd.

"Looking for someone?"

She gave him a sheepish glance. "Just wondering if your father was here."

"He's inside. Be back in a jiff."

By then they'd reached their destination. As they ap-

proached, he heard the name Hammerbilt, but the talk
died down as soon as they saw who he was bringing.

"Why, hello, Amy," Mimsy said. "Were your ears
burning? We were just talking about you."

"Oh?" She looked around the circle nervously.

"Just wondering if you had any inside info about the
plant. Whether we're going to get shut down or not."

A relieved expression crossed her face, but she shook
her head. "I haven't heard. I do know there's a group
from IAT coming to inspect it. That was arranged before
Fred . . ." she stumbled, couldn't say the words yet. "I'm
afraid I'm out of the loop now. With Fred . . . gone."

The women murmured sounds of sympathy, and
Mimsy patted Amy's hand. Over his mother's shoulder he
caught sight of what he'd been waiting for: Edie strolled
into the yard.

A sharp sense of possession hit him. Among the soft
crowd, the pastels, turquoises, and bright pinks, she was
an oasis of black. Dark hair, short black skirt, black tank.
All of which clung to her lithe body and sent another
spiky jab through his chest, his gut, and lower.

My woman.

Strong and indestructible. Nothing fragile about her.
The thought burst through his head as she turned and
found him. Across the lawn their gazes met and they
headed toward each other without a wave or a word. Just
a keen recognition of purpose. *This is why I'm here. For
you.*

They stopped within an inch of each other. Her eyes
glittered, and there was a sharpness about her face. A
wariness. Was his tough girl anxious?

He lifted a hand, tilted her head up by her chin, and turned it side to side. "Why look, it's Edie Swann."

She smiled. "Hello to you, too, lawman."

"No cuffs on you."

"I decided to turn myself in."

He nodded sagely. "Better that way." He wrapped an arm around her, squeezed her close, and said low, "Nervous?"

She tensed. "Should I be?"

He smiled down at her. "I don't know. You haven't met my mother yet."

"Oh, yes, I have."

It took a minute to remember. "That's right. The library. See? Nothing to be afraid of."

"Easy for you to say." She held up a paper bag. "Miranda here?"

"Miranda? Geez, woman, I thought you came for me."

He led her to the wading pool. Five or six kids were splashing and screaming. A clump of mothers stood by, half-watching the commotion and half-gossiping with each other. Bunny and Patty Jane were there, and they both eyed Edie as she approached the pool with him.

"Hey, Holt." Bunny gave him a friendly wave but before he could answer, a high screech pierced the air.

"The swan lady!"

Miranda bolted out of the pool and flung herself at Edie, smacking her with a wet bathing suit.

Edie didn't say a word about getting soaked. She hugged his daughter to her knees then knelt and smiled. "How in the world are you, Miranda?"

"Fine." She fingered the swan on Edie's shoulder. "My fattoo went away."

"Did it?"

Miranda nodded.

"Well that's lucky. Because otherwise you might have no place to put this." Edie pulled a handful of square papers from the bag. She peeled back a plastic covering off one square, dried a place on Miranda's arm, then turned the square over on the spot. She dampened the back with pool water, held it a few seconds, then slowly peeled it off.

Miranda's eyes widened. She gasped. On her arm was a small red heart. "Daddy, look. Look!" She ran to the pool to show everyone, and Edie rose slowly, watching. There was pleasure on her face. Contentment, even. Seeing it, seeing her with his daughter, filled him with deep warmth.

"My mother's going to have a fit," he said softly.

Edie turned from Miranda to him. "Is she?" There was dreamy satisfaction in her face.

"Yeah."

"Sorry."

"No, you're not."

In another minute they were surrounded by the rest of the kids, all demanding fattoos of their own. Miranda graciously consented to share, and Edie was willing to do the deed, but Bunny Carter didn't think it appropriate.

"Next thing you know they'll want to pierce their eyebrows," said Patty Jane.

"They're only temporary," said Edie mildly. "They'll wash off in a few days."

Taking their cue from Bunny and Patty Jane, the other

mothers shook their heads, but the kids took to jumping up and down and generally making such a fuss that some-one finally gave in. And once one capitulated, the rest followed.

Except for Bunny and Patty Jane, who took their screaming children by the hand and left.

Edie was tattooing the last child when Mimsy walked up. She took Holt aside.

"What in God's green earth is going on? Bunny Carter left in a huff, and Patty Jane said something about the Devil and talking to Reverend Parsley."

"It's nothing. Just two uptight people, that's all."

"What *is* that woman doing?" She looked beyond Holt to Edie.

Holt explained, and a frown settled over Mimsy's face. "I just got that darned thing cleaned off."

Holt put an arm around his mother. "I know. But look at Miranda." His daughter's face glowed. "How can that be wrong?"

Mimsy sighed. "I suppose you can't argue with happiness."

Holt gave his mother's shoulders a squeeze. "Thatta girl."

Mimsy shook off the embrace and shook a finger at Holt. "You make sure we have a chance to visit, now. I want to get to know that woman."

"Her name's Edie."

"Yes, I know. Edie."

"Or you could call her the swan lady."

Mimsy gave her son a long-suffering look. "I'll stick with Edie."

As if summoned, Edie finished the last tattoo. Holt beckoned, and she joined Holt and his mother.

Mimsy gave her an appraising look. "Are you trying to corrupt my grandchild?" And she was only half-kidding.

Holt winked at Edie, who smiled archly. "I'm doing my best."

"Well, I don't know how I feel about that," Mimsy said.

Holt slipped a hand into Edie's and squeezed encouragement. But Edie seemed to know instinctively not to take Mimsy seriously. She continued to smile. "I hope you're not against a little fun."

"Nannie, look!" Miranda ran up, breathing excitement. "It's a heart."

Mimsy's eyes crinkled in the corners. "That's because you're my sweetheart."

Miranda giggled and ran off.

"Well, you've certainly made a hit," Mimsy said. "Are you always so popular with children?"

Edie's smile faltered, but only for an instant. "I don't know. I don't know many. "

"But you like children?"

Holt sensed an interrogation coming up. "Mother—"

"I like Miranda," Edie said.

"I think we need to get something to eat." Holt tugged Edie away. Undeterred, Mimsy tagged along.

"And your parents? What do they do?"

Holt groaned, but Edie answered. "They're both dead," she said flatly.

That knocked him and his mother silent. But it made Holt wonder what else he didn't know about her. It seemed a lifetime ago, but something at the quarry had upset her and she'd dodged his questions. Then again, how much had he told her about himself? He hated talking about Cindy.

"I'm sorry," Mimsy said at last.

Edie plowed on, her face blank. "My mother died ten years ago. My father ten years before that."

"How awful. You must have been so young. Was he sick?"

She stiffened, and Holt tried to spare her. "Mom, that's enough."

"He died in a . . . a freak accident," Edie said. "My mother never got over it." They'd arrived at the long table laden with bowls and plates of food. Mimsy took Edie's hand and patted it.

"I'm sorry for all the losses you've had." Mimsy turned to Holt. "You make sure she eats, now."

"You know I will." Holt gave her a pointed look.

"I'm going. I'm going." She scurried off, still talking. "I'm glad we had a chance to talk, Edie. We'll do it again." A threat or a promise? Either way, he felt his girl had passed her first test.

Edie watched Mimsy Drennen shuffle off, leaving her alone with her son. Although they were surrounded by a swarm, she felt that solitude like an energy shield, walling her and Holt off from the rest. She looked through the barrier. Didn't see James, but felt his presence anyway. Hard to believe the loving family man could be the bomb that exploded her life.

But she'd vowed to take that power away from him, hadn't she? She opened her mouth, then closed it again. Saying she'd spill and actually spilling were suddenly two entirely different things. Besides, Holt looked happy. Relaxed. She hated to ruin that.

Yeah, right. *Coward.*

Holt handed her a plate. "Hungry?"

"I better be. Or I'll have your mother on my ass."

She was too agitated to eat, but she walked down the buffet anyway, plopping spoonfuls of food she didn't want onto a paper plate encased in a straw holder. Potato salad and coleslaw. Ambrosia. The standard fare for every American backyard bash. It was all so normal. Everyone was tricked out in summer colors. Yellow, turquoise, white. Kids running around in bathing suits, grass stuck to their bare feet. Why would any of these happy, normal people want to harm her?

Revenge was a two-way street, she realized. She wanted to find out what had happened to her father, but face it, she also wanted payback. Had come to town to exact it no matter the cost. Except she hadn't expected the cost to be life. Hers included.

She shivered in the heat, her jaw tense. Who was out there? Someone who wanted his own retaliation? Or someone who just wanted . . . her?

Mimsy broke from a circle of women and hurried to greet someone coming out the back door. James, carrying a couple of six-packs. Edie stiffened as Mimsy led him to the food table, where he dumped the beer into the coolers at either end.

Was it him? Was James the one after her? Her pulse sped up, and she tried to maneuver herself and Holt away, but Mimsy caught them.

"Have you met Edie?" she asked her husband.

Edie held her breath, waiting for some indication that

James was out to harm her. But nothing in his face signaled anything but civility. He straightened, lifted the Braves ball cap, and wiped his forehead with the back of his arm. "Sure I have. Nice to see you again, Edie."

To keep up the pretense, if it was pretense, Edie forced politeness out her mouth. "Looks like you've got quite a crowd for the game."

He nodded, looked around, came back to her. "Just the usual suspects."

Another casual reference or something with deeper meaning? Her heart was beating fast enough to fly, but no one else seemed to notice anything untoward. Holt was fishing in the cooler and Mimsy was fussing with the bowls on the table.

Another woman joined them. "James? Can I speak with you?"

"Sure, Amy."

But before she could, Mimsy said, "You know my son, Holt."

"Of course," the woman named Amy said. "He was so kind the night of Fred's death."

The name extinguished Edie's attempt to calm down. But surely there was more than one Fred in Redbud. More than one dead Fred?

"And this is Edie," Mimsy said. "Edie, this is Amy Lyle."

Edie greeted the woman, staring at her pale blue eyes and faded blonde hair. She didn't look like the wife of a town big shot. She wasn't wearing the latest Dana Buchman, but something she'd unearthed years ago from someplace like L.L. Bean. Some old faded thing she'd thrown on because she couldn't be bothered worrying about what she looked like. And what she looked like was frail and tired and sad.

A stab of guilt went through Edie. A stab of guilt she had no business feeling. Fred Lyle's death wasn't her fault. She wanted to cry it to the sky. *It wasn't her fault. It wasn't. Leave me alone, whoever you are! Leave me alone!*

Instead, she found herself saying the most unexpected thing. "I'm sorry about your husband, Mrs. Lyle."

"Thank you, dear."

Was James drilling a hole through her with his gaze? Or was it just her imagination?

Before she could decide, Fred Lyle's widow turned to the former chief of police. "James?"

"Why don't we go into the house," he said, and ushered her away.

With the house between her and James, Edie breathed a little easier. Mimsy left to greet another newcomer, and once more, Edie was alone with Holt.

Which only got her heart pumping again. Now. Do it now. Take the damn plunge down that black pit, and tell him. She heard the words in her head. *I'm the black angel, Holt darlin'. But those two dead guys—they really were accidents. I had nothing to do with them. I swear on my poor dead father's grave. Oh, and your daddy? The one you love so much, respect so much? Well, he may have tried to kill me.*

And if he believed that . . .

Uh huh.

"You all right?" Holt asked.

She nodded, unable to make her mouth work.

"You sure? You're not taking that grilling from my

mother too seriously, are you? Here—" He held up a bottle of Bud, and she washed away the words stuck in her throat with a long, cold hit.

"Better?"

"I'm good."

And maybe she was. Maybe everything would turn out all right. After all, whatever James knew, he wasn't telling. Yet. She'd just have to keep her distance. And check her bike every hour on the hour. Thank God, no one had died in the last few days, and hopefully—please, please, please—she'd seen the last of the black angels.

She took another swig off the bottle. The knot in her stomach loosened, and she thought about eating something.

Before she could pick up her plate, Holt's cell phone went off. He checked the number. "Gotta take this."

His face grow serious. Her hand started to tremble, and she abandoned her plate again.

"When?" Holt said into the phone. "Call Doc Ferguson. Okay, I'll be right there." He disconnected. Turned to Edie. "I'm sorry. I have to go."

"What happened?" Her voice was tight, her shoulders taut.

"It's Reverend Parsley." He started off at a fast walk, and Edie pursued, her heart halfway up her throat.

"What about him?"

"Looks like he's dead."

~24~

When Holt arrived at the Redbud Community Church, a small crowd had already gathered. Sam had called the Police Auxiliary, and Galen Crews was on guard duty outside the front door.

"What's going on, Chief?" someone called from the pack as Holt made his way up to the front door.

"That's what I'm about to find out." He bounded up the church steps two at a time and nodded to the gangly eighty-year-old who sat in a folding chair in front of the doors, tapping one long foot to some rhythm heard only by himself. He struggled to his feet, but Holt waved him back down.

"Any problems?" Holt asked.

"No, sir."

"Good. Don't let anyone in." Holt entered the church and met Sam inside the chapel. Without a word, she took him around the side, through a dressing room marked "men," and then out to the ramp leading down to the large baptismal pool. Reverend Parsley's wide bulk floated face down in the water, almost filling the space.

"Another heart attack?" Sam whispered.

"Could be." A bleak feeling took hold of Holt. "Who found him?"

Sam paused before responding. "Terry Bishop. His aunt is church secretary. Evidently he came to pick her up."

"Where are they?"

"Preacher's office. She was . . . well, she's old, and didn't take the news well."

Holt understood. The secretary was probably hysterical. "Pictures?" Holt asked.

Sam nodded to the camera the department had bought and never used except in training. It sat on a chair dragged into the pool area from somewhere else. "Got 'em."

"Every angle?"

She nodded.

"Okay. Get over to the office and make sure the two inside stay put."

After she'd gone, he examined the scene in front of him. The pool was at the back of the chancel where a small stained-glass window let in a stream of weak light. The water was an eerie sea green, reflecting the paint on the bottom and sides. It gave the pool a spooky air. Then again, maybe that was the purpose of a baptismal pool. To make you think you were washed with the spirit of God. And that was spooky, wasn't it? Except this one was full of the spirit of death. Calm. Quiet. No traces of blood in the water. Clear, clean, and final.

Holt took out a notepad, made his own sketch of the scene, and finished just as Doc Ferguson strode in.

"My God," the doctor said when he saw who it was. "What happened?"

"Hoping you could tell us."

The doctor was already examining the body. "Can I move him?"

"We've got our pictures."

They grabbed his feet, and between the two of them managed to turn him face up. Lividity had started, the blood pooling in the chest. Holt had seen a couple of drowning victims in Memphis. An accident and a suicide. Typically the body curls up in a partial fetal position with lividity in the face and neck. The preacher was in a dead man's float, which could mean one of two things. He hadn't drowned or he hadn't drowned in the pool. Rigor hadn't set in. Which meant he hadn't been dead long.

"Or it means the water kept it from setting in," Doc said. He was measuring water temperature, comparing it to the preacher's body temperature. "We'll see."

There were no signs of struggle or violence, except on the preacher's face. It had frozen into a grimace of fear or death or both. Natural causes or something more sinister? Ferguson knelt over the side, lifted Parsley's hands. No damage to the wrist area. No puncture wounds on the neck or face either.

"What do you think?" Holt asked.

"Can't be sure." He got off his knees, dried his hands on some paper towels. "Like I said, water sometimes disguises things. But on first glance I'd say it looks natural enough. He hasn't been dead long. An hour. Maybe two."

That would put time of death somewhere between four-thirty and five-thirty. A start.

"Heart attack?" Holt asked.

"Won't know until I get a closer look."

"He have a history of heart problems?" Holt said.

"He went out of town for his medical advice. Can't say I heard he did, but there's no telling." He looked around. "Okay if I get him out of there?"

Holt agreed and got the two men Doc had brought from the volunteer fire department. It took all four of them to heft the body out of the water and into a waiting body bag.

Holt watched them wheel the minister out, hoping the two men would be discreet about what they'd seen, and knowing word would get out no matter what he hoped.

He let out a breath. Time to talk to the witnesses.

Inside the preacher's office a desk and chair occupied one wall. Sam perched on the corner of the desk, arms crossed, gaze vigilant. In a corner, two armchairs were separated by a small table. The secretary was hunched in one of the armchairs, clutching a knot of tissue in one hand. Bookshelves lined the walls. Terry Bishop was slumped against one of them.

"Terry." Holt nodded to him.

"Chief." Terry nodded back.

"You want to tell me what you're doing here?"

He looked even more sullen, if that were possible. "Like I told Sam, I was here to pick up my aunt."

"So late in the day?"

"It's Tuesday," Terry said. "We always come on Tuesday. Same time. Ask anyone."

Holt looked to Sam, who murmured the woman's name.

"Miss Garvey?" He sat in the opposite chair. "That true?"

The secretary picked at a tissue in her hand. "I always come Tuesday evening. To do the bulletin for Wednesday's prayer meeting and to type up Reverend's sermon. Then Terry comes and sometimes we go to Claire's for dinner. And then we go home. He lives with me, you see. Only this time . . ." She worked the tissue again, unable to continue.

"Why does Terry pick you up? Don't you drive?"

"She drives," Terry said. "She lets me use her car while she's here."

"That true? Miz Garvey, is that true?"

The woman stared at Holt, but he had a feeling she wasn't seeing him. "He was just . . . there. Floating. Like he was on vacation." She shuddered and the glaze in her eyes went stormy. "He shouldn't be swimming in the baptistery." A tear leaked down one cheek, and she dabbed at it absently with the clump of tissue.

Holt tried again, taking her hand, and asking gently, "How did you get here today?"

She shuddered, but answered. "My nephew picked me up."

"Is that unusual? Can't you drive yourself?"

Terry took a step forward "I told you—"

"Shut it." Sam moved to intercept him.

"It's all right, dear." Miss Garvey seemed to get control of herself. She turned to Holt. "Terry's car needs a few repairs, so we have this arrangement. He takes me here, has the use of my car for a few hours, then picks me up."

"And what time did he drop you off?"

"A little after six." She collapsed against the chair again. Looked at Holt with watery eyes. "We'll have to clean the baptistery, don't you think?"

"I don't know, Miss Garvey."

"Purify it." She looked at her hands. A tear plopped into the tissue.

"Was there anyone else here when you arrived tonight?"

She shook her head.

"You're sure?"

She nodded.

Holt turned to Terry. "How about you? See anyone when you got here?"

"No."

"And when you found the preacher, he was face down in the pool?"

"I didn't touch him," Terry said. "I left him just the way I saw him."

"And how did you manage to be passing by the baptistery? It's not on the way to the office."

"It is if you come in the back."

"The back? Did your aunt let you in?"

He exchanged a look with his aunt. Reluctantly he said, "I have a key."

Holt scowled. "A key? What are you doing with a key to the church?"

"He cleans in the morning," his aunt said defensively. "Vacuums and such."

"You don't seem like the church-cleaning type," Sam said.

"The church needs cleaning," his aunt said. "It's honest work. And he needs the income."

"For those repairs," Sam said ironically.

Holt turned to the older woman again. "Any idea why the preacher was in the baptismal pool?"

She shook her head. "Unless he was trying to fix the

drain." She sniffed. "We had a baptism on Sunday. Little
Aaron Tewksbury. Do you know the Tewksburys? Such a
nice family." She exhaled a shuddery sigh. "It was beautiful. Truly. I wish you could have seen that little angel—"

"And something happened at the baptism?"

"Oh, no, it was perfect. Went off without a hitch. But
we drain the pool after each baptism, you see, and this
time the pool wouldn't drain. I guess . . . I guess he went
in there to see what the trouble was." Her voice cracked
and she blew her nose.

"Don't you have a custodian to do those kinds of
things?"

"We're a small church. Most of us volunteer. Money
for repairs is always scarce."

"What about your nephew?"

"I . . . I don't know." For a moment she looked confused and looked to Terry for help.

"I was getting around to it," Terry said defensively.

His aunt's expression firmed. "Yes, he should have
waited for Terry." She began to cry again. "I don't know
why he didn't wait for Terry. He liked doing things himself, but he should have waited."

"What about heart problems?" Holt asked. "Seizures?
Anything that could explain what might have happened
to him?"

She shook her head. "None that I heard of."

He asked the next question carefully. "Do you know
anyone who might want to hurt him?"

"Hurt the preacher?" The thought seemed unimagi-
nable to her. Then her eyes filled with surprise and fear.
"You don't think—dear Lord, you're not saying—"

"Had he received any threats? Had any arguments with anyone?"

Her face paled.

"What?" Holt leaned forward. "What is it?"

She hesitated, and he exchanged a look with Sam. "If you know anything, anything at all . . ."

"I'm not sure," she said. "It's probably nothing."

"You let me decide that."

She rose on shaky legs, leaned on Holt, while Sam opened the door. The two of them escorted her to the desk outside the minister's office, and Terry followed. She unlocked the top desk drawer and took out a small padded envelope, which she handed to Holt. He hefted it, feeling nothing more than the weight of the envelope. Whatever was inside, it wasn't much.

The top of the envelope had been slit open and taped back together. Holt grabbed a pair of scissors from a cupful of pens and cut the tape. Spilled the contents onto the desk.

A small black angel rolled out.

~25~

Though she'd seen it before, Miss Garvey gasped and covered her mouth as if the sight of the angel surprised her as much as it did the rest of them.

"Sweet Jesus." Terry took a step back.

"I'll be damned," Sam muttered.

Holt said nothing. His throat was too tight for speech. Three deaths, three black angels. Way too many for coincidence. Whatever had happened to Reverend Parsley, it was no accident.

Holt turned the envelope over, saw Parsley's church address. Showed it to Sam.

"It's addressed to Reverend Parsley," Sam said. "What's it doing in your desk?"

Miss Garvey looked shamefaced. "I didn't want to upset him, so I was waiting for the right time to . . . well, to give it to him."

"When did this come?"

"Last week," Miss Garvey said. "I do the mail on the days I'm here." She was wringing her hands again. "Did I do wrong? If I'd known . . ."

Terry rubbed her thin shoulders. "It's all right. I'm sure it wouldn't have mattered when you gave it to him."

"How do you know it wouldn't have mattered?" Sam asked sharply.

Terry flicked her a surly look. "I just meant if the reverend was marked for death, he was marked for death. Whether she gave him the marker or not."

His aunt gasped and started to shake again. Sam groaned, and Holt said, "I don't want to hear that kind of talk around town, Bishop. No one is marking anyone for death."

Terry shrugged and pulled his aunt closer. "Can we go home now? Aunt Ellen's tired."

Holt hesitated. As long as he knew Red's hours he knew where to find Terry, and his aunt did look weary. But he was loath to let them go yet.

Terry growled with impatience. "Look, Chief, you want to find out what happened to the preacher, just ask your girlfriend."

A jolt of astonishment rocked through Holt. "What?"

"You heard me. Your girlfriend—the tattooed lady."

Holt scowled. Leave it to Terry to pull a name out of the air and toss the blame there. "What the hell are you talking about?"

"She was here. This morning. I caught her rummaging around the reverend's office."

The air inside the office exploded with heat. Holt jerked forward. His hands reached for Bishop's throat. Miss Garvey screamed. Sam leaped between the two men.

"Chief!"

Holt ignored her, surging forward. "You shut your mouth," he said to Terry.

"Truth's truth," Terry taunted, safe behind Sam. "She even told me to watch out for the reverend. Like she knew something was going to happen to him."

"Shut up, Terry. Easy," Sam said to Holt, a hard hand on his chest.

Into the brief impasse, Holt's phone rang. He glared at Terry. Didn't move. The phone rang again. And again. The sound brought a semblance of normalcy, and Holt relaxed under Sam's hand.

"Get them out of here," he growled to his deputy, and walked away. By that time, the ringing had stopped. He reached for the phone to check the ID. Edie.

He pictured Terry. Heard his words. And somewhere deep inside Holt Drennen, a dark cloud shifted.

~26~

Edie disconnected the phone. She should leave Holt the hell alone, but patience had never been her strong suit. What had happened to Parsley? Had someone discovered the black angel she hadn't found? She leaned against the side of the Drennen house. Sweat filmed under her arms, and it wasn't from the heat. Had the angel of death struck on her behalf once again?

She shuddered. Why hadn't Holt answered his phone?

"Hello, Edie."

Edie's pulse shot up and she whirled around. She didn't know what she expected to find. The angel himself? The devil? Instead, Holt's father had come around the corner and was approaching her. With him was Fred Lyle's widow.

"Having a good time?" James Drennen said to Edie.

She nodded, her mouth too dry to answer.

"You remember Amy Lyle?"

"It's a nice party," Amy said.

Edie had to drum up some spit. "Yes, it is," she said at last.

She was aware of the blandness of their exchange, and the sharpness of everything left unsaid. Sorry about your husband. Sorry about whatever part I might have played in his death. Sorry, sorry, sorry.

The black angel rose in her mind, an effigy come to life. It swooped down on godzilla wings, the whoosh of their movement a thundering earthquake. The sound inside her head was so loud, she could barely stand it.

"Excuse me." She fled. Literally ran for her bike, scanning the skies as if any minute the huge black monster would appear, snatch her up and soar with her, higher and faster and faster and higher. Until she disappeared and only revenge was left.

Sam was surprised Holt didn't go back home after leaving the church. She usually took first shift with the paperwork. But this time, he followed her back to the office, jumpy as hell.

Not her. She always knew there was something funny with that woman. Eager to follow up on Terry's story, she asked Holt about bringing Edie into the office. He didn't answer.

"I'm happy to question her if you can't do it yourself," she said.

"I can do it just fine," he snapped. "If it was necessary. Which it isn't."

"But Terry said—"

"I know what Terry said, and Terry Bishop is a loud-mouthed drunk. Not much that comes out of him is worth listening to."

"Yeah but—"

"No buts, Sam."

"But—"

"I said—"

"Okay, okay." She hadn't expected him to be so stubborn. Had that witch gotten deeper into Holt than she'd thought? Hard to believe he'd let his sex life run his cop life. No, not hard to believe. Impossible. "You gonna call the staties?"

Another silent response.

"We got three mysterious deaths, Holt. And Redbud doesn't have the resources to pursue this kind of broad investigation." She waited, again got nothing. Jeez, you'd think he'd had a brain freeze. "I could call them if you want."

"No one's calling anyone," Holt barked. He threw down his pen, pushed away from his desk. "Enough for one night. We can finish up in the morning."

Sam stared. Wasn't like him to throw things. "That's okay. I don't mind staying."

"You gonna give me an argument about everything tonight? I said, we'll finish up tomorrow."

She shrugged, trying to hide her disapproval. "Sure, boss. Whatever."

He stalked out, not waiting for her to follow, and she sat there like a stupid grunt.

As far as flash-bastings go, she'd heard worse. Delivered worse if truth be told. But never from Holt. Being chewed out like that kind of hurt her feelings. Especially since she was just doing her job. And better than he was right now.

But she'd never disobeyed an order in her life. So she straightened her desk, set the paperwork neatly on top, then shut the lights.

Maybe a decent night's sleep would set his head back on his shoulders. Yeah, that's all he needed. A good night's sleep. Tomorrow he'd come in and do the right thing.

She locked up and headed for her car. Knocked herself upside the head for doubting him even a second. Holt always did the right thing. Her chest swelled a little, thinking about him. She was proud to be working beside him. Damn proud. He'd never let her down, and he never would. Especially not for some biker chick who'd probably never seen an iron in her life and wouldn't know what to do with one if she did.

After he left the office, Holt drove around aimlessly. He wasn't ready to go home. Needed time to cool down. Digest what Terry had said and what it implied.

He found himself heading for the cemetery and the black angel itself. The huge sculpture loomed over the Swanford headstone, its mammoth wings spread over the two graves on either side. Menacing ropes of thick hair swept back from a high forehead.

Holt stared at the fierce face. The eyes seemed to follow him everywhere. *Angel* seemed the wrong word, with its overtones of soft, womanly comfort. Nothing gentle or feminine about this creature. It emitted pure muscular fury.

An avenging angel.

He gazed up at the face like a supplicant at the foot of some fierce god. Who was it avenging? The answer seemed obvious. But what did Lyle, Runkle, and Parsley have to do with Charles Swanford? Lyle had run the plant, so that connection was clear. But the rest?

He gazed at the name on the headstone. It set something off inside him. Some familiar tug he didn't want to acknowledge. Swanford was damn close to Swann. Too damn close. For half a second he let suspicion ricochet around his head. What if Edie . . . ?

No, he wasn't going there. He was being ridiculous. How could she? Why would she? He was just letting Terry Bishop get to him.

He shut down those doubts all the way home. Paused a moment before getting out of the car to gaze at his parents' house. The house he grew up in. The house his daughter was growing up in. It didn't seem possible that something dark and evil could be walking the streets of his hometown.

Gloom settled over him as he walked in. His mother was in the kitchen cleaning up with a couple of other women.

"Well hey there, Holt." She shot him a smile as she wiped her hands on a dishtowel. "You hungry? You didn't get to eat much."

"I'll grab something later." He barely paused to greet the other women before heading into the den where his dad was picking up empties and dropping them into a plastic trash bag. The beer cans made a tinny rhythm as they clanked against one another.

"Miranda here?"

He shook his head. "Sleepover."

Holt nodded and sank into the couch.

"Trouble?"

Holt nodded. "Reverend Parsley."

"What?" The clanking stopped.

"Drowned in his own baptistery."

"My God." James sat beside Holt.

"Terry Bishop found him." And before he knew it, he was telling his father everything, including what Terry had said about Edie.

"I don't know what to think, Dad. It could all be a load of crap. Something Bishop said to get to me."

"But you're worried."

"At the very least, I have to ask her about it."

"I think that's a good idea. Look, when it comes down to it, what do you really know about her? She comes into town, makes friends with the local law, and suddenly people start dying."

Holt's earlier doubts resurfaced, but he didn't want to face them. "Dad, come on, you make it sound like Edie's some kind of crazy killer."

"Maybe she is." His dad paused and gave him a grave look. "I wasn't sure I was going to tell you this. Frankly, I didn't know how to tell you. Looks like I have no choice now." He paused for barely a breath. "Did you know Amy Lyle approached me about some private detective work? Seems Fred had a strange codicil to his will. A large bequest to one Eden, last name . . . Swanford. I'd bet the whole shebang that Edie Swann is really Eden Swanford."

Holt heard his father's words and didn't hear them. "That's . . . impossible." But now his suspicion at the cemetery reached in and gripped his heart like a fist.

"Is it?" James rose and led Holt to the back room that served as an office and Mimsy's ironing room. They made their way past the laundry basket, the ironing board, and the shirts on hangers waiting to be put away. Things he'd seen many times before, but now looked odd and out of place. James unlocked the top drawer of the desk jammed against one wall. He handed Holt a document. "Came yesterday."

A copy of a court order from the state of Pennsylvania, acknowledging a name change from Eden Swanford to Eden Swann.

Holt stared at it, the fist inside his chest squeezed so tight he had trouble taking in air. But even if he doubted the reality of the document, he couldn't doubt the evidence on her own skin. The serpent-entwined apple over her heart wasn't temptation, it was Eden. And the bird on her shoulder? A swan. Eden Swann.

Edie's emotional reaction at the quarry made perfect sense now. The story she'd told his mother. Parents dead, father of a freak accident. Some accident.

It killed him to give Terry Bishop any credit, but the image of the ominous black angel rose in Holt's mind. It loomed over the grave of Charles Swanford as well as the more recent deaths of Reverend Parsley, Dennis Runkle, and, of course, Fred Lyle.

The words blurred on the page, and the document began to tremble in his hand. He parked it quickly on the desk. "Fred Lyle had a heart attack. Are you saying Edie arranged it somehow?"

James put a hand on Holt's shoulder. It was strong and firm, a bulwark of reassurance. "I'm not saying anything, son. Just that now there's a connection. A human connection."

And though James didn't say it, Holt knew his dad was thinking it, because the thought was there in Holt's head, too. He didn't just have a connection. Now he had a reason. And if revenge wasn't enough, money was as good a motive for murder as any.

~27~

Edie couldn't think. She could hardly breathe. She sped back to Red's chased by a shadow so dark and expansive it blocked out the stars. She barely braked the bike before she hopped off and vaulted up the iron steps to her apartment door. She fumbled with the key, her hand shaking. Finally, she made it inside, and collapsed against the door in a quivering heap.

What was happening? Had she awakened some murderous demon in Redbud? The same demon that took her father?

She held her head in her hands. That was crazy talk. Devils, demons, angels of death. Insanity. She knew it, but couldn't stop the train from running on. Lunacy ran in her family, didn't it? Instability. Weakness. Was it her turn now?

Nausea circled in her gut, twisting and tightening and rising into her throat. She sprang up, ran for the tiny bathroom, flipped up the toilet seat. Vomited.

It caught her hard, pulsing and exploding out of her. The retching went on and on, but it didn't stop the terror.

Even when she was bled dry, exhausted and drained, she still shook, still sweated. Still didn't understand how anyone could know what was in her heart. And carry it out.

Was someone watching her? Following her? And did that someone know every detail of her past and all her secrets? She looked around wildly, as if whoever it could be was lurking in the shadows. But there was nothing. No one. Half-demented, she flung open the plastic curtain around the shower, metal holders screeching against the rod. Empty.

What was happening? Who was next? She hadn't delivered that last black angel to James. Would Holt's father be next anyway? Or would whoever was arranging these deaths let Holt know that his lover was responsible for those black angels?

She froze. Terry Bishop had seen her at the church. He'd blab to Holt, for sure. Oh, God. Would she rot in jail instead? Either way her life was over.

The thought shattered whatever calm she had left.

Only one thing to do. Get out. Now. Before anyone else died. Including her.

She staggered out of the bathroom, pulled the duffel down from the shelf and tossed it on the bed. Threw in her clothes, not bothering to fold anything. Piled on shoes and bras and jeans. She didn't even bother checking for what she might have left behind. Toothbrush, socks—whatever she missed, she'd replace when she got to wherever she was going.

She jerked the zipper, couldn't get it to close, jiggled the lumpy contents and when she still couldn't get the zipper up, yanked out whatever was on top.

She reached for the zipper pull, and into the crazed silence, a knock sounded on her door.

She froze.

"Edie!"

She couldn't see Holt. Not now. Not ever.

"Edie! Open up!"

She didn't move.

"Goddammit, Edie, I need to talk to you. Open the fucking door!"

She tried to squeeze herself small, so small he wouldn't know she was there, would go away and stay away. But he pounded the door again.

She looked around frantically. No place to hide. Could she jump out the window? If she broke a leg, she'd never get out of Redbud.

But the window was the only way out. She ran to open it. Raced back to the bed for the duffel.

The hell with her stuff. She could always buy more stuff.

Bolted back to the window. Opened it wider.

The door exploded inward.

She tried to dive through the open pane, but Holt was there in two strides, pulling her back by the neck of her shirt.

"Going somewhere, *Eden?*" He threw her on the bed and, with a heavy swipe, slammed the window shut. Then he grabbed the duffel and hurled it across the room. Shoes clattered out of the open top, a bra banged into the wall. T-shirts and jeans hurtled every which way, on a shelf, over the hotplate, curled around a chair leg.

And across the floor like a skater gone wild skittered

the tiny packet of black angels, spewing its contents over the room.

Edie looked at them with horror. Her dread was mirrored in Holt's face. He looked at her with disbelief. With hurt. With accusation. And finally, with cold knowledge.

"Turn around." The frigidity in his voice chilled her to the bone. She couldn't move.

"I said"—in one deft move, he flipped her so she was lying face down on the bed—"turn over." He yanked her arms behind her. Cold metal kissed her wrists. The snick of the locks closing around her hands sounded deafening in the silence. Roughly, he turned her over so she could face him.

"Eden Swanford, you are under arrest for the murders of Fred Lyle, Dennis Runkle, and Kenneth Parsley."

He yanked her to her feet. "You have the right to remain silent." Shoved her out the door. "Anything you say will be used against you." Down the metal steps. "You have the right to an attorney. If you can't afford a lawyer, one will be provided for you." A group of men were clumped outside the bar, smoking and laughing. The minute she stumbled into view, they shut up.

"Hey, Chief," one of them called, "what'd she do now? Hit you again?" They snickered, and Holt shoved her forward.

"Do you understand?"

She jerked away, whipped around to face him. "I understand everything."

"Good." He opened the door, put a hand on her head, and pushed her into the backseat of the car. The men outside Red's watched as he hauled her away.

~28~

Holt kept Edie up most of the night. Too angry to sleep himself, he paced the office, shooting wads of paper into a wastebasket for ten minutes before returning to the single cell where Edie looked out between the bars, staring coolly at him. Midnight. Two. Four in the morning. There she was, where he'd put her, like a wraith that needed neither sleep nor justification.

She freely admitted sending the black angels, but the rest she adamantly denied. "I didn't kill anyone."

Leaning against the wall across from the cell, he watched her closely. "But you knew about Fred Lyle's will."

She stretched out on the cot, hands behind her head, as if she couldn't be bothered with his persistence. "I still don't know about Fred Lyle's will. Why don't you fill me in?"

He took another tack. "Why change your name?" Over the course of the night, he'd asked her that a dozen times, and this time, as she had each time before, she told a variation of the same story. Eden Swanford was a sad, pathetic little girl and she didn't want to be her anymore.

"Why lie to me about it?"

"Eden Swann is my legal name. Everyone calls me Edie. I didn't lie."

"You knew who sent the black angels."

"That was none of your business."

"You made it my business when you killed those men."

"I told you—"

"Yeah, I know. A demon did it. A mysterious being working on your behalf."

"No, not on my behalf."

"You didn't want those men dead?"

"I wanted them to sweat, that's for sure. But dead? They're useless to me dead."

"Not if you wanted to use them for revenge."

She snapped to a sitting position, swiveled to face him. "Look, don't you get it yet? I wanted to shake them up. Get them ready to talk."

"To talk or to die?"

"Stop saying that."

"I'll stop when you start telling the truth."

She glared at him, and he scrubbed a hand over his face. He was tired of the runaround, but more pissed off than anything. He didn't have to lock her up. He shouldn't even have arrested her. But he wanted her on edge, and if she felt even the smallest bit of the betrayal he felt when he saw those black creatures tumble onto her floor, he'd cry hallelujah to the devil himself.

"Dammit, Holt. I am telling the truth and you know it.

Let me out of here. Go home. Look in on Miranda and get some sleep. Then we can go over all this tomorrow."

"And let you hightail it out of town? I don't think so."

"You took my keys."

He stabbed a finger at her. "And impounded your bike."

"See? It's not as if I can go anywhere."

He leaned against the wall across from the cell. Crossed his arms. He had no intention of letting her out. Not until her throat bled from begging. And maybe not even then.

"Okay, let's go back to the church. What were you doing there?"

"I told you. I was looking for the black angel. I was trying to take it back."

"Why?"

"Why do you think?"

"I think maybe you were planting something there, not taking it away."

"Like what?"

"You tell me. Something to implicate someone else."

"Like who, Holt? If I could have implicated someone else, wouldn't I have done it already? I love the enforced closeness, darlin', but I'd rather do it without bars."

He grunted, allowing her the point though he didn't want to. "If you didn't know something was going to happen, why did you warn Terry to watch out for Reverend Parsley?"

"I didn't know, I suspected. I told you, I was worried. Wouldn't you be? Wouldn't anyone?"

"Anyone with murder on their mind, yeah."

She glared at him.

"So why these three men?"

She groaned. "How many times do you have to hear it? Before she died my aunt Penny gave me a list of names. Men who visited my father during the last few weeks of his life. She didn't know why they came or what they said. If I could find that out—"

"What?"

"Maybe it would explain—"

"Why he killed himself?"

She nodded.

"No, I think you blame them for your father's death and killed them for it."

She grabbed her head. "I didn't kill them. How the hell could I find out what happened if they're all dead? Don't you see? It isn't me who wanted them dead. Someone didn't want me to find out what really happened."

"What really happened?" He lunged at the bars, grabbing them. "Your daddy embezzled money from Hammerbilt. He got caught. Couldn't face the consequences and offed himself. That's what really happened."

"You don't know anything about it."

"I know that your precious father jumped into oblivion and left you and your mother alone to face the whole town. I know that he was a weak coward."

"Shut up. Shut up!" She grabbed the bars from the other end and only the steel kept them apart. Her face was wild with denial and fury, the dark hair and brows a keen contrast to the high blush of her cheeks, the white of her neck. As alive in her passion to defend her father as she was in his arms.

He wanted to kiss her. He wanted to strangle her.

In either case he'd be able to touch her, which was what he wanted above all.

He cursed. Her stubbornness, his infatuation. The deep, deep endless pain inside his chest, as if someone had taken a machete, hacked through his ribs straight to his heart.

He stalked off. Back to his office. Back to the chair behind the desk. Breathe, man. Shake it off and breathe.

What was so damn attractive about Edie Swann anyway? Rat's nest she called hair, inked up and down her arms. She was a freak, a circus freak.

Yeah, and that freak was shaking up his life like nothing had since Cindy died.

Which was exactly the point, wasn't it? That itchy restlessness he shoved aside, the memories he buried—of dark alleys and the hyped-up rush of adrenaline from putting everything on the line. Wasn't he just a little tired of playing it safe?

And Edie was so far from safe she might as well be the grenade about to explode in front of him.

Maybe that was it. Not her at all, but the danger she represented. He grabbed on to that as if it was his last crumb of bread. Thought about all the other ways he could soothe his dormant thrill seeker. Bungie jumping off the nearest bridge. Hang gliding. Speedboat racing. Anything that didn't involve Eden Swann, black angels, or three dead men.

He closed his eyes, suddenly way beyond tired.

Holt didn't remember falling asleep, but he woke when someone shook him. And there he was, bones aching from being squashed in his desk chair, his father looking down at him.

"Jesus, Dad." He ran a hand over his face. Saw the time on the wall clock. 7:00 A.M.

"Morning," James said cheerfully. "Your mother sent over some coffee. Didn't want you poisoning yourself with the stuff here." He held up a thermos and a plastic container. "And some ham biscuits."

Holt grumbled, but his dad didn't seem to mind the crankiness. He set the thermos and container on the corner of the desk. Took a seat across from Holt. "Long night."

Holt unscrewed the thermos. The hot liquid steamed as he poured it into the top, and the aroma began to wake him up. He slid the coffee over to his dad, then poured some into a Styrofoam cup for himself. The liquid was hot and strong. It cleared his head but didn't take the ache away. "I arrested Edie."

James paused in the action of bringing the cup to his mouth. He hadn't slept much either, desperate to know what Holt would do with the information he'd been given, what Edie would tell him, if she knew anything to tell. He'd figured Holt would go straight to her, would question her. Hadn't expected him to arrest her.

"She's the source of the black angels."

James set down the cup altogether. Could he have lucked out at last? If Edie had sent all those black angels, she was Holt's prime suspect. "I'm sorry, son."

"Yeah, me, too."

"You got enough for an indictment?"

Holt shook his head. "Says she didn't do it, no surprise there. But her story was consistent all night long. And I can't place her at the scene of any of the deaths. And even if I could place her I don't know how she could've arranged any of them."

James nodded sympathetically, his mind racing. How to convict her without seeming to? "Look, Holt, I don't like to stick my nose in. This is your job now."

"But?"

"But are you sure you're talking murder? A heart attack, an allergic reaction, and a drowning could all have perfectly plausible explanations. The black angels could have nothing to do with any of it."

"A coincidence? Edie has a list of men connected to her father and three of them just happen to pop off while she's in town? Come on, Dad, you know better than that."

In a rush, the blood left James's body and pooled at his feet. "A list? She has a list of names? What names?"

Holt waved away the question. "Doesn't matter. They're all dead now."

"All of them?"

"Alan Butene—remember him? Fell off a ladder last year. Broke his neck. And then our three."

Anticipation beat a faint rhythm in his chest. "That's all?"

Holt peered at James closely. "Dad, you got something? Some connection between the names?"

James shook his head, buried his face in his coffee. "No, no. Just wondering. Thinking out loud. You said Butene was on the list and he fell off a ladder?"

"He was changing a light bulb at the top of the stairs. Tumbled right to the bottom. Neck broke. Died instantly."

"Another accident."

Holt shot his Dad a sharp look. "Had to be," Holt said. "The ladder must have been eighty years old."

"And Edie wasn't in town then."

"Okay, so I'll give her one. But the others?" Holt shook his head.

"You sound like you want her to be guilty." James picked his words carefully, trying not to let the hope shine through.

"What I want's irrelevant," Holt said flatly. "It's what's staring me in the face that counts."

"So what are you going to do?"

"The only thing I can do with the evidence I have. Let her go."

~29~

When someone finally came to unlock the cell, it wasn't Holt who set Edie free, but the deputy, Sam Fish. She was crisp and pressed in her starched uniform, her hair pulled back, her face bright-eyed and refreshed. The sight of her made Edie even more grumpy than she already was.

She stumbled out of the cell and into the sweeter-smelling air outside the jail room. "What happened to Holt?"

"Gone home."

No need for long explanations from Deputy Fish.

Edie grumbled. She couldn't help a flash of disappointment. Even in her dreams she'd been explaining herself to him, and the opposite urges to slap his face and throw herself on her knees and beg forgiveness were making her crazy.

"What about me?"

"What about you?" Sam countered. She led the way to the small office overburdened with its two desks, its steel filing cabinets, bulletin boards, chairs, and a long wooden bench against one wall.

"You just letting me go?"

"Why—you want to spend another night here?" Sam opened a desk drawer, took out an envelope, and dumped the contents on the desk. Edie's wallet, credit cards, keys.

Edie pocketed the first two, examined the last. It was lighter than it should be. "My bike key's not here."

Sam frowned, but there was something manufactured about it. "It's not? You sure?"

"Of course I'm sure."

The deputy shrugged. Sat in the big desk chair and leaned way back. "Maybe you didn't have them with you when the chief brought you in."

"I didn't have them with me, because Holt took them."

"Everything he confiscated was in that envelope."

"Everything except my bike key."

"Well . . ." She rocked back in the chair, clearly unperturbed. "They'll turn up." She grinned. "Eventually."

Eventually, my ass. "Tell Holt he can kiss my butt." She shoved the rest of her keys in her pocket and stalked off.

"Don't think he'd want to get that close anymore," Sam shouted after her.

Without her bike, Edie had to walk back to Red's. She would have called a cab, if there even was such a thing in this deadbeat of a town, but her cell phone was back in the room above the bar. And she'd be damned if she asked Deputy Dawg for anything, let alone use of the phone.

So she set her chin and started the tramp back. After her mostly sleepless night, she was so tired she could have slept a month. When she finally got to the alley behind Red's she clomped up the metal steps, opened the door, and crawled into bed.

And lay there, wide awake.

The night-long interrogation replayed in her head. The hurt and anger on Holt's face. The accusation. She tried to whip up some righteous indignation, but couldn't. Truth was, she deserved his condemnation. She'd lied. Betrayed his trust. It was her own goddamn fault if he thought her guilty.

Sure, there was a tiny pinprick of disappointment that he didn't believe in her despite appearances. But that wasn't the way the world worked. Not Edie Swann's world.

She sighed and rolled over. Thought about spending the rest of her life locked inside a jail cell. Couldn't believe it would come to that.

But if Holt didn't believe in her, who else in Redbud would?

A chill rolled over her. No one had believed in her father's innocence either. Was this what the black angel was all about? Standing over another Swanford sacrificed at the Redbud altar? Was she part of some great cosmic joke? A sick, twisted gag on the part of the fates?

Edie opened her eyes. Screw that. She sat up. Threw off the covers. She'd be damned if she would play the part of punch line for anyone, angel or devil. She would not throw herself over a cliff, would not go gently into a psych ward, and would not let Holt Drennen railroad her.

James nursed a cup of coffee at Claire's, trying to decide whether to be relieved or anxious that Edie hadn't named him. Was he even on her list? He hadn't received a black angel. Had she not gotten around to him? Or didn't she know about him? Was she, like him, loath to hurt Holt? Worse, would she use his name to get leverage over his son? And what would Holt do? Would his upright son bend the rules for his father?

James didn't want to find out.

He found himself remembering all the times he'd come home late to find his young son waiting up for him.

"You catch the bad guys, Dad?" he always asked, and James accepted the pride the question implied as natural.

"They show up here I will," he always replied.

And now he was one of those bad guys. Hell, had always been. No, not always. Only the last twenty years or so.

Sadness filled his throat, and he looked down at his coffee cup. All those baseball teams he'd coached, the football games he'd watched. The times spent with his son had been churning in his head like an endless video loop. Would everything he'd done be for nothing? He'd wanted his son to grow up strong and happy in a thriving town. Was that so wrong?

He caught a movement out of the corner of his eye. Red McClure waving to him. James nodded, and the bar owner took the gesture as an invitation. He slid into the seat across from James.

"Morning, Chief."

"Red."

Without asking, Darcy came with a coffeepot and a cup for Red. Her gigantic earrings swung as she filled their cups. Red ordered eggs, but James didn't have the stomach for food.

"Heard Holt arrested my bartender last night." Red shook his head. "Hell, half the town heard. Happened right outside the bar."

James nodded, trying to look sage but disinterested.

"I heard it's about Reverend Parsley and those black angels," Red prodded.

"You'll have to talk to Holt about that," James said.

Red nodded, but the worried look remained on his face. Darcy brought him his eggs, fried up with a side of bacon, and he gazed at the white and yellow eyes as if he was waiting for them to blink.

Tillman Crocker approached their table. A pudgy white-haired man with a gray mustache, he was Redbud's mayor.

"Hear your boy caught that black angel," Tillman said. "Had to hear it from Hattie Tuttle, too. Cleans the house once a week. Heard it from her boy, who saw the whole thing outside Red's last night." He turned to Red. "Works for you, does she?"

Red nodded. "Been released, too."

"Really?" The mayor frowned. "Don't know as I'm too happy about that. James? What do you think?"

"Holt brought her in for questioning. That's all."

"In handcuffs?" Tillman asked.

James held up his hand. "I'm not chief anymore, boys."

The mayor pursed his lips. "Well, I'll have to have a talk with Holt. Can't have a killer walking the streets." He looked pointedly at Red. "Or working for us."

"Now, Tillman," Red soothed. "If she was a killer, Holt wouldn't have let her go, ain't that right, Chief?"

James didn't have to answer because Tillman did.

"If she wasn't tied up in all this, he wouldn't have brought her in either." The mayor turned to James. "Your boy should have apprised me of this himself."

"It only happened last night," James said.

Tillman ran right over that. "Fact is, he should report to the whole city council."

"You'll have to work that out with him," James said.

"Don't think I won't," the mayor said. "Got a big delegation from IAT coming to town. Plant inspection. Now with Fred gone, we're not in as strong a position as we were. Can't have this hanging over us. Wouldn't want word to get back that Redbud's not safe. Isn't good for business."

Tillman left, and Red pushed his plate away. "Don't that man know about innocent until proven guilty?"

"He's not interested in proof," James said. "He knows that perception is reality. Especially in Redbud."

Red nodded glumly, put a few bills on the table, and left his untouched eggs congealing on the plate. James swiveled away from them and raised his coffee cup toward Darcy, who came over with the pot.

"Mayor's got a bee in his bonnet." She refilled James's cup. "Is it true what he's saying? Holt arrested that bartender last night for being the black angel?"

"He questioned and released her. That's all."

Darcy tsked. "Well, you know what they say—where there's smoke . . ."

James stared into the hot black liquid steaming in his cup. He felt the mist surround him, pushing him back to a time he didn't want to revisit.

The day they'd buried Charles Swanford had been hot as a blast furnace. He remembered sweating through his uniform. Evelyn Swanford's dress wilting around her thin frame. Her sister—what was her name? Penny. Penny Bellingham. Wiping her neck with a tissue. Everyone shuffling, trying to breathe the searing air, wanting the ceremony done so they could get back to their airconditioned cars.

And over them all, the looming presence of that enormous black angel.

Was it good for him that the town was about to paint Edie in its darkest colors? Would it mean the past was more likely to come out or less? With Lyle, Runkle, and Parsley gone, there was only one man left who could tell what happened. And he wasn't talking.

But that still left the problem of Amy Lyle. He hadn't told her that he'd found her Eden. Once he did, it could be the string that unraveled the ball. It wasn't enough to know who Eden was. Amy would want to know why Fred left her that money.

But James had already used the truth to loosen Holt's tie to Edie. Her identity was bound to come out. Better to control its release than let it run wild.

He felt for the cell phone at his waist and punched in Amy Lyle's number.

∽30∽

Perception or reality, Edie's growing notoriety proved the mayor wrong. Because it was good for business. At least for Red's business. The night after her arrest was the busiest since St. Patrick's Day. Seemed everyone wanted to glare at the black angel.

Edie felt the hostility like a stone wall she couldn't penetrate. Customers avoided the bar, preferring to be served by Lucy. But that didn't stop them from nudging each other and pointing at her. Even Howard and Russ sat at a table. She made a nickel in tips that night—slapped onto the bar by someone on his way out.

"Don't you pay no attention," Lucy muttered. "They'll come round."

After closing, Edie trudged up to her room. The door was spray painted with the word "killer," the last letter dripping white paint.

The next day she bought her own can of paint and added the word "smile" below the original.

Which didn't endear her to Red's customers. As days passed, business dried up. Some came anyway—it was a hike to the next town, where the nearest decent bar was. But some stopped at the Pay N Go on the way back from their shift and drank their six-packs at home.

A week after Sam Fish kicked Edie out of jail, Red's was abnormally quiet. Only a few customers scattered around the tables. The same group that had watched Holt haul her down the stairs in handcuffs sat in the corner nursing their beers and eyeing her balefully. Terry Bishop sat with them. Every time she looked over she found him watching her, a satisfied grimace on his face. She knew he'd been the one to tell Holt about running into her at the church. And Terry clearly couldn't be more pleased about it.

She stood behind the bar, swabbed a cloth up and down the already dry and shiny surface, and watched them watching her. How long would the freeze last? It was not only cutting into her own paycheck, but Lucy's and Red's, too. They'd both been terrific—Lucy for continuing to be her stalwart champion and Red for not firing her. But that couldn't last forever. Eventually he'd have to choose between his business and her. And she knew what his choice would be.

The front door swung open bringing with it a blast of hot night air. Behind it came a small, compact woman. Short hair in disarray, loose clothes soiled and wrinkled.

Amy Lyle.

She glanced around wildly, found what she was looking for, fixed on Edie. The entire room seemed to hold its breath.

"You should be ashamed," she said, shaking with rage. "To walk around like anyone else. And you"—she pointed a quivering finger at Red—"to let her. It's repulsive.

Sickening!" She swept over to the bar like a hurricane hurled her. "Murderer," she spat at Edie. "Murderer!" She slapped Edie, quick and fast and full of sting.

Edie iced over. The sound of the slap echoed in her brain and on her skin. Mrs. Lyle collapsed into horrible, hiccupping sobs, and Lucy rushed over, put an arm around her.

"It's okay, now, hon. You just sit down." She brought the widow to a table, but Amy refused to sit.

"Not here," she wept. "Not with her in the room."

Red hurried over. "Can I call someone?"

Amy Lyle sobbed harder. "No one to call," she wailed. "No one."

"Let me drive you home."

"She did it for the money," Amy said. "Don't you see?" She grabbed Red's arm, fingers clutching at his shirt. "She wanted Fred's money. And now she's got it. She's evil. Evil!"

"Come on, hon," Lucy soothed. "You let Red take you home." She helped her up and urged her toward the door. "That's right. Go on home."

"Maybe someone else should be going home." Terry Bishop stood up. Every gaze in the room swiveled to Edie. The grumble of assent was unmistakable.

Red stopped at the door, and turned to Edie. There was apology in his eyes, but also finality.

Edie shrugged, bitterness welling up. "You'll be short-handed," she said flatly.

"Not if the crowds stay away."

"I didn't do anything."

"Don't seem to matter much, does it?"

Ain't that the truth.

"Better give up the key to the upstairs room, too," Red said.

Son of a bitch.

She threw down the bar towel, and a cheer went up in the room.

~31~

Well, now," Doc Ferguson said, "this was a real puzzler."

Terrific. Holt frowned down at the sheeted body of Reverend Parsley. It had been over a week since the preacher had died. Holt had been on Ferguson's ass every day, but when he called at last, it was after midnight. Holt had been flat out, dead asleep, the kind of black, drugging slumber he'd fallen into right after Cindy died.

"Knew you wouldn't want to wait," Ferguson had said. There'd been excitement in his voice, and Holt had groaned, rubbed the sleep from his face, and said he'd be right there.

Now it was near one in the morning, and Doc was blathering about puzzles.

Was it too much to ask for a clear-cut cause of death? Holt would take drowning, stroke, heart attack, hell, he'd even take strangulation, then drowning. But puzzles he didn't want to hear about.

"Look, Doc, if it's too much for you, I can call the state ME."

"Hold on, hold on. Don't get your britches in a twist, I didn't say I haven't figured it out."

"So you do have a cause of death?"

"Well, he didn't drown. Water in his lungs was postmortem."

Holt's gut clenched. Accidental drowning would have been nice. It would have let Edie off the hook.

"And I couldn't find signs of a heart attack or stroke," Doc continued. "Nothing, you know . . . *natural*."

Holt's gut tightened. He didn't like the sound of that. But it was the perfect ending to the perfect hell of a week. Anger at Edie had given way to regret and a nagging hope that she was okay. He tried to bury it at work, doubling up on patrols, especially late at night when he missed her the most. He spent every spare minute going over his notes. Still found nothing to prove any of them was murder. Or any solid connection between the three men. Except Edie's angels.

The vise around Holt's middle tightened further. "If it wasn't nature, what was it?"

Ferguson pulled down the sheet to the reverend's neck. His face was blanched white, eyes closed, ugly black sutures around the incision in the front of his skull. Lifeless, soulless, a thing to be poked and prodded. Holt remembered the moment Cindy's breath stopped. He'd held her hand and watched life seep from her eyes. Felt glad for her release, guilty at the gladness, and bereft of everything. And days later, when the morticians had finished with her, she had been waxy and unreal, not Cindy at all. Just some creature that looked like his wife.

"No bruising anywhere," Doc said. "You noticed that at the scene."

"Uh huh."

"So there didn't seem to be any cause of death."

Holt stated the obvious. "Something killed him."

"Yup. And that's what I kept saying to myself. So I went over everything again. And finally—" he pointed to the minister's closed eyes. "Take a look."

Holt reached to open the eyelids.

"Not the eyes," Doc said, "the lids."

Holt gazed down at the reverend's closed eyelids. They looked normal to him. Maybe a bit redder than usual, but that could be Parsley's natural coloring.

"Petechial hemorrhaging. The purplish red spots on the lids. It's called petechial hemorrhaging."

Holt peered closer. The redness dissolved into tiny pixels of color. "And that's what killed him?"

"Hell, no, Chief. That's what *told* me what killed him. See, sometimes when the heart stops suddenly there's these"—Doc clenched the air with two hands—"muscle contractions, which cause the blood pressure to rise. And in certain circumstances the increased blood pressure forces the capillaries to release a small quantity of blood into the skin. Petechial hemorrhaging."

"And what are these 'certain circumstances'?"

"Electrocution. Particularly in a wet environment."

Holt stared at the doctor. "You're telling me he was electrocuted?"

"Uh huh. Death by electrocution is hard to determine. Not much morphological evidence. Had to do a bit of research."

"But you're sure?"

Doc nodded. "There was evidence of hemorrhaging in the membrane surrounding the lungs, too. You didn't find anything around the baptismal pool he could have used to electrocute himself accidentally?"

"You saw the same scene I did. Nothing there but the pool and him."

"No radio, electric screw driver? Even a microphone could do it. Was a preacher once, down in Texas, died that way. Just about to do a baptism, too."

Holt thought back. Saw the baptismal room, spare and dominated by the pool. Nothing in the water but the body. Nothing surrounding the pool but the ramp from the dressing room and the small expanse of floor. If Parsley had electrocuted himself, whatever he used would have still been there after he died. Which meant . . . someone else had to have engineered it.

Murder. The word echoed, unspoken, in the air.

It was difficult to imagine anyone arranging a heart attack or a lethal allergic reaction. But electrocuting someone? All you had to do was plug in a hair dryer and throw it in the water. Unplug it when the deed was done and take it away. A kid could do it.

Holt's mouth dried up. He now had the first concrete evidence that someone in Redbud had taken a life. Was that someone Edie?

She'd been there in the morning. She'd warned Terry, as if she knew something would happen to Parsley. She could have gone by the church on the way to the All-Star party, taken care of business, and still shown up at his house when she did. She'd been late, hadn't she? And keyed up when she got there. He'd attributed her nerves to the pressure of meeting his folks, but it could have been something else. Something far more lethal.

The thought that Edie had come to him right after killing Parsley turned his mouth sour and left him sick with revulsion. He wanted to believe there was another explanation for what had happened. But wanting and getting were two different things.

Edie didn't bother packing up. She didn't even take a change of clothes. She couldn't face seeing the room above Red's once more. She never was one to linger on a breakup. Never remained friends with her exes. Cut the ties and move on.

So the hell with Red and his freaking town. She counted her cash—enough to keep her in coffee and doughnuts if she was careful. Maybe a couple of nights in a motel. There was the Cloverleaf out on Highway Six. Not exactly walking distance. But Holt still had her bike and keys.

So if the town wanted her out, the town could damn well escort her out. And if it was too late for that, the town could put her up.

The municipal building was locked when she arrived. No surprise there. Except she'd heard that Holt was keeping late hours these days. So she set her butt down to wait. Didn't have to hang around long. Holt's headlights pulled into the parking strip in front of the building within half an hour.

It took him a few minutes to notice her. In the meantime, she had the luxury of watching him. His big body looked strained and tired. She had an impulse to run over, fling her arms around him, and tell him everything was going to be okay.

But it wasn't. The doom she'd lived with her whole life was closing around her, and he was pulling the drawstrings. She didn't want to surrender to fear, but seeing his powerful body and knowing it was ranged against her set her pulse banging. Is that what a warrior felt when he knew the enemy was not only worthy and capable but close? She didn't want to battle with Holt. She wanted him on her side, fighting for her. With her.

Knowing that wouldn't happen, that he believed the worst, sent a flutter of weakness up her legs and into her belly. Bad idea. Coming here had been a bad idea. She'd been all bravado and up yours, and hadn't thought it through. Hadn't realized what seeing him would do.

She jerked to her feet, hoping to slink away unnoticed, but the movement drew his attention. He stopped cold. A world of silence opened between them. Only a sledge-hammer could have smashed it, and Holt's was quiet and weary.

"What are you doing here?"

"Waiting for you."

He kept his distance, eyeing her. "Why?"

"I want you to arrest me."

His face congealed. He ran his tongue over his lips. "You're confessing?"

"No."

The freeze softened. He came to life, frowned, plowed ahead, and unlocked the door. "But you want to go to jail."

"No."

"Edie—"

"I don't *want* to go."

He opened the door to the police department, turned on the light, and threw his keys on the desk. They clattered into the quiet, a jangling, impatient sound that echoed the look he shot her.

"I have nowhere else to go."

He sat on a corner of the desk, crossed his arms, stared at her balefully. "You're kidding, right?"

"No."

"Something wrong with Red's?"

"He kicked me out."

"He kicked you—"

"Fired me first, of course. And since it's your fault for dragging me off in handcuffs in front of the whole damn town, I figure you owe me. And hell"—she laughed shortly—"it's where everyone thinks I belong anyway."

Holt took his time responding. Unraveled himself from the desk. Stood. Stepped closer. Pondered her thoughtfully.

"I'm sorry," he said.

"Are you?"

He shrugged.

"You find my bike keys?"

"Not yet."

"Lock me up, then."

"Edie—"

"It's jail or a park bench. And if it's a park bench you'll only arrest me for loitering, which means I'll end up back here anyway. Why don't we just cut out the middle step?"

He sighed. Grabbed a set of keys from a desk drawer. "Just for tonight."

She followed him into the cell room. "My keys going to turn up tomorrow?"

"We'll see."

Translation: not likely.

She threw herself on the cot, and he stood inside the

cell leaning against the bars. "You stop by the church on your way to my house the night of the party?"

Oh, God, not this again. "You know I didn't. Why?"

"Parsley was murdered, Edie. And I can prove it. The first one that can't be explained away as an accident or natural causes."

The news sent her bolting up. "I thought . . ." A wave of dizziness rattled her, and she put a hand to her head to steady herself. "I thought he drowned."

"Only looked like it." Holt eyed her coldly, accusation all over his face.

Oh, God. Tears ached in the back of her throat. Holt was close enough to touch, but farther away than the other side of the world. "I didn't do it, Holt."

"Do what?" His voice was soft, sad.

"Whatever. Whatever whoever did to make it look like he drowned." In her head she was pleading with him. *Believe me, Holt. Believe.* "Isn't it possible this death isn't connected to the others? Maybe they were what they appeared to be—a heart attack and a car wreck. And if that's true, why would I kill Parsley?"

"He was on your list. You sent him an angel. You even seemed to know something would happen."

"Suspected," she reminded him.

Silent now, he searched her face as if something there would determine her guilt or innocence if only he could probe deeply enough. Unable to face his doubt and that searing examination, she turned away.

"What do you know about Alan Butene?" he said at last.

She expected more hectoring, so the question took her by surprise. "Who?"

"Alan Butene."

It took a minute to register. "Just a name on a list, Holt."

"And you don't know anything about him?"

"I know he was the plant comptroller till he retired a couple of years ago. I know he's dead. Why?"

"Do you know how he died?"

"No."

"He fell off a ladder."

"So?"

"So he was the first accident."

"The first—oh." Possibility opened inside her. "No black angel either. What does that mean?"

"Means you weren't around. Means it was an accident. Means—I don't know what it means."

Silence settled between them again. Holt seemed to be examining the tile in the cell floor, and once again, she had the opportunity to stare at him. This time, she let the ache come. It was a yearning she must have been born with, she'd felt it so long—for acceptance, for arms to enclose her with esteem, for a place that was truly hers and not just a pull-out bed in the corner.

And then, when the longing threatened to become unbearable, she did as she always did. Set her jaw, raised her chin, placed the chip on her shoulder, and silently dared anyone to knock it off.

By that time, Holt had lifted his eyes and was studying her again.

"Maybe it means I had nothing to do with the others either," she said softly.

He looked directly at her. "Maybe."

"Do you know Mrs. Butene?"

"I do."

More silence. Edie didn't want to ask. Didn't want to risk an answer she wouldn't like. But desperation shoved like a bull at her back.

"So . . . does this mean"—she cleared her throat, the words sticking there—"that you believe me? That you don't think I killed anyone?"

Holt's mouth twisted. "It means I want to believe you, God help me."

Everything inside her wanted to whoop and holler, except something in his face stopped her.

"But?"

"But I have to prove it first."

~32~

Edie didn't know where Holt spent the night, except that it wasn't with her. Which was fine. After their conversation, he could be in Bangalore and she would have felt closer to him than she had in weeks. And this time when she woke inside Redbud's single jail cell, she wasn't staring at the scrubbed face of Deputy Fish, but at the green eyes of her boss.

"Rise and shine," he said.

She moaned and sat up. Rubbed the sleep from her face. "Is it noon yet?"

"It's just after six."

She slid into her shoes. "You're kidding." He opened the cell door and she passed in front of him on the way out. "Where am I supposed to go at six in the morning?"

"At least you can get more sleep. I've got work to do. And," he added casually, "a meeting with Hally Butene to arrange."

She stopped, eyes widening, and was tempted to fling herself into his arms. But he had a gleam in his eyes as if he knew it, so she yawned instead. "Great. When's it gonna be? Where does she live?"

He gathered his keys, checked his cell phone, patted his pockets for whatever else he never left without. "Let's go. I want to stop at Red's and get your stuff." He ushered her out of the office and into his car. This time she sat in the front.

"I don't need my stuff."

He shot her a glance. "You're going to live in those clothes forever? How about your teeth? Ever going to brush them again?"

"I can get whatever I need later." She paused. "Where are we going, by the way?"

"Highway 6."

Her brows shot up. "We're not meeting Hally Butene somewhere on Highway 6?"

He slowed, pulled into the alley behind the bar. "Not exactly."

He got out, and short of sitting there pouting, she had no choice but to get out, too. He tromped up the steel steps and she followed. He stopped when he saw the graffiti on the door.

"The smile is mine," she said.

He grunted, but whether in approval or condemnation she couldn't say.

Despite Red's demand, she still had her key. She unlocked the door and went inside.

The last time she and Holt had been there together, he'd arrested her. The anger and hurt of that encounter lingered in the corners as she stuffed her possessions into the duffel he'd thrown across the room. Neither one of them spoke. He perched himself in front of the door, as though he needed to guard it. His big body filled the room, and the stillness made his presence even larger. Everywhere she went—the small bathroom, the tiny closet—she was aware of his gaze following her. The accommodation they seemed to have come to the night before disappeared into the silence.

When she was done, he helped carry her bags down the stairs and threw them in the backseat of the car. Holt headed due east and onto Highway 6. Ten minutes later, he pulled up to the Cloverleaf.

"You're kidding," she said. "Mrs. Butene lives here?"

"No, but you do."

She stared at him.

"Look, you need a place to stay. I need to know you're not wandering the streets or disappearing into the sunset. And you can't sleep at the jail every night."

"At least give me back my bike so I won't be stranded."

"Come on, it's not like you're in the middle of the wilderness. There's a Waffle House half a mile up."

"Gee, thanks."

"You'll be safe. No one knows you're here. No spray-painting bogeymen to bother you."

"I can always rent a car to take me out of town."

"True. But an innocent woman doesn't run. You want to get to the bottom of this as much as anyone, right? Can't do that long distance."

She growled. "Whatever gave me the impression you were a nice guy?"

It took Holt all of five minutes to install her in one of the rooms. Seems he'd arranged it all before dragging her out there.

"Gotta run," he said when all her bags were inside and

scattered around the dingy room. "Mrs. Butene will probably be more receptive if I shower and shave."

"Yeah, good luck with that."

"Don't be so grumpy. I brought you a deck of cards and a crossword puzzle book." He nodded over to what passed as a dresser. A paper bag lay on top. "And there's always *General Hospital.*"

When he was gone Edie plopped backward onto the bed. She would have screamed if she wasn't too tired to open her mouth. She didn't even bother checking the sheets. Just closed her eyes and let the darkness take her.

~33~

Holt mused about his decision on the way home. He understood Edie's desire to believe in her father's innocence. The need to believe in hers was an unrelenting jackhammer inside him. He gnawed at the evidence, or lack thereof: He couldn't place her at the scene in any of the deaths. Even the explanation of her presence in Parsley's office made sense. Plus, it was hours before he died. And Holt would stake his life on her ignorance of Fred Lyle's will. But it all hinged on faith, and that was in the mind of the beholder. If he couldn't find some other suspect in Parsley's death, or some other explanation for the other two, Edie was still his only solid lead.

The first thing he heard when he got home was from Mimsy, who heard it from Carol Ann Baker, who heard it from Betsy Caldwell, who had kept Amy Lyle at her house after her disastrous foray into Red's the night before.

"Poor thing," Mimsy murmured, and Holt was pretty sure she didn't mean Edie.

The earliest Hally Butene could meet with him was that evening. All day, during neighborhood patrol, checking on the speed demons on the highway into town, behind his desk, wherever he was, Holt's skin prickled with anticipation. Something Mrs. Butene knew or said could be the key to freeing Edie.

By the time he finally pulled into the long driveway leading up to the Butene house he'd blocked out all possibilities except success. Somehow, some way, he was going to get what he needed from Hally Butene. This whole nightmare with Edie would be over, and they could go back to where they had left off.

On the way up, he couldn't help noticing the grounds needed mowing, the shrubs trimming—a far cry from when Holt had been there a year ago after Alan died. The property was built on a huge swath of Tennessee farmland. Probably too much for Mrs. Butene to keep up, especially with her Parkinson's.

At the moment, though, Hally appeared well able to care for herself, if not the homestead. As she'd been when she came to help Amy Lyle after her husband's death, she was well dressed, her chin-length white hair smoothed under, an ivory cardigan around her shoulders. The sight buoyed him. He needed her sharp and present.

She offered her hand, and he felt the tremor as she slipped it into his. Her head shook slightly, and her voice held the same gravelly precision he remembered. "It's good to see you again, Chief. And under much happier circumstances. Can I get you something to drink? Ice tea?"

He was itching to get started, but lubrication, even the nonalcoholic kind, gave them both something to do and would lower any lingering awkwardness. "Sure. Thank you."

He followed her into the kitchen, where tile and granite covered walls and counter, and watched her fill a tall glass with ice and tea and lemon. Her hands were shaky but capable.

"I see the grass needs cutting," Holt said as she poured a second glass for herself. "I could get someone out to do it, if you like."

She waved his offer away. "Oh, I'll get around to it. Alan thought nothing of lavishing money on the lawn. I'm afraid I'm a little more thrifty."

She led the way to a graciously furnished living room. A baby grand piano sat in one corner; a painting hung on the wall. Not your usual Redbud style of Wal-Mart and hand-me-down furnishings.

"Now, Chief Drennen, over the phone you mentioned something about my husband." She lifted her glass with dignity, despite the constant tremble, and took a sip, her gaze direct over the glass.

Holt plunged right in. "Your husband was comptroller at the Hammerbilt plant. He oversaw production, made sure the financials worked, that kind of thing. So he knew Charles Swanford."

A wary stillness overtook her, even as the tremors continued. "Swanford. Yes, of course. The embezzler." Holt bit back impatience as she looked down, picked at a small rip in the arm of the couch, then covered it with her hand. He assumed she'd "get around" to that, too, one of these days. "Poor man killed himself, didn't he?" she finally said. "Alan had been so shocked and upset. We all were. And not only for the personal tragedy. There was talk of consolidation and plant closings and everyone was on pins and needles waiting to see which factories would be shut down." She shuddered. "Not unlike now. Awful, awful time."

"I didn't realize there were corporate complications."

"Oh, I'm sure you've heard the story a million times now. What are they calling it? Globalization? Profits are faster and costs cheaper overseas. Everyone was worried. Especially after the whole Swanford mess."

"So, maybe it was a good thing he died."

She looked shocked. "That's a horrible thing to say."

"No truth to it?"

She sighed. "I don't know. I suppose . . . the cost of a trial, the publicity. Maybe in the long run it was better for the plant, but I can't think anyone would have said so at the time."

"Charles Swanford worked for your husband. Do you remember Alan talking about meeting with him?"

"I'm sure they met all the time."

"But nothing specific?"

"It was over twenty years ago. I wouldn't trust my memory."

Disappointed, Holt nodded and took another tack. "I know you and the Lyles were friends, but how well did your husband know Dennis Runkle?"

"Dennis? Oh, I'm sure they knew each other, but they didn't interact socially. Maybe a golf game here and there, but not on any regular basis."

"What about Reverend Parsley?"

"Well, we went to St. Edwards, the Episcopal church in Springfield, so I'm not sure Alan had much to do with him. But the community church was quite active in town, so I saw a lot of Ken." She shook her head in that wobbly fashion. "Hard to believe they're all gone. They say bad things come in threes. I'm not naturally superstitious, but still . . ."

A pinprick of panic touched Holt. He needed something, could not walk away without some tiny bit of information that would change everything. "Are you sure your husband didn't have business with all three of these men?"

"Business? No. Why?"

Holt was sweating, but he ignored it, hopeful that his next question would get Edie off the hook and worried it would implicate her further. He licked his lips. "Swanford had a daughter, Eden. Did your husband ever mention her, especially around the time he died? Might he have seen her or spoken to her? She goes by Swann now. Edie Swann."

A concerned expression crossed her face. "Edie Swann?" She frowned. "Isn't that the person who Amy Lyle—oh, my goodness. *She's* Eden Swanford?" Another wobbly head shake. "No, Alan never mentioned her. Why would he?"

"She has a list that contains the names of all the men who died. Including your husband's."

"A list?" She stared at him. "Are you saying there's some connection between these deaths and Alan's? But Alan fell off a ladder."

"And Fred had a heart attack, Runkle a car wreck, Parsley drowned. All accidents. Or made to look like them."

"Made to look—" A disturbed look crossed her face, and she rose. Ambled to a side table where she picked up a framed wedding photo. Her younger self next to a younger version of her husband. The couple smiled out from the frame. "I don't understand. How could—" She looked back at him. He saw tears in her eyes. "Are you telling me this Edie killed my Alan?"

"No." He held up his hands. "No. At least, that's what I'm trying to figure out."

"Well, I'm sure I would remember if Charles Swanford's daughter had suddenly showed up."

Holt took a photograph from his shirt pocket and placed it on the coffee table. It wasn't a great picture of Edie, but it was the only one he had. He'd taken it from the one Miranda had shot with his phone camera. That day at Claire's seemed a century ago.

"Recognize her?"

He didn't know he was holding his breath until Hally returned to the couch, scrutinized Edie's picture, and answered. "No. I'm afraid not."

He exhaled a huge breath. "You're sure?"

"I don't think I would have forgotten that remarkable face."

"And this?" He took one of Edie's angels out of his pocket. Handed it to Hally. "Have you ever seen one of these? Maybe in your husband's things?"

She rolled it around in her palm, examining it. "I heard about these, of course, but seen one here? Never."

"Did he mention receiving anything like this, or talk about Charles Swanford or the black angel?"

"No, Chief, absolutely not. Until all this crazy mess with the black angels I hadn't heard his name in years."

"What about your husband's behavior in the days before his death? Did he seem unusually agitated or secretive?"

"No, he seemed fine. His usual self." Her eyes welled up again. "I'm sorry." She took a tissue from the sleeve of her sweater and dabbed at her eyes. "It's been more than a year, and I thought I was over crying about Alan. But I still miss him." She got herself under control. The tissue disappeared and the solid gravel of her voice returned. "I'm afraid I haven't been much help."

Holt rose, excitement stirring. "More help than you know."

She brought herself to her feet. Smiled wistfully. "You know, when my husband got the job at Redbud, I thought he was dragging me to the ends of the earth. But there's something special about a small town."

"Not planning on selling, then?"

"Oh, no. Not if I can help it. I only hope my health holds out. And the money, of course. Illness is expensive, unfortunately." She gave him her hand again and walked him to the door.

"If you remember anything else, call me." He handed her a card. "Even if it seems small or unimportant."

She stood at the doorway and pulled her sweater closer as he drove off.

Was what she told him enough? God, he hoped so. No one could place Edie in Redbud at the time of Alan's death. And if she wasn't connected with it, maybe she wasn't connected with any of them. Maybe the deaths weren't even connected to each other. Or they were all connected, he just couldn't see how yet.

Except for Charles Swanford.

And Edie's angels.

～34～

It was after five when Edie woke. Her body clock still on bar time, she'd slept the entire day. Now, she stretched, sat up, stared at the motel room. She'd known a lot of motel rooms in her adult life. Drifting from town to town, staying in one sleazy place after another until she could find a job, rent a room, even occasionally an apartment. The tacky chipboard dressers, cheap all-in-one shower-tubs, the thin sheets with their lingering smell of cigarette smoke. It was all too familiar.

She thought about the ruin of her grandmother's house. What a little money and a lot of sweat could do. She could mow the swamp of a lawn, for one. Trim the bushes. Fix the tire swing. A couple of coats of paint could transform the exterior. And inside? She ticked off the tasks: refinish the wood floors, new wallpaper, new kitchen sink. Paint. Would it really take that much? A little love and care could work a large miracle, couldn't they?

She plopped back against the pillow. Congratulated herself on being the dumbest woman this side of Memphis. Her next home would probably be the state women's prison.

Besides, if she had the cash to buy a piece of property, Redbud should be the last place on earth she'd go. The town had gobbled up her father and was about to do the same to her.

And yet. And yet.

Miranda was in Redbud.

And Holt.

She punched the pillow. She should be planning her escape, not mooning over a life that would never happen. In a town she'd spent her whole life hating. And that now hated her.

She threw off the covers and jumped into the shower. Turned the water up hot and let it seep into every strand of hair, every inch of skin. And then, to make sure she was sharp-edged and straight-thinking, she turned off the hot and stood under the cold. Made herself count to ten before getting out. Shivering, she dried off, soaking the handkerchief that passed as a towel. By the time she was finished she buzzed with awareness, awake and ready for anything.

She rummaged in her duffel, pulled out a T-shirt, and dragged it over her head. Stepped into her denim skirt. Her cell rang as she zipped up.

Holt checking up on her? She didn't recognize the number, and the voice was female.

"Edie?"

Lucy.

"None other," Edie said.

"You doing okay?"

Bless her.

"What do you think?"

"Would I be asking if I knew?" There was genuine concern in the older woman's voice, and instantly Edie capped the sarcasm.

"Sorry. Little touchy these days."

"Can't hardly blame you. Where'd you go last night? I checked your room after we closed and you weren't there. You didn't spend the night wandering around, did you? After I checked the upstairs room I ran by the park. Didn't see you."

"I was safe and sound. In jail."

Lucy gasped. "Chief arrested you again?"

"Not exactly. But I made him put me up. Figured it was his fault I was suddenly homeless."

She snorted with what sounded close to awe. Or disbelief. "Edie Swann, you are something, you know that?"

"Yeah, whatever that is. An idiot?"

"A survivor."

"That supposed to be some kind of pep talk?"

"Just saying."

"What? That you don't think I killed anyone?"

"Did you?" The question came sharp and expectant, and Edie honored it by answering without hesitation.

"No."

She hmpfed. "What I thought. And what I said to Red last night. Gave him a real good talking to. He shouldn't have caved like that. No guts, that man. Just wanted to let you know I'll be working on him."

"Thanks. I think. Not sure I want the job back."

"Well, at least you'd be able to leave on your own terms. What about tonight? Guest of the city again?"

"No, Holt's got me stashed—" She paused. Holt said

no one knew where she was. Maybe it was better to keep it that way. "I'm good."

"You sure? You let me know if things fall apart again."

"Will do."

"Take care of yourself."

"Count on it. And Lucy?"

"Yeah?"

"Thanks for calling."

She chuckled. "You are welcome, missy. And don't let these small-town harpies get you down."

They disconnected, leaving Edie with a warm feeling. If Lucy believed her, maybe others did, too.

Clutching that small glimmer of light, she slipped on a pair of flip-flops. She was starving. Even the Waffle House sounded good. She grabbed some cash and the room key. Her hand was on the doorknob when the phone rang again. What now?

Again, the number was unfamiliar and so was the voice. "Miss Swann?"

"Yes."

"This is Bradley Cole, the late Fred Lyle's attorney."

Her hand around the phone clenched. The good feelings prompted by Lucy's call vanished. In their wake Amy Lyle's grief-fueled voice screeched in Edie's head. "Murderer!" The slap newly stung her cheek.

"Look, I'm sorry for Mrs. Lyle," she said stiffly, "but I can't help her." She clicked off. Shoved the phone in her pocket and slipped out of her room.

The phone rang again. She checked the ID. Cole and Tyrrell. She let it ring. Headed for the highway. Again, the phone rang. Annoyed, she answered. Maybe she hadn't been clear enough.

"Look, leave me alone. I didn't do anything to Mr. Lyle."

"That's not why I'm calling," Bradley Cole rushed to say. "Don't hang up. I promise it will be worth your while."

She stopped under the motel sign. A letter was missing, leaving the sign to read "loverleaf." She leaned against one of the signposts. "Is this about the will?"

Cole paused. "You know about the will?" He sounded shocked.

"I do now. Police chief mentioned it. Over and over. And over. Frankly, I still don't know. Just that I'm mentioned. For some ungodly reason, probably. And to Miss Eden Swanford, may she burn in hell along with her crook of a father."

"Actually, he left you a sizeable bequest."

She straightened. "What?"

"Could you come to my office tomorrow to discuss it?"

"Wait a minute. He left money? To me?"

"Yes." The single word contained a whole truckload of disapproval, which Edie ignored.

"But I didn't know the man."

"Evidently he knew you."

She swallowed. "I don't understand."

"Everything is contingent on you not having anything to do with his death, of course."

A flash of anger. "I told you—"

"We can discuss all of it when we meet. Tomorrow?"

"I don't know." She fingered the room key in her hand. "I don't have wheels."

"I can have a car pick you up. Behind Red McClure's bar, is that correct? Say, ten o'clock?"

Someone had been talking about her, but their information was a good twenty-four hours out of date. "Not Red's."

"Fine. Wherever you prefer." His voice was clipped and officious, and Edie couldn't help bristling. She didn't like being pushed and Bradley Cole was shoving her at warp speed.

"Look, things are a bit . . . up in the air at the moment. Can I call you?"

He paused a fraction of a second, but the tiny silence boomed with irritation. "Of course." He gave her the number. "But do it soon. The family would like to close this up."

The family. Again, Amy Lyle's face swam in front of Edie. She thought the other woman had been ranting that night at Red's, not even aware of what she was saying. But now . . .

Edie stared down the highway in the direction of the Waffle House. Her belly grumbled at the thought of food, but dinner didn't seem as appealing as it had a moment ago.

How much had Fred Lyle left her? And why? Hush money or blood money? Either way it came tainted.

She set off down the road. Dinner was an activity at least. She tramped the half-mile of blacktop, passing the ruins of Uncle Teddy's Variety Mart and a two-pump gas station that looked as if it had been there since the invention of the automobile.

What she couldn't do with a couple of thousand dollars. Buy a new clutch for her bike. A new pair of shit-

kickers. Those mothers were expensive. Or maybe she'd
throw it all into custom paint. One of those black-with-red
flame jobs. Or red with black angels. She couldn't help a
mischievous grin. Then she could take whatever was left
and hightail it out of hicksville.

If she wasn't in jail.

She pushed open the door to the Waffle House. The
smell of grease and food frying on a griddle hit her hard.
She swung up to a seat at the counter. Nodded to the waitress and ordered a burger and fries. Coffee to wash down
the grease.

Or she could use Fred Lyle's bequest as part of a down
payment on a broken-down shell of a house in the wilds
of Redbud.

The thought churned the food inside her stomach. That
was the second time in an hour she'd thought about settling down in Redbud. Dreaming was one thing, obses-
sion was another.

She bit into her burger, determined to drown herself in
bad food and obliterate anything else. She lingered over
her coffee, stretching out the meal as long as she could.
Nothing to look forward to but that motel room.

She paid her bill and headed out. Found herself
on the highway going in toward town. She walked
along the gravel edge, the occasional car buzzing by.
Past the gas station and Uncle Teddy's again. Past the
Cloverleaf.

Behind her, a souped-up engine boomed, and she
turned to see a ten-year-old Acura bearing down on her.
It zoomed past, close enough to take the hair off her legs.
She jumped back, gulping dust, lost her balance, heart
jamming.

God damn it to hell!

Fear drying her mouth, she watched taillights disappear. Must be going a hundred miles an hour, easy. No Acura she knew of could handle the road that way. Special delivery for her? She swallowed. Or paranoia raging?

Jittery, she got to her feet. Brushed off the gravel from her hands and knees. Looked around and saw nothing. No one. But dark was setting in. Just in case someone was sending her a message, she should get back to the motel. She even saw herself doing it, scurrying back to hide like a defenseless mouse.

Not likely.

She might have continued on bravado alone, but she wasn't stupid. She hugged the left side of the shoulder, staying as far from the road as possible. And she panned her surroundings making sure no one could pop up unannounced. Not a single other car rolled by. And the only creature she saw was a distant horse behind a fenced-in field.

Fifteen minutes later, the Hammerbilt sign lit up the horizon. She crossed the highway and stood against the wire fence that marked the outer edge of the plant property. Her hands clutching the metal, she peered in.

Across a flat expanse of grass and concrete, the factory complex stood stolid and unyielding. Lights around the property were just beginning to appear in the twilight. The compound dominated the skyline the way it dominated the town. And her own life. Years ago when she was too small to understand, something had happened in there. Something that had changed life forever.

Was her father really a thief? Hell of a legacy.

In the distance, a car exited the plant and headed her way. She stepped into the shadows, but even at a distance she could see this was no pimped-up street racer. Long and black with the windows darkened, the sedan looked official, as if it carried the Great Khan and his buddies. Two more cars followed, and the three proceeded past her toward town in a slow, pompous parade.

She'd heard there was a plant inspection on the horizon. Before her own notoriety, this assessment had vied with the black angels for the heavy chatter. These must be the VIPs, coming to judge the fitness of the town for further prosperity.

She leaned against the fence, suddenly tired. She'd come to Redbud to find the truth and set herself free. And now she was more entangled than ever. Suspected by some. Accused by others. Trapped. Literally.

She took her time returning to the motel. The sun finished setting and night crept into the sky. What was it about darkness that appealed to her? Things were muddled and unclear in the dark; any road seemed as likely as the next because all directions merged into one. Possibility dwelt at that fulcrum. In the dark, anything could happen.

But right now, nothing was happening. Nothing except the neon light of the "loverleaf" Motel, flashing its "vacancy" on and off. She walked under it, turned the corner to her room, inserted the key in the knob.

The door swung open.

Edie stood rooted. Stared at the mess inside. Blankets and sheets were strewn all over the floor. Her bags had been emptied, clothes, shoes, underwear scattered. The mattress was slashed down the middle, foam guts spilling into oceans of red. Blood everywhere. On the bed, the floor, her empty bags, her clothes. Blood dripped on the walls, oozed over the dresser.

And on the mirror above it, scrawled in red, was a message: "Die Killer."

~35~

It's paint," Holt said. "Red paint." He stooped down to the curb where Edie sat outside the motel room, tapping her foot impatiently. "It's not blood."

"That supposed to make me feel better?"

He'd come straight from the Butene place, the message Edie had left on his cell when he was inside ringing in his cars.

"There's blood all over," she'd repeated wildly.

He'd raced to the motel, calling Sam and ordering her out there. It seemed to take forever to get to his car. The drive felt like a week even at ninety miles an hour. Sure he'd find Edie dismembered, he was relieved to discover it was only her room that had been cut up. Though that was bad enough.

By the time he arrived, Sam had already secured the scene. She was inside now, taking pictures and prints. Leaving a scared and surly Edie to him.

"You said no one knew where I was," she said.

That was the disturbing part. "No one did."

"Someone did, Holt. Obviously. You must have told someone."

"Only my dad. In case something happened to me."

She paled. "Your dad?"

He frowned. "Yeah. My dad. Or do you think the former chief of Redbud came out here and did this?"

She opened her mouth. Clamped it shut.

"And the owner who I booked the room with. I doubt he'd vandalize his own room."

"What about the Acura?"

He shook his head. "One of the local kids, thinks he's James Dean. I'll talk to him."

A scrawny man with a thin mustache and a shirt hanging outside his pants came scurrying up. "Chief, about time. What are you going to do about this?"

Holt stood to greet him. "You Prewitt?"

The man nodded.

"Didn't I say no one was to know Miss Swann was here?"

"Sure. I remember." He glanced over at the open door of the motel room, where yellow tape blocked off the entry. "You know how much this is going to cost me?" He eyed Edie malevolently. "If I'd known it was her you wanted to stash, I wouldn't have been so helpful."

Holt glared. "What about employees? Maids, janitors, linen pickup."

"It ain't the Hilton, Chief," Prewitt said. "I got a woman comes in once a week. A couple of guys to vacuum now and again in between. I didn't tell a one of them. Swear it on a stack."

"Just give their names to the deputy inside."

Prewitt stalked off, and Holt turned back to Edie. "So what am I going to do with you now?"

"Nothing. I'm a big girl. I can do for myself."

"Like you did last night?"

"Give me back my bike and I'll be out of your hair."

Holt took a breath. Jumped into the fire with both feet. "How would you feel about coming home with me?"

Her head snapped up. Her eyes burned with dark glitter. "The black angel and the chief of police? Doesn't sound like that'd be a good career move."

"That's my problem, not yours. You have nowhere else to go and you'd be safe there."

"That's what you said about the motel."

"I doubt anyone's going to waltz into the chief's house and start throwing paint around."

She shuffled her feet. Looked down, then back up. Evaded his glance. "It's your family home. Your parents. Miranda—"

"Would die of excitement if the tattoo lady came to stay."

She stared past his shoulder. He saw yearning in her face, temptation. And caution, too. What was she afraid of?

"What?" he asked. He wanted to take her chin, turn her to face him. Rub his thumb along that stubborn jaw, kiss those obstinate lips, and force her to confess whatever was bothering her.

A thought occurred. It heated his face and he held up his hands. Took a step back. "I'm not going to touch you if that's what you're worried about."

Now she did look at him. But instead of being reassured, she scowled. "Thanks. Nice to know I'm so resistible."

"I only meant—"

"Yeah, I know what you meant. Things are a mess and we shouldn't screw them up even more by screw—"

"Chief!"

Sam ran over waving a piece of paper, Prewitt following.

"Mr. Prewitt here gave me that list of names." Sam was breathless—from her run over or from excitement. "Guess who's on it?" She handed the paper over to Holt. He scanned the short list.

Three names. The last one? Terry Bishop.

~36~

"Bring him in," Holt said grimly.

"Yes, sir!" Sam saluted, blushed to the tips of her ears, and jolted off. But not before eyeing Edie with a less than friendly look.

"This mean I won't be able to get the mess cleaned up?" Prewitt thumbed over his shoulder at Edie's room.

"Just for a day or two," Holt said. "And don't be handing out tickets or keys," he warned. "In fact, why don't I take any spares you have, just to make sure."

With a resigned shake of his head, Prewitt shuffled off, leaving her alone with Holt.

"So . . . we all set?" he said. "I can drop you off at the house before heading over to the office to talk to our mutual friend."

"Terry Bishop isn't my friend. Clearly."

"You had any run-ins with him besides at the church?"

She reviewed her association with Terry Bishop, couldn't see the harm in telling Holt everything. Nothing she'd said to Terry should have provoked this kind of violent response, but then, most people didn't like their secrets probed. And maybe Terry had his share.

"He was a regular at Red's."

"You piss him off there?" Holt said dryly. "Too much foam in his beer?"

"I know how to draw a beer, Holt."

"So—not the beer. What else?"

"I might have . . ."

"What?"

"Pushed him a little too hard."

"Pushed him how? You pack a wallop, I'll give you that, but you're still just a girl."

"I think—thought—he knew something about the plant. Some, I don't know, some dirt, I guess. I wanted him to tell me about it. I might have gotten a little . . . aggressive in my demands."

"You hit him?"

"No."

"Threaten him?"

"Not in so many words. But just asking about what he knows might be threat enough. If what he knows is personal. Or dangerous."

"Or both." They stared at each other, implications erupting between them like gunshots.

In the silence Prewitt ambled up. "There you go." He plopped two keys in Holt's hand. He indicated Edie. "She's got the last." Prewitt ambled away, and Holt closed up the room leaving the police tape intact over the doorway.

"Ready?" he asked when he finished.

"For what?" Edie said, knowing well enough what he wanted her to be ready for. But she wasn't going anywhere near his house. Or his father. Especially his father.

Before Holt could answer, his phone rang.

She exhaled. Reprieve.

Holt answered. Listened. Nodded. "Good work. No, I'll be there in half an hour. Gonna drop off Edie first. Any way you have to. Right." He disconnected, gave Edie a wry glance. "Seems Terry isn't too happy about his visit with the city's finest." He shoved the phone into a holder on his belt. "Come on. I'll call my mother on the way and have her set up the sofa bed in the den."

She braced herself. "I'm not going to your house, Holt."

He frowned. "I promise it's a lot more comfortable than the jail. Or a park bench."

"I've got another option."

"Yeah? What?"

The fewer people knew where she was, the better. "I'd rather not say."

Holt's frown deepened. "I don't give a rat's ass what you'd rather not say. You're not going anywhere I don't know about."

She shrugged. Remained silent. Why say anything? He'd only argue with her.

"I can cuff you to the sign over there." He nodded toward the motel sign. "Least I'll know where you'll be all night."

"Like I believe that. Empty threats, Holt. Beneath you."

He ran a hand through his hair. "Dammit, Edie, I can't let you go off on your own."

"Why not?"

"You know why not."

"Because I'm a person of interest in your murder case?"

"That, too."

"Because you'll miss me?"

"Because I'll worry about you." He crossed his arms, looked at her defensively. "Okay? You happy now? I said it. And I'll tell you another thing. I'll be damned if I let you put me through that. Lying awake wondering if you're hurt. Dead. I've been there. And I'm not going back."

She gazed up at the concern in his face. A warm flush of feeling jittered through her. Nice to have someone worry about her. Nice to have him worry about her.

"I'm going to Lucy's," she said.

"Lucy."

"From the bar. I think she'll put me up. Even if it's on the floor."

"You think?"

"Okay, I know she will. I just haven't asked her yet."

"For God's sake . . ."

"Look, I'm calling now, okay?" She already had her phone out. Punched in the number from Lucy's earlier phone call. Explained her situation to the older woman.

"Well, hell, girl," Lucy boomed in Edie's ear. "Come on over. It ain't the Biltmore but I've got a couch you're welcome to."

"Thanks. One last favor."

"Name it."

"Can you pick me up?" She told Lucy where she was and disconnected.

Holt looked at her. "I would have taken you over there."

"Yeah, can't think of anything less noticeable than the police chief driving up and dropping me off."

"I want an address and phone number."

"Okay. Fine. Whatever."

He grabbed her shoulders. "You are one stubborn witch, you know that?"

Like a live wire, his touch ignited her. She gazed up at him. His eyes glinted down at her.

"You just wanted me in your house," she said, *Your bed,* she wanted to say.

"Would that have been so bad?" His large, strong hands slid up her shoulders to her neck. "I could think of worse things." This while his hands smoothed over her jaw, gilded her cheeks, and finally, finally, finally found her lips.

Her mouth dried. Her whole body liquefied.

His thumb traced the line of her mouth. His gaze tracked the path of his thumb. She gasped. A little surprised breath.

Her own gaze stuck, too. On the sweet curve of his upper lip. The way the day's stubble speckled above it and across his cheek and jaw.

Was she breathing? She couldn't tell. Didn't care.

"Are you going to kiss me or what?"

"Mmm. Thinking about it."

"Less thought. More action."

He smiled. That curve grew sweeter. He pulled her around the corner, out of sight. Pushed her against the motel wall. His hands traveled up. They skimmed her face. Glided into her hair. His fingers swept the stuff away, and his hands, God, those hands, cupped the back of her head.

"I do love a woman who knows what she wants," he murmured. And said no more. Couldn't because his mouth was too busy elsewhere.

Oh, those sweet, sweet lips. That delicious throb of want pulsing deep inside. A universe of craving. She pressed against him, tighter and tighter, and he clutched at her body, desperate, like her, for more. He lifted her. High and up, way above him into the dark heavens, where all creation encircled them beneath the stars.

It took her breath away. Softened every bone. And, at the last, brought her to tears. Not out-and-out sobs, but a swift, unexpected swell.

Still holding her above him, he saw. "What?"

She shook her head. Couldn't speak.

He let her slide down his body, a slow, gorgeous glide that set off lovely explosions—pop, pop, pop—in her chest, her stomach, and lower.

When her feet were back on earth, his hand stroked her wet cheek. "Didn't mean to make you cry."

She smiled through the tears. "You didn't. It was just . . ." she swallowed. "So beautiful. You are"—she stuttered—"so—so beautiful."

"Hey, that's my line."

She laughed, and cried harder.

"Aw—it wasn't that bad, was it?" he said softly.

She shook her head. "I think . . ." She shuddered, looked helplessly around, then unable to escape, back at him. "Oh, God, I think . . ."

"What?"

"I think I'm in love with you." She clamped a hand over her mouth, like the words had leaped out without permission.

"Oh."

She gulped. Stared at him, tears still blurring her sight. "Is that it? Oh?"

"Oh, that."

She whacked him with the back of her hand. He grabbed it. Kissed her palm. She shuddered.

"It's okay to love me, Edie."

"No it isn't," she wailed. "You think I killed three people! How can I love someone who thinks I could do that?"

"Every couple has their issues."

"You think this is funny? It's not funny! It's a disaster! It's—" She stopped. Realized what he'd just said. "You think we're a couple?"

He pushed a strand of hair behind her ear. "A weirdly strange one maybe."

"But—"

"You think I'd invite you to my house, to live with my daughter, if I didn't believe in you?"

"But the black angels—"

"Yeah, they kind of stick in my craw. But I'm in love with you, so I'm not exactly objective."

She gasped.

Slowly, without trying, a wide grin spread across her face. He wagged a finger at her. "You disappoint me again, I'll take it back."

She whooped into the night.

Leaped, wrapped her arms around his neck, her legs around his waist. And kissed him hard just as Lucy drove up.

~37~

Holt wasn't happy about letting Edie go. He would have felt better with her at his house knowing his dad was there to look out for her. But she was adamant.

"I'm going with Lucy." They sat on the open back of Lucy's ancient pickup, and Edie squeezed his hand. Her legs, so much shorter than his, swung back and forth in the night. Lucy had politely made herself scarce, sitting in the truck cab with the windows closed while he and Edie hashed things out. The faint strains of Lynyrd Skynyrd drifted from the radio.

"I don't like it," Holt said.

"Yeah, you told me. About a thousand times."

He slung an arm around her shoulders. Something was going on with her. Something he couldn't put his finger on. "You sure you're telling me everything?"

She ducked her head. "I'm telling you I'll be fine."

He hugged her closer; the hug turned into a clinch. "Might have to hurt you if you aren't."

She pushed him away, jumped off, and he followed her to the cab.

"Be careful," he said when she'd settled into the seat.

"I'll take real good care of her," Lucy said. She handed him a scrap of paper with her address and phone number on it. "You can always reach me at Red's."

"Thanks." Holt pocketed the paper. He closed Edie's door and watched Lucy drive off.

He spent the ride back to town trying to get Edie out of his head so he could concentrate on Terry Bishop. If he could wrangle a confession out of him Edie would be cleared.

But his thoughts kept circling back to his woman. Her wide, soft mouth, her wild, soft body. The smell of her, spice and rain and exotic promises.

He had no business offering his home to her. She was the main suspect in a series of murders he was investigating. Talk about conflict of interest. But he couldn't help himself.

Hell, he didn't want to.

There it was again. That danger. If he kept this up, his job, his entire life in Redbud could be in jeopardy. And it wasn't just his life. Uprooting Miranda would be more than unkind. Children needed stability.

He pulled up to the square and parked in front of the municipal building. Sat with wrists draped over the steering wheel. Shook his head.

Would you look at him? Thinking about a future with a woman who might not have one. Unless, of course, he could figure out who killed three of Redbud's most prominent citizens. And it wasn't her.

Holt heard the wailing while he was still in the municipal building's hallway. Piercing, off-key, irritating.

The awful sound grew louder when he stepped into the office.

Terry Bishop sat in the middle of the room cuffed to a chair, howling like a dog who'd lost his tail. A floppy shirt hung over a wrinkled T-shirt, and his hair was pulled back into a grubby queue, which bounced as he sawed back and forth in the chair, drunk and loopy.

He grinned when he saw Holt. "Hey, Chief! How's your tattooed lady?" He laughed, and Holt exchanged a glance with Sam, who shrugged.

"Been like this since I picked him up," she said.

"Where was he?" Holt asked.

"Red's."

"How long?"

"Couple of hours, according to Red."

"And before that?"

"Home. His aunt verified. Said he was at the Cloverleaf earlier today."

"Hey—I'm right here," Terry interrupted. "And I ain't deaf neither."

Holt turned to him. Terry wanted to talk, Holt would let him. "What were you doing at the motel?"

"Working. Running the vacuum. Like always."

"What time did you leave?"

"I don't know. When I was done."

Sam came around the desk and perched on the edge. "Morning, afternoon, evening, Terry."

Terry responded, but sullenly. "Morning."

Holt drummed a finger on the back of his chair. So Terry could have seen Holt drop off Edie.

"Did you see Edie Swann there?"

"Maybe." He grinned. "A little love nest for you and the tattoo—"

"Shut up." Sam kicked at Terry's legs, unbalancing him. "Stick to the topic on hand. Did you go back to the motel tonight?"

He glared at her, straightened himself. Suddenly didn't seem as drunk as he had a minute ago. "Why should I?"

"Did you go back to the motel?" Holt repeated the question with more force.

Terry eyed Holt. "No."

Holt had had enough. He pushed his chair back and stood, towering over the prisoner. "Take off your shoes."

Terry looked as if Holt had asked him to take off his head. "What?"

"You heard him," Sam said. "Take off your shoes."

Terry grumbled, but used his toes to push his heels out of one, then the other of his cheap sneakers.

Sam picked one up, turned it over. Showed it to Holt. The run-down sneakers had a tread on the bottom. Holt examined the crevices. Found what he was looking for in the second shoe. Buried inside a cranny were dried streaks of red.

He looked from the shoe back to Terry. "You sure you don't want to tell me where you were before Red's?"

Terry looked between Holt and Sam and back to Holt.

"Did you go back to the motel, Terry?" Sam asked.

Terry remained silent.

"There's red paint on the bottom of your shoe," Holt said. "I bet we send it to the lab, it would match the red paint in Edie Swann's motel room."

Terry's face fell.

"Did you go back to the motel?" Sam asked again.

"I didn't do it," Terry said.

"Didn't do what?" Holt asked.

"Anything! Wreck her room. I found it that way. I swear. I was just going to talk to her. Knocked on the door and it opened."

"Convenient," Sam said dryly. "And you just had to go in."

"I thought she might be hurt or something."

Sam snorted. "Look at you—a regular good Samaritan."

Terry glowered at her. "I didn't do nothing."

"I wouldn't call criminal trespass nothing," Sam said.

That shut him up.

But Holt needed him talking. "What did you want to speak to Miss Swann about?"

Terry swung his gaze over to Holt. The glower was gone. He shrank in his chair as if trying to disappear. Which told Holt he was on to something.

"You said you wanted to talk to her. That's why you went over there, right? What about?"

Terry licked his lips.

Holt took his shot. "Something about Hammerbilt, maybe? Something important about the plant?"

Terry's eyes opened wide. "How did you—" He recovered himself. Straightened a little. Pressed his lips together.

Holt leaned in. "What's the deep dark secret, Terry?"

They waited. Gave Terry a few moments to think about answering. He didn't.

Sam threw up her hands. "I don't think he knows anything. I think he went over there with his mean streak and a can of paint."

"Shut up," Terry said to her. "You don't know nothing about it."

"I know you," Sam continued. "I been arresting you on and off for over a year now."

"What is it, Terry?" Holt said. "Did you go over with paint or with information?"

"Don't bother," Sam said to Holt. "We got him for trespassing. Paint on his shoes, we can make a case for the rest."

"I didn't do anything!"

"That's the song you always sing," Sam said. "You're a drunk, Terry. A drunk and a screw-up."

"Shut up."

"He's got nothing," Sam said to Holt, and to Terry, up close and in his face. "He is nothing."

"Shut up!" Terry cried. "I got plenty! And I want something for it! That's why I went over there, okay? I know she's got money. She's been hounding me about the plant. She wants something, she can pay for it."

Holt exchanged a look with Sam.

"She's a bartender," Holt said. "How much money could she have?"

Now that he'd blurted it all out, Terry was like a deflated balloon. "She got money from Lyle. Some kind of big cash thing. The whole town knows. Mrs. Lyle came to the bar and said so."

"And you were going to extort some of this cash from her in exchange for . . . what?"

Terry shuffled in his seat. Set his jaw. Holt was tired of the runaround. He grabbed Terry's chin. "For what?"

Terry yanked his head out of Holt's grasp. "I don't

know!" He shot Holt a surly look. "I was just going to take the money and get out of town."

"A drunk *and* a weasel," Sam said.

"And how about at the church, Terry? You do nothing there, too?"

Terry stared at Holt. A flash of surprise and fear crossed his face.

"Maybe you knew something about the reverend, too. And maybe he didn't want to pay you."

Terry shook his head. Violently. "No."

"You swear this time, too?" Sam said.

"It was her," Terry cried. "The black angel. She did it. Everyone knows."

Holt reined in his annoyance. "You see her do it?"

"No," he admitted.

"So it could've been you just as much as Miss Swann."

"But—"

"Wonder what they'd say at Red's if they knew you were there, too."

Terry's gaze darted around the room. He looked like a trapped rabbit.

Holt stood and nodded to Sam, who uncuffed Terry from the chair.

"You believe me?" Terry was astonished. He rose, rubbing his wrists.

"I don't know," Holt said. "I need some time to think about it."

Sam grabbed Terry's hands and recuffed him again. Terry yowled. "What the—"

She shoved him toward the back room and the jail cell. "Just making sure we know where we can find you."

He cursed all the way. Didn't even shut up after the cell clanked shut. Sam returned, pulling the door between the office and the cell room closed. She could still hear Terry going at it, but the noise was muffled enough to live with.

She checked her hands. No telling where Terry Bishop had been. She went to her desk, found the hand sanitizer, and drenched her hands with it. She was pleased with the way she and Holt had double-teamed Terry. Surely Holt would understand what she'd done on the way over. She'd done it for him. For the team. He'd see that. But despite the assurances to herself, what she'd done was sitting on her like a two-ton mortar.

She bit her lip, looked over at Holt. He was lost in thought, staring at nothing. "So? What do you think?"

His gaze shifted to hers as if he'd heard her voice but not her words. She repeated her question.

"As you so ably put it," he said, "Terry's a drunk and a weasel. He could have gone to the motel for the money, like he said, got pissed she wasn't there, and then wrecked the room."

Sam nodded. "Wouldn't put it past him." She hesitated, not sure how to broach the subject, then just came out with it. "And about the reverend? You weren't serious, were you? You don't really think Terry could have killed him?"

Holt rubbed the back of his neck. It had been a long, exhausting day, and he looked it. "I wish I knew, Sam."

See, she said silently. You need help. "What happened with Mrs. Butene?"

Holt recapped his conversation with Hally Butene. It

sounded like a lot of nothing to her. "So you're no closer to figuring out what happened?"

"I'm close enough to eliminate Edie from Butene's death."

"But you don't even know if that's connected to the three we're dealing with."

Holt sank into the chair behind his desk. Leaned back in his usual position but seemed far from relaxed. "No."

Sam nodded. Opened her mouth. Closed it again. Her heart was suddenly doing a crazy jig inside her chest.

"Something on your mind?" Holt asked.

How did that man always know what she was thinking? Not much of a poker face where he was concerned. "Not sure you want to hear it."

He gave her a resigned nod. "Might as well, Sam. Shoot."

She licked her lips, rolled herself toward Holt. Leaned forward. Told herself it was all for his own good and that he'd thank her. "Leaving aside what happened at the motel, why would Terry have anything to do with killing Reverend Parsley? As far as jobs go, Terry's not exactly the town workaholic. The reverend goes, maybe so does one of Terry's few means of employment."

"So he has no motive."

"Not from where I'm standing."

"What about the blackmail scenario?"

"What blackmail scenario? That's you reaching for something and coming up with smoke. If you don't mind me saying. Besides I can see Terry trying to extort cash out of a town newcomer, especially one who's become a pariah, but a minister? Someone well connected, with position and the power that goes with it? Terry's not brave enough. And what about Runkle and Lyle? There's no connection between Terry and either of them."

Holt jerked his chair to an upright position. Picked up a pencil and started tapping it on its eraser against the desk. Not a good sign.

"So, what are you saying?"

She took the plunge. "There's only one person connected to all three deaths. Only one person with any kind of motive in all three deaths. You know it. I know it. The whole town knows it."

"We don't make cases based on what the town 'knows' or thinks it knows."

Sam shook her head. Didn't want to say it, but had to. "You're too tied up with her. You're not thinking straight."

"All we have is circumstantial."

"Better than the big nothing we've got on anyone else."

He jolted to his feet. Shoved hands in his pockets. Paced away. She knew she could get him to see what was right in front of his face.

"Mayor called while you were out. He scheduled an emergency council meeting tomorrow. He wants you there to report on your progress. And he wants you to call in the state."

Holt stopped. Looked over at her as if an IED had exploded inside him. "The hell I will!" In two steps he was at her desk, braced against the edge, looming over it at her. "She didn't do it."

Sam remained motionless. "And you know this because . . . ?"

"Because . . ." He threw up his hands. "Because I just do."

She looked at him sadly. "Not good enough. And if you weren't so tangled up with her, you'd see it wasn't good enough either."

"I'm not calling in the TBI and that's it."

Sam crossed her arms. Raised her chin and stared him down. Her whole life she'd never gone against a superior officer. But this was different, she reminded himself. This was for his own good. "I figured you'd say that. So I did it for you. They'll be here tomorrow. Ten o'clock."

~38~

At ten, Lucy pulled her pickup into the No Parking zone in front of the building in downtown Nashville where Cole and Tyrrell had offices.

"Sure you don't want moral support?" she asked Edie.

A summer thunderstorm had threatened all the way in, leaving the sky a smear of charcoal. Skycrapers blocked out the little light left, turning the morning into eerie night. But it suited the mood. The mystery behind the strange bequest, the plunge, once more, into the muddy past.

Behind them, traffic hummed the way it never did in Redbud. For half a minute Edie pictured losing herself in the heavier flow of people inside the dark city. Wouldn't be hard. She'd wave good-bye to Lucy, enter the building, count to thirty, and exit again. Poof. She'd disappear.

But she'd leave behind too many things. Her innocence, for one. And for another . . . her mouth tingled with the remembered feel of Holt's kiss.

You're a fool, Edie Swann.

"Thanks," she said to Lucy. "But I wouldn't want to

rob you of a perfectly good shopping opportunity." She got out and plunged into the heart of the building.

The lawyers' offices were on the twenty-fourth floor. Her ears popped in the elevator, and she stared down at her feet. Her clothes had been trashed at the motel, leaving her with the denim mini and the T-shirt she had on the day before. But she'd been able to replace the flip-flops with a pair of sandals from Lucy, so at least her feet were presentable.

The office doors were thick and weighty. Entering them was like stepping into an inner sanctum. Puffed and stuffed, richly carpeted, the air leaden with silence. Bulky leather armchairs were trimmed with brass studs, and paintings of people in red hunting habits hung on the walls.

The receptionist was equal to the rest of the place. Not exactly a stuffed head on the wall, but the well-formed suit over her ample body, the heavy gold earrings and matching gold necklace did give the impression of red-faced jowled men gorging on roast beef.

Edie gave her name, and although the woman said nothing, she managed to look Edie over, taking in the short skirt, the rumpled shirt, and lingering ever so slightly on the pinup girl embossed on her arm.

Edie grinned. "I don't think he's expecting me."

She waited while the receptionist went to inform her boss that his ten o'clock had shown up after all.

Bradley Cole proved to be a big man, his girth made more so by the suit and vest he wore. He rose the minute she stepped into his office. Came around his desk, ostensibly to greet her.

But Edie stopped dead. Bradley Cole was not alone.

Sitting in the chair across from his large cherry desk was Amy Lyle.

Fred Lyle's widow looked at Edie coldly.

"You said you'd call," Cole said.

Impulsive, brash Edie. When would she learn? "Sorry," she said to no one in particular. Then turned to go. To run. To find a place—anyplace—where she could breathe.

"Stay." It was the first time Edie had heard Mrs. Lyle's voice since that night at the bar. A repeat wasn't exactly what Edie had in mind.

Her hand behind her on the doorknob, Edie scrunched up her nose. "Probably not a good idea. Too early in the day for physical violence."

Mrs. Lyle had the grace to look ashamed. She straightened in her chair, reshuffled her grasp on the purse in her lap. "I apologize for that," she said stiffly. "I wasn't myself."

"Still—"

"Amy, dear," Cole said gently, "maybe it would be better if we did this another time."

Amy dear looked directly at Edie. "Is that what you'd prefer, Miss Swanford?"

Edie recognized a challenge when she heard one. She dropped her hold on the knob, pulled her shoulders back. "It's Swann. And I'm fine if you are."

Silence. Then with a regal nod of her head, the widow indicated the other chair in front of Bradley Cole's desk. Slowly, Edie took the seat.

Cole himself regained the outsized leather chair behind his desk. Cleared his throat. Swiveled to reach for a stack of papers. Perused one.

"You are Eden Swanford, daughter of Charles and Evelyn?"

"I am. I was. Like I said, it's Swann now."

"And this is the court record of that name change?" He showed her a copy of the official document she had stashed away in a safety deposit box in Memphis.

"Yes."

"And you have some kind of proof of this?"

"I can produce the original. And there's always my driver's license."

"That will be fine."

She dug in her pocket, found the card, handed it over.

"Why did you change your name?" Amy Lyle spoke for the first time.

Edie shot the other woman a sideways glance. What did she owe her? All Edie had done was deliver a message. If Fred Lyle keeled over because of it, how was that her fault?

Uh huh.

"I didn't want to be Eden Swanford anymore," she said.

Amy's gaze bore into hers, asking without asking.

Edie sighed. "My father killed himself. My mother died in a psych ward. Swanford seemed like too big a package to carry around. Okay? That satisfy you?"

"I didn't know about your mother." The other woman's voice and body softened slightly.

"Not something I like to trumpet around."

"Miss Swann," Cole began, but Mrs. Lyle held up a hand.

"Tell me about her. Was she dark-haired like you?"

Edie gaped at the other woman warily. "Why? What difference does it make?"

"Indulge me."

"No, she was fair. My father was the dark one. Welsh, they tell me." Amy looked confused suddenly. "What?" Edie asked her.

She shook her head. "So you look like your father?"

"I guess."

She cleared her throat. "Did your mother ever . . . did she ever indicate . . . maybe not in so many words, but . . . hint perhaps that—" Amy turned to the attorney with a helpless wave of her hand and an imploring look.

Edie turned her attention to the lawyer.

"What Mrs. Lyle is trying to ask," Cole began, "is a question of . . . paternity. Did you ever doubt or did your mother or any other relative ever give you reason to doubt that your father was, well, your father?"

Edie blinked. What the hell . . . ? "No. And believe me, there were plenty of times growing up when I would have loved to know he wasn't"—she looked away, embarrassed to admit this—"you know, wasn't mine."

Another silence settled over the room. Broken, at last, by Mrs. Lyle.

"Then why—?"

Edie looked from her to the lawyer. "Why what?"

Bradley Cole clasped his hands over the stack of papers on his desk. "You know Mrs. Lyle's husband mentioned you in his will. I drew up the codicil myself."

"So?"

"So why did he do it?" Amy burst out. "If you weren't his—his child, why —"

"His child?"

"He declined to take me into his confidence when he asked me to add this to his will," Cole said. "Mrs. Lyle has no idea why her husband would leave so much money to a complete stranger. The natural assumption is—"

"Oh." Understanding dawned. "I see. A love child. Your husband and my mother." She nearly laughed. "No, my parents were devoted to each other. My mother completely fell apart when my father died. I mean unhinged. Entirely."

"And . . . you?"

"Me?"

"Were you and my husband . . ." She clutched the arm of the chair. Anguish edged her voice.

"No, no," Edie rushed to assure her. "Absolutely not. No. Never. I didn't even know him."

"Then why?" Amy Lyle cried. "Who were you to him?" Hurt and anger and frustration showed on her face.

A rush of unwanted compassion flooded Edie. She turned to Cole. "How much are we talking about?"

"A quarter of a million dollars," the lawyer replied succinctly.

The words hung in the air, suspended in disbelief. Edie opened her mouth, but only uttered a strangled squeak. Cole quickly poured a glass of water from a pitcher on a stand and handed it to Edie. She gulped it down.

"You had no idea," Amy Lyle said.

Edie shook her head. Found she could breathe again.

"And you have no clue why?"

"I have a theory," Edie managed to say at last. "But you're not going to like it. In fact, you should probably stick to the whole love child thing."

"I want to know the truth, Miss Swann." Amy kneaded her purse. "I need to know it."

"Okay, then. Here goes. I think Mr. Lyle had something to do with my father's death."

Bradley Cole's brows rose. Amy Lyle's gaze sharpened. "No," she said. "Impossible."

"What other explanation makes sense? It's blood money, Mrs. Lyle. Payoff for a guilty conscience."

"That's ridiculous."

"Is it?"

"You're saying my husband . . ." She shifted in her seat. Tried again. "You're implying that Fred—"

"Murdered my father. Yeah. That's it."

～39～

Edie and Lucy headed back to Redbud just as the storm finally broke. Rain fell in gulps that splattered on the windshield. Lucy had packed the crawl space behind the seats with bags from Ross and TJ Maxx, and Edie used the packages to put off the inevitable questions. It wasn't that she wanted to keep her meeting private, it was that she wasn't sure how she felt about it yet. So she thumbed over her shoulder at the parcels.

"You buy out the town?"

"Hell, yeah," Lucy said. "Not much point in coming all the way in without making a dent in the old bank account." She regaled Edie with a list of bargains, giving her a chance to think about Amy Lyle.

The woman's whole world had been flung upside down, and Edie couldn't help feeling . . . sorry. If anyone knew what losing their world was like, it was Edie. And she didn't wish that on anyone. Okay, maybe on the people responsible for taking hers.

Maybe.

Truth was, she hadn't realized what her headlong mission would do. That it might end up hurting people she didn't want to hurt. Or hurting them in ways she hadn't intended.

Mrs. Lyle hadn't fallen apart again, thank God. Not like that night in the bar. She'd clutched her purse as if it was the only thing holding her up, but she'd listened. Protested. Proclaimed her husband's innocence. But behind the denials there'd been a flicker of doubt. A doubt that might never be answered with certainty. Edie knew what it was like to live with that kind of doubt, too.

She shifted in her seat. Why did she never look before she leaped? Impulsive, headstrong, she could hear her aunt's voice now.

"The world's not as black and white as you'd like it to be, Eden Swanford. One day you're going to plow right into that truth."

She sighed. Damn Aunt Penny for being so right.

"Things didn't go your way?" Lucy said.

Edie looked over at the older woman.

"You sighed," Lucy explained. "Like the whole world was pressing you down. Sounded to me like the meeting didn't go too well."

"Amy Lyle was there."

"Uh oh."

"No, she was actually . . . nice. Apologized for the scene at the bar."

Lucy sniffed. "Too little, too late, in my opinion."

"She's got a lot going on right now."

"Well, look at you, all forgive and forget."

Edie smiled wryly. "Yeah, who'd have thought it?"

Lucy turned the windshield wipers to high. "So what now? You all fat and rich?"

"Fat? Hell no. Rich?" Edie thought about all those ze-roes. "I don't know. Doesn't seem right somehow. I never even met Fred Lyle."

"What are we talking about? In dollars and cents, I mean."

Edie told her.

"Jesus H. Christofaro," Lucy breathed, and for a mo-ment, the truck swerved along with Lucy's astonishment.

"Whoa—watch it."

"I am watching it. Damn road's slippery. And there's some asshole on my tail."

Edie turned around. Couldn't see too well in the rain. Looked like a black pickup of some sort. "Slow down, maybe he'll pass you."

But instead of passing, the truck butted right into their rear.

Lucy's smaller pickup swerved again, and she strug-gled to stay on the road.

"What the—? Hey—asshole!" Lucy shouted, and sped up.

The black truck butted their rear again. Harder.

"Jesus!" Edie thought of that Acura. If this was an-other stunt by the locals . . .

They got hit again.

Lucy's pickup headed for the shoulder. She spun the steering wheel, trying to correct the direction, but the tires slipped on the slick road.

Edie shouted. Lucy screamed. The pickup careened off the pavement, went over the road edge, and into the black abyss.

*   *   *

By two o'clock, the city council meeting was long over, and the state bureau of investigation, in the person of Agent Jackson Lodge, had made its appearance, taken possession of the Black Angel files, and relieved Holt of his duties regarding the case.

Sam was appalled.

"You're lucky I don't bring you up on charges of obstruction of justice," Lodge said to him. A small, compact man with an officious air, he was already rearranging things on Holt's desk.

"To be fair," Sam said, "the chief didn't know she was the Black Angel when he was . . . uh . . . fraternizing with her."

Holt shot her a shut-it look, but she felt awful about how Lodge was treating him. She hadn't intended to get Holt into more trouble. Exactly the opposite. *See, she told herself, that's what happens when you go outside the chain of command.*

"Sorry," she muttered. "About everything. I just . . . I didn't think he'd—"

"You did the right thing, Deputy," Lodge said.

Which was also true, and everyone knew it. But if she'd done the right thing, why did it feel so wrong? She looked over at Lodge. He was collecting all the writing utensils—pens, pencils, whiteboard markers—and putting them in Holt's coffee cup.

"Uh—that's the chief's—" Sam said.

Holt's phone cut her off. He answered, got a weird look on his face.

"Something wrong?" she asked him.

Immediately, his face cleared. "Miranda," he said, and

to Lodge, "My daughter. Do you mind?" He gestured toward the door.

Lodge shrugged. "By all means. Continue with your normal routine."

"Everything okay?" Sam asked.

"Oh, you know Miranda. Always some crisis." Holt dashed outside, and Sam was left with Lodge.

Without another word, the agent plopped himself into Holt's chair, leaned over Holt's desk, and began reading files.

~40~

Outside, Holt pulled his collar up against the rain and flew to his car. Edie's voice was wailing in his ear. "Holt, hurry. Please. Lucy is—God, she's hurt. Bad."

The lie he'd told Lodge and Sam would keep them out of his hair for a while. "What happened?"

In gulps and stutters, Edie told him about the ride home from Nashville in the rain, the attack by a black pickup. The fits and starts told him more about her condition than the words.

"Where are you?"

"I don't know," she wailed.

He started the engine, but couldn't move until he had some fix on her location. "You were heading back to Redbud. What highway did you take?" She told him. "Okay, that's good." He sped south, turned the siren on once he was clear of town. "Now look around. Any landmarks?"

"I can't see anything in this rain." She was stuttering. Adrenaline aftermath. Cold. Shock. Neither was a good sign.

"All right. Stay with me, Edie. I'm on my way. How long were you on the road before the truck hit?"

"Don't . . . know."

"Yeah, you do. Calm down. Count to thirty if you have to. Clear your head."

Silence.

"Edie!"

"I'm counting."

"Do it out loud."

"—eleven, twelve . . ." It took her to thirty-five until her voice steadied and she was breathing relatively normally.

"Okay, now think about the trip back. Were you on the road half an hour? Forty-five minutes?"

"Closer to thirty, I think."

"Good. I'll be there soon. Can you find a dry spot? Is there a tree nearby?"

"Don't want to leave Lucy."

"Okay. Just try to stay dry."

"Don't leave me."

"I won't. I'm right here." He wanted to keep her talking, keep her from passing out. "What were you doing in Nashville?"

"Fred Lyle's attorney. About the . . . the will. Amy Lyle, too."

"She was there? That must have been interesting."

"She didn't hit me."

"Good for her."

"I f-f-feel sorry for her."

"Now that's not the Edie I know and love."

"I was thinking."

"Yeah? About what?"

"The money. Should I k-k-keep it?"

"What would you do with it if you do?"

"Don't know."

"Buy a new bike?"

"Give up my . . . my girl?"

"A new sound system?"

"Uh huh." Her voice grew faint, and his alarm shot up.

"Edie?"

"Yeah, still here."

"What else could you do with Fred Lyle's money?"

"Buy . . . buy a house."

"A house, huh? Bet I know which one."

"Needs a lot . . . a lot of w-w-work." Her voice was fading.

"Yeah, but I've got two hands. You've got two hands."

Silence.

"Edie?"

More silence. He pressed down on the gas, kept the phone line open, and used the car radio to call for an ambulance.

He spotted the wreck an hour out of town. Flew off the road and onto the shoulder with a squeal of brakes. Bolted down the side of the embankment, sliding in mud and brush.

The truck was on its side, the driver's side embedded in the ground, the door open. Looked like Edie had managed to drag Lucy free—her body was outside the pickup, face down in the mud. Edie was lying next to her, passed out.

Holt checked both women for a pulse. Both alive, thank God, though Edie's was stronger than Lucy's. Looked like she'd broken a leg. No telling what else. He covered her with a blanket and poncho from his trunk, then put one over Edie. He ran to set up flares on the shoulder for the ambulance driver, then slid back down the dirt.

He slapped Edie's face lightly, coaxing her awake. She groaned, opened her eyes. Saw Holt, and started to cry. He scooped her up.

"You all right? Nothing broken?" His hands were searching, but he found nothing serious. Bruises and scrapes, the blood washing down her face and neck in the rain. "It's okay," he crooned. "You're okay."

A siren pierced through the rain, and seconds later, two EMTs were heading down the embankment into the gully. They did a fast assessment on Lucy, got her into a stretcher and, with Holt's help, up the mound and into the back of the emergency vehicle.

Holt helped Edie up the slippery dirt wall, where one of the EMTs gave her a quick once-over.

"I'm fine." She sat huddled in the wet blanket, half-in and half-out of Holt's car, and waved the EMT away. "Lucy needs you. Go. Go."

"I'll get her to the hospital," Holt assured the medical team.

The ambulance left, sirens blazing, and Holt got a dry blanket out for Edie, then tucked her into the car.

"You see anything of the driver?

She shook her head. "Too rainy."

"And the truck?"

"Full-sized. Black. That's it."

"You okay for a minute or two?"

She nodded, and Holt went back into the rain. Walked up and down the highway looking for tread marks or anything that might indicate the type of truck that had pushed

Lucy's pickup over the edge. But if there had been any evidence, the rain had washed it away.

Cursing the weather, he returned to his car, started the engine, and followed the ambulance.

Edie huddled into the blanket all the way to the county hospital. It was blazing hot outside, despite the rain, but cold shudders jolted her relentlessly. She couldn't get the picture of Lucy out of her mind. The blood on her face. The soft feel of her chest where the steering wheel had crushed it. The sick sight of the raw bone sticking out of her leg.

She closed her eyes, and started crying again.

"Dammit," she gulped, "Damn, damn, damn. Fucking God damn it."

Holt pulled over to the side of the road and pulled Edie close.

"Jesus," she stuttered through tears. "What good does crying do?" She pounded dully on his chest. "Why Lucy? What did she ever do to anyone?" She inhaled a huge, quivery breath, hiccupped, and swatted him away. "Go. I want to get to the hospital."

"Easy there, supergirl. We'll get there." He put the car in gear and set off again.

She squeezed her eyes shut, concentrated on breathing, and the tears soon stopped. But it was as if her heart had stopped, too. Or dried up. Cold and numb, she set her gaze straight ahead, trying not to feel anything.

The county hospital was ten miles outside Redbud. Edie pushed through the emergency room doors, and despite her protests, Holt insisted someone take a look at her. It was only later, when she saw herself in a mirror, that she realized her face was cut in several places, including a nasty one just over her right eyebrow that required stitches. She'd been thrown clear of the truck, and her body ached where she had landed, but for some inexplicable reason, she hadn't broken anything. Someone patched her up, but she didn't pay attention to who. All she wanted to hear about was Lucy.

She and Holt sat at the hospital while Lucy went into surgery. News of the accident spread somehow, the way all news seemed to spread in Redbud. Red showed up, and took a seat next to Edie in the waiting area. They didn't say anything except a lackluster greeting, but then no one was talking much. A nurse came around with papers to fill out.

"She have any relatives close by?" she asked.

"A son," Red said, surprising Edie, who hadn't known Lucy had children. "But he's in Atlanta."

"Can you get in touch with him?" the nurse asked.

Red shrugged, looked helpless. "I don't know."

"I'll find him," Holt said. He walked away to make the necessary phone calls.

A few minutes after he left, Sam Fish approached from another direction. As usual, her uniform was pressed and crisp, and she carried herself like a drill sergeant. A man accompanied her, small, neat, wearing a suit and an official air.

"Holt's making a phone call," Red said.

"We're not here for the chief," the man said. "I'm Agent Lodge, Tennessee Bureau of Investigation," he said, looking directly at Edie. "Ms. Swann?"

"Yes?" She looked between the two of them, saw Sam's gaze swivel away. Uh oh.

"Would you come with us?"

Edie didn't move. "Is it about the accident? Because I can tell you everything about it, I just want to make sure Lucy is—"

"It's not about the accident," Agent Lodge said. He nodded to Sam, who took out her cuffs and started to place them around Edie's wrists. She pulled them away.

"What are you doing?"

"Edie Swann, you are under arrest on suspicion of murder," Sam intoned, and not without a little smirk of satisfaction either.

Red rose.

"What?" Edie said. "You gotta be kidding."

Sam plunged in with the cuffs, and Edie struggled to keep them off her hands. "Don't touch me! You're not going to—" All the terror and rage from the accident exploded. She kicked and yelled, forcing Lodge to come in. Between the two of them they wrestled Edie down to the floor, where Lodge sat on her like she was a cow in a roping contest, wrenched her arms behind her back, and cuffed her.

The commotion brought nurses, hospital staff, and Holt to the waiting room. "Lodge, what the hell are you doing?"

Lodge pulled Edie to her feet. "What you should have done weeks ago."

"Someone just tried to kill her. Doesn't that prove she hasn't done anything?"

"Only proves feeling in Redbud's running high enough for someone to take the law into their own hands." He pushed Edie forward. "Let's go."

She whirled, head-butted him, and took off.

"Edie!" Holt went after her. But not before Lodge and Sam.

Red stuck his foot out, tripping Lodge and slowing his pursuit, but Sam tackled her a few feet away. She went down with a grunt that cut right through Holt.

He wrenched the deputy off, and Sam immediately started for her prisoner again. Holt stepped between them.

"Stand down, Deputy." Holt's command was hard and immutable, but she gazed uneasily between him and Lodge. "You work for me," Holt barked, "and I'm telling you to stand down."

Sam's face was red as a burn. Holt kept his gaze on her, commanding her attention. She should be embarrassed. Loyalty was everything, and she knew it. He should fire her ass for calling the TBI behind his back. But he needed an ally, and right now Sam was the only candidate. And he figured she owed him. Big time. So, he asked her silently, who's it gonna be—him or me? Lodge shook his head, but Sam thought about it and backed off.

Relieved, Holt turned to Edie. Supported her weight as she stood. He brushed the hair away from her face. "Dammit, Edie, you opened one of your cuts." He dabbed at it, and she winced. "No more, okay? I'll take care of this. I promise." He turned to Lodge. "What about bond?" Usually the warrant included bond.

"Judicial commissioner wanted to leave it up to the judge," Lodge said.

Holt cursed silently. That meant jail. "It'll only be a few days," he told Edie. "Just until the arraignment. I'll do what I can to speed things up. Go with them, okay? Everything's going to be all right."

"Yeah, sure it is."

Holt stepped back, and Sam reached for Edie. She jerked away, but walked out between Lodge and Sam. Holt followed close behind. At the door, Edie stopped, and turned to him.

"Tell Lucy I'm thinking about her."

Then they were out the door and into the rain.

~41~

Lodge took Edie to the county jail. It wasn't Brushy
Hollow, but it wasn't the room behind Holt's office either.
They threw her into a holding cell—a concrete room behind a massive steel door. The astringent smell of disin-
fectant couldn't cover the stench of ripe bodies and vomit.
A concrete bench extruded from the wall, both painted
the same dingy green. The room was lit with such sharp
intensity that every corner glowed nuclear. A window in
the steel door ensured that privacy was a thing of the past.
You can't run and you can't hide.

Three other prisoners were already there. One was snor-
ing on the floor, the other two ranged on the benches, spread
out like wolves protecting their territory. Cold, bored eyes
stared her down as she entered. Prostitutes, check kiters,
drunks? How many murderers? In their eyes, she could be
the worst of the lot. They watched Edie blatantly, waiting
to see what she would do. But she was too drained and
dispirited to fight over a seat. She settled into a corner and
huddled against the wall.

Ten minutes later, an officer called one of the women

out to be booked. It took a couple of hours to get to Edie. By that time, two more women had been added to the room, and Edie had taken a seat on the bench. The stench no longer bothered her, which was bothersome in itself. Whoever was sleeping on the floor continued to snore, despite the kicks she received as incentive to stop.

Eventually they called Edie out. The door buzzed, a high-pitched mosquito whine, then clicked to unlock. An officer stood in the doorway and escorted her to the booking room. She stood before a row of computers on a raised desk. It was so high off the ground, she had to tilt her head back to answer the questions put to her by the officers. Had she ever had hepatitis, HIV, heart disease? What was her birthday, spell her name. Has she ever been incarcerated in Corley County before?

She was photographed and fingerprinted. Unlike TV cops, these did the printing on a computer run by a technician who had to roll each finger just right over a photo plate. Evidently not an easy task, because they had to repeat the process eight out of ten times.

"First day?" Edie said.

But the jokes didn't come easily. This was real. Not some backwoods lockup but a serious jail for serious offenders.

They gave her a chance to use the phone, but she refused. Who could she call?

Back in the holding cell area, a female officer armored with latex gloves checked Edie's mouth and under her tongue to make sure she didn't have anything hidden there. Then she put Edie in a room with a shower and a grimy toilet and instructed her to clean off with the anti-lice soap provided. Before they gave her clothes, the officer had her raise her arms and turn slowly to show she had nothing on but skin. She was given a laundry bag that contained soap, toothpaste and brush, a comb, and a washrag. A rough towel, a sheet, and a scratchy blanket were added to the pile. The officer gave her further instructions, and Edie heard them from a distance. Four hours a week of recreation, an hour a week of visitation, but only after she'd been there three days.

Her hands were cuffed and she shuffled through a series of heavy green doors, all alike and all opened with the insect buzz and an electronic click that came from some central location. She trudged down the hallway, and into another concrete room, this one four times bigger than the tank. Twenty women were milling about. A television blared from one wall. Music from a radio was blasting from another speaker. Above all that din was the sound of talking.

Once again, the metal door shut behind her. Echoey, metallic, final. She glanced above. A central surveillance hub overlooked them with four guards watching everything. She avoided their eyes and found a seat at one of the steel tables built into the floor. They were low to the ground, like in kindergarten, and the seats—round stool tops—were attached.

The noise beat against her like a hard wave. In defense, she tried to conjure up the engulfing strains of Brahms, but her head couldn't keep the music going. She stared out at the mob, seeing little. Her father had died rather than face this. For the first time, she understood.

~42~

Holt tried using his badge to see Edie before she was booked, but no one was interested in bending the rules for him, especially with Agent Lodge there. The jail was run by the county sheriff's office, and news of his relationship to the prisoner had preceded him. His fellow officers managed to express their disapproval without actually voicing it, making him hang around the visitors' area like everyone else and then putting him off the way they put everyone off. No visitors in the first seventy-two hours. Which left him imagining every stupid thing she could have done to get herself in more trouble. Refusing to sign the fingerprint form, refusing to give up her clothes for the county's. Wising off, pushing back. Was she in solitary already?

He hunted down the court clerk and tried to get Edie's arraignment set for the next day, but the judge was on vacation until the beginning of next week, which pushed everything back. Edie wasn't getting out of jail any time soon.

Cursing, he bolted to his car. The rain had stopped; he

needed to examine the accident scene, start searching for the black pickup Edie had said attacked them. His cell rang on the way. It was Miranda's day camp. He was half an hour late for her pickup. Damn. How could he have forgotten?

Rapidly, he apologized to the camp director, told her he had an emergency, and would have someone pick up Miranda as soon as possible.

He called his mother on the fly, maneuvering the car out of the parking lot. No answer, either at home or on her cell. He tried his dad, but he couldn't pick up Miranda either.

"Busted a fan belt," his father said. "Stuck in Berding waiting for your mother to come get me."

Berding was about twenty miles south, on the road to Nashville. Same road Lucy and Edie had been on. A little farther and he would have seen the accident. "What are you doing there?"

James groaned. "Had this crazy notion of buying your mother that new washing machine she's been hectoring me about. Looks like I'll be buying a new fan belt instead."

"Okay. But tell Ma to turn on her cell. What's the point of having it if she never turns it on?"

Instead of going to the accident scene, Holt raced to the day camp at the county YMCA. On the way, he called Sam.

"Lodge there?" he said before she could even say hello.

"No," Sam replied.

"Good. I've got a favor to ask. Do a phone search of all the garages in the county. You're looking for a full-size black pickup with front-end damage. Anything you find, tell them to hold off on the repairs until I get there. And I'd appreciate your forgetting to mention it to our colleague from the state."

She sighed. "You're supposed to be off the case."

"The Black Angel murder case. This is attempted vehicular homicide."

"Look, I'm . . . I'm sorry about the way things turned out."

"Yeah, you should be."

She was silent, and he buried his anger. He needed her. "Look, stow the apologies, and do this for me instead. I'll take the heat if Lodge finds out."

"I can take my own heat," she bristled.

"That mean you'll do it?"

She paused, and Holt cursed at her silently.

"I'll let you know what I find out," she said at last. "Doesn't mean I think your gal pal is innocent," she added quickly.

"Doesn't have to."

They agreed to disagree, and disconnected. He pulled into the parking lot at the Y. Miranda was waiting for him under the portico over the entrance, the camp director at her side.

The minute Miranda saw his car, she ran out and climbed in.

"Where were you?" she demanded.

He waved to the camp director and took off. "Sorry, baby girl. Sometimes things happen."

"What kind of things?"

He glanced over at her blonde head, the beautifully fragile features she'd inherited from her mother, and wished more than anything that those things would stay clear of her. But they wouldn't. They never do. "Oh, just . . . things."

She pouted. "I don't like those things."

He sighed. Welcome to the world, Miss M. "Me neither." He ruffled her head, thought about Edie. "Me neither."

Holt managed to get Edie's arraignment bumped up a few days, but she was still inside longer than she should have been. He counted down the minutes until her seventy-two hours were up and was at the jail first thing.

Corley County had installed a new visitors' system the year before. He hadn't paid much attention to it, figured whatever was good for the jail was okay by him. But when he was brought to a video monitor and told to sit there until Edie showed up on it, he fumed. He wanted to see her in person, even if she was behind glass. Now they were separated by yards of building—hallways, cells, offices—she on her own stool somewhere else staring at a video picture of him. How could he trust that she was all right if he couldn't see for himself?

She wore what all the prisoners wore, shapeless neon orange jail clothes. The V-neck shirt hung on her slender frame like a big sister's. The oversized pants dragged. Inside the baggy clothes she looked listless and defeated, which scared him more than anything.

He tapped the screen and nodded toward her phone on the other side so she'd pick it up. "You okay?" he said when she did.

"Oh, sure."

Well, at least her sarcastic streak was still intact.

"Look, I'm here and working on this. Don't forget that."

"And Agent Lodge? What's he doing?"

He eyed her carefully. "Don't you give up on me, Edie Swann."

She shot him a tight smile. "Moi?"

He leaned in, wanting to get closer. But he only went out of frame and had to adjust back. Talking to her this way felt cold and distant, which was how it was supposed to feel. Institutional. Indifferent. Jail wasn't supposed to be fun, he knew that, but this was Edie. His Edie.

"I'm working on the truck. Sure you don't remember the make or model?"

She shook her head. "Too much rain. But definitely a full-sized black pickup."

"Okay, that's what we're looking for. Now, listen. I'm not going to let you rot in here, you got that? You'll be arraigned in a few days. Just a few more days, Edie, you can do that. And then you'll get bail and you'll be out."

She laughed. Short and definitely not sweet. "Swanfords have a history of getting a raw deal in this burg. What makes you think it'll be any different with me?"

"You're not guilty."

"Was he?"

Holt opened his mouth to say so, then closed it again. Everyone had proclaimed Charles Swanford's guilt. Then again, plenty of people wouldn't hesitate to proclaim Edie's. For the first time, Holt wondered. If everyone could be wrong about Edie couldn't they have been equally wrong about her father?

"I don't know," he said carefully.

"Maybe it's time we found out," Edie said.

A buzzer rang, signaling an end to their time. Unnaturally obedient, she stood, then shuffled out with the rest of the prisoners.

~43~

Amy Lyle heard about Edie's arrest the way most people heard about things in Redbud. Sherry Adams, a nurse at the county hospital, told her husband who worked at the hardware and had a piece of chess pie every afternoon at Claire's—where Emmalyn Brainerd was having coffee with her book group and overheard him talking about the ruckus at the hospital. She called Amy on her way home.

"About time someone did something about that woman," Emmalyn said.

"Thank you for calling," was all Amy said. She put down the phone and stared at the snowy piles fallen around her. She was on the floor in the middle of her husband's office. Surrounded by papers that went back two decades and more. Fred had been quite a packrat. Amy had been ready to box it all up and get rid of it, but she found herself riffling through everything to find whatever she could around June and July of 1989.

Mostly there were files of cost projections, profit and loss statements, budgets, quarterly reports from the plant. But there were also minutes from city council and Chamber of Commerce meetings and programs from long-ago Rotary assemblies.

And endless legal pads with notes and lots of side doodles. In the midst of it all words like conspire, cover, and prosecute popped up, traced over and over in heavy blue ink, individual letters turned into Martian flowers and monster gargoyles. Once, Charles Swanford's name appeared, underlined three times.

What did any of it mean? Fred was gone and Amy couldn't ask him. She pictured Edie Swann's fierce face, those dark eyes, the hair that never seemed to end. She'd had so much taken from her. Had Fred done the taking? Was the will his way of paying the girl back?

With a soft groan, Amy rose from the floor. Stepped over the piles of what had once been her husband's life, and went to find her phone.

A week after she was arrested, Edie was arraigned. Officers cuffed and chained her and a couple of other inmates, brought them out of the secure area into a hallway where they shuffled to the courtroom in their ugly, stiff jail clothes in a parade of humiliating orange. The minute she stepped into the corridor, her ears had to adjust to the quiet. Already the racket at the jail sounded more normal than the normal hush of life outside.

Holt was in the courtroom when she walked through the door. He gave her an encouraging smile, but it barely made a dent in the blur around her. She wasn't normally vain, but the thought of him seeing her dressed like a prisoner—up close and in person without benefit of a TV screen—sent deep currents of shame through her.

Prosecution called her a drifter with no ties to the community and asked for her to be remanded back to jail. But the judge set bail at a million dollars, which might as well have been no bail at all, as Edie had no way to raise that kind of money. She could have used the bequest from Fred Lyle, but her arrest put that in jeopardy.

It was all over in less time than it took to get her there. She was returned to her cell, and once more, the clamor of the concrete room vibrated against her skin. This time the postmodern symphony of disjointed noise was welcoming, comforting.

But a few hours later, just as she was settling in, they called her out again. Someone had paid her bail. She refused, not wanting Holt's savings for Miranda's future squandered on her. But the guard was insistent, so Edie left with her, guilt stalking her as they ambled down the hallway.

They returned the clothes she'd come in with, and she put them on. Her watch, rings, keys, wallet, all her personal effects were returned as well, and she signed a form saying so. She stumbled out of the prison and into the music of normal life.

As she'd expected, Holt was waiting for her, tall and strong in the sun. But there was someone beside him, someone she never thought she'd see again—a petite woman with fading blond hair. Amy Lyle.

~44~

Edie stopped short. She looked from Fred Lyle's widow to Holt, hurt tightening inside her. How could he have brought her? She walked past the two of them, but Holt stopped her.

"Edie, this is—"

"She knows who I am," Amy said crisply.

"Come to gloat?" Edie said.

"Actually, I've come to take you home."

Edie gaped at her.

Two corrections officers strolled by and gazed at them curiously. Holt took her by the arm. "Let's not talk here." He ushered her to his car, Amy Lyle in tow.

By the time they got there, Edie had control of herself again. "Wait a minute. Wait!" She untangled herself from Holt's grip and confronted Amy. "What did you say?"

Amy straightened her shoulders. "I think you heard me just fine."

"Why would I go anywhere with you?"

The other woman smiled. Almost as if she was enjoying this. "First of all, where else will you go? Your friend Lucy is—"

A warning shake of the head from Holt stopped her, but not before Edie saw it.

"What? What happened to Lucy?"

"We can talk about that later," Holt said.

Fear ran up Edie's spine. "Now."

"I'm sorry," Amy murmured to Holt. "I thought she knew."

"Knew what?" Edie cried, refusing to believe what she instinctively sensed was coming.

Holt moved, but it was Amy who put an arm around her. "She passed away yesterday," she said gently, and clasped Edie to her breast, a hot, tight hold that was as strange as it was meant to be comforting. This woman's body that Edie had never hugged before. This woman Edie barely knew. Holding her, saying awful, life-changing words. "I'm sorry. I'm so, so sorry." It was only then that the sounds made sense, the reality sank in.

Lucy. Dead. Oh, God.

The sun was high today, but Edie clearly remembered the rain, the huge black monster attacking from behind. Lucy's scream. Her bloodied, crushed body.

No, it couldn't be. It just couldn't.

"Let's get you home." Amy rubbed Edie's back, and Edie pulled away. Sank against the side of Holt's SUV.

"I don't understand," Edie said. Her body felt blood-less, dry and cracked as if all the fluid inside her had been siphoned off.

"Her chest wall was crushed," Holt said, "and they couldn't stop the bleeding."

A tear leaked out and she quickly scrubbed it away. She set her jaw. "Funeral?"

"Her son's taking her back to Atlanta for that."

Not even a chance to say good-bye. To beg forgiveness.

"It's not your fault," Holt said, reading her mind.

She didn't argue with him. She knew what she knew and felt that burden like a hundred-pound weight. The load threatened to crush her, so she straightened, shouldering it. Turned to Amy with suspicion. "Why do you want to take me home?"

"She paid your bail," Holt said.

Amy tsked. "You weren't supposed to tell her that." Amy took one of Edie's hands and squeezed it. "Why don't we go home. You can take a shower. I'll make us all some coffee. And then we can have a nice, long talk. And if you decide you don't want to stay, you don't have to."

Edie looked at Holt. He nodded. Opened the back door. Amy got in. And Edie, grief-stricken and confused, slid in beside her.

The shower felt wonderful. Private and hot and lots of fresh-smelling shampoo. The towel was fluffy, and when Edie dried off, she found her favorite pair of jeans and her most comfortable black tank waiting for her on the bed in the Lyle guest room.

Tears welled up when she saw the clothes. She held them up to her nose and inhaled the fragrance of cotton freshly washed in Tide or Cheer or anything other than institutional detergent. Her own things close to her skin, she found her way to the kitchen, where Amy was fussing with a coffeepot, and Holt was trying not to look too uncomfortable surrounded by all the yellow roses on the walls, the towels, and the countertop. He dwarfed the wrought-iron ice-cream-parlor chairs with their yellow seats that went with the round table in the breakfast nook, and the dainty teacup in front of him looked like a toy in his big hands. Her heart stopped at the fullness of his masculinity against the fussy room.

"Better?" Amy said to Edie. She carried a tray with more cups, the pot, and a plate of cookies to the table. Poured Edie a cup and set it in front of her.

"Much," Edie said. "Thanks."

Holt dove into the cookies, and no one said anything for chewing. Edie had never felt so hungry in her life. They'd fed her in jail, but this was ambrosia compared to the institutional stuff she'd been picking at for the last seven days. And that was nothing compared to the years of bad food that could be waiting for her. She shuddered and pushed the crumbs around on her plate. "I appreciate everything you've done, Mrs. Lyle."

"But you want to know why I did it?"

She risked a glance up. The other woman's face was calm and kind. "I hope it's not . . . well, not because of what happened at Red's. I thought we settled that."

"We did." Amy clasped her hands on the table. "But after we met at Bradley's office I pulled every scrap of paper my husband had saved over the years. And I have to tell you, it didn't make me feel better. Something happened when you were a child, some terrible thing, and to be honest, I didn't want to admit this, but I think my husband knew something about it. And he wanted to make it up to you somehow. That was his wish. How could I let you stay in jail when I had the means to help?"

"Does that mean you don't think I killed anyone?"

She hesitated. "Let's just say, I'm willing to suspend judgment. And in the meantime, you need a place to stay and I have plenty of room."

"Mrs. Lyle, you're pitting yourself against the whole town."

She patted Edie's hand. "Call me Amy. Please. And that's how small towns work. Kind of a mob mentality until someone takes a stand. Of course, it has to be someone of, shall we say, stature? I'm taking you under my wing, Edie Swann, so don't you worry about the town. You'll see." She rose to take the dishes to the sink. Edie gathered up the cups and followed her.

"There's one thing more," said Holt.

Edie handed the cups to Amy, who put them in the dishwasher. "No more, please. I don't think I could take another kindness today."

"Well, brace yourself, darlin', because one's coming. Mrs. Lyle—Amy—found the connection between our victims."

"It was simple, really," Amy said, her hands full of dish towel. "If I'd known you were looking so hard, I would have said something earlier."

Edie looked from her to Holt and back again. Anxious. Expectant.

"The city council," Amy said. "They all served on the city council together."

Edie frowned. She'd expected something . . . what? Diabolical? An underground cult? A Skull and Bones secret society? The city council was so mundane it was almost laughable. Yet here they were in an ordinary kitchen surrounded by dish towels and cookies, a place where meals were planned and prepared, where family gathered to be nurtured by them. And the three of them were discussing murder. Did the roses seem to wilt, the sunshine-yellow walls grow dim? Was it the darkness she carried with her? Or was it just the hidden truth of the universe? That evil was everywhere. Even here, in an everyday, sunny kitchen. Or a small-town city council.

"There must be dozens of people who've been on the city council," Edie pointed out.

"Not in 1989," Holt said.

A chill shook Edie. Nineteen-eighty-nine. The year her father died.

Was the shock on her face? Amy exchanged a concerned glance with Holt. "There's a lovely gazebo in the backyard," she said quietly. "Holt, why don't you show Edie where it is?"

She didn't feel like a stroll in the garden, but she didn't want to stay in the yellow kitchen either. Holt slung an arm around her shoulders and she let herself be guided out the back door into the warm summer evening. A cutting garden off to the side was a jumble of color, and the scent of newly mown grass hung in the air.

Edie inhaled, and the fragrance seemed to give her strength. "Pretty back here."

"Not as pretty as you."

But Edie wasn't up to compliments. She said nothing, just continued tramping over the yard, silent, shuttered.

The gazebo was a sweet thing with gingerbread trim and a bench inside. Edie couldn't make herself go in. She wanted quiet, loneliness, not this tricked-up terrace. She slid along the curved outside wall until she was at the back, facing a thick clump of woods bordering the property. It was dark back there, dark and cool and quiet, and she leaned against the side, head back, eyes closed.

Nineteen-eighty-nine. Two thousand nine. Her father dead. Her friend dead. She couldn't shake the portentousness of the dates, the parallels, the threat. What else did the black angel have waiting for her? Once again she felt the bike under her shimmy, heard the scream of skidding tires, the nauseated helplessness of flying through the air. Who wanted her dead?

"Shit," she mumbled. The grief and fear inside her hardened, and her voice rose. "Shit, shit, shit!!"

"Edie." Holt's voice was soft, his face gentle as he reached for her.

She shoved him away. "Don't!"

"Don't what?"

"Go all soft and cheesy on me. I need you hard and strong and angry as shit. Someone *killed* Lucy!" She grabbed her head as if that could somehow contain the impossible and make it real. "Oh, God. Oh, God." She was shivering uncontrollably, looking around wildly for an explanation, except there was none. Only her own misguided search for revenge.

"I'll find them. I swear." As if to confirm the vow, he wrapped his arms around her.

At first she fought the cage, struggling against his embrace. She had to hold on to her fury. Only that could overwhelm her terror.

But he wouldn't let go. He crooned and murmured and held her tight, and finally, like a pathetic, broken thing, she collapsed in his arms, pounding his chest as if to stop the sobs. The emotion turned her inside out, her heart raw, her bones aching. She sank to the ground, and he cushioned her, rocking and hushing and soothing.

Holt did for Edie what he did for Miranda. What he'd do for any lost child. He held her. Let her know there was one thing in her world that was solid and wouldn't go away. And when she was done, she leaned against him on the grass in the shadow of the woods. He stroked her hair, her neck, down her arms. Heard her breathing calm.

Then, minutes later, it picked up again. Only this time there was a different rhythm to it. An awareness. Of the two of them alone in the evening. It jacked up his own breathing. That was no child he held, but a true woman, heart and soul and curves that fit his hands. She twisted to face him, all dark, turbulent eyes and mass of hair, and her hand was on his jaw, her breath on his face.

And without a word, she pulled his mouth down to hers.

Heat fanned into a firestorm, an inferno he hadn't known he'd missed until he felt it again. Aah, this was what it was like. To want someone, to need her. To love her.

He lay them down, pulling her on top of him. Her breasts against his chest, her legs wrapped between his. How long had he waited for this? Eternities.

Her hands found his skin under his shirt, and he could wait no longer. He didn't have to. She pulled off his shirt, then her own. Slithered out of those amazing jeans, and got his off as well. Kissed him, fondled him, and slid him home inside her with a groan of pleasure that melted into his own.

Within two minutes he was ready, and he clutched handfuls of grass to keep from coming. But she sat up on top of him, primal and wild, her eyes closed, hair tumbling down her arched back. Her breasts bounced, her nipples jutted, and if it was possible to get harder, he did. She sucked her fingers, in and out and over again, and he clenched that grass tighter. Then she touched her breasts with those wet fingers, fondling the taut nipples, and the pleasure was so intense he couldn't take it. Not another minute, not another second, not another—

Unfair, his mind screamed as he exploded inside her. Unfair, as she pulled him into ecstasy.

He didn't know how long he lay there incapable of speaking, unable to move. Finally, she collapsed on top of him. Her hands roamed everywhere, gentle and sweet, and he drifted off holding her against him.

A soft moan woke him. He opened his eyes to the velvet gray of twilight. The air had cooled and a breeze blew against his bare skin. Edie was beside him on her back, one leg draped over his belly, the other spread wide. Her hand was deep between them, and she was squirming with pleasure.

A jolt of electricity hit him when he realized what she was doing.

He stroked her hair, fingers sinking into the thickness. "Want some help?"

She grunted. "I do all the work tonight," she said.

"Aw, let me." He nudged her hand aside, and she cracked open an eye.

"Just sit back and enjoy the show. Maybe you'll learn something."

He accepted her gift the way he accepted everything about her—as new and exciting. He watched her hips move, her fingers dance. It was rhythmic and beautiful.

And one of the sexiest things he'd ever seen. When she came, he watched her body pulse and contract, beckoning his own.

She made no protest when he slipped inside her. The tail end of those fierce contractions still pulsed. Their mouths met, wet and needy, and this time, their hips worked together. The moon rose and their bodies heated, slow and gentle, a long, caring waltz that ended on a tender sigh.

Afterward they lay looking up at the stars.

"Think Amy knows what we're doing out here?" Edie said.

He held her in the crook of his arm and enjoyed the primordial sensation of night wafting over their bodies. The woods crackled with katydids and hid their noise and their bodies from the neighbors. The gazebo hid them from the house, but it wouldn't be too hard to figure it out. "Probably. It was her idea."

Edie was silent for a long time, and Holt knew she was stewing about something. He waited, and she finally spoke. "Why do you think she's doing this?"

"She told you why."

"And you believe her?"

"There are a few good people in the world, Edie."

She nodded, but it wasn't convincing.

"We could sleep out here," she mused.

"The last time I slept in the backyard I was ten." He rolled onto his side to look at her, and she did the same. He ran a finger down her nose. "Besides, I have to take Miranda to camp tomorrow."

She sighed. "Okay. Another time." She sat up, pulled

her clothes over, and started getting dressed. He reached for his own stuff.

"City Hall opens at ten." He slipped his pants on. "Amy will take you and I'll meet you there."

She shoved her head and arms through the black tank. "What's in City Hall?"

"Council meeting minutes."

"You think if they were planning to kill someone they'd take notes?"

He shrugged. "We don't know that's what they did. And you never know."

He put his arm around her and walked her back to the house. It was full dark, the moon high and bright in the sky. He felt satiated and sleepy, as if he'd just consumed a huge meal and a full bottle of wine. He smiled to himself. Edie was like that. She filled him up, made him dizzy, and gave the world more luster.

He kissed her at the door, lingering over good-bye. Then watched as she let herself into the now-dark house.

~45~

Redbud had been collecting the minutes from city council meetings since 1947, so there were boxes and boxes of them, stacked in the basement of the municipal building. The centricity made it easier to get to, especially with Holt there. No one questioned his right to explore city documents, and no one said a word when he ushered the prime suspect in the Black Angel murders and the wife of one of her victims with him. Amy Lyle put a possessive arm around Edie's shoulders as they passed the city clerk, flashed her a cordial smile, and sang out, "Good morning, Barb. Choir practice this evening."

Barb nodded, gaze flicking back and forth between Amy and her companion. "S-see you there," she said.

Then they disappeared behind the basement door, the worst over with

"Let's see how fast that gets around," Amy whispered to Edie as they descended.

Concrete floor and walls shielded the underground room from the summer heat. It was cool down there. Industrial shelving marched across the underground room, row upon row of similar boxes. But Holt led the way to the council shelves easily.

"Reorganized when I had to make room for my case files." He cruised the boxes along one shelf, then stopped. "Pretty much know where everything is." He hauled down the boxes labeled 1980–1989.

Council met once a month, which meant twelve sets of minutes. But there were eighteen in 1989. Six additional meetings seemed to give further proof that something monumental had taken place in Redbud that year.

Holt divided up the file, handing each of them a small stack of pages, and they retreated to a corner where Holt had set up a card table and chairs.

Edie glanced down at the papers but the words blurred in front of her. She glanced over at Holt because she couldn't help it. The memory of the night before had stayed with her, a loving cocoon she didn't want to leave. Inside that space she was safe and warm. Protected. A false security maybe, but one she grabbed at anyway.

Holt looked up, caught her staring at him. Her heart expanded. That liquid electricity shot through her chest and between her legs.

"Amy, will you excuse us for a minute?" Holt asked, still staring at Edie, who couldn't tear her gaze away either.

The older woman began to rise. "Of course."

"No, no, don't go anywhere," Holt said, then leaned over and kissed Edie. The contact charged her body, filling and swelling her. She grabbed his shirt, holding on, drawing out the feel of his lips.

When they broke off at last, his mouth twisted into a

crooked grin. "Thought I'd better get that over with or we'd never get anything done."

Her face heated. She hadn't blushed in a long, long time. Which only made her blush even more. She cleared her throat, peeked at Amy. The other woman's eyes had welled with tears.

Instantly contrite, Edie apologized.

Amy shook her head. "Don't you dare." She rummaged in her purse, pulled out a crumpled tissue. Tamped her eyes with it. "It's just—I remember that." She gave Edie a watery smile that included Holt. "Lucky you."

Amy returned her tissue to her purse and they all returned to the twenty-year-old pages in front of them.

But not for long. A few minutes later, Holt threw down what he was reading. "Wait a minute." He looked at Edie, then Amy. "Who do you have present at your meeting?"

They read through the list of names. Four council members and a secretary to take the minutes. Three of the members were the three men connected with the Black Angel murders. The fourth was the previous mayor, now deceased. But in those six extra meetings there was a fifth: James Drennen.

"Your father?" Amy said.

Edie sat still as possible, hoping ridiculously that Holt would forget she was there.

"He was the chief of police," Amy added. "Of course he would be at the meetings."

"No." Holt shook his head. "That's not true. I mean, it's not normal procedure. I only attend those meetings twice a year. And that's to give a brief crime report."

Holt and Amy frowned, puzzled.

"Maybe in your dad's day it was different," Amy said.

"I don't think so," said Holt. "And even if it was, this is six times over the course of"—he shuffled through the reports—"a month."

Amy leaned forward, excited. "Look, whatever the reason, this is good. We don't have to go through the minutes. We can just ask James."

"The thing is," Holt said slowly, then stopped. He looked at Edie. That gaze seared her like a brand.

"The thing is what?" Amy asked.

"The thing is, you've been looking for a connection between these three men for a while now," Edie said softly.

Holt said nothing.

"Holt, it was years ago," Amy said. "Your father probably forgot."

"I'm sure that's all it is," Edie said. She put a hand over his, but he slid it away. She saw denial in his face, but also something else. Fear.

"Who is . . ." He stopped. Licked his lips. Started again. "Who's on your list?" he asked Edie.

"What list?" Amy said.

"You know who's on it," Edie told him. "Parsley, Runkle, Lyle, Butene."

"And?" Holt said.

Edie clenched her hands below the table. She looked down at the council minutes, unable to look at Holt.

"*And?*" he repeated. They all waited, the silence like dread.

At last Edie looked into the clouded green eyes of the last man in the world she wanted to hurt.

"And Drennen," he said to her. "Right? *Right*? Say it, damn you."

"Yes, Drennen. Okay? Yes, he's on the list."

"The only one left," Holt said with disbelief. "No wonder you didn't want to stay at my house." He pushed away from the table. "Oh, my God." How many times had he discussed the murders with his father? James had been the only one he'd told about Edie staying at the motel, too. A swirl of sickness overtook him. He grabbed on to the steel limbs of a bookshelf to steady himself.

What had his dad done?

And now, sweet Jesus, what was he going to do about it?

His brain swirled, making him dizzy. He was falling down, down, down, into an endless abyss, and as the black hole swallowed him up, his phone rang.

"I got those garages you wanted me to check," Sam said briskly.

"What?" His brain was too thick to make sense of what she said.

"The full-sized pickups? Remember? You asked me to check all the garages in the surrounding counties. Think I found what you're looking for. Black pickup over in Berding."

The shelving he was clutching bit into his hand even harder, but he couldn't feel anything. His father had a black pickup. And last he heard, it was in a garage in Berding. "You sure that's the only one?"

"Yup. Why? Something wrong?"

He could have laughed out loud. "No. Thanks."

"Want me to check it out?"

"No, I got it."

"Anything else?"

His hand was shaking. "Just," he swallowed. Sweat made the phone slippery. "Just keep me posted on what Lodge is doing."

A hand on his back made him jump. He whirled. Edie stood in front of him. Blood hammering in his head, he couldn't figure out how she got there. Where they were. What they'd been doing. But the confusion only lasted a moment. He glanced over her shoulder. They were alone.

"Where's Amy?"

"She made a tactful retreat to the ladies." She slipped her arms around his waist, put her head on his chest. But he only stood there, rigid against the comfort.

"Holt, I'm sorry. I'm so, so sorry."

He disentangled himself. "I gotta go." He was halfway across the basement before she could open her mouth, let alone respond.

"Okay," she said to the now-empty room. "No problem." She sank into one of the metal chairs at the card table. Drooped her head into her hands.

She should have told Holt.

Shoulda, woulda, coulda. Best-laid plans and all that crap.

Of course she'd held back. Easy to see why. The way he'd ripped himself away from her. As if she was poison. Or some contagious disease.

Well, she'd wanted the truth to come out. She just wished it hadn't slapped her so hard in the face when it did.

"Everything all right?" Amy Lyle's soft voice was at Edie's shoulder.

"I doubt it." Not if the look on Holt's face was any indication. She had a pretty good idea where he was going. Just didn't want to think about what would happen when he got there.

She turned to Amy. "Can you give me a lift?"

～46～

Holt drove like a demon chasing hell. He poured into the drive on the left side of the yellow and white house he'd grown up in, brakes squealing.

He slammed into the house. "Dad! *Dad!*"

His mother appeared from the kitchen wiping her hands on an apron. "What in the world? He's out back," she said.

He raced past her, through the kitchen and out the screen door, its habitual squeak like a scream in his head.

His father was painting the tool shed. Built in the thirties, it had been falling down until James had carefully restored it. Holt remembered helping on the weekends, sanding and hammering. Painting. Mimsy had insisted it match the house, so they'd given it a butter-yellow coat with white trim. It was the trim James was working on when Holt strode across the lawn.

His father shielded his eyes, saw him, and went back to painting.

"Early lunch?" James said.

"Why didn't you tell me you were on the city council at the same time as all the victims?"

The hand holding the paintbrush paused, but for so brief a time Holt wasn't sure it had stopped. "I didn't want you to know."

Not the answer Holt had hoped for. Fear tightened his belly. "Why? What happened back then?"

James was silent.

Holt broke through that wall with a battering ram. "Did you kill Edie's father?"

But his father reacted by not reacting. As if the question was usual, expected even. "Not in the way you're thinking."

"What way, then? Dammit, Dad, what did you do?" He grabbed the paintbrush out of his father's hand. White paint spattered their shirts and the yellow wood below the trim.

James gave him a hard, sad look. "I'll tell you what I didn't do, son. I didn't kill Runkle or Parsley, and that's all you need to know."

"What about Lucy Keel?" Holt snapped.

"What?"

"The truck that attacked Lucy and Edie on their way back from Nashville. Big black pickup. Just like yours." He looked at his father. The man he'd always respected. Whose son he'd always been proud to be. Now a pained expression crossed James's face. An expression that cut through Holt as well. He'd just accused his father of murder. The man who taught him how to be a man. "What did you do, Dad?" He raked his hands through his hair. "I can't believe we're even having this discussion. *Dad, what did you do?*"

Before James could respond, Edie's voice came out of nowhere. "Holt! Wait!"

He whirled. She was running around the side of the house, rushing down the lawn to them. How the hell did she get here?

"Get out of here," Holt told her. "This is none of your business."

"The hell it isn't." She tugged on his arm, but he didn't move. "Leave it, Holt. Forget it. It's only going to break your heart."

"Too late," Holt said. "Tell her, Dad. Tell her what your everyday ride is."

James said nothing.

"A black pickup," Holt supplied. "Full-size. Guess where it is? In the garage."

Edie gasped. Covered her gaping mouth with her hands.

"Still want me to forget it?" Holt asked. Edie said nothing. Only stared at James with reproach, her eyes wide with disbelief. "Yeah, didn't think so." Holt turned on his dad. "Where were you the afternoon Dennis Runkle wrecked his car?"

James looked down at the grass. Dots of white paint had landed there, too. "Here. Working on the shed. Hardware, buying paint. Supplies. Still got the receipts if you want them."

"And Parsley?"

"I was at the party—you know that."

"No—not the whole time you weren't. You disappeared. Went for ice."

"That's right."

"By way of the church?"

"By way of Myer's," James said quietly. "Ask him. I bought four bags of ice and we talked about the game because he was listening to it on that little TV he has in the corner and Chipper Jones had just hit a home run to tie the score."

"Dammit, Dad. You lied to me, pumped me for information, played on our relationship. Don't you think you owe me the truth now?"

"That is the truth, son."

"What about the other truth? What happened in 1989?"

Again, James didn't reply.

It was full day, almost noon, and the sun shone yellow and hot. But darkness seemed to gather and swirl around Holt. "What do you know about Edie's father?"

His own father remained mute, and Holt shoved him. "Say something, damn you!"

But it was Edie who spoke. "I don't care, Holt! I don't care anymore." She got between the two of them, stood in front of Holt's father as if he'd been the one wronged and not her. "Whatever happened, it's in the past. Can't we just leave it there? If I'd known digging it up would hurt so many people, I never would have come here. Oh, God, please Holt. Just leave it alone. My father's dead. Yours is still here and alive."

"Think I don't know that?" Holt snarled.

James stepped out from behind Edie, so she was no longer in the crossfire. "I'm sorry," he said to her.

Holt dove for his dad, spun him away "Don't say you're sorry to her! You let her get arrested. You let me arrest her!"

"I tried to get her to go away, Holt. Tried to save her.

But you're not one to take a hint, are you?" he said to Edie.

Holt gazed at his father through narrowed eyes. "You tried? What do you mean? How the hell did you—" He stared at his dad. Outrage surged over pain and disbelief. "That was you at the motel?"

James only gazed at him directly, confession enough.

"Oh, my God," Edie said. "Please don't tell me you're the one who tampered with my bike."

Holt whipped his head around to stare at her. "That was an acci—" A clutch of sickness grabbed his belly and crammed his throat. An accident like the rest.

His father was shaking his head, holding up his hands as if asking for peace. "I swear, I don't know anything about your—"

Before Holt knew he was doing it, he'd rammed his father against the tool shed. "Who are you?" Holt hauled his father up by the shirt front, shaking him. "Who the hell are you!"

"Holt, son, I didn't touch her bike."

"You could have killed her!" Almost on its own, Holt's right arm pulled back and punched forward. Connected with his father's chin. James went sprawling on the grass.

"Oh, God," Edie moaned.

"Holt!" His mother flew down the lawn. "What in heaven's name is going on? Dear Lord." She stooped to check her husband. Looked wildly up at her son. "Have you lost your mind?"

James groaned as he sat up, age and defeat in his rounded shoulders. His wife cradled him, looking up at her only son as if she'd never seen him before.

"Holt Drennen, you apologize to your father this minute."

"Hush, Mimsy," James said softly.

"I won't—"

"Yes, you will."

His mother's protests stopped dead. Out of the corner of his eye he saw Edie slink away. Sink onto a picnic table bench, head in her hands.

Holt ignored them all. James hadn't shielded himself. Hadn't lifted a finger to protect himself, let alone said anything in his defense. Not that there was anything to say.

Holt stared at the yard he knew so well. Remnants of a tree house James had built when Holt was nine still sat in the big maple in the corner. When Miranda was a few years older Holt had planned to fix it up for her. Forever in need of a new spring, the screen door at the back hung wide open as it always did when someone ran out without closing it. He'd loved this house his whole life, yet he'd married Cindy, eager to get away. How could he have forgotten that need to be on his own? The excitement of creating something that was his alone? He'd crawled back here a wounded dog. But he was long past healed.

"I'd appreciate your packing a bag for Miranda," Holt said stiffly to his mother. "We'll be leaving."

Mimsy shot to her feet. "What? Leaving? Where are you going?"

James struggled to stand, too. "Holt. Son. Don't do this. Not without cooling down some."

Mimsy's eyes filled. "What's happened? Please, someone, tell me what's happened."

Holt opened his mouth to tell her. That her husband

was knee deep in the murder of three of her fellow townspeople. That he'd likely killed Lucy Keel. Terrorized the woman Holt loved, and withheld information that could prove her innocent.

But the shock and distress in his mother's eyes were too powerful. He glanced over at James. He could hardly look at the man. "Let him explain it."

Holt began the long slog across the yard to the drive in front.

His mother called after him. "But . . . you can't take Miranda. This is the only home that child knows."

He managed to get around the corner without falling. He stumbled to the car, leaned hard against the roof, arms braced, head hung between. His legs were trembling, his shirt soaked through.

"Give me the keys. I'll drive."

Where had Edie come from? Oh, yeah. His mind filled with what had just happened. Nausea swirled at the back of his throat.

"And don't give me any crap about this being an official vehicle I can't drive," she added. "This is an emergency."

He looked over his shoulder at her. Black hair tumbling down her back, those big dark eyes full of sympathy and love.

But instead of bolstering him, it twisted inside him. His father had loved him, too. And Edie had betrayed him twice now.

Holt turned stiffly. Leaned against the car. "You should have told me."

"Why is that? So I could break your heart that much sooner?"

"Oh, so you withheld valuable information in a murder investigation to what—protect my tender feelings?"

Edie's face heated. "Okay, at first, yes, I didn't say anything because I didn't want you to know about the list and my connection with the angels. But then—"

"Then it was easier to keep on lying. Maybe because lying is a way of life with you."

The words cracked Edie's ribs in two, clean as an ax. And while she stood there speechless, bleeding inside, he got in the car and drove away.

~47~

Berding was one of those tiny towns that grew up along the old highways. Those mostly two-lane affairs, abandoned for the faster lanes of the interstate, were dotted with small towns, one blending into the other, then stretching into fields and out into town again. Holt had grown up with the names: Trenton, Three Corners, Goosefoot. They came fast, their main streets awash with the signs of businesses that had once been thriving. The AC Pajama Factory. Bradford Tractor and Farm Equipment. Even the Starlight Drive-in was nothing but dust and ghosts.

An Everest of rusted cars in an auto salvage yard signaled the entry to Berding. Next, a strip of stores set back from the highway were mostly empty windows except for a small antique-cum-consignment store called Pearl's. The most prosperous-looking building was Walker Funeral Home, a sturdy, red-brick building with a parking lot and a landscaped walk. Holt appreciated the irony of the mortician being the richest man in a dying town. Especially now when it seemed as if everything around him was dying, too. His family. His so-called love life.

The garage was on the far end of town. A single gas pump sat close to the road. A small shed perched behind the pump, attached to the garage, whose two open doors showed the lifts inside. A mechanic saw the car with its Redbud PD markings and came out wiping his hands on a grease rag. "You here about that truck I got a call on?"

Holt set his face, burying the pain behind hard lines. But he couldn't keep that pulse from slamming against his skin as the mechanic brought him to a side lot, where his father's big black pickup was parked.

He walked around the truck. Couldn't see any damage, especially the kind he'd have expected. "What's wrong with it?"

The mechanic scratched his head. "Busted fan belt."

Holt's jaw tightened. "Anyone pay you to say that?"

The man looked confused. "Pay me?"

"Let me see the paperwork."

The mechanic shuffled off, and while he was gone Holt bent to examine the front end of his father's truck. He rubbed fingers over a spot on the left end—a paint scratch and a small dent in the left-side bumper. Been there for months. Given the force needed to push Lucy off the road, he would have expected more. Much more.

He rose, flummoxed.

The mechanic jogged up, handed over a clipboard. Holt scanned it. *Fix fan belt, if possible. Install new if not.* There was a cost estimate, and his father's contact information.

"No front-end damage?" Holt asked.

"Front end? No sir."

"You sure."

"Look—alls we're supposed to do is fix the fan belt.

Thing was torn clear through. Waiting on a new one from the dealership. We'll put her in, truck'll be right as rain."

The mechanic headed back to work, and Holt leaned against the front of his father's truck. He scrubbed his face, relief making him almost shaky.

Jesus Christ in heaven, he didn't do it. His father hadn't killed Lucy.

He stared out at the garage, trying to ease the shakes, inhaling the metallic smell of engine parts, gas, and oil.

Which meant—what? That he hadn't messed with Edie's bike? Or with the three dead men?

Maybe.

But one thing he did know: There was another full-size black pickup with front-end damage out there. And someone else had been behind the wheel.

Holt had left Edie stranded, so she walked to Amy's, calling her on the way to fill her in.

"I called over to the Drennens' just to make sure everything was all right," she said when Edie arrived. "Mimsy was so upset. I could barely hear a word for the tears. Did Holt really hit his father? I can hardly believe it. Any chance this'll all blow over before the end of the day?"

"Probably not."

Amy tsked. "And he's taking Miranda? Just about broke Mimsy's heart to say it. Where in the world will he take that child? The only motel is the Cloverleaf"—she shuddered audibly—"and she can't go there."

So much had happened, Edie had forgotten Holt's determination to take Miranda and leave.

Amy's face brightened. "What about here? I've got the room. At least until he can figure out what to do."

"I don't know—"

"You don't want him here?"

"Oh, it's not me. I'm not sure he'd want to stay anywhere near me."

"What are you talking about? He's crazy about you."

"Yeah. Easy come, easy go." She told her what Holt had said.

Amy patted Edie's hand. "He was just lashing out and you were there. He didn't mean it."

"Felt like he meant it."

"Well, we've got enough trouble without fighting among ourselves." She rose and took Edie by the hand. "Come on, girl. We've got fences to mend."

Amy drove them to the municipal building where Holt's car was parked in front. Edie eyed it warily. "Might be better if I stayed here. Don't want to remind Deputy Fish or Agent Lodge of my existence."

"You want me to soften him up?"

"Yup."

"Coward."

"Yup."

But Amy smiled and went inside. She was gone long enough for Edie to get restless with concern. She got out of the car and leaned against it, breathing in the fresh air. Didn't look good if it was taking Amy so long to talk Holt into letting bygones be etc. etc.

While she was out there a car drove up and parked next to Holt's. Her heart sank when she saw who it was. Lodge.

He slammed the door, walked around Holt's car, scowling at her over the front end. "What are you doing loitering near the chief's car, Miss Swann?"

Her first instinct was to flip him off, but she remembered Amy, who believed in her and was counting on her to behave accordingly. So she answered. Not eagerly. And maybe not with all the respect Lodge assumed was his due, but she managed to keep her response short and sweet.

"Waiting."

Lodge narrowed his eyes. Seemed short and sweet wasn't his cup of Jack any more than wiseass was. He ordered her to turn around, and when she did, he slammed her against the car, spread her legs, and in full view of the town square, patted her down.

"I'm not carrying a weapon." The protest came out half-strangled, Lodge's heavy hand squelching her against the car.

"Like some in this town, I don't take your word on that," Lodge said. His hand ran up and down her legs, over her back and chest. He checked her pockets, found her keys and wallet and whatever spare lint was there. He should have been finished, but he kept her bent over, pressed even harder now that he had two hands to do it. "Now, you want to tell me what you're doing here?"

"She's waiting for me." Holt's voice came from the direction of the municipal building. It was tight and angry. "Let her up, Lodge."

"So you can coddle her? Or should I say cuddle?"

"I said," and now Holt sounded closer, "let her up."

Lodge was wrenched away, and Edie straightened with a small grunt of effort. Holt and Lodge were nose to nose, Amy looking on in dismay.

"You touch her again," Holt said, "I'll have you up on harassment."

"You keep favoring her, I'll have you up on obstruction of justice."

Across the square, a cluster of people gaped at the scene. Edie didn't care for her own reputation. She figured that was already shot. But Holt's was a different story.

"Don't you have to pick up Miranda from camp?" Edie hurried to say, and when he still stood rigid, daring Lodge to hit him or arrest him, or whatever he was itching to do, she said, "Holt? Miranda?"

Holt eased a step over, his gaze still on Lodge.

"Better enjoy her while you can, 'Chief,'" Lodge mocked the title. "She'll be headed for the women's prison soon."

The word *prison* sent a jitter of fear through Edie. But Holt only wrapped a firm hand around her arm and pulled her away from Lodge, who went into the building.

"What an awful man," Amy said, and no one argued with her. She turned to Holt. "Now, don't you worry about Miranda. I'll pick her up from camp and bring her back to the house."

"Not necessary," Holt said gruffly.

"It'll be my pleasure. You two need some alone time." She turned to Edie. "I'll see you later." She winked, and got in her car.

Edie looked at Holt. "What's going on?"

"Get in." Fury etched every tense line of his body, and for once she obeyed without question. He got in and drove off.

"Where we going?"

"Metaphorically? I don't have a clue."

Just what she needed. A little existential humor. "Literally."

But he wasn't interested. "That sonuvabitch ever does that to you again—"

"What are you going to do—hit him? Come on, Holt, there's more at stake here than my freedom. There's your job, Miranda's future. Don't blow it because of me."

"Yeah, why would I go and do that?" He snorted. "You don't think much of yourself, do you?"

"Didn't think you thought much of me either."

That shut him up, and they drove in silence. As the minutes ticked by time built a wall, brick by soundless brick, until Edie wanted to scream, if only to burst through. But it was Holt who spoke first.

"I, uh . . ." His voice sounded as if he had a live oak stuck in it, and he cleared his throat. "I've got a piece of news." He told her about his father's truck.

"So maybe he didn't mess with my bike, either," she said slowly, still absorbing what Holt had said. "Maybe it was an accident. A real one."

"That'd be a first."

A black hole opened up beneath Edie. She'd been so used to thinking of James as the villain, she didn't know what to think now. Except if James wasn't the bad guy . . . who was? She found herself staring out the window as if whoever it was might be lurking there. But all she saw were the familiar homey sights of Redbud. They sent a shiver through her.

"What now?" she asked, suddenly glad she was bottled up with Holt rather than on the streets where anything or anyone could get to her.

"We keep looking. There's another black pickup somewhere with front-end damage. We'll find it."

Before or after they sentenced her?

He drove her to Amy's house, and Edie wondered if Amy had asked him to stay, and whether he would. But she was afraid of the answer, so she said nothing. He parked and they sat there. He stared out the windshield, one wrist draped over the steering wheel.

"Look, Amy invited Miranda and me to bunk here for a while."

"She said she might."

He turned his head to gaze at her. "What do you think?"

"You asking permission?"

He thought about it. "I guess I am."

She shrugged. Why get stomped on again? "Up to you. Miranda needs a place to sleep."

"Miranda, huh?"

Her face heated, and she thought it was time to get out of that tight, closed space that smelled of leather and him. She opened the door. "Like I said, up to you."

He followed her into the house. Neither Amy nor Miranda was there, but they found a note in the kitchen saying Miranda was at a sleepover and Amy was at choir practice and then would be gone overnight. There was a chicken casserole in the fridge and a bottle of wine, which she told them to enjoy.

It was sweet and well meant, but so off-base it was embarrassing.

Holt was reading over her shoulder, his big body nearly enveloping her. Suddenly Edie realized how alone they were. Alone in this house that had seen joy and tragedy. That had nurtured a marriage and a family. The rootedness of the place seeped into her bones. How would it feel to live like this with him?

As if he'd read her mind, and wanted nothing to do with that cozy picture, he stepped back. "You going to be okay here tonight?"

She'd left it up to him, and it looked like he'd decided. "I think I can manage."

He nodded. "Anything happens I'll be at my office."

"Sure."

"Okay then." He shuffled, glanced around. "You call me."

She crossed her heart, held up a hand. "Will do."

"Okay."

"You said that already."

"Yeah. Right." He huffed out a breath, and walked out the back door.

As soon as he disappeared she was instantly sorry. She didn't want to leave it up to him. Not if it meant he'd go.

Ah hell.

"Holt!" She caught him at the car, his door unopened, looking back at the house as if he wasn't sure he wanted to leave either. "I can't eat a whole chicken casserole by myself."

~48~

Dinner started stiff and formal, both of them on their best behavior. Holt still looked out of place in Amy's kitchen, a giant in a field of tiny yellow flowers. But he seemed to prefer the kitchen to the dining room, because he set the table there while she warmed the casserole in the microwave. When it was ready, he held her chair for her.

She wasn't the shy type, but she felt shy all of a sudden. Sitting in the kitchen like old married folks gave her a glimpse of what might have been. And she wasn't sure she liked it. There'd be no yellow in her kitchen. Pink would be banished, too. If she had her way, it would be red and black, white and chrome. Like Beauty, her bike. So if Holt thought he'd tie her to yellow flowers and chicken casseroles and girly things . . .

She caught herself. Man, look at her all Martha Stewart, making plans. She gulped her glass of wine. Holt was watching her. Did he know what she'd been thinking? She flushed. Realized it, which made her face even hotter. What was wrong with her? She never blushed.

"I ever tell you about Mrs. Beasly's cat?"

The question was so random, it made her forget whatever she'd been fussing about a minute ago. "Who's Mrs. Beasly?"

He launched into the story, a tall tale about his first day as police chief, when he got a call from Mrs. Beasly, who'd since passed on. She was distraught because a stray cat had jumped through an open window and she said it was the spirit of her dead husband. "She kept calling it Merl, which was her dead husband's name," he said, and mimicked an elderly female southern drawl. " 'Chief, you come on over here and arrest that cat. Won't have no husband haunting me.' I'm sitting in my office, wondering how she knew that the cat was her husband, and whether my dad had maybe put her up to it but also wanting to make a good impression and all on my first day. So I check it out and sure enough, there's this cat, and his fur is colored into a big 'M' on his right side, like someone took a marker to him. I catch the cat and take it outside. Boy, am I feeling like a good Samaritan. Few hours later, Mrs. Beasly's on the horn, screeching at me about her husband again. I go back out there, same story. I catch the cat, put it outside. This happens like four more times, and I'm starting to think there's something to this haunting thing. After the fifth call, I get wise and pretend to drive away, only I turn the corner, get out, and double back. And there's Mrs. Beasly opening the window and letting the cat back in."

Edie smiled.

"There we go," he said softly. "That's what I've been waiting for." He held her gaze, and maybe it was the wine or maybe it was the look in his eyes, or maybe it was Mrs.

Beasly's cat. Whatever it was, all of a sudden the mood gentled.

"What'd you do?"

"Came back with some cat food. Stayed a while. Listened to her talk about her grandchildren."

She shook her head. "Anyone ever tell you you're a nice guy, Chief Drennen?"

"She kept the cat. Named him Beasly."

Edie put her fork down. "You're making that up."

He held up a hand. "Do nice guys lie?"

She stiffened, his words cooling the air between them and bringing Edie back to where they'd been hours ago. "Unlike me."

He looked stricken. "Aw, geez, Edie. No. Not what I meant." He pushed back in his chair, looked around the kitchen as if one of the flowers might pop out and rescue him.

She picked at the congealing casserole on her plate. "But you were right. I did lie to you."

"Truth isn't always as clean-cut as we'd like it to be. The point is—"

"The point is, this is screwed up."

"This?"

"You, me." She waved a hand between them. "Us. FUBAR. Fucked Up Beyond—"

"Repair. Yeah I know what it means."

"You're the law. I'm headed for jail." She shoved her plate away. "If that ain't FUBAR I don't know what is."

"Don't let that jerk get inside your head."

"Who—Lodge? I don't need him to remind me what's in front of my face."

He reached across the table and took her hand. His

skin felt warm, his fingers strong. It would be nice to stay there lulling herself into the false security of his touch.

"I'm gonna figure this out," he said.

"Before or after they fire you?"

He was silent. "It's only a job," he said at last.

She looked at their entwined fingers. "See, that's what I mean. You're a nice guy, so you'll fight to the death. Me? I've already hacked your family into pieces—"

"My father did that."

"Only because I showed up. And I'm not going to be the bullet that kills your career, too."

Holt watched her hand slip from his. It was a slow, simple gesture, her palm sliding across the ice-cream-parlor table, gliding around the half-empty casserole dish, the plates with food still on them, the napkins, glasses sweating from ice cubes—all the normal detritus of a home-cooked meal. But it felt as if he was watching something important disappear over the horizon. Something that would never return. Or if it did return it would never be the same.

He looked away. Felt his mouth twist into the semblance of a smile. "Thanks for dinner."

"You didn't eat much."

"Neither did you."

They sat for a moment, silence binding them and breaking them. Then he rose and made his way to the door. No good nights. No see ya laters either.

~49~

It took Holt a minute to recover from the earthquake he'd just survived. He sat in the car, hoping for another miracle. But when Edie didn't pop out the door and call him back a second time, he took off. Ended at his office, where he found a note from Sam saying Terry had made bond and been released.

Just as well. Holt wasn't in the mood to deal with Terry tonight. No, he was in the mood. The wrong mood.

He tossed his keys into the top desk drawer as always, saw the envelope with Edie's name scrawled on it. He tore it open. Her bike keys fell into his hand. Couldn't get away from her if he tried.

Itching to kick someone across the room, he kicked his chair instead. It went spinning and crashed into Sam's desk, toppling a neat pile of papers and a soft-sided black book with "Appointments" embossed in gold.

Fuck. He stared at the mess, exhaled a huge breath, and picked up the stuff, knowing she'd had it in a certain order, which he'd never be able to replicate. He set the appointment book on top, then thought better of it. It wasn't Sam's. She kept her appointments on her phone.

He opened it, saw Dennis Runkle's business card clipped to the inside front cover. So, they'd found it. He wondered when the hell Sam was going to get around to telling him.

The book was divided by day, each day with its own page. An index card marked the day of Runkle's death. He ran his finger down the page. Real estate appointments were listed by address; the one with Edie was 144 Dogwood. The next one was also on the east side of town. Not too far from Dogwood on Myrtle. Runkle must have grouped them together. Holt fixed on the house number, tapping the book. The address sounded familiar, though he didn't know why.

He was thinking of getting in the car and driving over there when it hit him. He knew who lived on Myrtle.

Terry Bishop.

The house on Myrtle was eerily menacing in the dark, its wide, beveled shape stabbing the moonlit sky. Holt climbed the steps and ducked into the blackness beneath the makeshift arch of overgrown shrubs a few feet from the front door. The house appeared on the other side, and if he'd been twenty years younger, he might have thought twice about knocking. His younger self would have imagined all sorts of gothic horrors behind the shadowy walls. But Holt was all grown up now and he knew the only horror waiting for him was Terry.

Ellen Garvey answered his knock, peering at him curiously. "Chief!" A hand went to her heart, her eyes scrunched into worry. "My goodness, has something else happened?"

"I'm looking for Terry, Miss Ellen."

She looked a little disheveled, as if she'd been lying down. At one point she'd applied a coat of red lipstick and it had blurred over her mouth and strayed over the lines of her lips, making her appear a little clownish. Holt felt sorry for her. She looked old and frail and now she had Terry to worry about.

"Sorry if I woke you."

She waved the apology away. "Oh, I was awake. Now tell me about Terry. Is he all right? He's not hurt, is he?"

Holt assured her that as far as he knew, Terry was fine. "I'd just like to talk to him."

"I was just about to go to bed, but . . ." She opened the door wider. "Come in, come in." She led the way to a small sitting room with a worn carpet and paint chipping off the walls, but no Terry.

"Please," Ellen said, "Sit down."

"That's okay. I won't be long. If I could just see Terry."

"I'm afraid he isn't in."

"Do you know where he is?"

"He's not in trouble again, is he?"

"I don't know, Miss Ellen. Did he happen to mention seeing Dennis Runkle the day he died?"

She looked taken aback. "Why ever would he?"

"He never mentioned Runkle at all?" Holt asked.

"Not that I recall. At least not until after he died. But then, so did everyone else." She shivered but there was a note of excitement to it. "That black angel business." She tsked. "All I heard about for days.

"Did Terry ever tell you he had some information about the Hammerbilt plant"?

"My goodness. Information? What kind of information?"

"Something . . . secret. Embarrassing maybe."

She shook her head. "Where in the world does that boy get these notions?" Fretful, she crumbled the cloth of her slacks. "I don't like to admit this, but my nephew tends to make himself more important than he is. It's a fault, I know, but he doesn't mean anything by it." She gave him a pleading look, as if asking him not to judge Terry too harshly.

Holt frowned. "Do you know where he is now?"

She shook her head again. "I believe he borrowed the car again. A young man needs a car," she said.

"You be careful now," he said sternly. "I know Terry's your nephew, but he's not always on the side of the angels."

"Well, I don't suppose any of us are," she said stiffly.

"I'd hate to see him take advantage of you," Holt said.

"You don't think . . ." She laughed nervously. "Surely Terry wouldn't hurt me."

Holt wasn't sure, but he also didn't want to alarm her. "You just call me if you need anything." He handed her a card.

Later, after Ellen had seen him out, he breathed in the night air, warm and overladen with the smell of vegetation, but still fresher than the mustiness of the old house.

He drove to Red's, but Terry wasn't there and hadn't been all night. He wasn't at the Cloverleaf either, and when Holt called Prewitt, the motel owner said he hadn't seen Terry in a week.

Stumped and not a little worried, Holt leaned against his car, stared out at the "loverleaf" sign, and shoved his hands in his pockets. His fingers traced the outline of a small set of keys, and he pulled them out. Edie's bike keys. He didn't remember putting them there, but then again, he didn't remember much except tossing his office.

Would she be awake? Of course she would, it was barely ten. Would she talk to him? After their awkward and aborted dinner, she probably wasn't too interested in seeing him again tonight. Hell, she wasn't interested in seeing him period. All in the name of his own good, of course.

Well, screw that.

He took off, keeping a close eye on the streets in case Terry or anyone else was where they shouldn't be. Didn't take long to get to Amy Lyle's house. Didn't take long to get anywhere in Redbud.

He pulled into the drive, parked the car in the same spot he'd left it a few hours ago. Made the same walk up to the door, bracing himself for the same reception.

She opened the door, surprise on her face.

"Yeah, I know," he said. "Didn't expect to see me so soon."

"Something wrong?"

"I got something for you."

Edie cocked her head. He was giving her a present? Not exactly what she'd expected after he left. It killed her to admit it, but despite what she'd said she was glad he'd come back. Stupid, of course. Downright idiotic. But who was she to tell her body not to get all neon glowy just looking at him?

"Hold out your hand."

"Holt—"

"Come on, hold out your hand."

She played along. Held her hand out, palm up. He dropped her bike keys into it.

Her gaze snapped to his. She searched his face but there was no sign he was punking her. "Really?"

"Really."

Still, she wasn't ready to accept. She leaned against the door jamb, the keys still sitting on top of her open palm as if they might bite if she got too close. "You're going to get in trouble for this, aren't you?"

"Nah."

"Yeah, you are. See? This is exactly what I meant."

"Will you just take the damn keys?"

It was selfish, but she couldn't hold out any longer. She closed her fist around the keys. The minute she did, he grabbed her hand and pulled her to the car. She barely got the door shut.

"Wait a minute!"

"Come on. I want to get this over with."

He bundled her into his car and drove downtown to the office. They got out and he led her around the corner and down the block to a small lot bordered by a chain-link fence. She grabbed a handful of wire and gazed in. Her bike sat in heavy chains against a post.

"What if I take off?"

"Then I'll hunt you down."

A fair enough bargain, especially since they both knew she wasn't going anywhere. Her stomach swirled and her heart spun with it. It seemed to take Holt forever to unlock the gate. Sick with excitement, she ran to the imprisoned Harley. Another eternity and he unlocked the chains.

She ran a shaky hand along the sleek body. Her chrome was dusty. "You need a bath, girl," she said to the machine. She switched on the "run" button, turned the key, and pushed the starter. The engine turned over, rumbling to life. That deep, throaty growl set off another electric wave inside her, an indescribable need to feel the road quake through her body. But before she could go anywhere, Holt's phone rang. He stepped away to take the call.

"What?" she asked when he returned. She was impatient to leave, anxious to feel the wind against her shoulders.

"A neighbor reported a break-in at the Community Church."

She pulled the passenger seat from a saddlebag. "I'll take you." She didn't wait for an answer, just fixed the suction cups to the fender. "Faster than going back for you car," she added.

He conceded the point and got on. When they were on the corner of East and Courthouse, he tapped her shoulder. She slowed to a stop. From there they could see the back of the church. A Saturn sat near the door.

"That's Ellen Garvey's car," Holt said.

Edie parked the bike and they crossed the street, instinctively moving fast and low. They crept to the back door. Slowly, Holt tried the handle; it turned.

Inside, the church was dark, but light spilled from a hallway up ahead. They inched toward it. Stopped at the corner. Flattened against the wall.

Holt peeked around the edge. Took Edie's hand and slithered around the corner. A few feet down the lighted hallway, a door stood open.

They snuck up to it. Gradually, Holt widened the opening until they could see inside. Brooms, mops, cleaning supplies. A janitor's closet.

And in the middle, sitting on an overturned metal pail, Terry Bishop was poring over a manila file.

~50~

Holt straightened, hands on hips next to Edie. "What you got there?"

Terry jumped sky high. The folder fell to the floor, papers spilled out. Edie grabbed them before Terry could. "What's this?" she asked.

Terry looked guiltily between them. He opened his mouth. Shut it again.

"Reports," Edie said, answering her own question. She flipped the pages. "Production stats from Hammerbilt. Daily. Weekly." She flipped more pages. "Monthly." She checked the top of the pages. "Look at the dates—1987, '88, '89." She exchanged a glance with Holt.

"Where'd you get this?" Holt asked Terry.

Terry's lips flattened. Holt grabbed a handful of Terry's shirt. "Answer the question. Where'd you get the file?"

"I found it."

"Uh huh. Where exactly did you 'find' it?"

He squirmed in his seat on the pail and finally admitted, "At Aunt Hannah's."

"What do you mean?" Holt said to Terry. "Where at your aunt's?"

"In her room."

Holt eyed Terry. He avoided the lawman's glance. "What were you doing in her room?" Holt asked.

Terry didn't reply.

Holt shook him. "What were you doing—"

"She was dead, okay? Wasn't going to need nothing. She had all these pins and necklaces and stuff. And I needed the money. I'm not gonna get stuck in this town for the rest of my life. I got plans."

Holt shoved him away with disgust. "Jesus, Terry. Stealing from the dead."

"What about the file?" Edie asked.

"Hidden in her closet. Behind a bunch of old-lady stuff. Hats and shoes and things."

"Why would she hide—"

"How should I know?" Terry said. "But I figured she wouldn't have hidden it if it wasn't important."

"Let me guess," Holt said. "This is what you wanted to talk to Edie about in the motel."

Terry flicked a hangdog look at Edie, shrugged, and nodded. "But I didn't wreck your stuff," he said.

"Yeah, I know," Edie said.

"You . . . you do?" Terry gaped as if it was inconceivable that anyone would believe him about anything.

"Does your aunt Ellen know about this?" Holt asked.

Terry looked horrified. "Hell, no."

Holt tapped his foot. Observed Terry sitting there. He had a two-day growth on his chin, a defensive look on his face. How Ellen Garvey could harbor even a small bit of affection for her nephew . . .

"Did you see Runkle on the day he died?" Holt asked.

Terry grew wary at the name of the dead real estate agent. "Sure didn't."

"Where were you that afternoon?"

Terry's eyes darted around the room. "Working at the motel. Call Prewitt. He'll tell you. I asked for an advance and the bastard wouldn't give it to me."

Holt pursed his lips. "Runkle had your address on his appointment book. Why is that, Terry? Are you sure you didn't have a meeting with him?"

"Hell, yes, I'm sure. I don't have meetings. I don't know why he had my address. Maybe he saw Aunt Ellen. She's been talking about selling the house. Maybe he met with her that day. Did you ask her?"

"I talked to her. She didn't mention it," Holt said dryly.

"Well, I don't know. I don't!" He shot Holt another defiant look.

"Funny how your name keeps turning up, though," Holt said. "First with the reverend. Now with Runkle."

"I didn't do anything to either one. I swear!" He jerked to his feet. "Can I go now?"

Holt held out his hand, fingers flicking a "gimme" gesture. "I want the key to the church."

"But I need it for the morning. So I can get in early and vacuum."

"Stop by my office. You can get it there. And return it there, too."

Terry looked pained, but he dug in his pocket and slammed the key into Holt's hand. "What about my papers?"

"They're not your papers, are they?" Holt said. "They belong to Hammerbilt."

"But—"

"Get going before I arrest you."

"For what?"

"I'll think of something."

Terry shot Holt one last complaining look, but the chief took a threatening step toward him, and Terry scurried out the door.

"Why do you think Hannah Garvey hid this?" Edie asked.

"Maybe they weren't hidden. Just stored. We're not dealing with a full tool box here, far as Terry's concerned."

"But why would she store them? Keep them even?"

"Who knows? When my father retired he brought a shitload of stuff with him. Most of it's still in boxes in the garage."

The mention of his father sobered them. Edie took Holt back to the municipal building where he locked the file inside a set of steel drawers.

"I spoke with the head of Hammerbilt's accounting department," Edie said. "Maybe he can figure out what those statements are." She scribbled Arlen Mayborne's name on a piece of scrap paper and handed it to Holt, who promised to call the plant in the morning.

Then there was nothing left to do but go home. They looked at each other from across the room, the same question burning in both their faces.

Holt came toward her. "Edie—"

She stepped back. "Thanks for my bike."

He kept on coming. "Give me another ride."

She moved back. "Not tonight."

"You're not going to make me sleep here, are you?"

"You come home with me, you know where we'll end up."

He closed in. "Doesn't sound so bad."

Her heels backed up against the wall. "Yeah, that's because you have some bizarre toss-me-over-the-ledge death wish."

She was trapped now, and he touched her hair, pushing a strand back. His head lowered, his mouth danced nearer and nearer.

With a groan, she ducked under his arm. Backed away fast. "Stop it. If you can't keep yourself out of trouble, I'll do it for you." She practically ran out the door.

"Gee, thanks Mom," he called after her, but didn't follow.

Free, she ran outside, revved her bike, and took off before she changed her mind.

The next morning Edie woke thinking about Holt. She lay in the bed in Amy Lyle's house, eyes closed, conjuring up a picture of him. His smell, his taste. Morning light filtered in through her closed lids, and she held the sensations tight, locking them into memory against the day she might be far away and need them.

The specter of prison hovered like a looming storm. The kind that darkened the sky for hours before the rain finally hit. She'd been right to keep her distance. But man, it would have been nice to have had him beside her in the morning.

She dragged herself into her clothes, made coffee, and drank it in Amy Lyle's kitchen. The note Amy had left was still on the counter, and Edie fingered it. She called

Amy on her cell, and when she didn't answer left a message thanking her. "Dinner's on me tonight, so let me know what time works for you."

She disconnected and went outside to check on her bike. Despite the rough treatment, she looked good. No damage, real or imagined. Edie rode over to Myer's, loaded up with cleaning supplies, and spent the morning wiping down the grit, polishing the chrome, and making Beauty shine. She stopped for lunch, finished off the casserole, then mounted the bike and set off.

The power of the machine rumbled beneath her, the hot summer air blew against her face and breasts. It seared her lungs, fueled her brain. The roar of speed rekindled her strength, as if she could navigate through life like that, always in command, always choosing her destination, how far and how fast. The sun was out, the sky a glorious blue, and the road beckoned.

A phone call woke Holt. His eyes were gritty and his face in the mirror over the sink was stubbled and worn, but he threw some cold water over himself and took off for Berding. The same mechanic came out from under a car and greeted him.

"Tow job," he said, pointing to the black pickup parked against the side of the garage. "Got the call early this morning from THP. State trooper found it abandoned. Thought you might be interested."

Interested was an understatement. The pickup was full-size, it was the right color, and the front end was smashed and flattened.

"You open this?" he asked the mechanic.

"No, sir," the mechanic said. "Didn't touch nothing except what we needed to tow it home."

He thanked the mechanic, got out a pair of latex gloves from his trunk, snapped them on, and opened the driver's-side door.

First thing Holt saw were rust stains on the floor of the driver's seat. Blood? He hoped so. Returning to the trunk, he got out his evidence kit, bagged some scrapings. He woke Sam up, gave her the VIN number, and told her to get down to the office and trace it. While he was waiting for a call back, he used a small, high-intensity flashlight to examine the rest of the interior. The force of the crash had snapped open the glove compartment and he could see it was empty. But he got several good prints off the cover. He ran the light up the seatback and seat, looking for extraneous fibers or cuts in the fabric. He felt for lumps or unusual shapes. Nothing front or back.

He'd just finished checking the truck bed and was under the hood when Sam's call came.

"Car's been reported stolen."

"Where?"

"Memphis."

Holt's pulse picked up. He still had plenty of contacts in Memphis.

"Want me to follow up?"

"No, I got it."

She made an irritated sound, but he was still only prepared to trust her so much. "I saw Runkle's appointment book got turned in. Nice of you to let me know."

"Look, it only came last night," she protested. "Was going to call this morning and tell you."

He didn't say anything. Was trying to decide whether

to believe her when she sighed, and said, "Watch your six, Chief."

Right. She was one to talk. If he'd been watching his back, she couldn't have slipped the dagger in. But he heard the regret in her voice, and knew one of these days she'd say so. And in the meantime, he still needed her.

So he kept his mouth shut and disconnected. Stared at the evidence bags he'd collected. Questions swirled in his head, and he headed for his car. Faster he dropped off the bags, faster he'd get answers.

~51~

Edie flew down the highway, following the curve of the country road. Patches of woods eased into plowed fields. Big black Anguses grazed against the green, as calm and content as she was exhilarated. The occasional home zipped by. Barns, pickups, horses.

All rooted to the earth she zoomed over.

She'd left Redbud in the dust behind her. Was determined to go as far as her gas tank would take her before turning back. Breathing in the hot stream as the air attacked her, she mocked her newly discovered inner Girl Scout. Because she could just keep going, couldn't she? Dye her hair, change her name. Run.

She smiled to herself. That Holt was a bad influence. Him and his laughing green eyes. His daughter, his parents, his own deep roots.

Running was the Swanford way. But she came to Redbud to challenge that tradition. To stand and fight

But she didn't know it would also mean stand and die.

She watched the road race by, tempted to slink away. Avoid the consequences. The razor wire, the institutional food, the kiddie tables. The whole enforced confinement of prison. She wanted to be here, free, soaring down the road.

She heard the siren then, checked her mirrors. Blue lights coming up fast behind her.

She pulled over. Watched Agent Lodge get out of his car and walk toward her.

Damn, damn, double damn.

"Turn around," he ordered. No howdy-do, no nothing.

Edie obeyed, groaned when the cuffs went around her wrists. "What's that for?"

"Stealing that bike and taking off. I can get your bail revoked for that." He patted her down, divested her of wallet, keys, cell phone.

"I didn't steal the bike. And I was just going for a ride."

"Uh huh." He strong-armed her toward his car.

"Wait a second. What about my bike?"

"I'll send someone to tow it in."

Great. And in the meantime, it was free bait for anyone who came along.

"Look, call Holt. He'll tell you I didn't steal the bike."

"Holt?" Lodge grunted. "That should be Chief Drennen. You got that man's pants so tied up he'd say anything."

"I'm telling you, I didn't—"

"You better hope you're lying, because I find out Chief Drennen released that vehicle to you, I'll charge him with aiding and abetting." He stuffed her into the backseat of the car. "Now shut up and sit back. I hear another sound from you, I'll add resisting arrest to all the other trouble you're in."

She gave the back of his seat an angry, frustrated kick and flounced back against the seat. Stupid son of a pig farmer, fish-faced frog wart, cocksucking asshole. But she didn't say so out loud.

He'd scared her about Holt. Even with all her good intentions she always seemed back here, his life in her hands.

Once they arrived in Redbud, Lodge dragged her out of the car, pushed her into the municipal building, past the mayor's office, and through the door that said Redbud Police.

Fish was there and rose to her feet when Edie stumbled into view. The flash of surprise in her eyes was quickly covered by professional impassiveness.

Lodge threw the deputy the keys. "Lock her up," he said.

Sam obeyed with typical efficiency. She walked Edie through the back door to the cell room. The minute they were alone, Edie stopped.

"Call Holt," she whispered.

Sam rolled her eyes. "The farther he stays away from you the better." She pushed Edie forward, but she dug in her heels.

"Just do it. Tell him not to let Lodge know he released my bike to me."

Sam's brows rose.

"Lodge is going to ask him, okay? So tell Holt not to admit it. Lodge threatened to charge him if he does."

Sam frowned. "But he did release the bike to you?"

"Yeah, but that's not the point. Tell him not to—"

"And you'd take the rap for stealing it?"

"I'm already in trouble. What's a little more?"

Sam eyed her. Nodded forward.

Edie walked into the cell. "So you'll call him?"

Sam closed the steel door and locked it. Edie clutched the bars.

"You'll do it?"

Sam walked away.

"Wait a minute. Deputy! Sam! Call him, Sam! Call him!"

But she disappeared behind the door, leaving Edie alone in the cell.

Sam returned to the office, where Lodge was ensconced behind Holt's desk. She hadn't seen much of Holt since Lodge had installed himself, and she missed him. Missed the trust that used to exist between them. Damn that woman. She'd come to town and turned everybody's life into a plate of slop. Messy, soggy, waterlogged.

But Sam was a sucker for sacrifice, and Edie had just offered to throw herself on her own sword. Sam looked over at Lodge, all official-looking and settled, proud of himself, she was sure, for having locked Edie up again. Well, they agreed on that, at least.

And yet.

Maybe she wasn't all bad, that Edie Swann. And the last thing Sam wanted was to give Lodge more ammo to use against Holt.

Huh. Wonder of wonders. Seems she and Edie had one thing in common after all.

Holt hightailed it to the state offices to drop off the blood and prints he'd collected from the pickup. The county had a coroner but no other forensic staff, so when necessary, he used the state facilities. He asked them to put a rush on it, and they promised, but they were big on promises and usually short on delivery. Who knew how long it would take to get any kind of ID? If an ID was even possible.

By the time he finished it was past noon. Which was when Sam called to tell him about Edie. He cursed under his breath, then told Sam to release her.

"I don't think that's a good idea, Chief."

"I'm not asking for your opinion, Deputy."

"What am I supposed to tell Lodge?"

"Nothing. Make yourself scarce. Go on patrol. Better yet, check out the site where the abandoned truck was found. Find me some trace evidence. Anything. I'll take care of Lodge."

"Or he'll take care of you," Sam grumbled and disconnected.

Edie leaped to her feet when Sam entered the cell room. "Did you tell him?"

"I told him," Sam said.

"And?"

She unlocked the door. "You're free to go."

"What?"

"You're free—"

"I heard you. How come?"

Sam frowned. "Friends in high places."

Neither one had to specify which friend she meant. "He gonna get in trouble for this?" Edie asked.

"Not my place to say. I'm just supposed to let you go."

"Not too happy about it, are you?"

"Not my place to say." She tossed her head with a disapproving jerk, which said it all anyway. "Come on. Before Lodge gets back."

"Don't suppose you'd give me a lift out to my bike?"

"Don't suppose I would," Sam said. She escorted Edie into the office, tossed over her possessions. Saw her out the office and out the building. Sam got in her cruiser and took off south.

Well, well, well. Deputy Fish. Who'da thunk it?

Shaking her head at the vagaries of womankind, Edie headed in the opposite direction, toward Myer's.

"Yo, Andy!" Edie peeked into the garage, looking for the mechanic. The place appeared deserted, but a disembodied voice answered.

"Who wants him?"

Edie walked further into the garage, then around the front of a Camaro, saw Burkett half-buried beneath. She bent down. "You get a tow call a few hours ago?"

Andy slid out on his pallet. Saw Edie. "That your bike out on Six?"

"You bring it in yet?"

"Nope. Had this to take care of first." He nodded toward the Chevy. "Something wrong with your Harley?"

"A little police harassment," she said, and then when Andy looked puzzled, "Never mind. Look, can I hitch a ride out there?"

"You don't need a tow?"

"I need a ride. But far as I'm concerned you can still charge Lodge for your time."

Andy thought about it. Wiped his hands on a grease rag. "Give me ten minutes."

While she waited, she tried Amy again. If things continued the way they were going, dinner didn't seem likely.

Edie tried the house and the cell, but got no answer at either, so she left messages and apologies at both places.

It took Andy twice as long to finish, and by the time she got out to the bike it was close to three. She thanked him for the lift, then headed south. There was a Piggly Wiggly in Thompsonville. She figured it wasn't too late to get dinner together, as long as it was just spaghetti and sauce in a jar. She bought a bag of salad stuff, too. A bottle of dressing. Some kind of premade garlic bread. She'd never been much of a cook. Hoped Amy would appreciate the gesture even if the food was store-bought.

She stuffed her saddlebags with the groceries and headed back to town. Wondered how many smokestacks Lodge had blown when he found her gone. Hoped Holt was nowhere near when they exploded.

Her phone rang just as she approached the center of town. To her surprise, it was Ellen Garvey, asking her to stop by.

Edie thought about her dinner preparations; she didn't want to disappoint Amy. "I could come later. After dinner. Or tomorrow." Provided she wasn't locked up again.

"Oh, dear." She sounded upset. "It's Terry —"

Edie's pulse quickened. "Something wrong?"

"I'm afraid—" The elderly woman hesitated. Had Terry done something? Had he hurt her?

"I'll be right there," Edie said.

She raced her bike to Myrtle Street, up the long, winding drive to the back of the house, and parked it there. Knocked on the back door. Like the front, the back was deep with overgrown trees and shrubs. Would take a month and a machete to clear it.

It took Ellen a few minutes to come to the door, during

which time Edie stamped impatiently, imagining all sorts
of things. But when she opened the door, Ellen looked
normal enough. Her lipstick was blotchy, but she wore another girlish dress, this one with wide padded shoulders.
But no bruises.

She gave Edie a small frown of disappointment.
"Oh, dear. You didn't have to come to the back like a
tradesman."

Relieved to see the older woman whole and unhurt,
Edie smiled. Plenty of people in Redbud thought a lot
worse of her. "Didn't want to leave my bike on the street."
She followed Ellen through a mud room and into the
kitchen. Saw nothing out of the ordinary. Confused, Edie
said, "Are you all right? Terry hasn't hurt you, has he?"

"Oh, no. Nothing like that." She beamed.

"Really? I thought—"

"I have something to show you." Ellen took Edie's
hand and brought her past the dining room where they'd
had lunch and into a small parlor.

The first thing she noticed was Terry asleep on the
old-fashioned sofa, his hands clasped over his heart like
a corpse. But before she could think too hard about that,
her gaze skated off him, and caught on the spectacle in
the middle of the room.

A round table was covered with a snowy cloth and a
dainty tea set. Cups and saucers rimmed in gold. Pinkie-
sized handles that looked as if they would shatter if you
breathed on them. Flanking a matching teapot was a
graceful creamer and a sugar bowl with miniature tongs
to pick up individual cubes. A tiered platter held tiny
cakes frosted prettily in pink, pale green, and yellow, and
crustless sandwiches cut into hearts and stars.

It was a fairy tale setup, something from another time, another world. And sitting at the table dressed in some kind of gauzy blouse that might have once belonged to her great-grandmother was a wide-eyed Miranda.

Can I have a pink one, now?" Miranda asked. She was squeezed in tight against the table, the heavy dining-room chair imprisoning her. "You said I could when she got here."

"Hush, child," Ellen said. And to Edie, "Do you like it?"

Edie blinked. Didn't know what to say. What was Miranda doing there? And where was Terry? "It's . . . it's lovely."

Ellen sighed happily. "It's been so long since I entertained."

"That's a . . . a pretty blouse you have on, Miranda," Edie said.

"Auntie Ellen gave it to me." She squirmed, eyes darting between Edie and Ellen as if sensing undercurrents she didn't understand.

"Auntie Ellen?" Edie didn't think the Drennens were related to the Garveys or Holt would have surely said so.

"Lent it to you, dear," Ellen said to Miranda. "For purposes of our party. You can't go to a tea party in those dreadful short pants."

Miranda looked cross and fidgeted again. "I'm hungry."

"Patience," Ellen said to her. "All ladies must learn patience. Lord knows I've had to."

"How did you get here?" Edie asked Miranda.

Miranda looked over at Ellen. "Daddy was busy. I don't know where Nannie and Pawpaw are. Auntie Ellen said we would have a party."

Ellen pulled a chair out for Edie. "Please, dear, do sit down."

But Edie sensed something wrong in the room. Ellen's eyes were bright enough to be tubercular, and Miranda . . . why was Holt's daughter here?

"On the phone you mentioned Terry."

Ellen sighed. "Yes, my poor nephew was beginning to be a problem. I understand he found some papers and turned them over to the police. He was drawing too much attention to us, you see." Ellen smiled. "And he does love sweets. Tends to overindulge. I think something he ate disagreed with him."

Edie swallowed. Why did that sound . . . ominous? Whatever was going on, she had a bad feeling about it. "This is really nice of you, Miss Ellen. But it's time for Miranda to go. She'll spoil her dinner."

She headed for the little girl, but Ellen got there first and blocked Edie's way. The older woman hovered over the child's chair and pursed her lips in a small frown. "But I've gone to so much trouble. And they're such small cakes. I'm sure one or two won't hurt. Well, perhaps a little," she added slyly. "But she really does want one, don't you, dear?"

Miranda nodded emphatically. "A pink one." She reached for the tier of pretty cake.

"Don't!" Edie cried, not sure why, but doing it anyway.

Miranda froze, and Ellen pressed the outstretched arm down. "Very wise," she said to Miranda. "Guests first." And looked sharply to the chair she'd pulled out for Edie.

Edie hesitated, unable to process what was happening. Was kindly, fragile Ellen Garvey threatening Miranda?

"Sit," she ordered, her voice neither kindly nor fragile.

Uneasiness threaded up Edie's spine, but she took the chair. She was probably misconstruing everything and besides, she didn't want to frighten Miranda.

"Now," Ellen said brightly. "Tea?" She picked up the pot and poured the hot brown liquid into the delicate cups. Held silver tongs over the dainty sugar bowl. "One lump or two?" Ellen watched intently as Edie made no move to pick up her cup. "You know, Dennis took three lumps in his tea. He always was a little self-indulgent. Even as a boy. Did you know we went to school together? All those pretty children he married, when there were perfectly decent women his own age. Did I tell you I had a beau? Alvin wanted to marry me, but I couldn't leave mother, could I?"

At the mention of Dennis Runkle's name, Edie's gaze snapped from the teacup to Ellen. The older woman's eyes glittered with malevolence.

"Dennis? Dennis Runkle? You served him tea? When?"

"Oh, when he came to talk about the house." Ellen gazed around with loathing. "I can't wait to get out of this musty old awful place. Dennis promised a brand new condo. Wouldn't that be fine? We had a lovely tea, and I fixed some wonderful lemon cookies. Dennis had four, can you imagine? Of course, I made sure to grind the peanuts up nice and fine. If you didn't know they were there you would hardly notice." She sighed happily. "He said they were delicious."

Edie chilled. Her stomach spun. She could hardly take in what the other woman was saying. It had to be impossible. Had to.

And yet, if Ellen was responsible for Runkle's death . . .

Unexpectedly, a path parted behind Edie's eyes. An endless road with bright blue skies and a way out of the terrible mess she was in. If the older woman was telling the truth, that is, and not spinning a schizophrenic tale. The way things were going it was probably the ramblings of a deranged mind, but Edie had to make sure. "You . . ." She licked her lips. Why were they so dry? "Did you . . . fix something for the reverend, too?"

Ellen smiled, a bizarre glitter in her eyes. "Oh, I didn't have to. There he was, the fat fool, trying to unplug the drain himself. It was like God talking to me. Giving me the opportunity, the idea. Has God ever spoken to you? It isn't pleasant, not like a tea party. It's filled with awe and . . . and might." Her voice dropped. A visible shudder ran through her. "Like a man touching me in all my secret places. Powerful. And exciting. And the church kitchen was only a few steps away. The waffle iron was right there. I didn't even have to hunt for it."

Ellen's words ricocheted inside Edie. Would anyone believe them? She was hearing it with her own two ears and she hardly believed them herself. "That was . . . that was lucky."

"Oh, no, my dear," Ellen said sternly. "Luck had nothing to do with it. Well, except for Mr. Butene. *That* was lucky."

The name registered with another jolt, but if the older woman noticed Edie's shock, she only plowed right over it.

"Perhaps that's too formal?" She frowned. "He was my father, you know. No, of course you didn't know. How could you? Mother kept it secret, even from me. But when she died, the payments stopped, you see. Now why else would Alan Butene pay Mother a monthly stipend if it wasn't for me? Of course, he denied it all. Laughed at me. Can you imagine?" She huffed. "I'm sure you would have been outraged, too. I needed that money to start my new life. And how was I to know the ladder wouldn't hold up under a good shaking?"

Edie swallowed a gasp.

"If you hadn't scared poor Fred Lyle to death I probably would still be here, old and unloved and unwanted by anyone," Ellen said. "But you gave me the idea."

Edie's stomach twisted again. If she could, she would have strangled herself for ever having come to Redbud.

But fault didn't matter now. What mattered was getting the truth into the open. Getting herself out of her own trap and getting Miranda home safe.

"Did you know angels are messengers of God?" Ellen babbled on, and while she did, Edie scanned the room, trying to recall the layout of the house, looking for the fastest route out. "Your black angels were my messengers. God wanted them to pay for the way they left me to dwindle inside this monster of a house. Mother worked her fingers to the bone for those men. And when she got sick, did they care? Did they come even once to see her? Why bother, she has Ellen to nurse her. Ellen can stay. Ellen can turn down every chance at happiness. College, husband, children. Ellen can do it. Always Ellen. Ellen, Ellen, Ellen. I was glad when she died. Glad!" Her voice shook with angry triumph, then brightened. "Now," she said. "Cake or sandwich?"

Edie swallowed. There were two doors leading from the parlor. Was the kitchen to the right or the left? "I'm really not hungry."

"Of course you are." Ellen indicated a plate. "Can't have you wandering around, denying your part in all this." She reached over and patted Edie's hand. "Poor dear, I know how sorry you are. My goodness, no one will blink an eye when you take the easy way out."

Dizzy with disbelief, Edie stared at the older woman.

Ellen sighed. "Miranda will have something, won't you dear?" With her free hand, she plucked a pink petit four from the tier and handed it to the child.

And now the reason for Miranda's presence became clear. Pulse pumping, Edie tried to intercept the cake, but Ellen had already squeezed it into Miranda's hand and was forcing it up toward her mouth. Miranda shrieked, and Edie did the only thing she could. She leaped and made a grab for Holt's daughter.

But Ellen was faster and nimbler than Edie could have imagined. Closer, too. She wrenched back Miranda's chair. It crashed to the floor, but not before Ellen snatched up the child. "There now," she cooed, holding Miranda tight, "we can have a fun time and eat lots of little pink cakes, can't we?"

Miranda squealed in terror, and a horrified Edie looked

on as Ellen danced away, the child in her arms, the tiny cake and whatever was inside it at Miranda's lips.

"Wait!" Edie cried. "Wait!"

Ellen stopped. Swung around to face Edie. "Yes?"

Edie could rush her. She could just knock the older woman down, grab Miranda and run. But would that . . . that thing get inside her mouth before Edie could get there? It would take less than half a second to smash it against the child's lips. If there was something in it, some, oh God, some terrible poison, and Miranda swallowed it . . . Edie couldn't take the chance. Not with Holt's daughter. Never with Holt's daughter.

She backed up to the table. Slid her teacup toward her. Ellen watched and didn't budge.

Oh, God. Edie closed her eyes in silent prayer to whatever was out there in the universe, and lifted the teacup.

"Go on," Ellen whispered hoarsely, her eyes fixed.

Edie tried not to swallow. Could whatever was in that tea seep through her body anyway? Her hand shook as she replaced the cup, making it clatter against the saucer.

"And now the cake," Ellen said in that same strained tone. "I made them specially for you."

No choice, now. She had to swallow. She downed the gulp she'd been holding and played her only card. "Not until you let Miranda go."

Ellen shook her head, clutched the child closer. Miranda shrieked.

"You're hurting her," Edie cried.

"No, my dear, you're hurting her." Ellen had to raise her voice over Miranda's howls. "You or Miranda—it's your choice, not mine."

"I want to go home," Miranda wailed. She squirmed

and screeched louder. "I want my daddy! I want my daddy!"

"Stop it! Stop it this instant!" Ellen said.

But Miranda kicked and pummeled the older woman with flailing arms, a wild, uncontrollable, slippery thing. Ellen ducked her head, tried to shift her hold to get a better grip. Instead, Miranda writhed, opening a gap. Immediately, she slithered down, out of Ellen's grasp.

Edie shot forward, seized Miranda's hand, and ran. Into the kitchen and out the back door. Swung Miranda up into her arms as they flew down the steps to the top of the drive where her bike was parked.

She shifted the child to her back. "Hold tight! Don't let go!"

The bike roared to life and she took off down the drive. The wind tore back her hair, and she prayed that whatever she'd swallowed wouldn't take effect until she got Miranda to safety.

~53~

Holt was examining the site where the abandoned pickup had been found when the call came. He answered it calmly, not thinking it could be the end of his world.

"This is County Hospital, Chief. We've got your daughter here."

He froze. "Miranda? Is she all right? What happened?"

"She seems to be fine. It's the woman with her. ID says Swann. Black hair, tattoos?"

Holt was already running toward his car. "What's wrong with Edie?"

"We're still trying to find out. She brought your daughter in, then collapsed in the emergency room. We'd like permission to check out your little girl."

"I'll be right there."

He waved to Sam, who was staring at him from across the field where the pickup had been abandoned. Yanked the car door open, set the siren, and took off, brakes squealing. He radioed Sam on the way, explained where he was going, then set all his concentration on getting there.

When he pulled up to the emergency room entrance,

he barely stopped before tumbling out and racing inside. He grabbed the first medical person he saw and spun her around.

"Miranda Drennen?"

But she directed him to the admissions desk. Mouth dry, palms sweaty, pulse bubbling, he ran to the desk.

"Daddy!"

Whirling, he got turned around just in time for his child to fling herself into his arms. Sobbing, she clung to his neck, and he held her tighter than he thought possible. She blubbered up a bunch of disjointed words. Swan lady, Auntie, pink ones.

"It's okay, baby doll. I'm here. Daddy's here." He continued to croon and cajole and hold on, more grateful than he'd ever been to have her whole and crying in his arms.

When she'd finally calmed down, and his own heart had stopped battering his chest, he saw his mother and father sitting quietly in the hard plastic chairs in the waiting room.

Seeing his father, a flash of hot anger shook him, then faded. At least Miranda hadn't been alone waiting for him.

He brought her over to them. Sat with her in his lap, and she curled into him, her thumb in her mouth. She hadn't done that in a long time.

He stroked her head, spoke to his mother. "Did she say what happened?"

"Couldn't get much out of her. Something about cake and how she didn't let go." He felt her hiccup against him.

"What about Edie?"

"They won't tell us anything."

"I don't think they know anything." His father spoke for the first time. Holt couldn't bring himself to look at him.

A few minutes later, Miranda was sound asleep. Carefully, Holt transferred the exhausted child to his mother's arms and went in search of Edie. He used his badge to get him to a weary doctor in scrubs.

"I think she's been poisoned," the doctor said.

Holt stared at him, appalled. "Poisoned?"

"Arsenic. Could be accidental. It happens. Has she been around pesticides, rat poison, anything like that?"

"I doubt it."

"Suicidal?"

Holt recalled the evening before. Nothing in her words or demeanor indicated she'd hit a low point. "No. Absolutely not."

The doctor shrugged. "That only leaves one other explanation."

Holt's thoughts hardened. Refused to go to that place where murder waited.

"She going to make it?" He braced himself, afraid of the answer.

"Don't know yet. We gave her Succimer. It's the antidote. If that doesn't work, there's Dimercaprol. It's more toxic, but it's there if we need it. A lot depends on how much she ingested and how fast we got to her."

"Can I see her?"

"You can, but she's not up for questions. She was convulsing, so we had to put her out."

Convulsing. He pushed past that image. "I just want to see her."

"Help yourself." The doctor led Holt to a curtained cubicle and left him there.

Edie was pale, her closed eyelids red-rimmed, the black lashes against her skin like winter branches against snow. He took her hand, straightened the fingers, stroked them. An IV was inserted in her arm, pumping medicine, vital liquids into her. How is it that the people he loved always ended up here—fighting for their lives on gurneys, plugged into machines, living off needles?

He set her hand back. Brushed a strand of hair back from her forehead. "Don't die on me, Edie Swann," he said softly. "Don't you dare die on me."

Back in the waiting room Miranda was still asleep on his mother's lap.

"Can you take her home?" Holt asked.

Mimsy didn't ask a single question or make an ounce of protest. "Of course," she said. "Did you see Edie?"

"Briefly. She's alive. For now."

"Oh, Holt, I'm so sorry," Mimsy said. "What on earth happened?"

"Someone poisoned her."

"What?" His father jolted to his feet.

"Oh, my God," his mother said at the same time. "Do you think . . . ?" She looked down at Miranda.

"She hasn't shown any signs of vomiting or an upset stomach, has she?"

"No."

"I don't know what happened, but she's probably okay. Best let the doctor check her out, though."

They woke her up and Holt stayed until the doctor had cleared Miranda. She got a lollipop for her trouble, and sucked on it greedily, still clinging desperately to her daddy.

"Auntie Ellen said I could have cake," Miranda said in a hurt little-girl voice. "But then she wouldn't give me any."

Holt stilled. Flicked a glance at his mother and back at his child. "Who is Auntie Ellen?"

"She picked me up early. She said you were busy."

His mind whirled, the name ricocheting inside his brain. *Ellen.*

"Is the swan lady coming home?" Miranda asked.

He answered, but he wasn't concentrating. All he could think about was that name. There was only one Ellen connected with all this. And if Ellen Garvey was involved, Terry couldn't be far behind. "Not yet," he said, stroking Miranda's hair absently. "She's still sick."

He swallowed. Protests hammered at him. Ellen Garvey was old. Old people don't do things like that. She was kind. She worked at the church, for God's sake. If Miranda was talking about Ellen Garvey, she must have been forced into doing whatever she did.

Or maybe Miranda got it wrong. How could he trust the word of a distressed five-year-old?

But then she repeated it. "Auntie Ellen wanted the swan lady to eat the cake but she wouldn't. And she wouldn't let me. And then we ran fast."

Outrage filled Holt, but he forced himself to stay calm. Anything else would upset Miranda even further. "Tell you what." He raised her chin and nuzzled her nose. "You go home with Grandma and we'll have cake for dinner. How's that?"

"Pink cake?"

"Pink, blue, whatever color you want."

"I want pink. With white flowers."

"You got it. Go with Nannie now, and I'll be home for cake." He tried to transfer her over but she clutched at him.

"Promise? I don't like Auntie Ellen."

Grimly, he tensed his jaw. "Me neither. You won't have to see her anymore. I promise. Go on now." He kissed her. "There's a brave girl."

He put her in the back of Mimsy's car. "I love you, baby girl."

"I love you, too, Daddy."

He waved as they drove off, tears welling in his eyes. Thank you, Edie, for keeping her safe. Thank you, thank you, thank you.

And now he allowed his fury to come. Hands fisted, he raced for his car. Pounded the wheel. Stupid, stupid, stupid. How could he not have seen it? Old people get confused and can be easily manipulated. But still . . .

Ellen had fed them cake? Poisoned cake? Bizarre as it sounded, that was the only sense he could make of his daughter's words. And where was Terry? Miranda hadn't mentioned him at all.

He sped off toward town, punching in phone numbers and barking at whoever answered until he'd tracked down Miranda's counselor. She was Darcy's youngest, so she wasn't hard to find.

"She had your card," the young woman said over the phone. "And a note on the back giving her permission to pick up Miranda. She works at the church; I was sure it was all right. I hope I didn't do anything wrong."

His hand tightened on the phone, and he felt like screaming. But he managed not to. "Just double-checking." It wasn't her fault for trusting someone she'd always known. Hadn't everyone?

He phoned Sam, told her what had happened, and had her meet him at the Garvey house. He wasn't sure what they'd find, but if Terry had somehow pressured his aunt to pick up Miranda, who knows what he'd be up to now that his plans had been thwarted.

Holt met Sam at the curb. He took out his weapon, signaled Sam to do the same.

"Expecting a fight?" she asked.

"Don't know what I'm expecting," he said grimly. "Terry could be holding his aunt hostage, or worse. He must be completely out of control. I want to be prepared. I'll take the front, you take the back," Holt said. "Don't want anyone running off on us."

"How's Edie?"

Holt looked at her, surprised she even cared. She reddened, then said, "I didn't ask anyone to kill her, Holt. Just wanted justice done."

"I don't know how she is." He took a breath. "Can't think about it now. Gotta concentrate on this."

She nodded and switched on her radio. "Look, been something I've wanted to say for a while."

"Can't it wait?"

"Probably. But we're going in armed and all, and, well, better get if off my chest now." She squared her shoulders. "Want to thank you for not firing me."

"I should have."

"I know."

"You're lucky you're a damn good deputy." He turned on his radio, too, then raised his weapon. "You go behind my back again, though . . ."

"No, sir. Won't happen again."

He eyed her. "Don't think you're through groveling."

Her mouth twitched, but she repressed the smile. "No, sir."

"Okay, enough said. Let's do this." He nodded for her

to take off. She walked up the drive and around back while Holt took the steps. Through the arched and overgrown shrubs and up to the front door.

He knocked.

No answer.

Knocked again. "Open up, Miss Ellen. It's Chief Drennen."

Still no answer.

"I'm going in," he radioed to Sam. "He could have her tied up in there. Meet you inside. Count of three." He counted down, kicked open the door, and crashed inside.

Except for the echo of his footsteps it was quiet as a tomb.

"Sam," he whispered into the radio. "Anything?"

"Negative," she said.

He made his way cautiously, room by room, leading with his weapon and clearing each one before moving on to the next. He made it past the dreary entryway, with its narrow set of stairs leading into a darkened second floor, then a front parlor whose French doors had been shut tight the last time he'd been there. When he got through he saw the room had been converted into a bedroom. A large, unmade hospital bed took up most of the space. Backing out, he headed deeper into the house.

He found the remains of a meal in the room he'd sat in with Ellen the other evening. Fancy teacups and cakes were scattered over a table in the middle. He poked at one with a pen. Pink, just as Miranda had said. An image of his frightened daughter rose up along with one of pale, lifeless Edie. Fury surged through him, and he gripped the pen so tightly it snapped in two.

Grimly, he surveyed the rest of the room. There were

clear signs of a struggle. A chair pushed back, another overturned. A teacup spilled. What in holy hell had happened here?

"Got something," Sam said into his radio. "Upstairs."

He tramped back to the front of the house and up the staircase. Sam was waiting in the hall outside an open door. She nodded with her head to the room, and he went in. Terry was on the floor.

"Dead," Sam said.

That threw Holt. If Terry was dead, he couldn't be the one pulling the strings. Which left . . . God, that was crazy. Pure unadulterated lunacy. "The aunt?"

"Don't know," Sam said. "Waited for you to check the rest of the rooms."

There were two more bedrooms up there. They found Ellen Garvey in the second one.

She lay on the bed dressed in a yellowed bridal gown. The flouncy skirt was spread wide, and a gauzy veil covered her head. Beneath it, her face was petrified in a grimace of agony. A dried-up bouquet lay at her side, her fingers frozen into monsterish, clutching claws.

Sam holstered her weapon. Let out a whistling breath. "Not my idea of a wedding night."

∽54∼

At ten, Holt left the endless paperwork at his desk and drove to the cemetery. By the look of the cloudless sky and the bright sun, it was going to be a scorcher. Not the day he'd pick to be standing around in the open, but everything had been arranged, so he couldn't do much about it now. And Edie would appreciate the irony. It had been hot the day her father was buried, too.

He parked outside the gates and walked to the gravesite. Passed the countless markers that represented the lifeblood of the town. Some of the names were familiar, families still pumping oxygen into Redbud. But there were also those long forgotten, the faded names dating back to 1842. Children dead before they could walk, mothers dead bearing them. Murderers and thieves as well as upright citizens. How many secrets lay buried in those graves?

Well, at least one was out in the open now. The blood evidence from the abandoned truck led to a thug who used to do yardwork for the Butenes. He didn't lose much time naming Hally Butene. Holt still remembered his disbelief, but when he went back to question Hally, he found Amy Lyle tied up and stuffed inside a closet.

"I thought Hally might remember something," Amy told Holt when she'd recovered from her ordeal. "Together we could figure out what happened."

"But she didn't want you poking around any more than she wanted Edie digging up the past."

Amy had shuddered. "Edie must have called me three or four times that day." Tears welled in her eyes. "She wanted to cook dinner for me."

Holt had squeezed her thin shoulders, still not understanding why Hally Butene had done what she did. But later, between her testimony and Arlen Mayborne's analysis of the file he'd taken off Terry, the whole story became clear.

The reports in the file reflected real production data, real profit-and-loss statements. Not the golden numbers Alan Butene, in his capacity as comptroller, showed IAT, the corporate parent. The reports in the file showed the factory losing money—a lot of money—its profits way down. In effect, the file was a second set of books. The real books.

Together with plant manager Fred Lyle, Alan had cooked up the scheme to doctor the reports in order to ensure the plant's survival during the period of corporate consolidation in the late 1980s.

But Edie's father found out, and threatened to tell the truth. Not only would that have put the plant in danger of closure, but discovery of the fraud would have meant the end of Butene's and Lyle's careers.

So they framed Charles Swanford. Holt discovered that Edie's father had been treated for depression at that time, and speculated that, faced with the power of his adversaries, his conviction that they could make good on their threats, the shame he must have felt as the town shunned him, and the impending loss of his own livelihood and freedom, Charles jumped into the quarry.

"Implicating Charles was supposed to be temporary," Hally Butene had explained in her gravelly voice while a tape recorder ran in the interview room. "A quick fix while they figured out what to do. But Charles jumped off that cliff."

"And attacking Edie?"

She'd looked away, ashamed. Her voice was more wobbly, her tremors worse—a sure sign of the stress she was under. But she refused to give in to them. She squared her shoulders as best she could and looked him in the eye, facing her confessor as well as her actions, he'd supposed. "I'm very sorry about that. It was stupid. Desperate and utterly stupid. But I panicked. I was terrified they'd take away Alan's pension if what he'd done came out. I'm afraid my husband wasn't as crafty with his own investments as he was with Hammerbilt's. The house and the pension are almost all I have left." She sighed. "I never meant to hurt anyone. I just wanted to scare Edie off. No excuse, of course." She gave a tiny, bitter laugh. "Things never do seem to go the way one planned, do they?"

But, as he pointed out, they'd gone that way for twenty years. Charles Swanford's suicide played right into the conspirators' hands. Between the mayor and the rest of the council they persuaded James to cover up the fraud For the good of the town.

"I did it, son," James told Holt in that same room at the police department. "I made the best decision I could. This town would have dried up and blown away if Hammerbilt had left."

"So you let Edie's family bear that burden."

"I wasn't proud of what I'd done, but I weighed the cost of the whole town against one family."

Hannah Garvey was part of it, too, the only one Alan trusted to keep track of the discussions at the council meetings. When Holt took a closer look, her name was there as secretary on every copy of the minutes.

Of course she wasn't as trustworthy as she must have appeared if she was blackmailing Butene. "I think she'd already started to get sick," James said, "and was frightened of not having the money to pay for medical care."

No wonder Alan Butene hadn't stewarded his holdings well. They were being systematically drained.

But how Ellen got the twisted idea that Alan was her father, Holt could only speculate. Probably couldn't imagine any other possibility. An analysis of Ellen's bank account revealed a huge dent in her income after her mother died. Alan must have figured the bleeding could stop, but Ellen had gotten used to the extra cash. She needed some reason to get the payments reinstated, so maybe she invented one. It wasn't so far-fetched. Hadn't Amy Lyle also thought the same thing about Edie?

And the arsenic could have fried her brain anyway. She'd been breathing and ingesting it for years as it flaked away from the paint on the walls. It's what she had used in the tea and cakes she prepared for the lethal tea party. Ground it up fine as dust.

On a hunch, he'd had Hannah's body exhumed. Sure enough, an autopsy revealed she'd died of arsenic poisoning, not the cancer everyone assumed. Her mother had been Ellen's first victim.

Closing in on the gravesite he'd come to see, he braced himself. Refused to get emotional. Plenty of time for that later. Instead, he busied himself with the details of the inspection. Walked around, examined everything. Was satisfied with what he found. The angel looked, well, like it was supposed to. And the newly turned earth of the Garvey graves was well away on the other side of the cemetery.

One last look, then he started back. He hoped he'd done the right thing. Hoped wherever they were the Swanfords would be pleased.

Holt had been right: the day did turn into a scorcher. But despite the heat, cars lined the road up to the cemetery and people streamed through the gates. Traffic was so bad, he called Sam out.

"Get your butt over to the cemetery, Deputy. Fast. We need traffic control." He turned on the siren and it burped on and off; a path parted for them. He drove through the gates, cruised slowly up to the site.

Unlike this morning, it was filled with people. Not just the expected, like Amy Lyle, but Andy Burkett, who had closed his garage and come, and Darcy, who had done the same with Claire's. Red was there, along with a group of regulars like Russ Elam and Howard Wayne, their Hammerbilt hats in their hands. The mayor was there, white hair glistening in the sun. He saw his mom's knitting pals, her book group, her poker players. And lots more he couldn't name. Except, of course, for Miranda, who was waving and jumping up and down in front of Mimsy. And James.

He stiffened at the sight of his father. Wasn't right, him

being there. He felt his father's eyes on him, even through
the windshield and across the distance. Sadness mixed
with the fury and made Holt look away. Maybe James's
presence was the most right of all.

He parked, sat for a moment, scanned the crowd. Said
a small prayer that this would all be okay, then turned to
his passenger. "You can open your eyes now."

Edie breathed out, nervous about what Holt was up to.
He'd picked her up at the hospital, and the minute she was
settled in the car he told her to close her eyes.

"Why?" she asked.

"Go on. You like surprises, don't you?"

But after everything that had happened, a nice long series of predictable would be a relief. Had Amy cooked up
some kind of welcome-home thing for her? She pictured
balloons and a "Welcome Home, Edie" banner scrawled
by Miranda. Edie had gotten plenty of her get-well cards
during the weeks she'd been in the hospital. The nurses
had taped them to the hospital walls, the portable tray,
even the IV stand until she didn't need it anymore. When
she was conscious finally, and then not only awake but
aware, they cheered her. So if Amy and Miranda had
planned a little something for her, Edie didn't want to disappoint them. She closed her eyes.

The drive seemed to take longer than it should have to
get to Amy's house, and she used the time to relax, or try
to. She was still weak, had lost like a hundred pounds,
and the littlest thing tired her out. But she was alive. Had
to be grateful for that.

"Edie," Holt said at last. "You can open your eyes
now."

She blinked them open.

No balloons. No "Welcome Home Edie" sign. No house at all. Just wall-to-wall people. All turned toward . . .

"What's going on? Why are we at the cemetery and what are all these people doing here?"

"They're here for you."

"For me?"

"Come on, I'll help you out."

She leaned on his arm and walked through the crowd. As they passed, people reached out to pat her back, touch her arm. And there were greetings, too. From complete strangers.

"Good to see you back."

"Glad you're well."

Red winked at her. Amy hugged her. Mimsy squeezed her hand, and Miranda insisted on being picked up.

"Not yet, darlin'," Holt said and swooped her up instead.

The only somber face in the crowd belonged to Holt's father. Holt paused in front of him, bristling, and James stepped back, silent and shamed.

Holt put Miranda on his shoulders, took Edie's hand. "Come on. I've got something to show you."

He led her to the one place in the cemetery she knew. This time her father's headstone was clean, and there were daisies and zinnias on his grave. Those weren't the only differences. The black angel was shrouded, covered with a thick tarp. She stared at it, then at Holt.

Mayor Crocker stepped forward, and the crowd hushed. "Miss Swann, you and yours have been wronged by this town, and we don't like that about ourselves. Can't change what happened, can only look forward with wiser eyes. We know it was your mother's dearest wish to clear

your father's name. You have now done so. And the town
thought, in honor of your father and to right our wrong,
we would complete your family's wish. We took up a collection, and . . ." He nodded, and a couple of men pulled
the tarp down.

Edie gaped.

"Oohh," Miranda said. "Pretty."

The angel *was* pretty. All snowy and pale and light.
Gone was the fierce, angry gargoyle. In its place was a
face softened by kindness and compassion. Wings curved
to embrace and shelter the wounded.

Edie didn't know what to say. She thought of her
mother, and her awful inhuman scream.

The crowd was silent, all eyes on her. Expecting . . .
what? Something. But what did she owe them? Any of
them?

Holt put an arm around her. "You okay?" he
whispered.

"This your idea?" she whispered back.

"Town hatched it up, like the mayor said. I only said
okay when they came to me with the idea."

She glanced up at the white angel. Smaller. Gentler
than the previous one. An angel of tenderness. Of pity in
its highest form. Carved into the folds of her robe was a
single word: mercy.

As if her mother had touched her hair and whispered,
thank you, the scream in Edie's head merged into a sigh
of contentment. She looked out into the crowd and saw
people who'd scorned her, but also people who'd stood by
her. For their sake as well as her own, she repeated her
mother's words.

"Thank you." She smiled, and a cheer went up.

*　　*　　*

Later, she stretched out in the gazebo with Holt, her head in his lap, her eyes closed. Miranda and Amy were in the cutting garden, and she could hear the music of Miranda's high-pitched voice as she chattered with the other woman.

Holt stroked the hair back from her forehead "You know, I never thanked you for saving Miranda's life."

"Mmm," was all she said.

"Guess this means you're sticking around."

She cracked open an eye, looked up at him.

"You save someone's life you're responsible for them," he said mildly.

She closed her eye.

"Now that there's no . . . barriers in the way," he continued. "No careers to lose, no more scandals to weather. No excuses."

"There is one thing," she murmured.

"Yeah? What's that?"

Miranda squealed and Edie sat up. She nodded to the side of the house where Holt's father was coming round the corner. "That."

"Pawpaw!" Miranda threw her arms around her grandfather's knees, but Holt rose and moved to the gazebo's entrance, stood there tense and rigid like a palace guard.

"Sit down, Holt," Edie said mildly. "I asked him to come."

He whipped around to face her. "You what?"

"You heard me."

His father gazed up at him from the yard. Amy whispered something to Miranda and pulled her toward the house.

And James began the tramp across the lawn toward the gazebo.

Holt was still positioned at the front, so James couldn't mount the two steps to enter.

"Hey, Edie." He nodded in her direction. "Holt." His gaze caught with his son's, and neither moved.

Edie watched them feel each other out. She didn't suppose she'd ever be a big fan of James Drennen's, but she wasn't going to blacklist him, either. Much as she'd like to. Ought to.

Holt might stick his chin out and hold on to stubbornness, but he was also sick at the breakup of his family. And what about Miranda? Edie couldn't bear the thought of Holt's child growing up with her world split in two as Edie's had been. Miranda needed her Nannie and Pawpaw as much as she needed her father.

"Come on up, James," Edie said. "Holt, get your butt out of the way."

Holt remained for half a second, then reluctantly gave way. He plunked himself down beside her and took her hand possessively, as if making sure James couldn't get close enough to chop it off.

James removed his ball cap, sat on the other side, tossing the hat nervously between his knees. No one said a word.

Geez. She was the injured party, wasn't she? If she could manage détente why couldn't they?

"Look, this is not going to work," Edie said finally. "I'm not going to be the reason you two never speak to each other again."

"No way is it your fault," Holt said.

"I'm not blaming you," James said at the same time.

"Well, I'm blaming myself. I know what you did hurt me," she said to James. "It was wrong. But the truth's out now—"

"Only because we forced it out of him," Holt said.

"I'm sorrier than I can say," James said. "To both of you. I know I can't change what's been done, but—"

"It's over," Edie said. "And everyone's paid a high enough price." She looked at Holt. "Do you really want to keep shelling out those dues?"

The two men eyed each other. Finally, James stood. "Thanks for trying, Edie." He tumbled down the gazebo's two steps to the yard.

Edie whacked Holt. "Don't let him go."

James turned at the bottom, gazed up at his son. "Oh, that's okay, Edie. One of these days he'll forgive me." His mouth twisted into the same crooked smile she'd seen on Holt's face. "Got to. No living with his mama if he won't." He put his hat on, pulled it low. "See you later?"

"Wouldn't miss it for the world," Edie said.

Holt turned to her. "What's he mean? What's happening later?"

"Your mama's cooking dinner for us."

Holt scowled. "I'm not having dinner with him."

"What about Miranda? You going to keep her from her grandparents the rest of her life?"

Holt said nothing, only set his jaw tighter. Well, she'd played the Miranda card, and that didn't work. She had one more ace left.

"You want me to stick around? Well, I can't do that if it means you'll always cross the street when you see your folks coming. I'll be like a pebble under your shoe—al-

ways a reminder of why the road between you isn't smooth.
I won't do that. I won't hurt Miranda that way. Or you."

Holt's mouth compressed into a grim line. He looked
at his father. James shook his head.

"She don't mean it, son."

"Don't I?" Edie said. She crossed her arms over her
chest.

"Don't," James said. "Please. I'm in enough trouble
without you threatening to leave because of me." He stuck
his cap on his head. "Look, I'm going. No one has to come
for dinner tonight. We got time to work things out." He
started across the lawn.

But Edie continued to look at Holt. "What's it gonna
be, Chief? A life with grudges or a life with me?"

"You're a damn pain in the ass," Holt said.

"Don't I know it."

Holt sighed. Bounded down the steps. "Dad! Wait
up!"

She watched Holt jog over the grass toward his father.
They spoke briefly. Shook hands. She closed her eyes
in relief. Collapsed against the gazebo bench, suddenly
sweating from effort. Man, peacemaking was hard work.

Holt returned, and lurked in the entrance. "Happy
now?"

"You?"

He grunted. "But I'm still not going to dinner."

Edie sighed. "Yeah, you are. Because I'm still all weak
and wobbly and if you don't I'll be stressed out, and it'll
hamper my recovery."

He scowled at her.

"You don't want to hamper my recovery, do you?"

"How long you think that trick's gonna last?"

She shrugged happily. "Long as it has to, I guess. Come on, now. Sit back down and fiddle with my hair again. It's not easy being poisoned."

Miranda came out of the house and clambered up the steps, an ice-cream bar dripping down her shirt. "I want another ride."

"Mmm," Edie said, "me, too."

She turned to her daddy. "Can we?"

"Soon," he said, and hauled her up beside him.

"How soon?"

Edie drifted off to the sound of father and daughter negotiating. A couple of days and Edie figured she'd be ready to get on the bike again. Feel that rumble of power beneath her. She even knew where she'd go for that first ride.

She hadn't told Holt yet, hadn't told anyone. But she'd used some of the money Fred had given her as a down payment on a broken-down house with an old tire swing in the yard. Miranda was going to love that swing.

And she and Holt would fix up the house. Clean out the old memories and make new ones. She'd take off her shoes and plant her feet. Feel what it was like to finally have her roots.

If that got too confining? She and Holt and Miranda and whoever else came along could hop on their bikes and go for a nice, long ride. And when that was over, something would always be waiting at the end of the road. Home.

AUTHOR'S NOTE

This book was inspired by the legend of the black angel in Oakland Cemetery in Iowa City. For more on the legend, see Ghosts of the Prairie—Behind the Legends at http://www.prairieghosts.com/oakland.html. For more on how the legend evolved into *One Deadly Sin*, visit my Web site at www.anniesolomon.net.

Dear Reader,

Have I got something to share with you. It's the story of Mitch Hancock, a man living on the run, his identity so lethal its discovery could unleash a nightmare of horror on himself and his innocent daughter, Julia. Unfortunately, since Mitch is in one of my books, things don't go the way he planned. Which is lucky for you, because that's only the beginning of what I hope will be a page-turning story of love, sacrifice, and murder.

To whet your appetite for my next book, here's the event that kicks everything off.

The day Sarah Jean Miles jumped into the Forbidden River was sunny and warm for October. The trees along River Road were splashed with crimson and rust, and even as she stood on the bridge staring down at the dark, swirling water, Sarah Jean knew it was a glorious day.

She just didn't care. Glorious days were for the other eighth-grade girls. The ones who knew how to put on eyeliner and flatiron their hair. Who could giggle with the boys without blushing. Who wore bras and had MySpace pages with lots of friends.

Sarah Jean would never be one of those girls. She would never be anything.

She realized this in a moment of clarity on the bridge.

She would never be anything. Not because she couldn't be, but because she didn't want to be. She only wanted the sun to go away and the blackness to come and cover her.

And the water was so very dark. It swayed and circled around itself, beckoning like a pair of open arms. It made her drowsy. She could hardly take her eyes away.

Except that a sound jolted her. It came from a distance, slowly penetrating like the heart of a dream. She looked over her shoulder, a reluctant, gradual slide, as if her head was still tethered to the water below.

A truck was coming over the bridge. A black pickup.

She watched it come, a creature from another world. Land-based, sunlit.

Choose, her mind told her. You have to choose.

Her head, rubber-banded as it was to the river, turned back. Had she climbed the railing? She didn't remember. But there she was, high above the water.

The truck had stopped. Someone was getting out, waving arms. Shouting.

But all she could hear was the voice of the water. She flew through the air to greet it. And when it claimed her, she sank deep in the river's cold, bottomless embrace.

Happy reading!

Annie Solomon

THE DISH

Where authors give you the inside scoop!

♥ ♥ ♥ ♥ ♥ ♥ ♥ ♥ ♥ ♥ ♥ ♥ ♥ ♥

From the desk of Elizabeth Hoyt

Gentle Reader,

Whilst researching my latest novel, TO BEGUILE A BEAST (on sale now), I came across the following document, which was written in a Suspiciously Familiar hand. I append it here for Your Amusement.

THE GENTEEL LADY'S GUIDE TO CLEANING CASTLES

Written for the Express Purpose of Guiding the Lady of Quality who may, through no fault of her own, be hiding under an Assumed Name in a Very Dirty Castle Indeed.

1. If at all possible, the Genteel Lady should choose a very dirty castle *not* inhabited by a Male (one cannot use the word *Gentleman!*) of a foul and disagreeable disposition.
2. Even if the Male in question is rather attractive otherwise.
3. An apron, preferably in a becoming shade of light blue or rose, is important.

4. The Genteel Lady should immediately hire a large and competent staff—even if it is against the express wishes of the Disagreeable Male. Remember: if the Disagreeable Male knew anything about cleaning, his castle wouldn't be in such a deplorable state in the first place.

5. Tea is harder to make than one might imagine.

6. Beware birds' nests hiding in the chimney!

7. The Genteel Lady should never deliver the Disagreeable Male's luncheon to him in his tower study by herself. This may result in the Lady and the Male being closeted together—alone!

8. Should the Genteel Lady dismiss the Above Advice, she should not under any circumstances participate in a Passionate Embrace with the Disagreeable Male.

9. Even if he is no longer Quite So Disagreeable.

10. Finally, the Genteel Lady should never, ever engage in an Affair d'Coeur with the Master of the Castle. In doing so she puts not only her virtue in peril, but also her heart.

Yours Most Sincerely,

Elizabeth Hoyt

www.elizabethhoyt.com

♥ ♥ ♥ ♥ . ♥ ♥   ♥

From the desk of Annie Solomon

Dear Reader,

Everyone always asks me where I get my ideas. Sometimes I get them straight from the newspaper. Or a song lyric might start an idea rolling. Places often give me ideas, especially if they're new to me. But in the case of my latest, ONE DEADLY SIN (on sale now), the idea for the book came from a tour guide to Iowa.

My brother was moving, which was sad because we live next door to each other, and also happy, because it meant he was taking a job that was exciting and challenging and something he always wanted to do. As a parting gift, someone had given him a guide to interesting places in Iowa, and while flipping through it one day—trying to ignore the boxes that were piling up in his living room—I happened across a famous midwestern legend about a monument in an Iowa cemetery. A monument that supposedly turned black overnight because the man buried beneath it was guilty of crimes of the heart.

That got me thinking. What if the person buried beneath the angel was innocent? What if someone wanted to prove it? What if proving it cost that someone his or her life?

That's the nugget that got me started on Edie Swann, the tattooed, Harley-riding heroine of ONE DEADLY SIN.

They say you can't go home again. For Edie, going home is murder. Out to revenge her father's long-ago death, she's caught in her own trap by a maniac who wants to see the sins of the past paid in full. With Edie's blood.

You can check out an excerpt on my Web site, www. anniesolomon.net. You'll also find more on the legend that started the story circling in my head. And while you're there, don't forget to check out my blog for behind-the-scenes stories in the life of a writer.

Happy Reading!

Annie Solomon

♥ ♥ ♥ ♥ ♥ ♥ ♥ ♥ ♥ ♥ ♥ ♥ ♥

From the desk of Lillian Feisty

Dear Reader,

Have you ever had a crush on a rock star? Have you ever watched *American Idol* and your heart began to pitter-patter as you saw a performer belt out a song, straight from his gut? Have you ever stared at a musician's fingers as he strummed his guitar and thought, "Wouldn't it be fabulous to be tied up by that rock star as he did wicked things to me?"

Or maybe that's just me.

It all started when I heard Robert Plant. I'd never even seen him, but when I listened to him sing I fell in love with his voice. He sounded so soulful, so sexy. I wondered why he wanted someone to squeeze his lemon, but my mom assured me it was because he liked a citrusy tea. Being thirteen, I believed her. It didn't stop my crush, though. I'd just lie on my bed, listening to Led Zeppelin, in bliss. And when I caught sight of Plant onstage, swinging his hips in those low-slung jeans, I was toast. I never got over my fascination with musicians, and I suspect few of us do.

Enter Mark St. Crow, the hero in my May release, BOUND TO PLEASE. Mark's a hot, tattooed musician with a tendency to, well, tie women up and do wicked things to them. Of course, I couldn't make his life easy so I made Mark fall for Ruby Scott, an event planner who longs for stability and all the things Mark's lifestyle could never allow. Oh, I admit it was fun torturing them both (even though they sometimes liked it), and while I did so I got to live out my not-so-secret rock-star crush, with a heavy dose of spicy romance thrown in.

I hope you enjoy BOUND TO PLEASE! You can find out more information about me and my writing at www.lillianfeisty.com.

Lilli Feisty

Want to know more about romances at Grand Central Publishing and Forever? Get the scoop online!

GRAND CENTRAL PUBLISHING'S ROMANCE HOME PAGE

Visit us at www.hachettebookgroup.com/romance for all the latest news, reviews, and chapter excerpts!

NEW AND UPCOMING TITLES

Each month we feature our new titles and reader favorites.

CONTESTS AND GIVEAWAYS

We give away galleys, autographed copies, and all kinds of fun stuff.

AUTHOR INFO

You'll find bios, articles, and links to personal Web sites for all your favorite authors—and so much more!

THE BUZZ

Sign up for our monthly romance newsletter, and be the first to read all about it!